BOOKS BY BRAD MAGNARELLA

THE XGENERATION SERIES
You Don't Know Me
The Watchers
Silent Generation
Pressure Drop
Cry Little Sister
Greatest Good
Dead Hand

THE PRISONER AND THE SUN
Escape
Lights and Shadows
Final Passage

XGENERATION 1

You Don't Know Me

by Brad Magnarella

1

Gainesville, Florida
Sunday, August 26, 1984
8:05 a.m.

Scott Spruel leaned nearer the window and parted his bedroom blinds a little more, not wanting to lose her. She had already set a canvas bag in her sister Margaret's car and disappeared down her driveway, to the garage side of her house—the side he couldn't see.

"C'mon, c'mon, c'mon," he whispered.

He stole a look back to the car, where Margaret was sorting through the trunk. A red cooler came out then went back in along with a tasseled blanket and a second canvas bag, this one with sandals poking out.

Scott resumed his vigil over the distant driveway, the blinds trembling above his ink-stained fingers. He hoped to see her again—*had* to see her again—if only for a moment. Of course he told himself that every time, didn't he? *If only for a moment.* But what did he ever do with those moments? He could never make his legs move toward her, could not even premeditate the words he would say or how he would say them. He'd once spent half a day in front of his mirror trying out his greeting: "Hi, Janis," followed by an easygoing smile. He gave up when all he could manage was a Jokeresque parody of a grin.

A hopeless sigh steamed the glass. It had been a long summer.

Something flickered beyond the blur—a flame. Heart pounding, Scott wiped the window clean, wiped her into view.

Janis Graystone.

Her fiery-red ponytail swished over the straps of her white tank top as she jogged into view on lean, athletic legs. She bounced a soccer ball along the asphalt driveway, an act as natural for her as chewing gum. The sound reached Scott's ears a split second after each impact. It was the distance, that impossible distance between his house and hers—one hundred fifty yards, give or take

He began to sigh again but clamped his breath off.

Janis stopped where the driveway met the cul-de-sac and, before Margaret could prevent it, punted the ball. The ball disappeared into the car's trunk. Margaret said something, body thrust sternly forward, but Janis ignored her, raising her arms at her feat.

Silent laughter parted Scott's lips from his braces. For a moment, it felt as though he and Janis were connected again, time and space snapping away. But then she was climbing into the passenger's seat and closing the door. Margaret slammed the trunk closed and joined her on the driver's side. To Scott's ears, the faint start and rev of the engine signaled another opportunity slipping away.

The Honda Prelude rounded the cul-de-sac and came straight toward Scott, whose house faced the short street on which the Graystones lived. He drew back into the darkness before stopping himself.

"Who are you kidding?" he mumbled. "She's not going to notice you."

After all, she hadn't noticed him since the end of fifth grade, more than three years earlier. Why would she start now? He pushed his glasses to the bridge of his nose and parted the plastic blinds once more.

When the dark blue car arrived at the top of the street, morning light illuminated Janis's face. A clean glow shone over the pull of her hair, her perfect brow, cheeks Scott could only imagine himself caressing, her full lower lip. The light caught the depth and pensiveness of her chestnut eyes as well, even as they squinted. It was the most clearly he had seen her in years.

Then the car turned, and the square of sunlight slid from Janis, and only the street remained.

Scott let the blinds snap closed. It took several seconds for the green glow of his computer to reclaim his bedroom, to redefine the heaps of clutter around him. He swiveled back to the blinking cursor on his TRS-80. With burning, sleep-deprived eyes, he scanned the lines of commands and responses that had delivered him to his present point, the same lines he had been staring at since late the night before. The modem clicked and hummed.

"If you want true power," Scott whispered to himself, "you have to finish this. You have to go back inside."

He hesitated before closing his eyes. Behind his sealed lids, he was startled to find an afterimage of Janis's face, no less stunning for being a negative. But by then, his consciousness was already squeezing through the computer modem, being shot along the network. And though Scott struggled to hold on to her image, it was soon lost to a cold and bewildering storm of data and electrical current.

2

Crescent Beach, Florida
Later that day

"Do you ever think we're being watched?" Janis asked.

She lifted her head from her soccer ball and squinted past her toes, still slick with sunblock, to where the beach crowd thinned near the crash and rumble of the ocean. For the first time, she and Margaret had the beach blanket to themselves, and she knew it wouldn't last. Beyond her feet and off to the right, her sister's three friends squealed and pranced from the water's edge in new bikinis. The bright pastel colors made them hard to miss. They would probably be running back this way any minute.

"Well, we *are* at the beach," Margaret said.

Janis turned onto her elbow. In contrast to her airhead friends, her older sister lay in quiet repose, brunette hair tucked into a neat bun that cushioned her head and opened her lithe neck to the sun. Black Wayfarers hid her eyes. When the breeze stirred, the strings of her apple-red bikini fluttered against her hip.

"Not here, I mean," Janis said. "In the neighborhood. At home. I keep having this feeling that we're—"

"Being watched? Like the song?"

Janis groaned. She had walked right into that one. "Somebody's Watching Me" had played on the boom box a half hour before, the deejay at I-100 FM using a creepy ghoul's voice when he recapped the song and artist.

"Not funny," she said.

"Couldn't resist. Go on."

"All right, but no more jokes. This is serious."

The corner of Margaret's glossy lips tipped into a half-smile. She sat up and checked her stomach before dripping tanning oil into her hand and spreading it around her golden belly.

Janis became aware of her own stomach starting to burn and reached for the sunblock. "There are just these ... dreams I keep having," she said, rubbing a dollop above then below her lime-green bottoms. She tested the fading bruise on the side of her thigh—softball casualty. "But they're not dreams. Not exactly. They're more like out-of-body experiences."

"Out-of-what?"

"I think that's what they're called."

"If you say so."

Janis capped the sunblock and searched her sister's face. She was wading into the paranormal, which wasn't exactly her thing and was much less Margaret's. But with the experiences happening almost nightly now, Janis needed to confide in someone, even if that someone was her ultra-pragmatic sister.

"Anyways, in these dreams, these experiences, I'm suddenly awake, and I'm standing in the backyard. And there's this strange energy all around me: *whoosh-whoosh-whoosh*. Like the wind's blowing but deeper and ... rougher, I guess."

Janis waved her hands around her head in demonstration, but Margaret was on her back again, the sun shining along her slender legs and glinting off toenails painted red to match her bikini.

"How can you be awake if you're asleep?"

"That's just it. When it happens, I'm as awake as I am now. But my body's still in bed. I mean, I can't feel my body, but I know I'm not actually standing out in the backyard."

"Maybe you're sleepwalking. Mom says I used to sleepwalk."

"Wouldn't I wake up in the morning with crud on my feet if—"

"People do strange things when they sleepwalk. I read about this guy from California who mowed his entire lawn, front and back. And he didn't remember a thing when he woke up."

"What does that have to do with—"

"Only found out because his neighbors called the police. You know, the noise of the mower."

"Margaret!"

"Oh," she cut in again, "and he was buck naked."

Janis snort-laughed. Margaret joined her, her own laughter illuminating the backward tilt of her face. Disney couldn't have animated a more perfect laugh. The only things missing were the little woodland creatures. But Janis only half begrudged Margaret her laugh, especially since her sister didn't seem to let it out often enough.

"All right." Margaret cleared her throat and retucked her bun beneath her head. "I'll give you that you're somehow awake in the backyard while asleep in bed. But what does that have to do with being watched?"

"I...," Janis began, then pressed a loose strand of hair to her nose. That's where things got tricky.

6

She didn't always remember the out-of-body experiences—not in detail, anyway. A dream would often intrude then another and another, such that by morning, she could only dimly remember the experience. All that remained were whatever impressions still lingered in her memory, faint and ghostly. And that's what Janis felt at that moment, what she had been feeling all day: a spine-needling impression that someone had been watching.

And hadn't there been a smell? Cigarette smoke? Or maybe she was confusing last night's experience with the present.

The approaching surfer took a final pull on his stub, then flicked it away, not looking where it landed. A blue tattoo stained his upper arm: a dagger piercing a heart. The surfer behind him was sharp faced and darkly freckled, his nose coated in silver zinc. Janis peeked toward Margaret and began drawing her legs in.

The surfers swaggered toward the blanket as though meaning to trample over it. They stopped at the last moment, propping their boards on end. Tattoo glanced along Janis's legs then turned his gaze back on Margaret. He tossed his slick, sandy hair to the side, his stubbly cheeks swelling around a pair of hard dimples.

Margaret raised her Wayfarers a half inch, then lowered them.

"Move along, boys," she said.

The surfers' smiles faltered. It was the way she had said it: no nonsense, her tone sounding older than her seventeen years. Freckles whispered something near Tattoo's ear, drawing a stupid leer.

Janis suddenly felt naked in her two-piece and turned onto her side, pulling her knees in even more. The xylophonic beats of Bananarama's "Cruel Summer" popped from the boom box, but there was no fun in them. Janis peered toward the ocean, wishing Margaret's friends were crowding the blanket again, giggles and all. It figured. Now that they were needed, they were nowhere to be found.

"Whoa, babe," Tattoo said. His ragged wetsuit was peeled below his navel, and the neoprene arms flopped around his thighs as he gave his hair another toss. "What's that all about? Can't a dude admire the scenery?"

His friend sniggered, and the two of them edged closer. Tattoo could have been cute, Janis thought, but there was a crudeness in his manner, in the way they were both standing, hips thrust forward. She imagined it would only take a few beers for them to become dangerous. The tip of Tattoo's board dripped water near Margaret's feet as he staggered a step nearer.

They'd probably already had a few.

"Admire it somewhere else," Margaret said, still on her back. Then added, "*Dude.*"

"Or what? Gonna choke us with those fine legs?"

Their laughter landed like blades in Janis's stomach. Margaret rose onto her elbows. She raised her sunglasses again, propping them over her teased bangs. Her sea-green eyes studied the surfers sternly.

"Oooh," Tattoo said, waggling his fingers in feigned fear. "A man-eater."

Freckles sniggered, the oily silver glistening along the blade of his nose.

Margaret's eyes didn't flinch.

"Oh, c'mon, baby. Don't be like that." Tattoo pushed his board toward Freckles and planted a sand-caked foot on the blanket. "I'm just trying to make some conversation." It came out *convershashum.*

When Janis looked up, Freckles was grinning down at her. The tip of his tongue emerged, worm-like, and ran across his mottled lips. Janis edged toward her sister. But now Tattoo was planting his hand like he meant to lower himself between them, the muscles bunching across his upper back. Margaret didn't shrink from him. Neither did her gaze waver from his face.

"I said *move along*."

Janis imagined herself lifting the red Igloo cooler behind them, using her knee to help boost it higher, the dozen-odd cans of Tab slish-sloshing in the melting ice. She imagined dropping—no, slamming—it on the side of Tattoo's head.

But as Janis tensed to move, the muscles across Tattoo's back softened.

"...the hell?" he muttered.

Like a movie reel being played in reverse, he rose from his three-point stance to his knees, to his feet, and shuffled backward until he was beside Freckles again. His jaw hung to one side, as though he was uncertain of what he was doing. Freckles's tongue crawled back into his mouth.

Janis followed their squinting gazes toward Margaret. Her no-nonsense expression hadn't changed ... except for her eyes. A deeper shade of green grew inside them, seeming to hold Tattoo. Freckles, too.

Ten seconds passed. Twenty. A dry click sounded from Tattoo's throat. Freckles shivered. The two of them had diminished, their boards no longer penetrating the space above the blanket, their hard arms deflated. Or maybe it only seemed that way because Janis could sense how badly they wanted to leave. They were just waiting for the excuse, waiting for Margaret to release them.

Freckles glanced down at Janis, his expression the plea of a lost child.

Janis looked around, the shouts from a volleyball game, the crash of the surf—Bananarama, even—sounding hard to her, raw. She hadn't even wanted to come to the beach that day. She'd originally planned to spend the morning in goalie gloves and a practice jersey, beaming a soccer ball off the garage door. ("So bring your ball," Margaret had told her. "Problem solved.") Now, trapped between Margaret and the surfers, her stomach twisting into knots, Janis tried to imagine herself seventy miles inland, the driveway at her feet, the woods at her back, slinging the soccer ball toward the garage door, gathering the rebound...

Margaret gave a small sigh and lowered her shades.

"My sister and I were talking." She pronounced every syllable as though explaining the concept to a pair of slow children. "You know, having a *con-ver-sa-tion*. And you interrupted us. May we finish now?"

"Uh, yeah ... whatever," Tattoo said hoarsely, already turning. His board collided into Freckles's as the two of them wheeled in opposite directions.

A small part of Janis wanted to laugh. She cringed and curled her toes instead.

The surfers straightened themselves out and made for the boardwalk, Freckles stammering an apology over his shoulder. Margaret adjusted her top and lay back down, frowning as though the whole episode had been nothing more than a minor irritation.

"How do you do that?" Janis asked.

"Do what?"

"That. Getting people to do whatever you want?"

Margaret shrugged. "I just tell them."

Janis watched the surfers disappear beyond the dunes separating the beach from the public restrooms. It was true. Margaret always told people what she wanted, and nine times out of ten, she seemed to get it: an A in the few cases where she'd earned a B+, a speeding warning instead of a hefty fine and points, another curfew extension from Dad. And her job. Even though she was the youngest salesperson at the JC Penney in the mall, she earned the fattest commissions by far, more than double anyone else's. She'd already been promised a management position after graduation, a position she declined, thanks but no thanks. Business school called.

But what just happened? What was that?

"Don't worry about them," Margaret said. Janis caught herself staring at the place where the surfers had disappeared. "They were jerks. Worse than jerks. Pigs. And they *did* interrupt us. You were telling me about a dream?"

Janis felt herself nod, but before she could reassemble her thoughts, Margaret's friends burst onto the blanket: "Did you, like, see that girl's hair?" "What a total *disaster*." "It's like she set it with a waffle maker!"

Margaret rose and brushed her legs off, scolding the girls for tracking sand onto the blanket. At five foot ten, she stood a full head taller than her friends. When she got them settled, she drew several quarters from her canvas bag and announced she was going up to the pay phones to call her boyfriend, Kevin. She set off through the patchwork maze of beach towels and glistening sunbathers while Janis tried to come up with an excuse to tag along.

Before that could happen, Heather swiveled toward her. "Feather Heather," Janis still thought of her, because of her blond Farrah Fawcett 'do. She'd trimmed it shorter over the years, but the neat center part, highlights, and flipped out sides had never quite gone away.

Heather plucked up the book at Janis's hip and held it at arm's length. "Eww," she said, making a face. "Summer reading?"

Janis started to shake her head, then stopped. She *had* been assigned summer reading, but this wasn't *1984*. It was *The Outsiders*, a book she'd already read twice but grabbed off her bookshelf anyway. There was something in the urban edginess that captivated her, something in the idea of kids her age—Ponyboy and Johnny—having to go it alone in that kind of world while somehow managing to "stay golden." It wasn't Sweet Valley High, that was for sure.

It also wasn't something Heather would ever understand.

"Yeah," Janis said. "Summer reading."

"Who's your freshman English teacher?"

"It's not Mr. Adams, is it?" Tina asked hopefully. She had pulled a *Flashdance*-style workout shirt over her blue bikini and begun fumigating her dark, voluminous hair with Aqua Net. Janis squinted and held her breath as the mist blew past, the chemical tang finding the back of her mouth anyway.

"Tina had, like, the biggest crush on Mr. Adams," Heather explained.

"You thought he was hot, too!"

Janis cleared her throat. "Fern," she said. "Mrs. Fern."

"She's *totally* weird," Tina said.

"Weird?" Janis asked. "How so?"

"Like, forget the teachers." Heather waved her hand. "They're all weird."

"For sure," Tina said. "The important question is..."

Janis's face began to burn. She knew what was coming.

"...do you have a *boyfriend* yet?"

Kelly's crimped hair shook as she giggled.

"Well, no ... I mean..." Janis hoped her cheeks weren't as red as they felt. "I play a lot of sports, so I don't really have time..."

The girls pressed nearer. Janis winced, trying her best to endure their close company. They were Margaret's friends, after all, and high school seniors. But the truth was, she would have traded them for her fellow summer-league outfielders in an instant. At least she could *communicate* with them, especially Samantha, her best friend. Samantha would be starting Thirteenth Street High tomorrow too, but bummer of bummers, wasn't going to be in any of her classes.

"So, like, listen," Heather said, turning a serious face on her. "If you're going to start out on the right foot, there are a few groups of guys you totally need to know about. First, avoid the losers."

"Losers?"

"Yeah," Tina said. "The ones in black. Heavy metal shirts. Commando pants. Gross, stringy hair."

"Pizza-faced burnouts," Kelly added with a giggle.

"They park on Titan Terrace behind the school and smoke cloves," Heather said, "among other things. Get mixed up with that crew and you can, like, kiss your reputation goodbye."

"Forever," Tina added gravely.

Janis looked around for Margaret.

"So right, forget about them," Heather said, taking Janis's arm. "The group you totally want to start with are the preps. They're clean, well-dressed, have money, so you're, like, guaranteed a good date. Not some cheap park-and-grope."

"Janis said she's into *sports*." Tina pronounced it as though it was a foreign word. "She'd probably have better luck with the jocks."

Janis tuned the girls out as they went back and forth on whether she was better suited for a prep, a jock, or some hybrid of the two. She squinted past them to the surf, where the heads of swimmers bobbed like buoys and waves frothed toward shore, some carrying surfers. Farther out, the water had turned the color of gunmetal. Black clouds churned against the horizon. From deep inside one mass, lightening flashed. Janis squinted, trying to gauge whether or not the clouds were moving inland.

"Whatever!" Heather relented with a loud sigh and took Janis's arm again. "The point is, preps are for sure where you want to start. And there *are* preps among the jocks." She shot a narrow look at Tina. "Nice ones, too."

"Anyway, after preps and jocks, the pickings are pretty slim," Tina said. "Though it doesn't hurt to flirt with the nerds now and again."

"Why would you do that?" Janis asked.

"To get help with your math."

The others nodded wisely. It took Janis a second to realize they were serious and another to decide that the last five minutes had been a complete waste of her life. She found herself wishing again that she'd stayed home.

"What kind of nonsense are you filling my sister's head with?"

The girls spun from her so abruptly that Janis felt like she was being dropped. It was a relief, though. She had been getting that prickly, pressed-in feeling she sometimes got around large crowds. She squinted up at Margaret, who stood over them looking toward the ocean.

Margaret clapped her hands briskly. "We've got about ten minutes to pack it in, girls. A storm's coming."

Janis slept most of the ride home, her sluggish rest textured by the grit of salt and dreams of black thunderheads. She awakened when Feather Heather, their last drop-off, hugged Margaret through the window and jogged up her parents' walkway.

"See you tomorrow," Heather called over her shoulder.

Janis yawned and looked over her ruddy arms, which stung when she stretched them. SPF 20 or no, the sun had done a number on them.

"Did you have a good time?" Margaret asked as she swung from Heather's neighborhood. They had beaten the storm inland, and now the setting sun filtered through the canopy of oak trees, flashing the car with golden light. Margaret smiled and squeezed Janis's knee, not waiting for her answer. "My little sister. I can't believe you're going to be a Thirteenth Street Titan tomorrow."

Janis winced, watching the blanched spots on her knee turn red again. Her legs had fared little better than her arms. "Yeah, me neither."

"Don't worry about whatever Heather and the others told you." Margaret sighed and shook her head. "They're boy crazy, so I can only guess. Take care of yourself first, and the boy thing will take care of itself. Just look at me and Kevin..." Her voice trailed off.

When Janis peered over, she found her sister's gaze lingering on the rearview mirror.

"So it *was* him," Margaret said.

"Who? Kevin?" Janis asked, turning.

"No, no, I saw his car in the lot when I went to call Kevin. It was parked a little down from ours. He's been behind us most of the way home." Margaret returned her gaze to the road. "Never struck me as the beach type."

"*Who?*"

"Mr. Leonard."

"Leonard?" Janis echoed.

"Yeah, from the neighborhood."

And now Janis could see the bug-eyed Datsun some three or four cars back. A faint queasiness gripped her and she faced forward again, slumping down. Sweat broke around her throat.

"Is something the matter?" Margaret asked.

"Nuh-uh," Janis answered quickly.

Then why are you losing it? She pressed her hand to her chest as if that could suppress the escalating thuds. Her body was reacting to his name, to the fact that he was behind them. *But why?* It wasn't like her to freak out. If she were alone, she might have slapped herself.

Margaret slowed toward the landscaped island and wooden sign that announced their neighborhood: OAKWOOD. Janis peeked into the passenger-side mirror in time to see the signal light on the green hatchback flashing. She imagined Mr. Leonard's long, pale brow looming over the wheel, his yellow-tinted glasses tracking the turn into Oakwood. Tracking them, maybe.

Then, for no apparent reason, Janis imagined his lips holding a cigarette.

Only there was a reason.

Janis sat upright as if she *had* slapped herself, her thoughts sharpening to points. The experience last night. The dream-that-wasn't-a-dream. In it, the orange tip of a cigarette had illuminated a pair of glasses. Yes, yes, she remembered that now. Someone had been watching. From the house behind theirs, the one on Oakwood's main street, up ahead on the left.

The house where Mr. Leonard lived.

Janis peered beyond Margaret as they drew nearer the dark brown house. It stood two stories tall, its windows seeming to possess a disturbing sense of sight now, a disturbing *knowing*. The windows were bracketed by false shutters the color of old yellow teeth, the same color as the front door. Looking on them, Janis felt an acute ache inside her own jaw—and in her right side, for some reason. She jerked when the garage door gave a lurch. It ratcheted upward like a gaping mouth.

"Janis?"

Janis turned from her sister's concerned face to peer into the passenger-side mirror again. She watched the Datsun slow, then angle sharply into the driveway and disappear from sight.

3

Scott Spruel's glasses clicked against something. His eyes opened to a green-pixelated blur and his lungs to a broth of computer fumes. He pushed himself from the computer screen—vertebrae popping in a line—until he met the chair's felt backrest. Gasping, he swiveled toward the window.

All of the cars in his subdivision had a distinctive sound, a *signature*, and Scott had come to recognize the Prelude's, to anticipate its return. He parted two of the blinds, as he had done that morning, but now peered onto a street cast in tea-colored light and steep shadows.

Cripes, how long have I been gone?

Before Scott could twist his watch right-side up, Margaret's car was passing in front of his house, turning down the short street. It circled the cul-de-sac, tires swishing against the blacktop, and eased to a stop in front of the Graystones'. Seconds later, Janis stepped from the car, her hair still up in a ponytail, but her face now ruddy with sun. Scott imagined the warmth of the beach across her shoulders.

He sat up straighter, his lips beginning to move: *Hi, Janis.*

Janis disappeared behind the car's open trunk door and reappeared seconds later, canvas bag slung over her shoulder, soccer ball tucked inside her elbow. She backed toward the driveway and cocked a hip beneath the ball as she waited for Margaret to close up the car.

Enjoying your last day of freedom? he asked in his head. *Yeah, me too. Are you nervous about high school? Don't be. They say it's just like middle school, only astronomically harder.* Scott gritted his teeth. *("Astronomically," you dipshit? "Astronomically?") And look on the bright side. We can count our remaining years of incarceration on one hand. Or, more precisely, on one of E.T.'s hands. With his ... um ... four fingers.*

"God, you're hopeless," Scott muttered.

He drove his imaginary self away from Janis with a twelve-pronged flog.

Janis started up the semi-circular driveway, Margaret joining her. A cabbage palm centerpieced their front lawn, and Scott had to crane his neck to keep Janis in view. When she arrived on the front porch, she paused, her ponytail swishing as she looked around. Then she disappeared inside the house after Margaret.

Scott released the blinds. Another opportunity gone.

He sagged back toward his computer, picking at the handwritten notes piled in small drifts around the equipment on his desk. He fought to concentrate, his mind reeling from Janis's entrance into his world, from her just as sudden removal. He selected a random scrap of graph paper and held it up to his glasses: ARPANet command lines he'd copped from a hacking board, nothing that was going to help him here. He tossed the paper aside. No, he was deeper in than that.

He blinked and read to the bottom of the screen:

```
. . . . .

. . . . .

- Open

WELCOME  TO  STLA-TAC  -  ARMY  INFORMATION  SYSTEMS
COMMAND - ST. LOUIS

  **FOR OFFICIAL USE ONLY**

  **TRESPASSERS WILL BE PROSECUTED**

  - Login?

  > sys2428

  - Password?

  > ggt925
```

Only one digit remained in the password, one decisive digit.

Scott swallowed the bitter bite of adrenaline. He had taken special care to mask his modem call through a series of innocuous 1-800 numbers. But this caller wasn't acting innocuously, far from it. He was dialing into no-no land.

Once more, Scott closed his eyes and concentrated on the modem. A part of his mind—his consciousness, he supposed—began twining in on itself like copper filaments inside a tapering cable. The twists came sharper, tighter, his world constricting toward a suffocating darkness.

Hold on for a few more seconds...

His head felt like it was being crushed inside a compactor.

A few more seconds to ... true ... power...

At last he was forced through what felt like a pinpoint. He burst into a chaotic beyond.

Scott could still sense himself sitting at his desk, his fingers resting on the blocks of keys, but his immediate experience, his *reality*, was that of speed, of supercharged distances. He shot along the telecommunication lines, frames, and mechanical switches, *becoming* the connection: Gainesville to Jacksonville, then along a major trunk line to Atlanta. Within milliseconds, he was in the St. Louis area, cascading down local loops to the Army Information Systems Command, his latest and—if he succeeded—greatest hack.

The perfect job for Stiletto.

Of all his Dungeons & Dragons characters, Stiletto remained Scott's guilty favorite. An 18th-level thief, Stiletto had a bad habit of getting into places he wasn't supposed to get into and accessing things he wasn't supposed to access. In one campaign, he'd hidden away his teammates' magical items and then ransomed them back for leadership. Craig and Chun refused to role-play with him for months after, but Scott didn't see what the big deal was. He hadn't kept their items, hadn't pawned them for gold or platinum pieces. No, he'd only wanted to see whether he *could* do it—and with a pair of killer rolls on a twenty-sided die, he *had*.

Just like now. Scott only wanted to see whether he could do it: slip past Uncle Sam's sentry, snoop around a little to prove he'd been there, and then leave for good. The campaign secure under his belt, nothing stolen or damaged, no one the wiser.

And that would be enough.

Scott concentrated, grounding himself in the data current. He imagined himself as Stiletto, crouched before a forbidden gate, peering into an elaborate locking mechanism. Scott owned a real lock-picking kit, something he'd sent away for the year before and then put into practice on every pin- and disc-tumbler system he could get his hands on. He imagined himself drawing the tools from his belt, inserting his favorite pick, listening, feeling...

Far away, Scott's finger punched a key. He trained his thoughts on the modem, on "beaming out," and in a shot, his consciousness returned to his body. The screen swam into focus.

And there it was:

```
- Password?
> ggt9251
```

His index finger hovered over the RETURN key, but Scott already knew. He didn't need to press the key to find out. He was on the brink of breaking inside the information system for the United States Army.

The power!

"Scott?"

His knees banged into the bottom of the desk. "Cripes!" he cried, rubbing his thighs and twisting toward the door. Inside the growing shaft of light loomed his mother's barrel-sized silhouette. J.R., their toy poodle, stood beside her in a knitted dog sweater, rattling with nervous energy. Scott threw his hand to his brow as his mother flipped on the light switch, his heart still racing.

"Don't you knock?" he muttered.

"What was that, mister?"

Scott's throat constricted as he swallowed his words. She stared at him another moment, her eyes like black tacks, then nodded. *That's what I thought*, said the nod. She shot her gaze around the room.

"Have you been in here all day?"

"No." Scott walked his legs further under the desk where she wouldn't see his pajama bottoms.

"Do you think Lee Iacocca got to where he is by shutting himself in a sty and playing computer games all day?"

Scott shrugged. He had no idea who Lee Iacocca was.

Nose wrinkled, his mother shuffled sideways into the cluttered space, just far enough to hold out the cordless phone. "Wayne's on the line." Her frown supplied the *again*. "And your father's late bringing home dinner, but he's on his way." *Again*.

Scott took the phone. "Could you, um—would you please cut the light on the way out?"

His mother's chest swelled as though she were going to say something more, maybe insist he clean his room—she'd been on him about it all summer—but she only huffed and turned. J.R. used the opportunity to squirt through the closing door without her seeing. He wasn't allowed in the bedrooms and stood trembling, watching Scott with liquid eyes. "I won't tell if you won't," Scott said, which set J.R.'s cotton-ball tail into a frenzy of beating.

When Scott lifted the phone to his ear, he felt his exhaustion. "Hey, Wayne."

"Oh man, you missed a *killer* one." Wayne's first words always exploded from the receiver as if he couldn't get them out quickly enough. "I dungeon-mastered the entire *Dragonlance* manual, and Craig and Chun gained a *ton* of experience points. They're way beyond any of your characters, Scott-o. And I mean *way* beyond. Light years. It's going to take four or five campaigns to even catch them, assuming they're just sitting around on their asses." He laughed his annoying, chopped laugh. "I guess you won't be leading any more parties anytime soon. And you can forget about trying to steal their charmed boots again because—"

"I hacked Army Information."

A low, buzzing silence grew on the line. Scott imagined Wayne's fingers pausing over his threadbare mustache, mid-stroke.

"When?"

"This weekend. Just now. It's why I skipped out on D&D."

"Yeah, right."

But Scott could hear the strain in Wayne's voice, the deflating sense of his superiority.

"I'm looking at it, Wayne-o. Want a print-out?"

"How?"

Scott opened his mouth to answer, then paused.

Scott had met Wayne in the seventh grade while wandering through the gymnasium at the school's annual science fair. He'd stopped in front of a tri-paneled display crookedly stenciled "Blue Boxing: The Future of Telephony." Beneath the display sat a jerry-rigged circuit board and beside the circuit board, the smirking owner.

"Can that thing really make free calls anywhere in the world?" Scott asked. He had read about blue boxes in a science and technology magazine.

The smirker stroked the peach fuzz across his pursed upper lip like a prepubescent James Bond villain. "Meet me at the pay phones after school," he replied, "and you'll find out."

Two things happened for Scott that day. He found a kindred spirit in Wayne, and the national phone network—"Ma Bell" before the January breakup—became an obsession, the sweating-in-your-sleep kind. Over the next several months, Scott memorized the network's hierarchy, from the small local exchanges all the way to the Class 1s in cool-sounding places like White Plains, New York and San Bernardino, California. From phone phreaking, Wayne introduced him to the wonderful world of ARPANet and computer hacking.

Sometime in the eighth grade, Scott's knowledge surpassed Wayne's. Wayne, who had anointed himself high priest of the Creekside Middle School brainiacs (or nerd heap, depending on who you talked to), went ballistic, demanding Scott scrap every bit of info he'd ever supplied him. But by then, Scott knew most of the dial-up numbers and logins by heart. Some he had gotten from Wayne, others from party lines and hacker boards. The rest…

Well, the rest he had just started feeling.

"The boards," Scott heard himself telling Wayne. J.R., fresh from rummaging through the closet, clambered onto Scott's lap, and he cradled the dog against his bare stomach. "I got the login and password from a board, one of Goblin's posts."

"Goblin? He's not dumb enough to post that kind of intel, not after the FBI crackdown. So let's agree that you're getting it off a message board is total crapola. What does that leave us?" Wayne began humming the Jeopardy theme song. "Oh, wait, wait, I know! You *felt* it."

Scott pressed his lips together.

"Oh, just spit it out, half-wit."

Scott sighed. "We've been over this. I enter the network. I listen. I feel. That's all I can tell you. I don't know how it happens, I don't know why it works. It just does. If you can't accept it, that's your problem."

Another long, buzzing silence.

"Share everything."

"What?"

"That was the promise, the Hacker's Pact. *Share everything*." Wayne's voice trembled over the line. "I-I'm the one who got you into phreaking. I'm the one who turned you onto hacking. And you keep pulling this … this crap! I'm going to ask you one more time. How did you get in?"

"I just told you."

"Ass-wad."

The line clicked. Scott set the phone aside to help J.R. squirm out of his stupid dog sweater. Freed from his knitted bondage, J.R. leaped into a pile of clothes and proceeded to dig out a bed.

Scott pushed himself from his desk. When his knees cracked, he realized it was the first time he'd stood since the night before, some twenty hours earlier. He staggered through a scatter of empty RC Cola cans, edged past his clothes-draped dresser, between teetering boxes of comic books (the one thing for which he actually had a semi-coherent system of organization) and found his bed. He stretched to his full length, his heels reaching beyond the end of a mattress he had outgrown, featuring a faded Buck Rogers fitted sheet with Twiki the robot. Overhead, model spaceships swung on threads from the AC vent.

With a gangly leg, Scott pushed aside a couple of Bell South technical manuals, and with the other, a copy of *1984*, which he had yet to even crack. *Crap. School tomorrow.* Which meant the summer's hacking marathons were over.

He dropped his glasses on his chest and rubbed his eyes with the heels of his palms, making stars explode across his vision. He tried telling himself he'd still have nights and weekends, but the notion only depressed him. The thought of sitting through seven classes, computerless, modemless, in a new school, surrounded by a new class of cretins bent on making his life hell...

But Janis will be there.

Her sunlit face from that morning glimmered in his mind's eye. Scott laced his fingers behind his stiff hair, reveling and suffering in the image. It seemed impossible that a younger version of the same girl used to speak to him, smirk at his jokes, sock him in the shoulder, hold his hand.

Forgetting his hack and his fight with Wayne, Scott drew his softest pillow around and nuzzled against it. Still holding the image of

Janis's face, he tried to imagine the feel of his fingers running through her hair, holding her cheek. He closed his eyes. Slowly, he began pressing his lips to the pillow.

A hard rap sounded on the door. "Dinner!"

Scott thrashed to a sitting position, terrified his mother had opened the door, relieved to find she had not this time. He waited for her sharp footfalls to retreat down the carpeted hallway before kicking out of his pajama bottoms and pulling on a pair of shorts and a mismatched collared shirt. He went to his computer and stared down on it.

Once more, his finger hovered over the RETURN key.

This time, he punched it.

```
· · · · ·
· · · · ·
** WELCOME **
Sunday, 24-AUG-84 5:13pm-PDT
>
```

The fatigue left Scott's body at once. He started to laugh. He had done it. Barely fourteen years old, and he was privy to the stuff of Matthew Broderick movies and hacker dreams.

He typed in **HELP** to be sure, watching as all of the possible commands marched down his screen. And because he was an administrator (so far as the system knew), an extra column scrolled out, listing his root privileges. Scott thumped his sternum with his fist, cringing a little at the force of the blow. But there it was: the power to create or delete accounts, change passwords, destroy files—hell, shut down the entire system if he wanted to.

Instead, Scott reached across to power up his printer. This one would go into the box at the back of his closet along with the others. Proof. Sweet, indisputable proof. But when his elbow knocked over the cordless phone, the consequences of bragging to Wayne about the hack gut-punched the rush right out of him.

Dumb. Really frigging dumb.

Because to lose Wayne as a best friend wasn't just to lose Wayne. Wayne would turn Craig and Chun against him as well. He had done it before. And how was that for starting high school, which was going to suck as it was? Computerless, modemless, and now friendless.

Scott eyed the phone, hesitated, then hit the speed dial for Wayne. He listened to the tones pulse out and waited for the ring.

But before the phone *could* ring, he mashed the phone off. Scott stood frozen. The receiver droned in his hand. The monitor in front of him, with its incriminating command lines, flashed with each hard swish of blood inside his ears. Scott exited Army Information, logged out of ARPANet, and, in a fury of typing, deleted the backdoor account he and Wayne had created.

He turned everything off, even his modem.

Especially his modem.

The room went dark. Behind his desk, Scott squirmed inside the snake's nest of cords, yanking every plug from the power strip, already begging his parents' forgiveness in his mind. He kept hearing—no, *feeling*—that interval between the final pulses for Wayne's number and the ring. A matter of milliseconds, probably, but it didn't matter. It had been milliseconds too long.

When he stood, the room wavered around him. The corner street light came on, illuminating his blinds. When something damp touched his calf, Scott nearly screamed. J.R. nosed him again and then gave a tentative lick. Scott collapsed to his haunches, the life gone from his legs. He rubbed the stiff curls around J.R.'s vanity collar.

"This is bad, buddy," Scott mumbled. "Really bad."

Because those milliseconds too long meant one thing to Scott, and one thing only. His phone line, his calls, his hacks—it was all being monitored.

4

"How well do you know Mr. Leonard?" Janis asked.

Her mother's face appeared over the top of the mustard-colored refrigerator door. Even from across the kitchen table, Janis could see lines forming between her brows. "Mr. Leonard?"

"The neighbor behind us," Janis said.

Her mother disappeared inside the refrigerator again. Janis edged her gaze to her father, who had paused mid-chew to listen to the evening news on the TV. Margaret appeared equally absorbed in the anchor, who spoke gravely over their dinner: "NATO is proceeding with plans to deploy six hundred new American missiles in Europe. The comments came following the Soviet Union's announcement Saturday that it had conducted successful tests of its ground-launched cruise missiles."

Their father grunted and resumed eating.

"Well, they both seem nice enough," her mother said, closing the refrigerator door and returning with a fresh bowl of grated cheddar.

She was wearing tan slacks and a print blouse—modern housewife attire, she called it. "Tend to keep to themselves. Why do you ask?"

Because I think Mr. Leonard has been watching us.

"Just curious," Janis said, gesturing impatiently for her mother to sit and eat. Everyone else was almost done with their first taco while her mother had yet to even start dressing hers.

"Did he say something to you?"

Janis shook her head and pretended to become interested in the news. Her mother, who made it a habit to stress over everything, remained staring at her, the worry lines spreading around her pale blue eyes now.

Should never have opened my mouth, Janis thought as she crunched into her taco.

The news segment ended, and the ubiquitous commercial for Viper Industries came on: "In these challenging times, the security of the United States and its citizens cannot be underfunded. Call your congressperson and ask them to hasten approval of the V-III missile system, the next generation of—"

Her father muted the television. "What was that about Mr. Leonard?"

Oh, for the love of...

"He was at the beach today," Margaret answered for Janis—a not uncommon occurrence, especially when her sister had no idea what was being discussed. "I just hope he covered that chrome dome of his."

Their father began spooning ground beef into the bottom of his second taco. He was staid-faced, with stiff gray hair receding blade-like above tanned temples. Their mother was younger, with Dee Wallace blond hair, but paler than their father, more careworn. They had met in college as many couples did—only he had been her political science professor, more than ten years her senior.

"When does soccer start?" he asked.

"Tryouts in four weeks," Janis replied, grateful for the change of topic.

"Think you're ready?"

"I will be. Gonna put in an hour of garage practice after dinner and a half-hour of dive and rolls in the side yard. Samantha's coming over this weekend so we can practice up in the Grove."

"Atta girl," he said, winking. He had lettered in three sports in college, and though he never said so, Janis could tell he was pleased one of his daughters had inherited his passion for athletics. And that, in turn, pleased Janis.

The news came back on, and he unmuted the television.

"...on a campaign stop in Ohio, President Reagan answered questions about a proposed summit with the Soviet Union."

"Our governments have had serious differences," Reagan said from an outdoor lectern, the wind tossing graying strands of hair from his steep side part. "But I stand by what I have said repeatedly: If their government wants peace, there will be peace." As he gripped the sides of the lectern, his grandfatherly voice began to shake. "Russians, hear this: A nuclear war cannot be won and must never be fought. The only value in our two nations possessing nuclear weapons is to ensure they will never be used."

"So far," the anchor concluded, "the Soviet leadership has expressed no willingness to meet."

"And they're not going to," Janis's father said. "Secretary Chernenko is as rooted in moldy Soviet-think as his predecessor."

"Oh, we don't know that," her mother whispered, the lines around her eyes seeming to grow taut. She looked from her husband to Janis, trying to smile, then down to her plate.

That night, Janis had the dream again, the *experience*.

But another dream preceded it, and in this one, she was back on the beach blanket, the soccer ball beneath her head. People were everywhere, the beach even more crowded than it had been that day. Margaret's friends were talking too close, debating about the hottest member of Duran Duran. "Rio" blared from the boom box, but it sounded warped—one moment chipmunk speed, the next slow and nauseating. Janis got up and pushed her way past Margaret's friends toward the sound of the surf. Underfoot, the sand firmed and dampened, making a sucking sound each time her foot flexed.

Soon, she found herself alone before the ocean. But the ocean looked larger, more daunting, and she squinted to see the faint line of the horizon. Across all of that water was no change, no point of reference, just endless gunmetal gray—like the sky. Janis hugged her shoulders and began to shiver. The season was no longer summer but pale winter.

She turned, seeking warmth, seeking people. Most of all, she sought Margaret. But Margaret was nowhere; the beach stood empty. Miles of sand rose, coarse and untrammeled, into dunes of wild sea grass.

Something flashed and rumbled. Janis spun back around. Far off over the ocean gathered the same black clouds that had threatened earlier, but these clouds were rising into a column ... an hourglass? The top began to bloom. No, not an hourglass, Janis saw in dawning terror.

A mushroom.

A low line of clouds blasted inland. A blistering wind dashed through her hair. The mushroom cloud grew taller, its cap more corpulent, rivaling the very ocean for size.

"Margaret!" she cried, but it came out a murmur.

The air stung Janis's nostrils as if something toxic were burning. She fled from the water, knowing only that she needed to get away, needed to escape inland. A fireball smashed into the beach to her right. Globules of melted sand splashed up. Another fireball landed to her left, and Janis screamed because she knew the next one was going to be the one to strike her. And moments later, as her legs swam against the inexorable pull of the sand, it did.

The sound—a walloping roar inside both ears—jolted Janis awake.

But she was not in her bed.

She stood in her backyard, beside the island of oak trees and azalea bushes. English ivy crept ink-like from the house, curling into tendrils near her toes. Vibrations coursed the length of her body and thrummed inside her head: *WHOOSH-WHOOSH-WHOOSH*. It was the same feeling she'd had in similar dreams that summer.

Similar out-of-body experiences.

Keep it together, she told herself. *Just keep it together.*

The backyard was dark, the household asleep. Janis guessed it was after midnight because no light shone from her father's study or bathroom. It dawned on her that she would also be inside, sleeping. And yet here she was, out in the yard, shimmering shapes playing across her vision.

When she first began to experience this state, she couldn't move or see. The shimmering shapes were as chaotic as the energies that ravaged her senses. *Am I dead?* she had asked herself the first time. *Is this hell?* Janis had prayed with everything she had that she be delivered from her wraithlike state and be restored to life. She started to panic when she remained paralyzed, but soon the vibrations faded, and cool, familiar sheets had enfolded her legs.

Now, with a little concentration, Janis made herself light. She giggled as her feet lifted from the grass. Free from gravity—or whatever passed for gravity here—Janis hovered above the lawn and began to drift its length, weaving around one plant island and then another.

Janis loved flying dreams, but she wasn't dreaming. She knew this because of the plastic egg. She had discovered it in the nest of ferns one night, near the clothesline. A purple egg, faded and spotted with dirt, half buried—one she and Margaret must have missed during a childhood Easter egg hunt.

A week had gone by before Janis remembered the experience with the plastic egg, sparked by a trip to a McDonald's during one of her softball camps. A couple of her teammates had gone into the play area and waded into the pit of colored balls. Colored *plastic* balls. That's all it had taken. For the rest of the camp, whenever Janis could remember, she repeated to herself, *plastic egg, clothesline, ferns.* Back home, Janis didn't even change out of her cleats. The egg was not in the exact spot, no. And it was yellow instead of purple. But what did that matter? It was *there*: half buried, spotted with dirt— like in the experience. She twisted it open and found two quarters. Now and again, she would retrieve the egg from the top drawer of her dresser and give it a little shake, the rattle of coins erasing her daytime doubts.

But she wasn't doubting now.

Janis neared the tall bushes that formed the boundary between their yard and the neighbor's and floated to a stop. In all of her experiences, the bushes were as far as she had gone—as far as she *could* go, it seemed. She extended an arm into the dark leaves and felt it being repulsed: a charge rebuffing another like charge. The harder Janis pushed, the harder the field shoved back on her.

All right, she conceded. *I'm not going to win this one.*

She drifted backward and lifted her face to where oak branches dipped and Spanish moss hung like beards. An urge came over her to perch on one of the branches and watch the night hum and crackle around her. Janis rotated as she rose, streams of energy seeming to trail out beneath her. When her gaze reached above the rear line of bushes, she froze.

The back of the Leonards' house appeared like a dark, dreadful creature emerging from the earth. But it was not the house that chilled her. It was the shadow of a human figure on the high deck and the point of light that smoldered red. The same light she had seen the night before and in the same place—at the height of the figure's head.

The light dimmed and fell. She pictured the threads of smoke snaking over the dark sloping yard, fording the cement culvert between their properties, filtering through the leaves. She did not know if she possessed smell in this state, but she imagined the low scent of the cigarette anyway.

When the point of light rose and smoldered again, it glinted against a pair of glasses.

The previous night, the same sight had driven Janis back to her body, back to her bed. But now she remained hovering. He couldn't see her after all. She was insubstantial, incorporeal. She drew courage from that vocabulary word—*incorporeal.* Drifting nearer the shrubbery, she peered past the leafy tops. The red spot of light rose and burned again. The lenses they illuminated were perfectly round.

Forward-facing.

And she could feel it too, somehow, the concentration coming from his shadow, the intent. This was not a person on a casual smoke break. Mr. Leonard was watching just as he had likely been watching at the beach that day, the throngs of beach-goers his shield, as the darkness was now.

But *why* was he watching?

Janis sifted through what little she knew of him. He had lived in the house as long as she had been aware of him. He had a wife, a pale woman with dust-colored hair, who stayed inside. No kids that Janis knew of. Sometimes he substitute taught. She'd seen him in the halls of her middle school as recently as last year, his dress shirt crumpled, his thinning wreath of hair in mild disarray, as if he were always filling in on short notice. He'd even subbed her history class once, his lecture voice thin and quavering. He never quite looked anyone in the eye, either, always down and to one side. So why was he watching now?

Margaret.

Her sister's name sprang into Janis's mind. Had he noticed her at school just as the surfers had noticed her on the beach that day? Had he become interested in her? Infatuated? Mr. Leonard had to be at least twenty years older than Margaret, but Janis's father had warned them about "sickos" during one of his serious talks. Was Mr. Leonard a sicko?

The tip of the cigarette inflamed his lenses again.

Janis started to withdraw, then stopped. *Incorporeal,* she repeated. *I am incorporeal.* As if to underline the affirmation, the energies that coursed throughout her intensified. Janis dove down and felt her way along the bushes, palpating with ethereal hands, probing for an opening. It felt crucial that she discover what he was up to, before something happened.

The barrier rebuffed her again and again and—

Her arm plunged through a place in the leaves that appeared just as thick as any other spot but did not feel like-charged. She withdrew her arm and felt the soft pull of a force that seemed reluctant to release her. An opposite charge. Even as Janis leaned away, she found herself reaching forward again, anticipating the fascinating tug on her fingertips.

And if I go through, what then? Will I be able to return?

Or would she become trapped on the outside, barred from her yard, her home, the bedroom where she slept … her own body? Beyond the leaves, the tip of the cigarette smoldered red again. Janis hesitated then let herself be pulled through in a cold and silent *whoosh*.

5

Spruel household
The next morning
6:36 a.m.

"What in the world were you doing in the garage last night?"

Scott jolted awake. He found himself at the kitchen table, one hand pushing his jaw askew, his other hand barely clinging to the end of a spoon. The spoon teetered over the rim of a bowl of soggy Golden Grahams. Dribbles of honey-colored milk spotted the plastic place mat.

He blinked up at his mom. "Huh?"

"You heard me, mister."

She clopped across their all-white kitchen to the freezer, pulled out an oat bran muffin, set it on a plate, clopped to the microwave, and jabbed the panel with her thumb. The microwave roared like a vacuum cleaner.

She leaned against the counter, facing Scott in her orange skirt suit. Arms crossed, she raised her freshly stenciled eyebrows. It was her Don't Mess with Me look. Scott cleared his throat and tried to sit straighter. His vision swam with sleep or, rather, the severe lack of it—four hours, maybe.

"My computer," he mumbled.

"What about your computer? And enunciate when you speak."

"It's not working." His cereal dissolved to mush when he stirred it. "Something with the motherboard, I think."

"Well, no wonder. With you on that thing all the time, it probably overheated."

"I brought it to the storeroom to fix."

"What storeroom?"

Yeah, what storeroom, genius? Wasn't that the whole point of bringing it back there? To hide it?

"In the garage," he replied, too spent to lie.

His mother gave a sharp laugh. She clopped to the chair at the kitchen table where her white leather briefcase hung and began flicking through the files of houses she'd be showing that day. She yanked a folder halfway out and then slid it, knife-like, back into place.

"I'm surprised you could even get back there. Your father with his ... *junk* piled floor to ceiling. I've given him a deadline. Thanksgiving. Everything has to be out of that garage by Thanksgiving, or so help me God, I'll have it hauled to the fill." She knifed another folder home. "And don't think I won't."

Scott's impulse was to defend his father, but he remained silent—as usual. Anyway, what she said was true. For all intents and purposes, his father was a hopeless, and pointless, junk collector. Lampshades, lawn chairs, lawn darts, rolls of linoleum, it didn't matter. If it was a deal, his father bought it. And then promptly stored it in the garage.

"I can't even remember the last time I parked in there." She found the folder she was hunting and flicked through its papers, repeatedly wetting the edge of her thumb. "Imagine that. The luxury of parking a car in the one place for which it was actually intended."

Scott grunted and slurped his cereal.

He was awake now, but it was a temple-boring wakefulness. After mining a tunnel through the garage last night and carrying his incriminating computer equipment, printouts, floppy disks, and Bell manuals to the rear storeroom, it was after two o'clock in the morning. He wasn't even able to manage one last check of his bedroom to see if he had missed anything. Fully dressed, he collapsed into sleep, only to dream his door was being kicked in. The FBI always raided in the wee hours, went the rumor. So you couldn't warn your hacker friends.

The microwave *beep-beep-beep*ed at the same moment his mother patted the files down and snapped her briefcase closed. "All right," she said, slinging the briefcase over her shoulder. "I put three dollars on the mantelpiece for your lunch. If there's any change, I want it. Mr. Shine might come this afternoon to weed. Tell him I'll have his check this weekend."

She wrapped the steaming muffin in aluminum foil, took a bite from the end, and patted her short, dark hair.

"And wake your father before you leave."

For the first time that morning, Scott became aware of the choked snores from the living room. After pizza last night, his father had fallen asleep on the couch, trying to watch his three rentals from Video World, action-comedies from the sounds of them. His volcanic laughter had erupted on and off until about a quarter to one, then ended abruptly.

"Yeah, all right," Scott said to his mother.

But she'd already seized her thermos of Ultra Slim-Fast and was halfway to the front door.

The early morning, though dim, felt raw against Scott's eyes. The front yard was empty, the street still. No swarm of black Crown Victorias parked helter-skelter over his lawn, which Scott had dreamed as well. He staggered down the street, wearing an oversized backpack into which he'd dropped some mechanical pencils, a scientific calculator, two sheaves of paper, a green Trapper Keeper, and his unread copy of *1984*. The backpack, one of his father's finds, had sagged to the backs of Scott's knees the year before; now it barely touched the hemlines of Scott's shorts. His summer growth spurt had been more vigorous than he realized.

He approached Oakwood's main intersection—no cars coming—and scuttled across. But he didn't stand beside the stop sign as the letter sent by the school had instructed. Instead, he studied the Pattersons' driveway, where a pair of tall bushes flanked the garage door. The nearer bush looked fuller. A moment later, he was crouched behind it, peering through the leaves at the intersection.

He shrugged off his backpack and held up his calculator-wristwatch. 7:02 a.m. He was probably safe unless the FBI decided to come for him at school or bide their time until the weekend, when they would have a better chance of catching him asleep.

That's how the FBI had nailed hackers all summer long. The thing of it was, the hackers Scott knew from the boards were harmless, not out to bring the system to its knees or start thermonuclear warfare (as if they could). To them, hacking was a challenge. It was learning how systems worked and then becoming master of those systems. It was sports for nerds. Scott had never scored a goal or a touchdown or swatted a home run—and probably never would. But he couldn't imagine any of those matching the rush of a successful hack.

Or the terror.

Scott watched cars pause at the stop signs, then cruise down the hill toward Sixteenth Avenue, their taillights as red and bleary as his eyes felt. Most of the cars he recognized, many of them just by the hum of their engines, the cut of their tires: Volkswagen Rabbit, Chevy Chevette, turd-brown Toyota Tercel. Most recognizable were those cars that came from the Meadows, the subdivision where Scott lived. Less familiar were the ones puttering up from the Downs or coasting down from the Grove, where the biggest houses were. The Grove also featured a field with a playground, where Scott used to venture—until Jesse Hoag snapped his arm.

Scott's hand went to the place above his right wrist where the bone had healed into a lump. It still swelled when he slept on it wrong, and it ached a little this morning. But his mind was preoccupied with his phone call to Wayne from the night before, those extra milliseconds between the final pulse and the ring.

How long had the FBI been monitoring him?

That Scott was too young for prison offered little consolation. He could still end up in juvie, and juvie would mean the worst abuses he had suffered during his ten years of public schooling added together and squared. He thought about all of the playground fights, the humiliating wedgies, the two times he'd had his head crammed in a bathroom toilet and flushed on.

His ears burned. No, he wouldn't do well in juvie.

And what about Wayne? With his Napoleonic size and D&D-themed insults, where he'd throw his face forward, lips pursed ("You're not a Night *Hag*," he'd once informed Scott during a spat.

"You're a Night *Fag*."), Wayne wouldn't last a day. And if the feds had a tap on the Spruels' line, chances were good they'd have one on Wayne's as well. Scott needed to warn him. The problem was, Wayne would want to know how he knew about the tap, and then they'd be right back to what caused their fall out in the first place.

Ass-wad, he heard Wayne saying.

Scott unzipped the small pocket on his backpack, took out his Thirteenth Street High class schedule, unfolded it, and ran his finger down the first column. Advanced Computer Programming. Third period.

He would have to figure out some way to warn him then without—

A thundering belch echoed from the Downs before falling into a guttural chop-chop-chop-chop. *Crap*. The sound came nearer. Scott crammed his schedule into his backpack and crouched low to the bush, checking to see that every part of him was concealed.

A minute later, the black car trundled into view. Not a Crown Victoria but a 1970 Chevy Chevelle. The car idled at the stop sign, the chop of its engine like crude laughter. Scott didn't need to see through the homemade tint job to know who was behind the wheel. The collapse of the car's frame toward the driver's side told him everything: Jesse Hoag, all three hundred pounds of him—the same three hundred pounds that had snapped his arm the summer before.

The Chevelle continued *chop-chop-chopp*ing, its wheels compressed to the pavement, not moving. When a minute passed, Scott became certain that he was spotted. He darted his gaze to the left. Could he get over the Pattersons' wooden fence in time, knock on the sliding glass door hard enough to awaken one or both of them, convince them to let him in?

Jesse was too big to give chase, but Creed Bast would be in the car with him. So would Creed's younger brother, Tyler. Both of them had tormented Scott at one time or another—and why not? Unlike Wayne, Scott knew the game; he knew the score. He was among the weakest and geekiest. He wore thick glasses and carried an inhaler until just last year. Worst of all, he owned a pair of legs that did everything but what he wanted them to do, especially in times of stress. The qualities had singled him out of the healthy herd long ago. Made him fair prey.

Beyond the bush, the Chevelle ripped another belch and idled. Scott inhaled a lungful of exhaust. Were they toying with him, daring him to step out? Scott tried to swallow the hard lump in his throat, afraid he might start blubbering like the last time they'd cornered him.

When the passenger-side door swung open, heavy-metal music blasted out. From a swirling fog of smoke, blue-tinted John Lennon shades appeared. The rest of Creed's narrow face followed. He'd grown his hair longer, Scott saw. The dirty blond hair fell from a black bowler hat that sat high on his head. Creed looked around, then said something over his shoulder.

One of his slender black boots landed on the pavement.

Scott slid his gaze to the Pattersons' fence and ran his dried-out tongue over his braces. It was now or never. Once Creed's second boot hit the pavement, Scott wasn't going to be able to outrun him, much less get himself up and over the fence. Scott rose to his haunches.

Creed draped his hair behind his ears. Then he snorted and hawked something into the street. His boot and glasses disappeared back into the fog, and the door slammed closed, muffling the music.

Scott sobbed once as he let out his air.

Huge brakes cawed, and a chrome yellow nose drew up behind the Chevelle. Two minutes late, but it was here, thank God. Scott stood from his crouch, ready to make for the school bus whenever the folding door flopped open. But the door wasn't opening. The bus tooted twice at the obstructing car, waited, then blew one long, exasperated honk.

A meaty hand appeared above the Chevelle on the driver's side, its middle finger extended.

The kids on the bus begin to stand. Some lowered their rectangular windows and craned their heads out. Scott squinted to see inside the car's windows. If Jesse and the others were looking away from him, he would go for it, slip down, sidle up to the bus, get the driver's attention...

The bus lurched forward. It heaved around the Chevelle, narrowly missing its rear bumper, blasted another long honk, and rumbled down the main hill. Scott wasn't sure, but he thought he glimpsed the female driver extending her own middle finger. The bus disappeared from his view.

The driver will not stop for students who give chase, the letter from the school warned.

Not that Scott would have. Above the metal music, he heard raw laughter. The Chevelle gunned blue smoke and slogged out into the intersection after the bus, the frame squealing against the left front tire rim.

When the coast was clear, Scott emerged from behind the bush and stood for a moment in the lingering haze. Then he crossed the intersection and made for home. He hoped his father hadn't fallen back asleep. He was going to need a ride to his new year of hell.

6

"New developments," the man said.

"Yes?"

"The boy hacked into a high-security military site yesterday."

"Hm," the woman responded. "Are we talking computer skills or something more?"

"Sounds like something more. We'll continue to monitor."

"And the girl?"

"Some irregular energies manifested around her house last night."

"Same pattern as the..."

"Ones throughout the summer?" the man said. "Yes. Only stronger."

"Your orders, sir?"

"Remain vigilant."

7

Wendy's Restaurant
Lunchtime

"How's it going so far?" Margaret asked, plucking up one of Janis's fries.

Janis hunched her shoulders to her ears as Feather Heather squealed over something being said at the next table. It was the beach all over again, but instead of bikinis, everyone was in high fashion: Chic, Gloria Vanderbilt, Sassoon, Guess. Janis had agreed to wear jeans, even though it seemed ridiculous—Florida, late August ... *hello?*—but she drew the line at the shoulder-padded number Margaret had tried to push on her, opting for a softball T-shirt instead.

How's it going? Let's see ... I don't know anyone in any of my classes. My one opportunity to spend with friends was preempted by your decision that I should eat out with The Seniors. And I'm starting to get that rash-like feeling I get around big crowds. Other than that, it's going great.

"I started off with four killers." Janis popped her last bite of burger into her mouth and washed it down with a sip of Coke. "Thought I was going to get a break with P.E., but all the guy could talk about was the F's he gave out. Oh, and the time he made some big, burly football player cry."

Margaret smirked. "The legendary Coach Coffer."

"You don't have him!" Feather Heather cried, spinning to face Janis.

"God help you," Tina said, and the girls fell away into laughter.

Janis grimaced.

"He talks tough, but he's not so bad," Margaret said. "Just do what he says, and you'll be fine. There will be plenty of ditzes and doofuses for him to make examples of. It's not like Thirteenth Street High is in short supply. Case in point." Her eyes cut to a table where three boy-men were competing to put away their three-quarter pound triples in record time. Jocks, Janis guessed.

The boys' cheese- and mayonnaise-smeared jaws smacked and churned until, at last, a boy with a blond crew-cut pounded the table with both fists, then opened his mouth to show he was finished. A chorus of cheers rose above feminine protests of "How immature!" and "Grody!" that only made the guys at the table laugh harder. All except for the one who hadn't participated. His lips were pressed into a grin, but his indigo eyes winced.

"Blake Farrier," Heather said from beside her.

"Who?"

"The boy you're, like, staring at."

Janis's cheeks started to burn. "I wasn't staring at anyone."

"Sure you weren't." Heather nudged her with a bony elbow. "But in case you were, I hear he's as sweet as he is cute. I could totally put a word in—"

Janis spun toward her. "Don't you dare!"

"Oops," Heather whispered. "Like, I think you just got his attention."

Janis lifted her face. Sure enough, Blake was looking right at her. Janis's immediate instinct was to feel terrified, but his eyes were cool, a little mesmerizing. Now a smile reached them, a soft-dimpled smile that seemed to say, *Hey, I'm a little out of place here, too.* Janis tried to smile back but dropped her gaze to the scatter of fries across her tray, the spell broken.

Heather nudged her again. "Sure you don't want me to channel my inner Chuck Woolery and make a *love connection?*"

"Oh, leave her alone," Margaret said.

Heather opened her mouth to say something more but then relented with a sigh. When Janis peeked past her, Blake's head was turned. Soft ridges of muscles showed through his pink Polo shirt.

"Hey, did you have a nightmare last night?" Margaret asked.

Janis blinked. "Huh?"

"I heard you yell, I don't know, around one a.m. I almost went to check on you, but you only did it the one time."

Janis felt her stomach lurch. "I ... I did?"

A huge mushroom cloud sprang up in her mind's eye, like one in that television movie last year, *The Morning After*, about a Soviet nuclear attack on the United States. She watched the cloud swell and blister, sensing its tremendous heat. She began to smell it, even, a smell of death and—

"Oh, before I forget."

Janis found herself staring at Margaret, who was snapping her fingers.

"Alpha meeting this Friday at lunchtime. Don't make other plans. Understood?"

It took a moment for her sister's words to compute. When they did, Janis stifled a groan. Alpha was a service/social organization for girls—scratch that—for *popular* girls. This would be Margaret's second year as the club's president.

"Alpha has its share of athletes, and it's never been a problem," Margaret said, preempting Janis. "It's not going to interfere with your soccer or softball or whatever other games you decide to play."

"*Sports.*"

Janis was also tempted to throw in that cheerleaders, while athletic, maybe, were not athletes—not as far as she was concerned. But she bit her tongue. She felt a little more forgiving toward Margaret today. A little more ... protective? In her gut, it seemed like the right word. But why would Margaret need protection? Something to do with the nightmare? Janis fought to think, but all she could dredge up were fragmented images of cockroaches and rotten sacking. Her mind recoiled from them.

"Understood?" Margaret said. "Friday at lunchtime. Don't forget."

Students poured from the classrooms on all sides of Scott, like water through just-opened sluice gates. He fidgeted with his watch and adjusted his glasses, but his legs remained rooted. To that point, he had known more or less where to go, first period to second to third to fourth, the crumpled schedule his compass. But now, with the start of lunch, he hadn't the slightest idea where to aim himself.

"I've got shotgun!"

Scott flinched before realizing the guy with the orange, flipped-up collar was talking about riding in the front seat of someone's car. A group of girls followed closely, shoes clacking, gum smacking, making loud plans for the Wendy's salad bar.

Scott let the girls' raspberry scent pull him into their wake, into the general flow. He tried to make himself just another droplet in the gushing current. *Nothing to see here, folks.* Then it dawned on him that the current he'd entered was pulling him toward the senior parking lot.

You have no car, Scott. No ride, either.

His head still buzzing with sleep deprivation, he stopped and wheeled to go back the way he had come. He didn't see the solid guy in the pink Polo shirt until it was too late. The impact knocked Scott sideways and as he danced a circle to stay upright, he felt the guy moving in.

Here we go.

Scott cringed and raised a forearm. But when Pink Shirt grabbed him, it was to help steady him. "Oh, man, I totally didn't see you," he said, his brow furrowing above indigo eyes. "You all right?"

Scott fixed his glasses. "Yeah. I'm fine."

"Cool, man." He clapped Scott's shoulder. "Catch you later." Pink Shirt resumed his athletic trot down the hallway. Scott stared after him, as stunned by the collision as by the fact the guy hadn't called him *geek* or *dweeb* or just pummeled him outright.

Around Scott, the flow of students tapered to trickles. He craned his neck, hoping to spot Craig or Chun, even Wayne. But whatever plans they had made for lunch hadn't found Scott's ears—by design, of course.

Things had gone badly that morning in their computer programming class. When Scott had attempted to sit beside him, Wayne threw his backpack over the seat and refused to look up. And when Scott proceeded to try and warn him about the phone tap,

Wayne closed his smudged-in eyes, plugged both ears, and gave him the "la-la-la" treatment. Scott ended up spending the period on the far side of the room, drafting his warning on a piece of paper and then passing it to him. But no dice there, either. Wayne's mustache curled into a snarl and, with one hand, he crumpled the paper into a wad. Then, on his way out of the classroom, Craig and Chun following like obedient lap dogs, he spiked it into the trashcan.

Now, with the last cries of the lunch rush tailing off, Scott gave up his search for his friends and watched his gray tennis shoes scuff over the concrete. He followed an outdoor hallway that ran perpendicular to the school's four wings and led to the auditorium. Above the metal doors, a banner with purple lettering read: WELCOME TINY TITANS – CLASS OF '88!

Scott's mind crunched the numbers. *Four school years. One hundred forty-four weeks. Seven hundred twenty days. Five thousand forty class periods.* He dropped his gaze from the banner, swallowing his despair.

Twin pay phones stood off to the right of the doors, and Scott scuffed toward them. Reaching back, he fished his hand into the smaller pocket of his backpack until he found a quarter. He lifted the receiver on the rightmost phone and dropped the quarter into the slot. He dialed a random 376- number, listened until the line began to ring, and hung up. The phone coughed his quarter into the change receptacle. Scott started over, this time with another random 376- number. He did this twice more.

Finally, he dialed his own number, another 376- number. Scott listened and replaced the receiver promptly.

Damn.

All of the numbers he had just called were located on the same exchange. And as he'd expected—and as *should* have been the case—

all of the delays before the start of the ring lasted roughly the same. Except for the delay on his own home number. Just like last night, the difference could have been measured in milliseconds, but it was there, just long enough for him to notice.

Someone was still listening.

You need Wayne.

Scott hesitated before nodding to himself. Wayne had hacked the phone network before. Using a clean line—Craig's or Chun's, maybe—Wayne could do it again. He could discover when the order for the tap had been placed and by whom. Only one teensy little problem. The last time Wayne had accused Scott of holding back info, he'd gone a month without speaking to him.

"Must be wanting to talk to someone pretty bad, calling so many times."

Scott's hand jerked, and the quarter he had been drawing from the change receptacle spilled to the ground. It wasn't just the suddenness of the voice, but the sense that the person had been behind him the whole time. Scott peeked around. Hands the color of dusty teakwood drew up a pair of blue pant legs. The man had been pushing a cart with a metal trashcan. Several garbage bags hung like drapes from the mouth of the can while a broom and a long pick for stabbing stray trash leaned against it. The man reached for the quarter, which was rolling in dying circles near his paint-spattered work shoes.

Breathe, Scott. Just a custodian.

With a chuckle like dry wind, the custodian captured the quarter between his thumb and third finger. His upper back remained slightly hunched when he straightened. A flat-topped straw hat shaded his black-weathered face, where a row of teeth shone white and straight. The man held the quarter out, the tails side showing. And now Scott recognized him.

"Mr. Shine?"

Mr. Shine was his yardman—the yardman for several families in Oakwood, in fact. Scott was so used to seeing him in cuffed brown trousers and suspenders that his mind was still trying to reconcile that image with the coveralls. But the rich brown gaze was unmistakable, the gaze of someone from another era, an era of sun-bleached dirt roads and wooden porches. *Old Florida*. That's how Mr. Shine struck him.

Mr. Shine smiled as Scott reached for the quarter. "Better hol' to her tight, or next time I'm liable to keep her." His eyes squinted when he chuckled. "Course, maybe I already kept her."

Mr. Shine snapped the fingers holding the quarter—a fast, dry sound—and Scott watched the quarter disappear. Mr. Shine showed his large, calloused palm, then the knotted darkness of the back of his hand, also empty.

"How did you—?"

When Mr. Shine snapped his fingers again, the quarter reappeared right where it had been, except now with the heads-side showing. A laugh of disbelief escaped Scott's throat. He pressed his glasses to his face and stooped toward the coin, still trying to figure out what Mr. Shine had done.

"Don't worry. I ain't gonna make her jump again."

Mr. Shine handed the quarter to Scott, who took it between his own thumb and third finger. Scott began to execute a slow snap, watching the quarter rise between his first and middle fingers.

"Now *you* don't go makin' her jump." He nodded past Scott. "You need her lots worse than me, seems."

Heat scaled Scott's cheeks. "Oh, I was just, um"—he turned his face toward the pay phones and then back to Mr. Shine—"just trying to call home."

"You forget the number?" Light twinkled from his eyes.

Before Scott could come up with another half-truth, Mr. Shine leaned into the cart, setting the wheels into wobbling motion. "You have you'self a fine day, sir," he called over his shoulder.

"Thanks, Mr. Shine. You too."

"Oh, and 'round here they call me Geech. Ain't my name, but just so's you know."

Scott looked from Mr. Shine's limping, receding figure down to the quarter. He turned it from heads to tails and back. All the years Mr. Shine had worked in their yard and that marked the first time they had really talked. Scott considered this as he pocketed the quarter and wandered off in search of lunch.

8

Janis reached fifth period typing between the warning bell and final bell, out of breath and with the first stabs of a stomach cramp. Eating off campus was liberating, sure, but she'd never had to sprint to get to her next class at Creekside Middle School.

The desks sat in pairs, and the sight of twenty-odd sets of eyes peering over the enormous Smith Coronas unnerved Janis. She scanned the room for a place to park herself, thankful her hair had darkened a shade over the last years. She still harbored adrenaline-spiked memories of other kids, boys especially, taunting her on the first day of elementary school each year, calling her Strawberry Shortcake. Not that she hadn't eventually straightened them out with her fists. Her temper had once been as storied as her bright hair.

Now, a pair of sniggers made the nape of her neck bristle. Her gaze darted toward the source, a boy with a pug nose and shades parked on the top of his head of tight blond curls. But his sniggers weren't meant for her. He was leaning toward the punk-rock girl seated in front of him, poised to set a wad of gum atop one of her blade-like spikes of black hair.

"Hey!" Janis called.

The guy jerked his arm back. The girl, who had been oblivious, turned from the window, one knee hugged to her chest. Janis looked on her gaunt, pale face painted with black lipstick and funeral-dark eye shadow. It was a face Janis had seen once that day already, though she couldn't remember where. She approached the empty desk beside her.

"Seat taken?" Janis asked.

The girl shrugged a shoulder. "Knock yourself out."

Janis thanked her and shot a warning look at Blondie, who had popped the gum back into his mouth and dropped his shades. Janis stowed her books under the desk and glanced around. The final bell rang, but the teacher's desk remained empty.

Janis cleared her throat. "I'm Janis."

The girl lifted her dark, hooded gaze. "Star," she said.

And then Janis remembered. "Right, you're in my American history class. Second period."

That would be Advanced Placement *American history, Janis. And here you'd figured her for a burnout.*

Star tensed her lips and eyes into something like a smile, then looked away. Janis's gaze fell to the black Chuck Taylor perched on Star's chair. Messages and little pictures covered the high top's graying rubber. *Question Everything!* the toe commanded. It seemed her typing neighbor was into skulls and ravens as well.

"Used to be called Americanism versus communism," Star said.

"I'm sorry?"

"Our history class."

Star dropped her foot from the chair and smoothed her ruffled skirt. Beneath the black skirt, she wore black tights. A green-checked flannel shirt hung from her rail-thin torso. Janis wondered what her own father would do if she ever tried to leave the house like that. And it went beyond the clothes and makeup. Janis, who had been allowed her first piercing only last year, counted eight black studs around Star's right ear.

"The legislature passed a law back in the sixties forcing the high schools to teach anti-communism. They were afraid we'd reject American consumerism if they didn't. Isn't that something? Using the same kind of indoctrinating as the Soviet Union—the *evil empire*—to cheer our system and crap all over theirs." She snorted and began nipping at a black-painted pinky nail.

Janis frowned and tried her best to appear thoughtful.

"They only repealed the law last year," Star went on. "Said it was outdated, and they're probably right. We've got MTV now and 'Where's the beef?' "

Janis nodded, thankful she'd tossed her Wendy's cup on her way in from the senior parking lot.

"Do you watch MTV?"

"Um, I've *watched* it," Janis said, "but I wouldn't say I watch it."

"Cable's first nonstop commercial. The new opiate for the teen masses. And it's not just music they're pushing. Take a look around. It's clothing, accessories. Telling you what to eat, what to smell like, how to act. How to *think*." She snorted again. "Everyone wants their MTV. Can't get enough of it."

Janis glanced around at the other desks she might have taken.

"And everyone thought Big Brother was going to be government. Turns out it's big business."

"Seems a tad dramatic," Janis muttered.

Black flames seemed to burst behind Star's eyes, burning away any lingering impressions of despondency. "Oh, really?" Her gaze searched all over Janis before latching onto her pants. "Guess jeans. What did those cost you? Better yet, *why* did you buy them?"

Heads turned at Star's raised voice, and Janis fought to not bring her hair around to her nose, wishing she'd never opened her mouth. She wished, too, she hadn't let Margaret dress her that morning.

"My older sister," she answered honestly.

Star's black-rimmed stare remained large and frightening. Janis tried to think of something better to say but couldn't. After several seconds, the black flames relented. Star's makeup grew dark around her eyes again. She gave a tired smile and looked down.

Just as their typing teacher arrived, a short woman with a round, pleasant face, Star mumbled, "Yeah, I had one of those once."

Scott balanced the paper plates of pizza on hand and wrist, and found a seat inside the sprawling root system of an oak tree. The day had warmed to ninety degrees, easy. He scooted back until he was against the tree and beneath its shade. With the breeze, it was almost pleasant. He cracked his grape soda, slurped the foam, and set the can atop a flat knot on the root to his right. Long banners of Spanish moss swayed overhead.

This isn't so bad.

At Creekside Middle School, lunch had to be taken inside their sour-smelling cafeteria every day, no exceptions. That's where Scott fell victim to the most humiliating "pranks."

Ha ha! Look, everyone! The dork's dropped his tray again!

Scott took a large, cheesy bite of pizza and glanced down at his lap. This shirt was clean, but the stains that had never come off his others told the story: faded squiggles of spaghetti sauce, spots of broccoli juice—the sloppy joe stains were especially gory, making it look like he had given gastric birth to an alien fetus. The steak and gravy only left mud-like impressions. And that's what he had told his mother on that occasion, that he'd fallen in mud, because he didn't dare tell her he was being bullied. He'd already learned that lesson.

"Oh, stop crying!" she told him when he'd gone sobbing to her one night, unable to sleep for the dread of another school day. "If you can't stand up to *children*, how are you ever going to call yourself a *man*?"

But Scott never stood up to them, not when it happened. He knew that's what the cretins were hoping for, could see it in their glinting eyes. No, he waited until he got home and was seated in front of his computer.

Who was that who upended my tray today? Cam Moser? Well whadd'ya know? Cam's in the student directory. How about we change the class code on that phone number from personal to pay. Got twenty-five cents, Cam? Because that's what that annoying recording is going to ask you to deposit every time you try to place a call from your Touch-Tone. Let's see how hard you laugh over that one. Hope it drives you and your family straight to the flipping nut house.

Clickety-clack and *voilá!*

The pleasure Scott would feel was grandiose and guilty, not unlike when he assumed his Stiletto identity in D&D campaigns. There, like in real life, his powers were predicated on going unseen, on being a slink. He would never tell anyone that he was behind the phone tampering, not even when he would hear the cretins grumbling at lunch and he wanted to stand and declare, "Yes, it was me! Behold the power I wield over your puny lives!"

But now Scott recalled his summer spent at his computer, in the darkness, alone. He gazed at the other students spread over the lawn, their chatter as bright as the day. With high school, Scott had expected the worst: middle school on anabolic steroids. It had never dawned on him that the students here had other concerns besides making his life miserable. He remembered the solid guy in the pink shirt. ("I totally didn't see you. You all right?")

Then he thought of Mr. Shine and the quarter he'd vanished, then reappeared—now tails, now heads.

In a snap another thought came to Scott: maybe he could belong, for a change. He felt he was already being accepted by his lunchtime peers for the simple reason that, like with Pink Shirt, they were tolerating his presence. They weren't singling him out, anyway. Not like in middle school. Scott's back stretched straight, and for the first time that day, he experienced his full height.

Maybe he could—

The thought fell apart. A black Chevelle was parked on Titan Terrace ahead of the shimmering food trucks, where the road curved near the tennis courts. Scott hadn't noticed the car when he was waiting in line. Now he held his aching wrist as Jesse's recollected voice rose over him.

Bring him over here. Let's see how well he pulls his bullshit phone pranks with one arm.

The car lurched. Creed, with his narrow face and black bowler hat, leapt from the passenger's side. Tyler emerged behind him. The car was leaning way off kilter, as if it was trying to kiss the curb. Creed and his brother sauntered around to the driver's side, where an elbow the size of a pig's rump propped on the windowsill. Above the elbow, smoke steamed out in a jet. Scott couldn't hear what they were saying, not from his distance. Jesse heaved his arm up, cigarette smoke trailing from his fist. Creed and Tyler lit their own cigarettes, hands cupped to their mouths. The other students gave them a wide berth.

Scott tightened his grip on his wrist as though willing himself to hold his ground, to not care if they spotted him.

But when Creed's face turned in his direction, Scott dropped his pizza. He scrambled to rescue it from the sandy ground, but managed only to knock over his grape soda, which promptly fizzed away. He left everything where it fell, found one of his pack straps, and slung it over his shoulder.

His knees jimmied like loose hinges, but he didn't stop until he reached his fifth period class—honors trig—fifteen minutes before it was scheduled to begin. He took a seat in the rear corner of the empty classroom, the front of his shirt spotted with sweat, his lungs wheezing for air.

9

The start of seventh period found Janis speed walking down A-wing, scanning the room numbers above the doors for her final class. English was the one course she was actually looking forward to. Of course, she had also been looking forward to P.E. until Coach "Two F's" murdered any and all hope that the class might actually be fun. So she didn't get her hopes up now even though she enjoyed reading almost as much as she loved sports. She had actually gotten into *1984*, creepy though it was. A world in which the government watched everything, controlled everything, all the way down to the thoughts in your head.

Turns out it's big business.

Janis broke into a jog, notebooks braced to her chest. First day or not, she felt the pulse-pounding dread of being the only one wandering the hallways after the final bell. And with that thought, an image of a barren beach came to her mind. The dream last night? *Room A-14.* She'd have to think about it later.

Janis stepped past the threshold and stopped. She'd expected to find the entire classroom seated and silent, the teacher suspending her lecture for the latecomer. Instead, students stood around the rear of the room, backpacks slung over shoulders, books still in hand. Janis followed their bemused gazes to the chalkboard, where in great big letters a message read DO NOT SIT!

The first two words were underlined twice for emphasis.

Mrs. Fern—the teacher Margaret's friends had said was weird—was nowhere to be seen. Janis scanned faces, disappointed to find another class without any of her friends. That was the thing about taking almost all advanced placement courses. During registration, guidance counselors had advised freshmen to take no more than one AP course their first year, two tops. Five was considered loony tunes.

But it wasn't as if she had a choice. Going all the way back to elementary school, her father made sure she was in the highest level of every subject—Margaret, too. He had the teachers give them extra work when he thought they were finishing their homework too quickly (Janis learned to slow way down); signed them up for intelligence camps each summer; and starting in the sixth grade, he enrolled them in an after-school program at the Center for Foreign Language Study until both could speak German and Russian reasonably well. "They're diplomatic languages," he explained whenever Janis would complain about having to go—as though their being diplomatic languages was reason enough. Her father would ignore her grumbles that none of her other friends had to learn even one "diplomatic language," much less two.

Janis was surprised to spot one of those former friends in the English classroom. Amy Pavoni. She stood near the bookcase in a tight circle with two other girls, flipping her bouffant of hair from side to side. In matching blue prep-school outfits and berets, the three were all but declaring their little clique closed for the day, if not the school year. It was just as well. Janis couldn't stand them. Beside Amy was Autumn, a long, lean clothing model, and Alicia, an aspiring actress with Phoebe Cates eyes. All three had hair the color of dark chocolate. The "A-Mazings," they had started calling themselves in middle school. Janis could think of a name far more fitting that also began with an A and a hyphen.

Janis gave a small wave when Amy glanced over, regretting it even as it was happening. Amy's response was to look her up and down and then decide she wasn't there. She pressed closer to her group and whispered something. A second later, Alicia and Autumn turned and made similar assessments, Alicia rolling her eyes.

Amy lived one neighborhood over from Janis, and the two of them had been best friends throughout elementary school. They had even held a joint birthday party at the Skating Palace in fourth grade. But in sixth grade, Amy joined the Teen Board at the mall while Janis channeled her after-school energies into softball and soccer. They were still friendly, still stopped and spoke in the halls—until Amy fell in with the other two. Not long after, Janis found a note in her locker:

Softball is for lesbians.

It wasn't signed, but it was Amy's handwriting (never mind that she'd played softball herself once). From then on, Amy wouldn't acknowledge her, not even with a nod of her head.

Janis pressed her lips together. It seemed little had changed.

Beyond the A's, Janis was dismayed to discover Star again. She was perched on the horizontal bookcase like one of the skeletal ravens depicted on her shoes. She hadn't spoken another word the rest of typing class—not about her sister, not about anything. Maybe she was a couple olives short of a pizza. Whatever the case, Janis decided that sitting beside her in one class was more than charitable.

She sidled away until she had a tall student between them. She was preparing to peek back, to see if Star had seen her, when the tall student spoke.

"H-hi, Janis."

Janis raised her gaze and then stared a moment, recognizing and not recognizing the bespectacled face and distressed head of brown hair. Her gaze fell to his crumpled blue shirt, then returned to his glasses, which went crooked when he smiled. And then it clicked. He lived up the street from her, though she couldn't remember the last time she'd seen him. Last school year, maybe? It was hard to say. He had turned into one of those quiet types who were easy to miss. But whenever it had been, he was much taller now.

"Scott?" she asked to be sure.

He made a choked sound and coughed into his fist, then pushed up his glasses and opened his mouth to try again.

The closet door inside the classroom flew open. Janis spun around. A woman who looked to be in her sixties sprang into the room, a wave of silver hair following her. Off to Janis's left, the A's screamed. The woman skidded to a stop at the teacher's desk, her skirt of multi-colored patches billowing out, and shot her gaze from the columns of empty desks to the students at the rear of the room. She adjusted her glasses from the sides, magnifying her eyes.

"Well, drat! I was sure I'd catch one of you at a desk."

She turned and wiped the DO NOT SIT! message away with an eraser, then brushed her hands together and wheeled toward the classroom again. Her owl eyes blinked twice before closing. She stood there straight, chin lifted, silent. Behind Janis, a couple of titters arose. Mrs. Fern brought a long finger to her lips. The titters broke off.

"Is there a Mr. Dougherty here?"

A block-shaped boy to Janis's right peered to each side as he inched forward. "Present," he said.

"Oh, hush with the *present*. This isn't a roll call. Let's see ... Dougherty, a variant of D*oherty*, probably. Irish. Of course it would have originally been O Dochartaigh or something close." The globes of her shuttered eyes moved back and forth as if she read all of this from the inside of her eyelids. "Unfortunately, the name means 'obstructive.' Are you an obstructive sort, Mr. Dougherty?"

"No, ma'am," he answered.

"Well, we can't take any chances. It's there in your name after all. And quit it with the *ma'am*. I'll start looking for my mother, and she's ten years buried. Chop-chop! To the head of the class with you."

Dougherty made his way to the desk where she stood, the fingers of one hand balanced on the desktop. When Mrs. Fern stepped away, Dougherty snuck a look back and twirled his finger around an ear.

"Obstructive *and* disrespectful, I see," Mrs. Fern remarked.

Dougherty jumped, but so did most of the rest of the classroom. She couldn't have seen anything. Her magnified eyelids hadn't parted, not even in the slightest. The back of Dougherty's neck broke out in red splotches, and he began to stammer, but Mrs. Fern held her palm out for silence. No one laughed this time. Her eyes were reading the inside of her lids again.

"Miss Pavoni?"

"Presen—I mean, here." Amy stepped primly from her clan.

"Is that an Italian name?"

"Yes, I'm Italian on my father's side. My grandfather arrived on Ellis Island, New York in 1934 when he was twelve..."

Janis tensed her jaw. To anyone they deemed beneath them—which was almost everyone—Amy and her friends were dismissive and cruel. And still they were awarded Good Citizenship awards by hoodwinking their teachers with the same saccharine-speak Amy was spooning out now.

"...The immigration service held him there because there was a tuberculosis outbreak and—"

"Do you know the Italian word for peacock?"

Amy scratched her elbow, her cheeks beginning to flush. "Well, I'm not sure *exactly*, but the Italian word for bird is—"

"It's *pavone*, Miss Pavoni—with an *e* instead of an *i*. But pronounced almost the same. *Pavone. Pavoni.* Peacock. It was first used as a nickname for a proud person. Someone who thought too much of herself. Now, I'm willing to bet that quality has winnowed over the generations since being ascribed to your family, if not disappeared altogether. But a bet is never a sure thing. How about this desk here, far from the windows where your reflection in the glass could pose a distraction."

When Janis snort-laughed into her hand, she thought she saw the corner of Mrs. Fern's lips turn up slightly. Amy glared at Janis and stomped to her seat, the façade gone. She glanced over her shoulder at her friends, sensing perhaps that she was not going to be sitting with them.

Amy would have been right. For the next thirty minutes, Mrs. Fern divined qualities from the origins of the students' names and seated them accordingly. Alicia went to the back of the classroom (Joiner was an occupational surname for a carpenter, and Mrs. Fern wanted a good vantage for Alicia to monitor the state of the wooden desks). And Autumn was given a window seat (because Warren was Germanic for "guard," and Autumn was to cry out at the first approach of anyone suspicious or untoward). Both of them had huffed and rolled their eyes and later tried to exchange a note before Mrs. Fern—

her eyes still sealed—plucked the message away, disappearing it into an unseen pocket in her skirt.

It was the most unusual seating system Janis had ever witnessed—and also the most entertaining. Finally, she was one of only two students left standing.

"Graystone," Mrs. Fern said.

"Yes?"

"Nothing too revelatory about that name. Nothing too much to glean. English in origin. Self-explanatory, really. And yet I sense there's something more to you." She stood silently for a moment. "And your first name, Miss Graystone, is...?"

"Janis."

The twin globes of Mrs. Fern's eyes seemed to swell beneath her lids. "Ah, yes. Now we have something to work with. Janis, a derivative of Jane, perhaps, but also a variation of *Janus*, who was a Roman god. A god of two faces."

At this, Amy sniggered from her desk.

"But not two-faced in the sense of duplicity, oh no," Mrs. Fern continued. "Janus is a powerful god, a diviner. A god of doorways. Think of *Janu*-ary. One face looking to the past. The other peering ahead, to the future. But we speak not just of doorways in the sense of time. No, there is also the doorway between here and there."

Mrs. Fern's head bobbed slowly. Janis had been anticipating having her name explained, but now she became uncomfortably warm. She curled her toes inside her white Keds, alternating feet.

"The doorway between this world and another. Yes, *another*. One not quite seen, perhaps?" When her eyes opened, it felt to Janis as if they were poised to swallow her. "Isn't that right, Miss Graystone?"

But Janis couldn't make a sound because she remembered why she had felt protective toward Margaret at lunch. She remembered what had happened the night before. The dream, the experience...

In a torrent of horrifying images, she remembered it all.

"This desk in the very middle of the classroom will suit a Janis quite perfectly, I would think."

But Janis did not go to the desk Mrs. Fern was opening her arm toward. She turned from the classroom and fled.

10

Mr. Shine stood before Scott, chuckling and holding out a quarter. "Ain't much magic to making her jump. Jus' a little diligence. A little patience." His brown eyes flashed sky blue as he snapped his fingers. The quarter changed from tails to heads. "Go on and try for you'self."

Scott accepted the quarter from Mr. Shine, whose eyes had settled to brown again, and snapped it between his own fingers.

The quarter disappeared.

"Not bad, young blood. Not bad at all," Mr. Shine said. "Course, it ain't gonna happen overnight, but look at you!"

When Scott looked down, he was wearing a full-body uniform, dark blue except for what appeared to be a pair of Speedos and boots, both yellow. Above a broad red belt, abdominal muscles showed beneath the uniform's fabric in interlocking columns. He was no longer Scott Spruel, he realized, but his favorite comic book character: Scott Summers of the X-Men.

Smiling, Scott began to feel for his cyclopean visor.

Brakes cawed, and Scott jerked awake to find the school bus approaching his stop. After disembarking, he stood a moment, squinting into the heat, watching the bus rumble away. He turned to the bush beside the Pattersons' garage door, the one he'd hidden behind that morning. Maybe it was because of the dream he was still emerging from, or because he'd made it through his first day of high school intact, but in the light of midafternoon, everything appeared more promising.

Scott crossed the street, then ran the rest of the block home, rejuvenated, his arms and legs fueled by hope. One of Scott's hopes was that if the FBI hadn't come down on his head, it was because they didn't have enough evidence or didn't consider his crimes criminal enough. There were still no Crown Victorias in his yard, anyway. Scott let himself in the front door using the key kept on a string around his neck. He dropped his backpack in the hallway and, without breaking stride, headed toward his room, J.R. yipping circles around his feet.

The solution, Scott told himself, was to leave his equipment in the storage room in the garage and give his extracurricular activities a rest for a while, take a hacking hiatus—a long one if need be.

But standing inside his doorway, Scott could see that was going to be easier said than done. His brain still harbored a compulsion to beeline to his computer desk, flip on his equipment, and launch into his latest hack, the behavioral groove well established and deep. Scott leaned his arms on the back of his office chair and stared down at the naked desk. There would be no more navigating the networks, no head-splitting challenges, no fist-pumping victories. He was out of "The Game," as some hackers called it. At least until he was no longer a person of interest.

You need Wayne.

Scott picked up the cordless phone and punched his number. The exchange and suffix pulsed out—a pause a few milliseconds too long—then a ring. With one hand, Scott ushered J.R. from the room, letting him keep the stick of pizza crust he'd foraged from beneath the bed, and closed the door. On the eighth ring, Scott hung up. Either Wayne had divined it was him, or he wasn't home yet.

Scott scrubbed a hand over his face and drew up his blinds. Light flooded the bedroom, causing him to frown in thought. Something seemed out of place, and it wasn't that the walls were bare from his having yanked down the hand-drawn Bell schematics the night before.

Then it hit him.

The room belonged to somebody barely out of elementary school, a child. So much of his attention the last three years had focused on Ma Bell, ARPANet, D&D, and comic books that he had neglected the fact that he was growing up. Today, he'd been the tallest in almost all of his classes, but nothing in his room reflected that growth. And after the revelation at lunchtime that he was among a more mature, more accepting breed of student, he didn't want to remain in childhood any longer. He didn't want to hide behind his computer. He wanted to belong.

Especially after his encounter with Janis.

Scott?

He drew a Glad Bag from the box his mother had given him, whipped the bag open, and pushed a scatter of RC Cola cans into its mouth. At the start of the day, he had imagined himself dropping into bed upon returning home and zonking out until eight or nine o'clock that night. But now that he *was* home, he found himself incapable of sitting still, much less nodding off. Because with the memory of

Janis still swimming through his thoughts, he believed he could do this now, that he could remake himself. That he *could* belong.

Now tails, now heads.

Scott?

Yes, he had seen her. Better, she'd come and stood beside him before the start of seventh-period English. The flaming cascade of hair that, for so long, he could only watch from a distance, had been right there, at his shoulder. In that first moment, the classroom revolving around him, he'd had to summon almost all of his nerve to compose himself and then the rest to get her name past his stuttering lips. But he *had* gotten it out. He'd spoken to her, and that seemed a victory in itself—one more monumental than all of the printouts in his hidden box of hacks.

And she'd spoken his name, too.

Scott?

That one word, the texture of it, the breath behind it, were now the most precious things in the world to him. He'd been preparing to ask her how her day was going. Hard to screw up. But his throat succumbed to what felt like a seismic tremor, and the words became Larry, Moe, and Curly jammed inside a doorway. Then the teacher jumped out of the closet.

As students spun, Scott's eyes remained fixed on Janis, the swirl of her hair, the excited shine of her eyes. When the teacher started in with her seating system, he had to bite back a grin. It was no alphabetical system, which would have doomed the names Graystone and Spruel to distant rows. No, it was something different. Something unique. Scott didn't understand it entirely, but he stood a chance of sitting next to her—or close, anyway.

"Spruel," Mrs. Fern said. "A derivative of Spurling, most likely. And not nearly as lowly as it sounds. The name means 'little sparrow.'"

And she proceeded to seat him as far as possible from another student whose name meant "great cat." That received a tide of laughter from the class and a pretty smile from Janis—teeth and all. Scott returned the smile. It was crooked and brace-faced, he knew, but he didn't care. Having her smile at him was right up there with hearing her speak his name. He would not be forgetting either for a long time.

But then something had happened.

Scott stopped pushing trash into the bag long enough to stand and gaze outside. The cul-de-sac in front of the Graystones' house stood empty. Margaret's car was still gone. He bounced the Glad Bag against his knee.

When the teacher had gotten to Janis, she talked about a Roman god and doorways—Scott remembered that. And then he watched Janis's face change, going from open and bright one moment to tense and pale the next. It was as if she had aged—not outwardly but inwardly, as if she'd acquired all of the cares and concerns of an adult in a matter of seconds.

She ran from the classroom.

Whispers rose. Necks craned. Scott imagined himself going after her, seeing if she was all right. It's what Scott Summers of the X-Men would have done. He would have pursued his red-haired love, his Jean Grey. But Scott Spruel was no Cyclops, he found out. That would have required something he didn't have. *Gallantry? Courage? A working spine?*

He just sat there and craned his neck like the others.

Mrs. Fern appeared unperturbed. "Now, now, settle down," she said, closing her eyes again. "Our goddess of doorways just needs a little fresh air. A moment to reorient. She'll return shortly."

By the time the final student had been seated and the course syllabus distributed, Janis had returned. She smiled tightly and said something about becoming lightheaded. She still looked pale to Scott, especially around her eyes. And when she took her seat (two rows from him, damn it all), her hair looked as though it had lost some of its luster as well. Amy, a student from their middle school, muttered "faker." When Scott turned, she leveled a hard stare at him. The stare reminded him so much of his mother's that he lowered his eyes and turned back around.

After class, Scott had been determined to ask Janis if she was okay. He followed her the entire length of A-wing before losing his nerve and veering off toward the bus circle. *Tomorrow.*

And that was the amazing thing, he thought. He had tomorrow, the next day—every day for the rest of the school year. He didn't have a seat beside her, no, but he shared a class with her. A class with the same peculiar teacher, the same reading list—things to talk about. For the first time since they were kids, he would no longer have to resign himself to gazing helplessly on her from his bedroom window.

Scott sighed and dropped the Glad Bag by the window. He pulled a comic book from one of the boxes beside his bookshelf and retired with it onto his bed, his pillows piled three deep under his head.

His favorite comic book artist was John Byrne, and Scott's acquisitions for the last three years followed his career through Marvel Comics: old issues of *The Avengers*, *Captain America*, *Daredevil*, *Iron Fist*, *The Amazing Spiderman*. Byrne was currently illustrating the *Fantastic Four*, since issue #232, so that collection was ongoing. And last year, he had started this cool new series about a Canadian superhero team called *Alpha Flight*.

But Scott's favorite John Byrne series by far—by light years— was *The X-Men*, issues #108 to #143. Those issues had everything, cool characters, awesome powers, riveting storylines, and all of them illustrated and co-plotted by John Byrne. The issues Scott liked the most, the ones he had absolutely fallen into were the ones with Scott

Summers and Jean Grey, also known as Cyclops and Phoenix. Scott would start the series at #108, read until Cyclops and Phoenix each presumed the other dead in issue #113, then skip to where they were reunited on Muir Island in issue #126.

He would read and reread the panels when it was just the two of them speaking intimately—before the power of the Dark Phoenix corrupted Jean. And maybe it was his knowing that their time together was short, that they only had those few precious panels, that made the panels seem to Scott sadder and more special than anything in his real life.

He opened issue #132 to one of those pages.

Byrne had stopped drawing *The X-Men* more than three years ago, so Scott had to track down old issues. Some he'd acquired at The Time Machine, others at comic book conventions. Now he owned the entire series, save one: issue #137, the issue where the X-Men fight to save Jean's life. And without it, he didn't feel quite complete. It was less a break in the collection than a hole in the complexity of feelings he had taken from the series and projected onto Janis and himself.

He squinted his glasses up and drew issue #132 closer to his face. He was at the page where Jean Grey interrupts Scott's meeting with Angel. They're on the top of a stone mesa in New Mexico. Angel leaves, and now it's just Scott Summers and Jean. She spreads out a picnic blanket. They speak. They kiss. Four issues later, Scott proposes to her.

Jean Grey-Summers.

Scott rested the comic book on his chest and closed his eyes.

Janis Graystone-Spruel.

Someday, maybe. If he could transform himself. If he could leave Stiletto for Scott Summers. If he could become that person who would pursue Janis down a hallway and ask if she were all right.

Now tails, now heads.

Just maybe.

And that was the final, hopeful thought he carried headlong into sleep, a sleep so sudden and profound that he didn't stir at the sound of Jesse Hoag's Chevelle creeping past his house only minutes later.

11

"You know, it sort of defeats the purpose when you drown your yogurt in chocolate syrup and Gummi Bears." Margaret aimed her plastic spoon toward Janis's cup before dipping it back into her own—plain vanilla, no toppings. "We might as well have gone out for ice cream."

Janis watched her sister's lips ply a layer of frozen yogurt from her spoon. Maybe it was this gesture, the angle of Margaret's head, the small hunch of her shoulders, that made her seem young to Janis. Vulnerable, even.

"I have to tell you something," Janis said.

"Oh, right." Margaret sat up, appearing to remember why they had come to TCBY. She'd blabbed the whole car ride over. "What's up?"

"It's..." Janis took a deep breath, wondering where to begin. "Do you remember how you said you saw Mr. Leonard's car at the beach yesterday? And then we saw him behind us on the way home?"

Margaret nodded, eyebrows raised in question.

"I think he was following us."

Margaret laughed and brought the spoon back to her lips.

"I'm serious, Margaret."

"On what basis?"

Janis couldn't tell her about the experience last night. Just like at the beach yesterday, Margaret wouldn't understand, wouldn't believe her. And who could blame her? The whole thing sounded insane, but Janis still needed to warn her.

"I woke up last night from a bad dream. A dream where Tiger was hit by a car," Janis lied. Tiger was their gray tabby cat. "It was just a dream, I know, but I went out to look for her anyway."

"What time?" Margaret asked, narrowing her eyes.

"I don't know—twelve thirty, one? Anyway, when I got to the backyard, I could see Mr. Leonard out on his deck smoking a cigarette."

"So?"

"He was staring at our house, Margaret. Over the tops of the bushes. I could see his glasses."

"He probably heard you walking around."

"I don't think so." *I was incorporeal.*

"Janis, his deck faces our backyard. So he comes out and smokes at night. His wife probably doesn't want him doing it in bed, which is smart. Lots of house fires start that way." Margaret's spoon scraped the bottom of her Styrofoam cup. "What is it with you and this obsession with being watched anyway?"

"It's not an obsession. It's a feeling. A..." Janis searched for a stronger word. "A *strong* feeling."

Margaret shook her head.

"Just promise me you'll be careful."

"So what you're saying is that Mr. Leonard—*our* Mr. Leonard—is dangerous all of a sudden? Why now? He's lived there since before we moved in. Plus, he's around students all the time, and he hasn't done anything to any of them."

Not that we know of.

Janis rescued a drowning Gummi Bear from her melting yogurt and then ate it. She didn't have a good answer for Margaret. She only knew what she couldn't tell her, what she had seen the night before, what she had discovered when she'd gone through the bushes into his backyard.

"Seriously, Janis. Where is this coming from?"

When Janis looked up, her older sister had finished and set her cup aside. Margaret sat regarding her, hands folded on the table, no longer young, no longer vulnerable. And those eyes...

"Just promise me," Janis repeated, straining to recall what they were even talking about. "That's all I'm asking."

Margaret sighed and lowered her gaze to Janis's half-finished cup. "All right, I promise I won't let the big, bad Mr. Leonard get me. Now hurry it up. I have to stop by the drugstore for some poster board before it closes."

In the parking lot, Margaret spoke over the car's roof as she fished for her keys. "Was Tiger okay?"

"Tiger?" Janis had to think for a moment. "Oh, yeah. She's fine."

Janis stood in her bedroom in a long cotton T-shirt. Next door, she could hear Margaret settling into bed. Her father was the only one still up. Janis pictured him in the study down the hallway, his reading glasses perched near the end of his nose.

Janis had finished what little homework she'd been assigned and already spoken to Samantha on the phone, each recapping her first day of school and making plans to meet for lunch. She had tied up the ends of her day—her normal life, as she'd come to think of it—and now stood contemplating this alternate life that claimed her when she fell to sleep each night.

There is also the doorway between here and there.

And that's what it felt like to Janis. That she was looking down, not at a bed with soft printed sheets and a light summer comforter, but at the doorway Mrs. Fern had spoken of.

The doorway between this world and another.

And looking down at it, Janis felt small and afraid. To draw back the covers and step inside was to go to a place she wasn't sure she wanted to go to anymore. And could she even trust what she saw and experienced there?

Janis stepped around her bed to her dresser. Trophies lined its top—gold-painted statuettes of girls dribbling soccer balls, wielding bats, and fielding deep flies on marble pedestals. She parted the medals that hung like necklaces around the tallest trophies and pulled open her top-right drawer. From behind a container holding a medley of loose change, team patches, and movie-ticket stubs, she drew out the plastic Easter egg. Two quarters shifted inside.

She carried it to her desk, where her books and folders with her finished homework sat in a neat pile. Upon setting it down, she gave the egg a spin. Janis watched it rotate, her chin on the back of her hands.

Yellow instead of purple.

Not the same color, no. Not in the exact same spot. But it had been there, her guarantor that the experiences were real.

Or were they?

Of all the Easter egg hunts they had done over the years, weren't the chances good that at least one or two eggs had gone undiscovered? It wasn't like her parents took an annual inventory. And where would the eggs be most likely to turn up? In the places hardest to see, of course. In areas of dense growth.

Inside the ferns.

Maybe somewhere in her subconscious mind, she'd already reasoned that out. And maybe that's all these nocturnal experiences were: voyages into her subconscious mind. Vivid, perhaps, but not happening *out there* at all. Instead, it was taking place inside her head.

Janis gave the egg another spin.

Whoosh.

The force that pulled her through the bushes last night had stretched her, made her feel long and charged. The vibrations tightened, rattling like charged ball bearings inside her head, down her body. She feared for a moment that the energy was going to force her apart, cast her into pieces. Even her mind, in her panic, felt like it was about to be blown like shot pellets.

Then, in a gasp, she was through.

She found herself hovering over the cement culvert that ran from the large cylindrical opening beneath the street and divided their backyards. Janis raised her face to the Leonards' house. A chain-link fence bordered the steep, unkempt yard. On the back deck stood a slender shadow. The cigarette that had earlier illuminated Mr. Leonard's glasses was gone. Had he sensed something and ground it out? Could he sense *her*?

She sank to the slanted wall of the culvert and watched through the tall grass along the fence.

She felt his vigilance as he stood there. Yes, an energy surrounded him, raw, and perhaps a little conflicted. Was this his desire for her sister, for Margaret? The thought made Janis's insides crawl.

She drifted down the culvert to the lower boundary of his property, continuing to monitor him to make sure his gaze wasn't following her. Then she went for it. The chain-link pattern of the fence offered brief resistance, and she was through. She was in his yard. Above her, Mr. Leonard yawned, his head tilting back. She crouched deeper into the grass. It seemed impossible that he couldn't hear the energy that whooshed and crackled around her.

A flare made Janis jump. On the deck, Mr. Leonard's brow shone pumpkin orange. Then he shook out the match, and only the ember and its reflection against his lenses remained.

Off to Janis's right, a woodshed leaned with the slope of the lawn. A stack of rotten logs huddled against its far side where a shingled roof jutted out. Janis waited for the cigarette to float to Mr. Leonard's face again, waited for the small ember to swell on his inhalation, and then shot behind the shed. She hovered, one hand resting against the shed's back wall.

When she peered around, she found Mr. Leonard in the same place but in profile. A chill rippled through her. What in the world was she doing here? What was she hoping to discover? That he was monitoring their house was clear. That he'd followed Margaret to the beach that day was also clear.

But is he dangerous?

Yes, that's what she needed to know—whether he was dangerous, whether he was capable of hurting Margaret, whether he'd hurt anyone before. Another student, maybe.

The side of the shed facing the house consisted of a double door held closed by a locked bolt. A bolt? Surely he would keep his expensive tools in the garage, not out in some decrepit woodshed. She concentrated in the same manner as when she wanted to float and pressed herself against the plywood siding. She encountered a layer of resistance, like the skin around a soap bubble, before popping inside the black confines of the shed.

When she concentrated again, the woodshed illuminated for her in little flickers, like a failing bulb determined to hold on. Shelves lined opposite ends of the shed. A heap of kindling rose from the floor, over what looked like old sacking. Cockroaches glistened chocolate-brown among the sticks and twigs. Janis recoiled. She could handle snakes, spiders, and other creepy crawlies, no problem—she'd even kept some in jars as a kid—but she *detested* cockroaches.

She gazed along the shelves, whose contents looked unremarkable: a bow saw with rusted teeth, lengths of frayed rope, a pair of stiff, weathered work gloves—the sorts of things one would expect to find in an old woodshed. Which made the bolt seem even more out of place.

She pushed out her light. Blond lengths of timber reinforced the inside. Thick silver bolts secured them. From the outside, the shed looked like it would topple from the breeze of someone walking past, but peering around, Janis believed it would stand up to the fury of a category four. Between two pieces of sacking that didn't quite overlap, Janis made out a concrete floor.

She reached toward it with her hands. She couldn't pick up anything in this state, she'd discovered, but she did possess a penetrating sense of touch. It was how she'd found the plastic egg in the ferns. Her hands encountered the cement. The slab went down inches, then feet.

It was not meant as a foundation for the shed, Janis realized, but a ceiling for whatever lay below. She withdrew her hands and hovered in thought. She'd learned about fallout shelters in school, but Janis had never seen one. She just assumed they weren't around anymore, not in 1984, or if they were, that they'd been converted into things like storage basements, wine cellars...

(torture chambers).

If it was a shelter, there would need to be an entrance, and she hadn't felt one. Unless...

When Janis moved nearer the kindling pile, roaches skittered beneath the sacking. Could they see her? She glanced toward the door. No gaps around the frame, no space where the double door met in the middle, where whatever light she might be casting would flicker out.

Calm down, Janis. You're safe. Incorporeal, remember?

Squinting, she reached through the sticks and rotten sacking. Cockroaches scurried around her hands. She was about to draw her hands back when they encountered something metallic in the cement. She felt along its edges. It was smooth and shaped like a manhole cover.

A lid.

The realization that there *was* a hidden room underground fell over her like ice water. She pressed against the metal lid. But like when she tried to pass through the bushes bordering her lawn, her progress was barred. This obstruction felt different, though—not like charge repelling like charge but an electrical barrier, fiery and unyielding. She redoubled her concentration.

The field gave a little.

The wooden door to the shed began to rattle. She hadn't heard his footsteps patter down the steps of the deck or cut through the grass, but she could hear the scraping sound of a key inside the lock.

She fell against the back wall of the shed, her mental commands colliding into one another: *Pass though the wall, Janis! Concentrate! Pass through the wall! C'mon, Janis! Concentrate, dammit!*

But the skin of the shed's wall held this time. There was no pop...

Other than the bolt's release.

Red terror blotted over Janis's senses like a swarm of cockroaches, flapping their oily wings, spilling down her back, cocooning her arms and legs. It was like those first out-of-body experiences when she couldn't move, couldn't act. Now the same horrible thoughts assailed her:

What if I can't return? What if I'm trapped on the other side of that barrier, trapped inside this shed?

The door swung open, and Mr. Leonard's face loomed from the night like an executioner's.

WHOOOOOSH.

Janis jerked upright in her bed, heart thundering, cotton T-shirt warm and soaked through. But it wasn't sweat she felt. It was urine. For the first time since she was five years old, Janis had wet herself.

Janis grimaced as she gazed at the rotating plastic egg. She remembered the fear and shame of stripping her shirt and sheets the night before, tiptoeing the length of the house to the laundry room, starting the Kenmore, taking a quick, furtive shower, later moving her sheets to the dryer, then back to her bedroom, and at last drifting off, where the memory of the experience receded from her conscious mind like a wretched creature down a slippery hole, deep beneath the ground.

But Mrs. Fern's words from that afternoon had ripped through Janis's amnesia, resurrecting the vision of Mr. Leonard's looming face, spurring her flight from the classroom.

Now, as Janis chewed the inside of her cheek, two competing questions chewed at her mind: What was beneath Mr. Leonard's shed? And had the experience even happened to begin with?

Janis glanced at her clock radio and sighed. She should have been in bed an hour ago. When she gathered the egg, the back of her hand ached from supporting her chin. She carried the egg to the dresser and returned it to the top drawer.

Yellow instead of purple.

She closed the drawer tight. Last night's experience hadn't happened, she decided. Like with the egg, it had been a product of her subconscious mind, manifesting the very things she'd expected to see and terrifying herself in the process. The next time she found herself in the backyard, she would will herself back to bed. She would never put herself through another experience like that again.

With that, Janis climbed beneath her covers and turned out the lamp at her bedside. But she didn't fall asleep, not right away. A niggling thought came to her as she massaged her hand. She had spun the plastic egg several times in the half hour she'd spent recounting the experience. But how many times had she actually moved her hands from beneath her chin to do so? Every time? Every *single* time?

Enough, Janis.

She turned over and closed her eyes again, and this time she did find sleep.

12

Thirteenth Street High
Friday, August 31
Lunchtime

"You can do this," Scott said into the rust-speckled mirror. Outside the metal door, he could hear the final calls of students headed to lunch. The bathroom stalls and cracked latrines at his back stood vacant. "It's just an informational meeting. One informational meeting. You go in, you listen, you size it up. If it feels wrong, you're done. You don't have to go back."

But it will be a risk, a voice whispered. *Being seen will be a risk.*

Scott considered that as he looked back at his pallid face. No one had messed with him all week, or even given him a second look. And now he was threatening that invisibility, threatening to stand out. Informational meeting or not, he might as well be wearing a sandwich board that announced: *I want to be like you guys!* And on the back side: *Please accept me!*

Scott knew something about healthy herds. They didn't take well to misfits worming into their ranks. As he worked to flatten a few stubborn sprays of hair, he reminded himself of the progress he had made that week...

After crashing following that first day of school (and sleeping straight through the night), he had rebounded Tuesday afternoon and cleaned the rest of his room. Gone were the relics of his childhood: the Buck Rogers sheets, the plastic models, a View-Master whose lever had jammed years before, his Atari 2600, eight binders of Scratch 'n' Sniff Stickers, stacks of *Encyclopedia Brown, Choose Your Own Adventure,* and *Mad Libs,* as well as a medley of dog-eared magazines he'd stopped reading when he was eleven: *3-2-1 Contact!* and *Cracked* among them. He filled four Glad Bags and dragged them to the garage.

Immediately, his room felt twice as spacious. It smelled better, too. He proceeded to vacuum and dust in places that no instrument of cleaning had touched in years. But that had been the easy part.

What about his Star Wars figures, his *D&D* manuals and modules, not to mention his comic books? He made a deal with himself. He would box them all and place them in his closet. If by Christmas he hadn't gotten them back out, he would sell them to the last. All except for his John Byrne collection—he could still read those.

On Wednesday, he had tackled his clothing. All of the stained middle school—era shirts and shorts were goners, along with most of the rest of his clothes. He'd been amused to find a mashed-up pair of Spider Man Underoos behind the bottom drawer of his dresser. He held the diminutive red undies to his waist and then tossed them in the discard pile.

The following evening, Thursday, he had stood in front of his closet mirror, stripped to the waist. His room was clean, his clothes sorted out until he could go shopping for more. It was time for Scott

Spruel himself. After deciding he needed his hair trimmed on the sides and grown a little longer in back, he touched his forehead. The acne eruptions were fewer than last year, he decided. Even so, he pledged to wash his face twice a day and get back on his Retin-A regimen—something that had fallen to the wayside that summer.

And the rest of him? He examined his body with the clinical eye of Professor X: his lanky neck, his sallow, sunken chest, stark ribs, arms that hung long and thin at his sides, promising harm to no living thing. He rubbed his right forearm. A slight angle showed where the bones had healed (yes, Jesse had snapped *both* his ulna and radius), a permanent deformity now. Anger flared from the pit of his stomach, the anger that he had not been able to stop them.

Do it again, and it's gonna be both arms, you little piss stain, Jesse had promised.

He needed bulk. He needed mass. Scott Summers of the X-Men was no Incredible Hulk, but he was solid. He kept in shape. Scott Spruel of Oakwood, meanwhile, had never touched a barbell, much less lifted one. Back in his room, he broke his promise and fished a handful of non–John Byrne comics from the closet, plopped in the chair at his desk, and began flipping through them. After a couple of minutes, he found what he was looking for:

HEY, WIMP! I'M TALKING TO YOU!
REMAKE YOUR BODY IN 15 MINUTES A DAY!

It was the full page ad with Bud Body, "The Finest Specimen of Manhood," standing in what looked like his underwear, fists on his glistening hips, glowering out of the page like he'd just as soon beat you senseless as bestow on you the glories of his strength and conditioning program.

"Bulk out your back, puff up your pecs, strengthen your arms and legs. My easy-to-follow, SCIENTIFIC method will make you fitter, faster, and MORE DESIRABLE than you ever dreamed possible!"

Scott made sure it was one of his rattier comics before taking an X-acto knife to the small order form for the booklet. It was a start, he had figured, and would only cost him five bucks plus shipping…

Standing back from the rust-speckled glass of the C-wing bathroom, Scott examined the tuck of his green Izod inside his belted khakis. He turned one way and the other, made a couple of adjustments, and then stooped to rub away a smudge near the lacing of one of his Docksiders.

He removed his thick glasses, folding them with a decisive clack, and nodded at the mirror.

"You can do this."

The room was a chaos of motion and voices, and for a moment Scott considered feigning surprise with his hands (*Oops! Wrong room!*) and backing out, resuming his stiff walk down the D-wing corridor and over to the food trucks, where he would eat alone as he had done every day that week. And that was the thought that stopped him: eating alone again.

He lowered his head and stepped into the room.

"Hey!" someone called to his left. Scott froze, waiting for the inevitable, *What do you think you're doing here?*

When he turned, the person he beheld was brown haired and blurry, nearly faceless. He was sitting at a table near the door with four other faceless people. Scott went to push up his glasses before remembering he wasn't wearing them.

"You rushing Gamma?" the voice asked.

"Y-yeah." Scott cleared his throat. "Yes."

"You're gonna need one of these." Scott felt a piece of paper being pushed into his hands. "It's a permission slip. Have it signed by a 'rent and back here by the next meeting. Go on and take a seat. Pledges in the back."

Scott nodded. "Thanks."

There were other young men's service/social clubs at Thirteenth Street High, but Gamma was considered the premier. That part didn't matter so much to Scott. In fact, he would have preferred it if the club were of more middling status, to improve his chances of getting in. No, what mattered most was that Gamma was the brother organization of Alpha, the club to which Janis's sister belonged (he'd seen her hanging posters on Tuesday to announce their first meeting). And Scott was gambling that if Margaret was a member, Janis would be pledging, too.

Like big sis, like little sis. He hoped.

Scott clutched the strap of his backpack and made his way between two columns of desks, his sternum stiff, breaths paper thin. Volleys of masculine voices shot through an air thick with cologne. Several Gamma members were parked on desktops, but without his glasses, Scott couldn't see how they were looking at him, or whether they were even looking at him to begin with. Being half-blind had its advantages. It made the room and everyone inside it seem spectral, not quite real—like he was there and not there at the same time.

He edged to the back and joined the other hopeful pledges, where it was decidedly quieter. He wondered if anyone from his middle school had come. He hoped not. He picked a desk in the last row, stumbling around it before getting himself seated.

"SHUT THE HELL UP!"

Scott jittered and dropped his backpack. The louder conversations at the front of the room wound down. Members climbed from their desktops. Scott peeked to either side to find the other dozen or so pledges sitting ramrod straight.

"SHUT IT, I SAID!"

Scott drew his glasses from his pocket and, keeping them folded, snuck a lens over his right eye. A stocky guy with a blond buzz cut paced the front of the room, arms bowed. His clenched face shriveled Scott's insides. Was this the president? Was this the guy he was going to have to answer to?

"All right," Buzz Cut said, his face decompressing into a sidelong smile. "That's better."

Laughter from the front rows.

"Now, stay shutted the hell up." Buzz Cut leaned his butt against the ledge of the chalkboard, his thick arms folded.

Someone stood up from the table in front, a taller, more refined-looking member of what Scott surmised to be the club's officers. He strode to the front of the room in a stylish white Oxford, a silver pen jutting from the brown sweep of hair above his ear. "Thank you, Britt. That was ... colorful." Then he spoke to the room: "The sergeant at arms has called the first meeting to order."

"Hear! Hear!" someone shouted.

The sergeant at arms paused in his return to the table to glare at the shouter, which evoked more laughter.

"All right, guys," the tall speaker said. "For those who don't know, I'm Grant Sidwell, president of Gamma." He went on to introduce the other officers, who half rose from their seats at the table in turn. Scott made a point of repeating their names inside his head, but with his heart still pumping at a breathless rate and the dry bite of terror in his mouth, the names abandoned him seconds later.

Grant went into some administrative items, clearly meant for current members, and Scott couldn't concentrate on those either. His eyes were going from officer to officer, struck by how *adult* they looked. One of them even had a mustache, not one of Wayne's threadbare numbers, but the real Tom Selleck deal. And they were all stylish and sturdy in a way that Scott could only dream of. All day, his own shirt had been shifting and chaffing in odd places, requiring constant readjustment. But with these guys, there was no effort, none at all. It was like their clothes *knew* they belonged inside them. And with that thought, Scott understood how ridiculous his presence was. He didn't belong here. He would never belong here.

"A show of hands if you're planning to pledge this year," Grant called.

Heads turned in the front as the pledges' hands went up around Scott. He was late in realizing that he was still holding his glasses to his face. He fumbled them into his lap, went to reach for them, and then shot his arm up instead.

Grant began counting the hands off with the tip of his pen.

Scott's gaze found the large intercom box on the wall above Grant's head. Without his glasses, it looked like a manila blur, but it was something to focus on, something to keep his mind from the craning stares of the Gamma members, from his own doubting thoughts.

His head began to spin.

It was a familiar sensation, the filaments of his consciousness winding around one another, harder, sharper...

But here?

His world twined tighter, dimming to the brink of darkness, before bursting open. Scott scattershot over the intercom system, box to box, then down a stepwise series of branches to the main trunk, where the system was rooted, probably somewhere inside the school's main office.

Scott braced himself against the stinging current and tried to reverse course, but it was like swimming upstream, the energy less linear, more turbulent. Perhaps it was the age of the system, the dry cracks in the rubber insulation. He stopped straining and imagined the intercom in the meeting room as he'd last seen it: a manila blur. He focused on it, just like he would do with his modem at home, felt his consciousness gathering there...

The report sounded like a cross between a fart and a shotgun blast.

Scott blinked from his seat in the rear of the classroom. At the head of the room, Grant had fallen into a crouch, his pen still held out, his other arm thrown up over his head. Everyone else was staring at the intercom box above him. Glasses to his eyes, Scott's gaze went there, too. The box emitted a final petering raspberry from its smoking speaker, then fell silent.

Heat washed over Scott's face.

The laughter was sudden and riotous. Britt, the sergeant at arms, stood from the table. But rather than restore order, he waved a hand near his backside in exaggerated motions. "I swear, it wasn't me this time!"

Grant straightened and swept his fingers through his hair. He peeked back toward the intercom in disapproval, then cleared his throat into his fist. "All right, everyone, return to order." Then to the back of the classroom: "You can put your hand down."

Scott made a convulsive sound when he realized Grant meant him. He hugged his arm to his side.

"The Gamma pledge term is thirteen weeks." The laughter quieted to guffaws. "I'm not going to sugarcoat it. They are thirteen *demanding* weeks. But do everything you're asked as a pledge, and you're in. You're a brother. It's that straightforward. And once you're a Gamma, you're a Gamma for life."

"And if Britt can do it, anyone can," someone called to the back.

That revived the laughter and had the other officers restraining the sergeant at arms as he pretended to want to climb over the table to get at his heckler. Scott smiled at his antics, and for the first time since walking through the door, he felt the knot in his stomach begin to loosen.

Do everything you're asked as a pledge, and you're in. You're a brother.

A roll sheet found its way to his desk. Scott signed it and passed it along.

When the laughter subsided, Grant had another question for the pledges: "How many of you have been eating lunch off campus?"

All of the pledges' hands went up, and once more, Scott's hand joined theirs. Not true, of course. But who would know? He became worried when snickers began to pop off like bottle caps.

"Well, as of next week, that stops," Grant announced. Scott could feel the questioning looks of the other pledges as they lowered their arms. "In the cafeteria, there's a special table for Gamma pledges, and that's where you'll be eating. You will partake of the good food that our lunchroom ladies prepare each day but that no one has the good manners to appreciate. As representatives of Gamma, *you* will appreciate that food, and you will appreciate them. You will do so by eating every bite. I don't care if it looks and tastes like regurgitated cow cud. At the end of the lunch hour, a brother will stop by to inspect your trays. And don't try to get cute and dump your food beforehand, or it'll be two trays the next time."

"Someone's always watching!" a voice warned.

"But here's the most important part," Grant went on. "When you return your tray, you're to stick your head through the service window and thank the ladies for your meal, and you will do so with sincerity. Understood?"

"Yes," the pledges answered in unison.

Scott swallowed. Just when he thought he'd escaped the cafeteria and its depravities—the food not the least of them—he was being ordered right back into that ghetto.

"In addition to daily lunch in the cafeteria, you are all required to dress in what we call 'Standards.' Dress slacks, dress shoes, dress shirt, and a tie. Your Sunday best. Blazers optional."

Grant signaled to one of the officers, who began passing something toward the back of the room. With his glasses in his lap, it was all a blur to Scott.

"These are your Gamma letters," Grant said when they began arriving. "They will complete your attire. You will wear them every day, and you must wear them so that they are *visible*—not inside your shirts. That way, your brothers can identify you around campus."

More snickers.

Scott took his giant laminated L and turned it one way and the other before setting it flat on his desk. If he decided to go through with this—the cafeteria, Standards, a giant Greek letter around his neck—there would be no going back into the shadows. Not at Thirteenth Street High.

"Any questions?" Grant asked.

Do you really want to do this? the same voice whispered in Scott's ear. *It's an even bigger risk than you first thought.*

"It all starts the day after Labor Day," Grant said after no one spoke up. "And the next meeting is a week from today, when you'll be assigned your big brother. Be sure to bring back your permission slips. We'll need those. The other requirements for your term are spelled out in these pledge packets. Make sure you grab one on your way out. Good luck."

The sergeant at arms rose from the table and stalked to the front of the room. "DISMISSED!" he bellowed, throwing his arms out. "NOW GET THE HELL OUTTA HERE! ALL OF YOU!"

This time, Scott laughed with the others.

13

After school

The garage door was solid. It didn't rattle when the soccer ball *thunked* against it, which made the rebounds come off hard and fast. And because of the paneled design of the door, the ball would often career from it at erratic angles: to the right, to the left, straight up in a spinning pop.

Perfect for a goalie in training.

Janis sprinted beneath the latest pop-up, elbows tucked to her sides, the webbing of her goalie gloves spread wide.

Watch the ball into your possession, she thought, in mantra. *Always watch the ball into your possession.*

Her squinting eyes tracked it to her arms, and she cinched the ball to her chest, crouching protectively. She straightened and returned to her starting spot. Clamping the taut ball between her knees, she wiped sweat from her brow and tightened her ponytail.

The temperature had climbed into the upper nineties again, and her pores gasped inside her long-sleeved polyester jersey. But she loved the training, even the suffering that went with it. It was who she was, it was where she belonged, not in *Alpha*. She grimaced. Even the thought of the word tasted bad.

Janis had shown up early to the first meeting that day with the sole intent of telling Margaret she wasn't going to be joining and wouldn't even be staying for the rest of the meeting. *Sorry, but Alpha just isn't for me.* Margaret had been in the middle of organizing packets and patting them into neat stacks when Janis arrived at the meeting room.

"Where's your lunch?" Margaret asked, hardly glancing up. A few members were eating near the front of the classroom, Feather Heather, Tina, and Kelly among them, their desks pushed together.

"I'm sorry, Margaret..." Janis lowered her voice, "but I can't."

"Can't what?"

"Do this. I have to leave."

Margaret looked up from her counting and, for an instant, it felt to Janis as if her sister's green eyes were around her head. It wasn't an unpleasant feeling but strange and disorienting. Similar to what happens before falling asleep, when your thoughts begin to dissolve a little.

"Oh, march your little bottom to the back and stop being silly."

And surprisingly, Janis found herself doing just that. Her thoughts on Alpha hadn't changed, no, but asserting herself before Margaret felt like too much trouble, as if the lead of resistance had melted from her will.

Better just to go along with it.

Janis picked out a desk in the very back and watched the classroom fill with the type of girls she swore she'd never become.

Most clacked in on high heels, their hair and makeup *way* overdone. The older members squealed and clapped their hands when they spotted Janis, but she knew it was only because she was Margaret's little sister. Celebrity by relation. She raised one hand in response, her resentment at being there seeping back by degrees.

Aspiring pledges entered too, dolled up and doe-eyed, Margaret directing them to the back. They steered clear of where Janis sat, probably because her own fashion sense that day amounted to athletic shorts and a Jordache T-shirt. She might as well have had leprous tumors. Of course, they didn't know she was Margaret's sis—

Janis nearly choked.

Amy, Alicia, and Autumn entered the room in virtual lockstep. In their pleated skirts, pink Argyle vests, and matching socks, they looked like a three-headed creature. A hydra. They filed toward the rear of the room, flashing smiles and waving to the older members pageant-style. Janis slid down in her seat and swore at herself. Why in the world hadn't she left when she'd had the chance?

The Amy-Alicia-Autumn hydra stopped at the row of desks in front of hers, a gust of hyperfloral perfume enveloping Janis, and sat three across. They didn't deign to look back. Big surprise there. The backs of their brunette heads perked up as Margaret called the meeting to order.

The informational meeting was pretty much what Janis had expected: *we do service work, we host social events, we represent the school in the community, blah blah blah.* The single highlight was when the intercom blew and the room erupted into screams. But the hysteria was short lived, and the meeting resumed with the Alpha pledge term. Lunch in the cafeteria? Dressing up every day? Janis slouched in her chair. Not for her. *Definitely* not for her.

And to have to do it with the Amy-Alicia-Autumn hydra? *For. Get. It.* Janis was sure the feeling was mutual on their end.

But then something weird happened. As the meeting broke up and the three A's stood from their desks, Amy, her former best friend, turned and looked at her. "Hey," she said and smiled. Not a polished, practiced smile, but one that pouched a little at the ends with, what, contrition?

Stunned, Janis returned the greeting with a hoarse "hey" of her own. It marked the first exchange they'd had in almost three years, their first one since Janis had found the note in her locker.

(*Softball is for lesbians.*)

And then Amy had turned back to her friends, and the exchange ended.

Out in her driveway, Janis palmed the soccer ball against her wrist and shook her head. She heaved the ball at the garage door, harder than she meant to. The ball caught the left side of an upper panel and careened off to Janis's right. She had already begun a stutter step in that direction and lunged with her right arm. The impact stung her fingertips, but the ball was tipped off course, cleared of the imaginary goal. Janis checked her stumbling momentum with her hand and watched the ball dribble off into the side yard.

At first, Amy's gesture had perplexed Janis. But by the end of typing class, the obvious dawned on her: she was Margaret's sister; Margaret was Alpha's president; the three A's wanted to get into Alpha; hence, the three A's believed they needed to make nice with Janis.

And there you had it, folks. Nothing more or less complicated.

Janis followed the ball into the side yard, where the garden hose lay in a loose coil. She tugged off her gloves and shoved up her sleeves. The water that gurgled from the hose was still cold from the last time and felt wonderful flowing over her head. She tilted the nozzle up so the water pushed against her face, then took a long drink as the water trickled beneath her jersey, cooling her body in little rivulets.

After tightening the spigot, Janis gathered the soccer ball and sat with it cross-legged inside the wall of shade along the edge of the yard. She traced the ball's hexagonal seams with her fingers. All around her, the late afternoon heat rattled and droned with insect sounds...

And then drilling.

It was the same drilling that had been whining on and off while she practiced, but Janis hadn't given it much thought; she couldn't tell where it was even coming from. But now she could. She left her ball in the shade and followed the sound to the back line of bushes. Beyond the leaves, she could make out someone in a white T-shirt. Janis sank to one knee and pushed aside a low bough.

Mr. Leonard was standing in front of his woodshed, his back to her. He was bracing the farther shed door open about a foot while, with his other hand, he operated a drill powered by a long orange cable running up to his house. Narrow straps of muscle stood from the back of his sunburned neck. It was her first time seeing him since the dream (*experience*).

But she felt no fear, not in the light of day.

Janis shifted her attention from Mr. Leonard to the shed. It was decrepit and leaned with the lawn, just as it had in her dream. But of course she'd seen the shed before, like when she and Margaret used to roller skate down the culvert. Her mind had obviously kept the image on file and then called it up when, in her dream, she had ventured into his backyard.

But what about the inside?

The drill rattled to a stop. Mr. Leonard wiped a hand against his hip and began to turn. Janis released the bough and drew back. Through the leaves, she watched him set the drill on a folding chair. She reopened her sight line just as he shut the shed door and locked it with a key.

So there *was* a bolt.

But she could have noticed this feature from the culvert as well. Not consciously, maybe, but her mind could still have recorded the detail and stored it away.

Mr. Leonard tugged on both doors, peering up and down the frame. He turned back to the chair and began gathering his things. Something small went into the front pocket of his cut-off jeans. Then he scooped up what must have been screws by the way he palmed them. *Parts of the old lock?*

The idea made the damp skin beneath Janis's jersey bunch into gooseflesh. *Sunday night you dream he catches you in his shed. Five days later he changes the lock...*

She watched him unplug and disarm the drill and then shove it into the waist of his shorts in the back.

When Mr. Leonard turned toward her, Janis was too slow to release the bough. Like an exposed animal, she froze. He squinted around, his yellow-bespectacled gaze appearing to hesitate on the spot where she knelt. A second later, he turned and hiked toward the house, gathering the extension cord around his arm in sharp, strong gestures. He didn't look at all like a hapless substitute. No, he appeared capable—capable in a way that made him far creepier.

That night, Janis sat up with her back against the headboard, telling herself she would quit reading at the end of the chapter and turn off her light. In English that week, they'd finished their discussion of *1984*, and Mrs. Fern had assigned them *To Kill a Mockingbird*. "No book better contrasts the imagined realm of children with the stark and consequential world of adults," she had declared. "And none better collides them." Janis couldn't say how, but she felt that Mrs. Fern had intended the message for her.

She was at the nerve-wracking part where the kids sneak over to Boo Radley's house at night when a pair of taps sounded on her bedroom door. Janis gasped and pressed the book to her chest.

"Come in," she called, her heart still thudding.

Probably Margaret, home from her date with Kevin. The rest of the Graystone clan had spent the evening with bowls of popcorn, watching a rental from Video World: a Tim Conway and Don Knotts spoof. Movie night on Friday was a Graystone tradition, a reward for their week of work.

But it wasn't Margaret. When Janis looked over, she found her mother slipping ghost-like into the room, one hand to the chest of her cotton nightgown. She smiled and moved toward her in a way that seemed apologetic.

"I saw your light on," she whispered.

"What are you still doing up?" Janis asked.

"I could ask the same of you. It's almost midnight."

Janis held the book up. "Just some reading for next week."

Janis's mother took the book and sat with it on the edge of the bed. "Harper Lee. I would have been about your age when I read this." She seemed to reflect on that for a moment before smiling and handing the book back to Janis.

"Is everything all right?" Janis asked.

"I just woke up and couldn't fall back to sleep. Normally, I go to the kitchen table and read until I'm tired again, but when I saw your light on ... I thought maybe you were having some trouble sleeping, too."

Her mother's low voice sounded lonely to Janis, but she told herself her mother was trying not to wake the rest of the house.

"No, I'm fine, Mom."

"You would tell me if you weren't? If anything was the matter?" She touched Janis's cheek and smoothed the hair around her ear, like she used to do when Janis was a little girl.

Janis looked into her mother's eyes. For a moment, she considered telling her about the dreams, about her fear of falling asleep. But Janis knew it would only make her mother worry for her, and what could she do anyway?

"Well, there is this whole thing with Alpha." Janis cut her eyes to the wall separating her bedroom from Margaret's. "She just doesn't get that I don't want anything to do with it."

Her mother chuckled, more with her body than her voice. "Deciding what's best for others is your sister's way of showing her affection. She's a lot like your father that way."

Her mother looked down in a manner suggesting she hadn't meant to say the last part. But Janis saw she was right about Margaret—and her father. And in this realization, her heart suffered a pang of what could only be described as jealousy. Ever since she was little, Janis had tried to emulate her father—his strength, his even-spokenness, his athleticism—so to now see this stronger semblance between Margaret and him felt strange.

"You know, I started school this week, too," her mother said.

"Wait, what?" Janis sat up. She tried to read the soft upturn of her mother's lips.

"It's a biology class. We meet twice a week at the community college, Tuesday and Thursday mornings."

"Biology? When did this happen?"

The smile continued to spread over her mother's face, as if it had been wanting to express itself for a long time. "You know how Samantha's mother is a special education teacher? Works with the elementary school kids? Well, it's what I'd like to do someday."

"That's great, Mom. But why haven't you said anything?"

The smile lingered across her mother's lips, then slipped away. "Your father and I decided to do it this way for now ... just a class or two a semester until you graduate high school. And then if I'm still interested, we'll see about the full-time program at the university."

"That's so great." She took her mother's hand and squeezed it. She had always seen her mother as ... well, a *mother*. But she had been a student once, too. A serious one. "Really. I'm proud of you."

"Thanks, hon." Moisture glistened in the corners of her mother's eyes as she squeezed back. "Well, I'll leave you alone with Scout and Jem." She planted a kiss on Janis's forehead. "Don't stay up too much longer."

"I won't, Mom. G'night."

Halfway to the door, her mother turned, her hand pressing the collar of her gown flat. "What were you doing by the bushes this afternoon? In the backyard?"

"Oh, I heard Mr. Leonard drilling. I just wanted to see what he was up to."

"I see."

"Is that all right?"

"The Leonards are ... private people. Your father and I have always thought it best that we respect their privacy." She looked like she was going to say something more but instead glanced around the room. Her gaze touched on the posters tacked to Janis's walls: the Tampa Bay Rowdies, U.S. women's softball, a flag-draped Bruce Springsteen. When her gaze returned to Janis, she was smiling that apologetic smile again. Or was it sorrowful?

"All right, then. Sleep well, hon."

But Janis did not sleep well. As she was drifting off, she dreamed she was creeping up to Boo Radley's front door at night, just as Jem had been doing in the book. Janis didn't want to, but it was as though some inimical whisper compelled her, telling her she had to. The door loomed closer, not old and gray, but a suburban shade of yellow. As Janis reached forward to knock, it swung inward.

A pale hand seized her wrist and pulled her into the darkness.

It took Janis another hour to fall back asleep.

14

Thirteenth Street High
Tuesday, September 4
Third Period

Scott was waiting for the computer at his station to boot up when a high, sneering voice pierced the classroom doorway: "Even *with* a plasma effect, the electrical pulses would have to be *sustained*, dill weed!"

Wayne brushed past, bumping Scott with his backpack. Craig and Chun followed closely. By the time they took their seats across the room, Scott gathered that they were debating whether or not a lightsaber could be built using present-day technology. Scott caught himself cocking an ear before realizing that was just what Wayne wanted: for him to feel left out.

Scott had left several phone messages for Wayne that weekend. None had been returned. He sighed and pressed himself to his feet. This had gone on long enough. He weaved past the intervening computer stations, stooped over Wayne's shoulder, and spoke through his teeth.

"Can we drop the whole Scott Spruel Doesn't Exist thing already? This is getting way past lame."

Wayne turned his head one way, then the other, his back to Scott.

"Did you hear something, men?"

Craig's eyes flickered toward Scott as he shook his large head, his feathery blond hair in disarray. Chun fingered the purple mole above his right nostril and lowered his face. His black bowl cut shuddered with quick rotations.

"Hmm, must be the interference from the simultaneous boot-up of three systems," Wayne said. "Just ignore it, men, and those annoying noises will go away."

"I hope you realize how stupid you sound."

Wayne wheeled to face Scott, his mustache bristling above twisted lips. Small, smudged-in eyes looked him up and down. Scott braced for a blow to the stomach, but Wayne's narrow shoulders began to shudder with laughter. "Talk about *stupid!* Who dressed you in pink this morning? Miss Pac-Man?"

Scott glanced down at his Standards: Miami-pink shirt, pressed white slacks, penny loafers. He smoothed his purple and blue paisley tie, heat crackling up his neck. "Yeah, well…"

"And what's this?" Wayne grabbed the laminated letter around his neck. "The sign of The Secret Order of I'm The World's Biggest Ignoramus?" He unleashed more spitting laughter.

"It stands for *Gamma*. It's a men's organization, something you wouldn't know anything about, you—you hacking neophyte."

Wayne went rigid. "What did you call me?"

In his anger, Scott had gone straight for Wayne's doomsday button. He glanced over at Craig and Chun. They looked back with wide-eyed expressions that said, *Now you've done it.*

"Just forget it," Scott said.

He tried to draw away, but Wayne still had the other end of the letter in his grip. The glint of condescension in his eyes sharpened to blades of jealousy.

"Let go," Scott said.

Wayne mimicked him in falsetto: "*Let go.*"

"Let go, I said. You're gonna tear it!"

"*You're gonna tear it.*"

Scott had hoped to resolve their dispute with the same command and maturity as Scott Summers of the X-Men. But here they were, grappling for a laminated letter like a pair of first graders. All that was missing were the glue sticks and round-tipped scissors. Scott glanced back to make sure the other students weren't watching and found them standing in a semicircle, all glasses and unkempt hair. He seized Wayne's fingers and tried to pry them away.

"I just wanted to warn you about a tap," he whispered as they struggled. "There's one on my line ... might be one on yours."

"Crap on your tap." Wayne jerked his arm, and the string around Scott's neck snapped. They both looked at the letter in Wayne's hand, an "oh, shit" flitting across Wayne's eyes. Then he scrunched up his face and flung the letter away. It flapped over the heads of the onlookers.

Scott stared at Wayne, klaxons blaring between his temples. His first instinct was to seize his throat. Instead, he leveled a trembling finger at Wayne's nose.

"We're through," he said. "I mean it."

"*I mean it,*" Wayne echoed, waggling his head. Several students tittered, including Craig and Chun.

Scott wheeled to hunt for his letter.

Janis stood on tiptoes outside the peeled-paint metal door, trying without success to peer through its mesh window. She knew about the defunct room from when Margaret had pledged. It contained a couple of small tables, a non-working refrigerator, and a countertop with broken cabinets and mouse holes. The room's official name was the Teacher's Dining Room, a relic of some bygone era. Now it was Where the Alpha Pledges Ate Lunch.

Janis sighed through her nose and seized the door handle. *Let's get this over with.* Hinges squealed, and the pledging class, crowded around the two pushed-together tables, blinked up at her from the darkness like well-heeled tomb robbers. The room's lights didn't work either.

"Sorry I'm late," Janis muttered, letting the door swing closed behind her.

Chair legs scraped, and when Janis's eyes adjusted to the gloom, a narrow wedge of table had opened up for her. She was glad to see it wasn't beside the Amy-Alicia-Autumn hydra. It was bad enough having to miss her lunches with her friends, but being confined to a room with her archenemies...

"Just as well for you," Amy chirped. "It gave us time to spruce up the room a little. You should have *smelled* this place ten minutes ago."

Janis didn't lend her voice to the flutters of laughter. Instead, she unpacked her lunch bag. Apparently the three A's had been holding court before Janis's arrival because they resumed chattering to their rapt audience about life in front of the cameras. Janis took a despondent bite from her bologna-and-mayonnaise sandwich and examined the stained ceiling for roach activity. Never in a million years would she have imagined experiencing the place herself. And yet, thanks to whatever power Margaret wielded over her thoughts, here she was.

Yay for me.

The stuffiness of her outfit—slacks and a flipping *blouse*—made her shift and fidget in the half light. She had drawn the line at hanging a giant laminated A around her neck. If it meant demerits, so much the better. Maybe she wouldn't get in.

"So what do you think, Janis?"

She looked over to find the round whites of Amy's eyes peering back at her.

"What do I think about what?"

"About getting together this weekend. The whole pledge class."

"No thanks." Janis took a sip of Capri Sun and pretended to become interested in the writing on the metallic pouch. The other pledges fell silent. Of course to them, *she* was the stuck-up bitch.

"Oh, are you busy this weekend?" Amy asked.

Janis was, actually. She had plans to practice up in the Grove again with Samantha.

"Not really."

"Well, think about it." Amy's voice sounded a half octave higher than natural. "You still have my number, right?" She didn't wait for Janis to answer before turning to the other pledges and listing the places they might meet up. Naturally, the food court in the mall topped the list.

Janis pushed the last bite of sandwich into her mouth and scooted her chair out. She had fulfilled the requirement. She'd eaten with the other pledges. No one had said anything about sitting there the entire lunch period. Heads turned as she stooped for her books. Before the door could swing closed behind her, she heard Amy telling the others she would be right back.

Great.

Janis sped up, but Amy caught her near the auditorium.

"Hey," Amy called, out of breath.

Janis swung around but didn't speak. She began wadding up the paper bag that had held her lunch.

"Look..." Amy watched Janis's hands. "I just ... I was hoping we could put the past behind us. You know, start over."

Janis shot the balled-up bag past Amy's head, rimming it into a metal trashcan.

Amy flinched then looked back at Janis. "Can't you say something?"

"How about I write it down on a piece of paper and slip it into your locker when no one's around?"

The space between Amy's eyebrows wrinkled into a W.

"Oh, come off it," Janis said. "I know it was you."

"You know what was me?"

Janis turned to leave.

"All right, wait!" Amy hustled to catch her. "I was eleven years old. It was immature and ... and mean." Her eyes glistened above cheeks still soft with baby fat. "I don't know why I did it."

Janis pointed her chin toward the door they had come from. "I do. They were sitting next to you."

Amy lowered her eyes. "I've changed," she said softly. "We all have."

"Oh, really?" Janis tapped her foot. "On Monday, you and the A-hol—the other two look at me like I'm something you just stepped in. Then Friday rolls around, and suddenly it's time we all kissed and made up? That could only mean that whatever *change* you're talking about happened in a matter of four days."

Amy didn't say anything.

"Hmm ... wonder what *that* could've been." Janis made a point of staring straight at the red Greek letter against Amy's chest.

"All right. You're still angry. I get it." She started to touch the A, then clasped her hands in front of her. "I deserve it."

For the first time, Janis sensed her former friend didn't like what she had done. It was in her stance, the inflection of her voice. Amy began to walk away. And now something in her surrender—the totality of it—struck a chord in Janis. She opened her mouth, knowing she would probably regret it.

"I'm not going to say anything to Margaret," Janis called. "If that's what you're worried about."

The fact was, she'd never planned to say anything to Margaret. If Amy and the others got in, so what? It wasn't her club. She wanted nothing to do with it, in fact. But at least with the information, Amy could stop making a pretense of being her friend again.

"All right?" Janis called when Amy didn't answer.

Amy turned partway and nodded. And in that glimpse of her face, Janis saw she was crying.

Scott threw his hand over his mouth and shrunk back. There was a quality of sour milk to the smell, of a cold metal railing that had been handled too much. But worse than the smell itself were the associations it dredged up in Scott's mind.

Memories of torment, mostly.

He swallowed hard and stepped all the way into the cafeteria. The metal door slammed shut behind him. Scott faced an industrial-blue room made cavernous by the absence of students, a far cry from the crowded chaos of Creekside Middle School, anyway. At a table off to his right, two students with rattails faced off in a game of pencil breaks, the splintering *thwacks* echoing the length of the cafeteria.

It didn't take long for Scott to spot several pledges seated on the far side of the room, Gamma letters dangling over their steaming lunches. The faint clatter of trays called Scott's attention to a doorway across from him. He fingered the string holding his Gamma letter (knotted in two places now, thanks to Wayne) and joined the short lunch line.

Just as he had last year, he selected his milk carton from a damp bin and his food from a despondent-looking tray lineup. He separated a dollar from the three his mother had left for him and handed it to the sallow grandmother at the register. As he pocketed the change, he realized that one advantage of eating in the cafeteria was that he would profit ten dollars at the end of each week. Money to buy cologne with ... or take Janis out on a date.

His cheeks flushed as he turned with his tray.

The pledges were engrossed in a spirited discussion when Scott arrived at the table, and he managed to seat himself unnoticed. He pressed up his glasses (thin metal frames now, courtesy of the one-hour vision store in the mall) and craned his neck like a periscope.

"...and he made me drop right there and give him twenty!"

"That's nothing," said another pledge. "I had to run two laps around the practice field and got crud all over my shoes. *And* I was late for first period."

"Next thing you know, they'll order us to kneel while they use our ties as toilet paper."

That got some laughter, and Scott was glad to see that the disgruntled joker was short and pudgy with an Ovaltine-colored bowl cut, not of the same physical stock as the officers he'd observed at Friday's meeting.

There was hope for him yet.

"What about you, Stretch?" Ovaltine asked. "What've they made you do?"

It took Scott a moment to realize the boy was addressing him. The rest of the pledges turned. His ears prickling savagely, Scott lowered his eyes and retracted his neck like a tortoise.

"Oh, um..." The truth was, he hadn't been made to do anything yet. "Push-ups."

The others grunted and nodded in understanding, all except for the tall pledge who sat across from Scott and ate quietly. He seemed to be the only one without sweat stains in the armpits of his dress shirt. A minor miracle. And then Scott recognized him. It was the same guy he'd collided with on the first day of school. Only Pink Shirt's top was now blue.

"All right, guys," he said once he'd finished chewing. The table fell silent. "Like it or not, this is going to be our life for the next thirteen weeks. We can either sit here grumbling over who has it the worst, or we can say, 'You're not going to break my resolve.' Because that's exactly what this is—a test of our resolve, our character. But more, it's a test of us as a pledging class."

The solidity of his words struck Scott first, then the words themselves. Why couldn't he talk like that? Scott watched the speaker's intent blue eyes, his easy smile, the way his fraternal gestures included the entire table.

"I say we make a pact right here. A pact that we're going to complete our pledge term—the thirteen of us." He bent toward his backpack and reappeared with a sheet of college-ruled paper. He took a couple of minutes to write something across the top, then slid the paper and pen over to Scott. It read:

The Pact

I hereby promise to do everything required of me as a pledging brother. I understand that failure to do so will result in letting down not only myself but also my fellow brothers. If I am ever on the verge of giving up, I promise to first seek out a pledging brother for counsel and support. And if I see a pledging brother in crisis, I promise to do everything in my power to help him.

The "Lucky" Thirteen are:
Blake Farrier 372-8731

Scott followed the speaker's example and printed his name and phone number under the statement. The sheet went around the table and at last came back to Blake.

"Good deal," he said. "I'm going to see about printing these off and getting everyone a copy."

Scott peeked around, then cleared his throat. "I have a computer. I-I could type it up and print off copies." *Correction,* he thought. *Your computer is stowed away until someone decides you aren't worth the hassle of a tap. Meaning you'll have to use the library computer.*

"Even better," Blake said. "Thanks, Scott."

Scott's chest swelled as he took the piece of paper from Blake and stowed it importantly inside his own backpack.

The pledges now talked of other things, Scott soaking in the laughter and fraternal chatter. He marveled at how much could change in a week, how much *had* changed. Last Monday, he was a computer dweeb and recluse, harried by thoughts of phone taps, federal agents, and the ghosts of middle school past. Now he was in high school and a member of The Lucky Thirteen. He was sitting across from a football star, he soon learned, and was among a group who'd just sworn to help him pledge into the school's premier club.

The pudgy pledge ("Just call me Sweet Pea—everyone does eventually") pretended to count on his fingers. "One down, and let's see ... only fifty-nine more cafeteria lunches to go!"

When Scott looked down at his clean tray amid the laughter, he realized that he hadn't even minded the cafeteria fare, and he said so. The others agreed—Blake, too. An older brother came by to inspect their trays and dismiss them. And when Scott poked his head through the service window to thank the lunchroom ladies, he could not have been more sincere.

"I wouldn't have wanted to eat lunch anywhere else today," he told them.

15

As school let out, Janis hurried to the sidewalk outside the front office. She knew Amy's mother picked her up in front of the school. If she found Amy alone, she would ask if she were all right, tell her she was forgiven. Ruse or no, Janis just wanted the whole thing off her conscience. She didn't want to have to think about Amy's crumbling look back anymore.

But Amy, who had entered English class solo, her face pale and puffy, wasn't solo now. When she appeared in front of the auditorium, she was in Autumn and Alicia's company. They chatted for a minute before something made Amy rear her head to the sky in a fit of laughter.

Well there you have it, Miss Gullibility.

Janis wheeled around and stomped toward where Margaret was parked. *Stupid, stupid, stupid!* She should have known better than to believe anything that came off of Amy's forked tongue. She switched her books from one arm to the other and had only gone a few paces when someone called her.

"Hey—uh, Janis is it?"

She spun. "*What?*"

Behind her, someone knelt to the sidewalk.

"I, um, I think you dropped this."

When he stood, Janis recognized the boy with the indigo eyes who had been at Wendy's last week. Blake—yes, she remembered his name—Blake Farrier. In fact, she'd repeated the name to herself a few times since. Though she hadn't told anyone, not even Samantha, the name had come to feel good in her thoughts. But, oh God, had she just snapped at him?

"I'm so sorry," she blurted. "I didn't know ... I thought you were..."

He laughed. "I think it fell out of your folder there."

Janis saw he was holding her Alpha letter. He stepped forward and slid it back inside the folder so she wouldn't have to adjust the books in her arms. For a moment, his crisp, clean fragrance was around her. His cheeks dimpled softly when he smiled.

"Thanks," she said.

"Shouldn't you be wearing that?" Before she could answer, he leaned in and lowered his voice. "Don't worry, I won't tell anyone. Technically, I should be wearing mine, too."

Janis took her turn to smile. "Your Alpha letter?"

His light fragrance whisked back around her when he laughed.

She nodded at his blue shirt and tie. "I'm not sure it goes so well with..."

"Nope, you're right. Guess color coordination's not my thing." He took a smiling breath then stopped and shook his head. "I'm sorry. I haven't introduced myself. I'm Blake."

I know. The words almost slipped out when she tucked her books to take his hand. "Janis," she said.

His grip was firm and kind.

"Janis," he repeated. "As in Graystone?"

She fought off a grimace as she nodded. *Once more, Margaret's good name precedes you.*

"Let's see, star outfielder, stellar goalie..."

Confusion creased her brow.

Blake laughed. "I read the paper."

"Oh, that." Janis's pulse quickened.

The *Gainesville Sun* had done a piece on her that summer, one that took up half the front page of the sports section. Thanks to her dad, the article now hung in a frame above her trophies.

"Well, welcome to Thirteenth Street High. I have to go and get ready for practice, but..." Blake indicated the string of her Alpha letter dangling from her armful of books. "I guess this won't be our last meeting."

"No, I guess not," she said. "Thanks again."

As Janis watched him turn and step into an assured balls-of-his-feet gait that was somehow unassuming at the same time, she wondered whether pledging Alpha was such a bad move after all.

Biting her smile, she turned toward the parking lot to find Margaret.

At the library's circulation desk, thirteen printed copies of The Pact in hand, Scott asked to use the phone to call his father. Mrs. Norris, who looked as if she'd been shut inside the library since the Woodrow

Wilson administration, sniffed and turned the phone around just enough for him to read the message taped to its base: "Not For Student Use." A small lock secured the phone's rotary dial. The chains from the head librarian's horn-rimmed glasses swayed with the wattled skin at her neck as she stepped past him with a stack of books. Scott waited until she was out of sight, then lifted the phone.

Dial tone? Perfecto.

Using his abilities, he concentrated into the system. Several seconds later, he had a ring.

"Hey, Scottie!" A gasp for breath. "Whaddya say?"

His father owned a prosthetics practice in northwest Gainesville, and Scott imagined him standing there, brown tie thrown over his shoulder, the bulging belly of his shirt smeared with plaster.

"I stayed late at school to work on something," Scott murmured into the cupped mouthpiece. "Any chance you could swing over and give me a ride home?"

"Hold on."

Scott craned his head toward the back of the library, listening for Mrs. Norris's return.

At last, his father came back on. "Can you give me fifteen minutes?"

So, thirty minutes. "Sure. I'll be in front of the school."

Outside the library, the campus looked deserted. The slanting sunlight Scott stepped into threw a long, lone shadow behind him, as though mocking his solitude. Scott should have seen it as a warning, but he didn't.

At his locker, he swapped some books from his backpack, remembering to grab *To Kill a Mockingbird* this time. He ambled along the school's four wings, half expecting—half hoping—to spot Mr. Shine pushing his cart. But Mr. Shine had apparently gone home as well.

Scott wandered behind the gymnasium and joined the few spectators—parents and girlfriends, he guessed—along a low wall in front of the grunting, thudding practice field. In the middle distance, a player launched a football in a long arc toward several players sprinting downfield. The thrower was too far away to tell, but Scott wanted to believe he was Blake, one of his new Gamma friends.

The Fall Jamboree was that Friday. The other pledges would probably be going. Janis, too. But the home stadium was across town, and Scott's parents wouldn't want to drive him both ways. A sleepover at Wayne's might have offered consolation, but Scott didn't even have that to fall back on.

We're through. I mean it.

He was wondering if he would come to regret those words when a cadence of chanting broke up the thought. Scott squinted. The sound was coming from a part of the field away to his right, hidden from view by the tennis courts. Scott hiked up his backpack and trekked over. When he reached the corner of the fenced-in courts, he peered around.

Whoa.

The dozen or so chanting cheerleaders pumped their fists, rose into human towers, rotated, and disassembled. Midriff-baring tops and short shorts showed off glistening abdomens and muscled legs. Scott allowed the stunning sight to bombard his retinas—until he realized he was gawking in plain view.

He slinked along the chain-link fence to its far side and entered the empty courts. Just as he'd hoped, the green windbreak covering most of the fence was opaque enough that it was easier to see out than in. Inside, he was all but invisible. Scott glanced at his watch as he hurried across the courts toward the chants. He still had fifteen minutes until his dad arrived.

He slung his backpack over the end of a pole that stretched the farthest tennis net, then reclined against the pole itself, one knee pulled in. The cheerleaders pumped their arms in unison.

"WHO ARE WE? THE MIGH-TY TITANS!"

This, my friend, is the life.

"WHO CAN BEAT US? NO ONE CAN!"

The cheerleaders broke off into leaps and high kicks, then clapped their hands as they reassembled. For Scott, it felt like even more of a shame that he wouldn't be going to the Jamboree that Friday. Maybe he could—

Metal rattled behind him as the gate to the tennis courts latched closed. By the time Scott turned around, Jesse Hoag was nearly to the center court, Creed and Tyler Bast not far behind.

16

Jesse Hoag was even more massive than Scott remembered. Or maybe he only appeared so because Scott was still sitting against the post, unable to draw his feet underneath himself. The asphalt court trembled with each of Jesse's closing footfalls. Scott's gaze shot from Jesse's fists, which swished at his sides like wrecking balls, to his face. Gobs of grease held his dark hair out of his eyes—sober gray eyes that appeared at odds with his sinister smile.

That got Scott moving.

He sprang up and promptly tripped over his own feet, stumbling backward into the fence. While he struggled to right his splayed legs, the cheerleaders launched into a new chant:

"THAT'S OUR TEAM! GO, TEAM! GO!"

Jesse stepped onto the last of the three tennis courts—Scott's court. Tyler had lingered behind, standing guard near the gate, the only way in or out. Creed circled around the other side of the tennis net, ensuring that Scott had nowhere to run.

"We were starting to think you'd left Dodge," Jesse said. "We've got some unfinished business, you and me."

I don't know about any business.

Scott heard the words, but he only managed to mouth them, his tongue flicking around a bed of desiccated flesh, like a beached fish. It was the calmness with which Jesse had spoken, the coldness, as though he was just there to do a job. Scott knew what that job was. He seized the place where his right forearm bent. The lump of healed bone had begun to ache as if someone were needling the marrow with a shard of ice.

Jesse's eyes shifted toward Creed, who in the next instant appeared at Scott's shoulder, his hand locked around Scott's upper arm. When Scott turned, he was staring into a pair of blue-tinted John Lennon glasses.

How in the world did he move so fast?

Scott tried to shake him off.

"Don't make me get nasty," Creed whispered, tightening his grip.

And now Scott felt the rim of Creed's bowler hat against his temple ... and something else, thin and sharp, against his neck. Scott froze. Moving only his eyes, he tried to see where Creed's hand disappeared beneath his chin. *A knife?* The idea almost made Scott giggle because any other sound would have made him lose it. *He's holding a knife to my throat.*

"WHO ARE WE? THE MIGH-TY TITANS! WHO CAN BEAT US? NO ONE CAN!"

Scott's eyes shifted toward the chants.

"One peep out of those pipes, fuck face," Creed whispered, "and they're as good as diced."

Scott looked up to where Jesse had stopped two feet in front of him. His eyes, deep set and gray, were assessing him, taking measurements, particularly of his arms. Scott could almost hear the slow, clanking cogs of Jesse's brain. He was calculating breaking points.

"Do you remember what I said?" Jesse asked.

"About whu-whu-what?"

"'Do it again, and it'll be both arms.' Do you remember me saying that?"

Scott started to shake his head before remembering Creed's knife at his throat. "I didn't do it," he murmured, trying to hold his Adam's apple in. "God, I swear—whatever it is, I didn't do it."

But he had done it.

Maybe it was having to spend last summer in a plaster cast. Or maybe it was lying to his mother about what had happened to his arm and listening to her huff as she drove him to the Emergency Care Center. *A klutz,* she'd no doubt been thinking. *Just like his father.* Or maybe it was knowing that he hadn't been able to stop them, had been too chicken to even try. Maybe that's what had driven him to what he did.

"Ever been beaten by a tire iron?" Jesse asked.

"No."

"Do you know what that feels like?"

"N-no."

"The old man thought it was me making all those long-distance calls, running up the phone bill. I told him it wasn't, but he didn't believe me. Called me a lying sack of you-know-what. Said if I couldn't come up with the money, he was gonna take it out on my hide. A few hubcap jobs, a few trips to the pawn shop, and we're good, you follow? We're square, me and my old man. Everything's cool. 'Cept the thing was, it happened again the next month. This time, the bill was twenty pages long. He caught me coming home. It was at night. I'd just parked the car, and he was waiting by the garage door in the dark."

Jesse pushed up the sleeve on his black Metallica T-shirt. A brown blotch stained the meat of his upper arm. "That was his first good shot," Jesse said. "The second one caught me here." He mashed away his upper lip with a hammer-sized thumb to reveal a missing molar. "Third one got me in the skull. Here." He rapped his knuckles hard against the side of his own head.

Scott had heard about Jesse's father, about the drinking. But he had no idea...

"I'm sorry," Scott managed and then began shaking, "but it whu-whu-wasn't me! G-god, it wasn't m-me!"

"And Creed and Tyler here," Jesse continued in a calm voice, "well, the phone company hit them with a delinquency. Cut their service. Their mother about lost it. Wouldn't come out of her room for days. Isn't that right, Creed?"

"Fuckin' A," Creed whispered.

Scott remembered hacking the central office that day last summer, remembered taking over Jesse's and Creed's phone lines. He had started dialing country codes and phone numbers, one after another: South Africa, Australia, Japan, Nepal—calls where the connection fee alone was worth a prime cut of steak. Over several days, Scott had kept a running tab in his head. When the dollar amounts climbed into the hundreds, he made himself stop, figuring they were even.

Apparently, Jesse figured differently. His hand swallowed Scott's wrist—the left one this time.

"Good thing is, you know what to expect." A hint of a grin returned to Jesse's face.

Jesse's thumb, which was almost as thick as Scott's forearm, bore down. A deep ache bloomed beneath the pressure. Scott winced, lips pressed together, determined not to cry. He imagined the latticework of bone—cortical bone, he'd heard it called, *his* cortical bone— beginning to collapse where Jesse pressed. At any moment, it was going to snap. He would hear it. And that seemed to Scott the worst part: that he would hear his own bone snap. Again.

"Holy shit!" Creed cried. "He's pissing himself!"

It was true, Scott realized. His bladder had just bailed, turned to Jell-O, said, "The hell with it." Nothing was contracting to hold anything in. Scott felt the urine matting his pant leg, soaking inside his sock. When he glanced down, he caught it seeping over his right loafer. Creed tried to dance away from the spreading pool. Jesse scuffed back a step as well, his grip faltering.

That was all Scott needed.

He wrenched his arm down at the same time he shoved Creed, propelling himself into the first gangly steps of flight. Jesse lunged, but Scott had enough prescience to arch his back. The fingers that sought him raked his shirt.

Scott turned toward the gate. Tyler, who had sauntered a short distance away, scrambled to get back into position. A cigarette fell from his mouth, and he stumbled for a moment, arms flailing inside his dusky jean jacket. He regained his balance and closed the distance to the gate in four scampering steps.

So much for that.

Scott veered toward the court's baseline, arms pumping, his paisley tie streaming over a shoulder.

Behind him, Creed swore, still down. Good. But Jesse was chasing him. Scott could feel his footfalls rumbling through the asphalt, gaining momentum. Scott sped past the baseline and straight for the fence.

C'mon, legs. Don't fudge on me now!

And he leapt.

He rattled against the fence and latched on. But his grip on the chain linking was shallow because of the windbreak. And only one of his shoes had a toehold. The other slipped against the fabric.

"Help!" he cried. "Helllp!"

The chanting from the field to his left continued unabated.

Scott clawed and pulled, stabbing the toes of his shoes inside the chain-link diamonds like crampons. Upward movement! He stretched an arm until his fingers curled over the top of the windbreak. The fingers of his other hand grasped the chain linking just shy of the top bar.

Creed grabbed one of his ankles.

What the—? Three seconds ago, he'd been halfway across the court on his backside. But Scott knew Creed's grip, thin and steely. And when Scott peered down, he saw the curtains of his dirty blond hair thrashing like Saint Vitus. Creed had always been fast, but that was entering the realm of super speed. Scott jerked and kicked. Behind Creed, Jesse pulled up to the baseline, chest heaving.

"Hold still, goddammit!" Creed shouted.

Metal glinted in Creed's other hand but not from a knife, Scott saw. The blades belonged to the studded leather glove Creed wore. One long blade extended from the index finger, a second from the thumb. Creed drew the glove back, but with Scott's next kick, Creed stumbled backward holding an empty loafer.

Humming with adrenaline, Scott pulled with both arms. He heaved his legs up frog-like until he was perched atop the windbreak, out of reach. His eyes cut up and down Titan Terrace, where there was...

(*crap*)

...absolutely no one.

"Help!"

The fence pitched backward. Jesse had two of the fence's poles inside his fists. Scott watched the pole to his left uproot from its foundation in a burst of cement. *Great. Super strength and super speed on the same team.* His own power? Navigating telecommunication lines while his body remained behind, limp and defenseless. Hardly an equalizer.

Scott clamped the top bar of the fence under his armpit and threw a leg over. If he could just roll over the rest of the way, fall into the lawn, stumble toward the practice fields...

Jesse ripped the other pole free. Its conical base of cement and earth scraped over the green asphalt. The fence leaned inward. Scott had to contract even the tiniest muscles in his fingers and toes to maintain his hold.

Creed's reedy laughter pierced the afternoon heat.

Scott closed his eyes in resignation. And he'd been having such a good day: the lunch with the Gamma pledges, The Pact, the growing feeling that he, Scott Spruel, belonged at Thirteenth Street High. Now, here he was, clinging to the top of a fence, being pursued by three future convicts, marinating in his own urine—and drooping.

Jesse's hand clamped around his neck. "Let go," he ordered.

Stale tobacco breath broke against Scott's face. He opened his eyes and stared into Jesse's huge nostrils. Warped chain linking billowed around them. Jesse's other hand seized the bar to which Scott clung.

"I said, let it go."

When Jesse squeezed, the bones in Scott's neck crunched together. His body went numb. He had been clasping the top of the fence snugly to his ribcage, but now he could hardly feel it. Was it slipping from his hold? Scott cried out, but not from that thought. Something was spiking through the numbness.

"Ow!" Jesse hollered.

The fence vaulted up several feet and bobbed. When Scott looked down, he found Jesse clenching his hand. Scott squirmed over the fence top, his neck sore, but sensation prickling back into his body in little electrical shocks.

"You're dead!" Creed yelled.

Anticipating his escape, Scott held up his fist to Creed, thought about it, and then popped out his middle finger. Suicidal? Maybe, but man, it felt good. And with one leg over, he was already halfway home. It was just a matter of—

A jag of metal snagged the crotch of his pants. Threads popped as Scott strained, but the fence wouldn't release him. He looked toward the gate, expecting to find it swung wide, Tyler running around to intercept him. But Tyler was still at his post, withdrawing his arm from beneath the windbreak for some reason. When the fence beneath him shook, Scott didn't have to look to see Creed climbing toward him. Scott wriggled and whimpered, a fish on a hook.

"You're mine now, you little shit," Creed whispered from inches away.

Make that a fish fillet on a hook.

The door to the courts banged open. A tall man in blue coveralls and a straw hat appeared. In two steps, he had a wad of Tyler's bleached hair and most of his ear inside his thick hand.

Scott stopped struggling and sagged in relief.

"What in the hell is going on in here?" Mr. Shine yelled, eyes blazing. He marched Tyler toward where Creed had leapt back down to the court. Tyler winced and staggered to keep up with his hair.

Creed showed his glove with the twin blades and began circling to Mr. Shine's left. "There's no trash in here, Geech, which means it ain't none of your business. You follow?"

Still holding his hand, Jesse stood to his full height. "Yeah, go home."

"Looks like I a'ready done made it my business," Mr. Shine said, "and I'll go home when I'm damn ready." He shoved Tyler toward Jesse and, with as much speed as he'd reappeared Scott's quarter the other day, produced a garbage pick from behind his back. Except this one looked longer than the one Scott had seen on his cart, sharper. Of course, last week the pick wasn't being wielded like a spear. Mr. Shine's teeth flashed white as he pointed it toward Creed.

Creed looked cross-eyed toward the pick's tip as he retreated to Jesse's side. Both held their palms out now, as if trying to placate a lunatic. A fresh pink line seared one of Jesse's hands.

"We weren't doing nothin'." Jesse's voice was suddenly high. "Just trying to help our friend."

"Yeah, dummy was goofing around up there and got stuck," Creed put in. "We kept tellin' him not to—"

"Don't story me, boy!" With the pick, Mr. Shine motioned toward the gate. "Git on out o' here."

Jesse and Creed looked at one another. Tyler stood at their backs, rubbing the side of his head.

"Git, I said. This ain't no place to be horsin' around."

Creed swiped his bowler hat from the ground, then sauntered toward the exit. Jesse grumbled and followed. Tyler took up the rear. Mr. Shine held out the pick as if he were herding cattle, and Scott had no doubt he would prod any that went wayward. The three didn't appear to have any doubt either. They were almost to the gate when Jesse turned his head. His pitted gray eyes found Scott's.

"Help's a funny thing," he said. "I wouldn't count on it showing up the next time."

"Go on!" Mr. Shine said.

When the three were outside, Mr. Shine retreated toward Scott, then slid the pick through a strap on the back of his coveralls. Scott unhooked his pants easily now that he wasn't being pursued, and he scaled down the fence.

When he dropped to the court, Mr. Shine supported him around the waist. "You all right?" His eyes were dark with concern.

"Just shaken up." Scott wiped his nose. He hoped Mr. Shine couldn't see that he'd wet himself.

"I don't know what you did to get them riled," he said, looking on the destroyed section of fence. "But them's some ba-a-ad company. Need to watch yourself. Keep to you own business, hear?"

"Yeah."

"All right. You got someone coming for you?"

"My dad." He retrieved his backpack and pushed his sopping foot into his tossed-off loafer. "He's going to pick me up in front."

"Well, c'mon then. I'll walk you over." Mr. Shine clapped his large hand on Scott's shoulder. "But remember now what I said 'bout your business. Them boys is nobody to be messing with."

Scott nodded. He didn't need to be told a second time.

17

Thirteenth Street High practice fields
Friday, September 28
3:34 p.m.

J anis bounced on her toes and then paced in front of the goal line. Cinching up her gloves, she flexed her fingers and bounced again. She felt springy. She felt good. If it weren't for her damned nerves…

"Ready?" one of the assistant coaches asked, bringing a whistle to her teeth.

Janis nodded, blowing a strand of hair from her eyes. She crouched and surveyed the four players about fifteen yards out from the goal. That afternoon marked the end of the first week of tryouts, and the coaches had opened the varsity tryouts to all grades. Janis rocked from one leg to the other. She had dominated the junior varsity tryouts that week.

The whistle blew.

But these weren't junior varsity players.

The first shot came low and hard to Janis's left. She dove and punched it away, skipped to her feet, and scrambled back to the center of the goal line. The next shot came straight at her, a bullet. She watched it into her stomach—*umph!*—and rolled it off to the assistant. The third shot went high and to her right. She followed it for a step, then let it sail over the goal. The spank of the final shot sounded quickly—too quickly—and the ball was already on its way to the opposite goalpost.

I'm not going to get there.

But like a ghost image, so faint she might have imagined it, Janis saw the ball careening off the post and angling toward the other side for a score. The image came to her in an instant. Janis pulled up, and when the actual ball did career off the post, she was there to collect it.

The assistant coach blew her whistle. "Good anticipation, Janis." Then to the four girls, she yelled, "Reset!"

The drill continued for the next thirty minutes. After set shots, the four girls dribbled and shot, seeming to come nearer the goal each time. Janis understood their frustration. They were aspiring varsity players after all—some of them seniors—and a freshman was denying them goal after needed goal. But the truth was, Janis could anticipate them, sometimes seeing the ball's trajectory, sometimes just sensing it and reacting, like a reflex. And with every shot she tipped up, punched away, or watched into her possession, her confidence grew.

A few got past her. But only a very few.

When the coach blew the whistle for the final time, Janis's hands were numb. Her thighs burned with fatigue. The air didn't scorch as it had in August, but her face still felt like it was on fire. She also had the beginnings of a headache, twin screws in her temples. The assistant coach dismissed the other players, then consulted with Coach Hall, who had walked over to observe the last few rounds.

Janis pulled the stopper on the Gatorade sports bottle she'd parked next to the goalpost and squeezed a jet of warm water into her mouth. Her thin gold chain with its crucifix pendant had wriggled out during the drill, and she tucked it back beneath her collar. The chain had been a gift from her father for her thirteenth birthday. She touched it through her jersey as she watched the two coaches confer.

At last, Coach Hall tucked her clipboard under her arm and walked toward Janis. Her red cap was pulled low over aviator sunglasses, the rest of her face a bed of frown lines.

"Go on and wrap up today's practice with the other freshmen," she said when she reached Janis.

In the sunglasses' reflection, Janis's lips quivered once. She nodded. "Okay."

"But I want you back here Monday. You're going to finish tryouts with varsity."

This time, Janis's lips tried their hardest not to smile.

"It's all the work you put in," her father said.

Janis took another swallow of Coke and rested her arm on the windowsill. The late-day air felt good billowing around her, stealing away her perspiration. Her father had had the celebratory can of soda waiting for her when he pulled in to pick her up. He'd never doubted the news would be good.

"But now isn't the time to rest on your laurels," he counseled. "If anything, you have to be more prepared than ever."

They pulled up to a light. When her father looked over, a thin mesh of wrinkles grew around his eyes, which was how he smiled. He shook her dusty knee where, for the first time, Janis noticed a dark patch of blood.

"But I know you know that."

"Yeah, don't worry. I'm not expecting next week to be any easier."

"Good, Janis." He turned back to the road. "Not enough people think that way. There are far too many receiving perks in this country through no diligence of their own. Too many government programs enabling that kind of ethos. They're well intentioned, I'm sure, but self-defeating. Motivation, initiative..." He waved his hand. "That's all done away with. And now we're facing skyrocketing debt and a workforce that can't compete with the Germanys and Japans anymore. It's why we're supporting Reagan again."

"Mom, too?"

Her mother hadn't been crazy about staking the Reagan/Bush '84 sign in the front lawn.

"Well, your mother's coming around. The sixties left a bit of a stain on her thinking, I'm afraid."

As Janis lowered the can from her lips, she thought of the way her mother had smiled that night when, in a low voice, she shared her plans to return to school. Janis glanced over at her father. For the first time, she felt a wall going up over the part of herself that had always accepted his conservative opinions as holy writ.

"Star says the debt is because the Republicans are spending money on missiles we don't need and giving tax breaks to their rich friends. They want us to believe it's because of welfare spending, but it's really not."

"This Star is a friend from school?"

Janis made herself nod.

"What Star needs to understand is that her country is responding to an aggressor that has vast nuclear armaments and has sworn our annihilation more than once. Her country is doing its best to protect her."

"She says that's a lie, too."

They were passing a short strip mall with a convenience store and Laundromat, and her father swerved in. The car bounced against the drive, its bottom scraping the cement incline. Janis gasped and held her Coke up to keep it from spilling. The car cut into a space at the far end of the building that fronted a cinderblock wall. When her father pulled the emergency brake and looked over, his face was so solemn that Janis feared for a moment he was going to slap her. Not that he ever had.

"What is it?" Her eyes felt huge above her quivering lips. The last mouthful of Coke had turned sour on her tongue. She watched her father's nostrils dilate, his eyes pressing into hers.

"We knew that in high school you were going to be exposed to people with different opinions, different views of the world. It was why your mother and I were so demanding of you and your sister growing up. We wanted you to develop the capacity to think for yourselves. And you've done that. Your mother and I are very proud of who you and Margaret have become."

But even as he said this, his face remained stern, his wiry brows nearly touching.

"For some reason, people often get swept up in movements and ideologies that sound moral and righteous but that are, in fact, defeatist. Defeatist for themselves—defeatist for their country. This happens even to intelligent people."

"I wasn't saying I believed what Star said." A lump swelled in Janis's throat. "I was just telling you..."

"I know." He closed his eyes and exhaled. His brows drew apart. "But now that you've heard your friend's version, I think it's important that you hear the truth, even if it scares you. You're old enough now."

Janis watched her father's face, which looked gray and grave in a way she'd never seen.

"You're familiar with the Cold War, of course. You've studied its history in school."

"Yes," she said, but wasn't sure her father heard.

"In the late years of World War II, the U.S. and the Soviet Union teamed up to defeat Hitler and Nazi Germany. Americans advanced through Western Europe, the Soviets through Eastern Europe. They met at the River Elbe in Germany. Your grandfather was at the meeting point, in fact—your mother's father. You were too young to remember, but he would tell stories about sharing photos and hand-rolled cigarettes with the Soviet rifle division in the spring of 1945."

Her father gazed through the windshield as he spoke, and Janis wondered whether he was thinking about his own service in Korea, something he rarely talked about.

"But it was an alliance of convenience, you see. After World War II, the Soviet Army remained in Eastern Europe, which had been Stalin's plan all along. Where he didn't expand the Soviet border, he installed puppet regimes in countries like Poland, Hungary, half of Germany. It's why there's an East and West Germany and a wall dividing Berlin. Communist governments, Janis. No democracy, no free will. Everything controlled by the state. The United States, meanwhile, sent billions in Marshall funds to rebuild Western Europe and bulwark its governments from the spread of Soviet influence."

In the past, whenever her father used to lecture her like this, Janis would have to fight the compulsion to roll her eyes, but there in the car, she could barely breathe. Like stones being set on her chest, his words bore weight.

"An arms race followed. More and deadlier missiles. The advent of the hydrogen bomb, a thousand times more powerful than its atomic predecessors. By the 1950s, the U.S. and the Soviet Union had hundreds of nuclear weapons pointed at one another. Did you learn the concept of Mutually Assured Destruction? MAD? It was the idea that a massive launch from one side could be answered with a massive counter-launch from the other. Both countries would be obliterated, you see? Which meant neither country could strike first. And this has been the basis for our *peace* for the last thirty years. But that may be changing."

"How?" The question caught in Janis's throat.

"The Russians have more sophisticated weapons than was previously believed, for one. They pulled ahead in the arms race, and now Reagan is determined to pull even. But it's not just a matter of numbers anymore. Something else is happening."

Janis was barely aware of cars coming in and out of the lot, their headlights washing past them and illuminating the dark dumpster that seemed to be squatting in the weeds beside them in wait.

"There are voices in the Soviet Politburo talking now as if a nuclear war *can* be won. That could be bluster, of course. But it could also mean they've discovered a method for launching a first strike that would go undetected until it was too late. Or perhaps they have the means to neutralize a counterstrike. Either way, there would be no retaliation. No Mutually Assured Destruction."

The cinderblock wall beyond their windshield was dingy and littered with graffiti: crude messages about what this or that person would do, complete with phone numbers—the sort of thing that would normally have turned Janis crimson, especially with her dad beside her. But now the messages barely registered. She didn't think he was seeing them either.

Janis's fingers felt for her crucifix.

"I'm not telling you this to frighten you. I'm..." He took a breath and then a long look at her face. "You're extremely intelligent, Janis. Extremely capable. You and your sister, both. And if this standoff continues to escalate, why, you may be called on one day to help your country. That's why I'm telling you."

Her father looked at her for another moment, then started the car and put it in reverse. By the time they rejoined the traffic on Sixteenth Avenue, her father seemed himself again, but everything around them—the entire world—felt different to Janis, as if it had fallen under a dark pall.

He snapped his fingers. "I almost forgot about movie night. Should we swing by Video World and pick up a rental?" He glanced down at the clock display. "There's still time before dinner."

"Oh, I'm going to the homecoming game tonight, remember?" Janis's voice felt far away, as though someone else was saying the words. "And then sleeping over at Samantha's."

"Right, right..."

She peeked over to find her father facing straight ahead. Yes, he looked himself again, but knowing what he *could* look like made him look different, somehow. Though she tried, Janis couldn't wipe away how he'd appeared only a minute before. She couldn't forget what she'd seen on his face as he stared at the cinderblock wall. Fear. She had seen her father's fear.

And that upset her more than anything he could have told her.

"You all right?"

"Hmm?" Janis looked over at her best friend. She and Samantha were sitting at the top of the football stands in their softball-league jackets from the year before, the shouting of the student body surging and crashing beneath them like a restless surf. A cool gust of wind blew Janis's hair across her face while Samantha's boyish brown hair only fluttered.

"You've barely said two words tonight. Everything cool?"

"Yeah." Janis pushed her hair back. "Just tired."

On the field, the Ocala team kicked off the ball. It was late in the fourth quarter, and Thirteenth Street High was way ahead. Shrill screams rose around them again as Thirteenth Street's return man ran the ball to the fifty. Cheerleaders high kicked and showed their shining teeth. A hyper group of freshmen boys turned around and demanded high fives.

Janis held her hands up, numb to the ensuing smacks.

"You're not holding something back on me, are you?" Samantha asked.

There would be no retaliation. No mutually assured destruction.

Janis thought for a second before shaking her head. Her friendship with Samantha had been founded on their passion for sports, not strange dreams or dark musings on the Cold War.

"Hey, isn't that your man?"

For the first time that night, Blake was putting on his helmet and attaching the chin strap. Coach Coffer shouted something in his ear and shoved him onto the field. Blake jogged toward the huddle.

"Cute butt." Samantha nudged Janis.

Janis could only nod vaguely. She had finally broken down that week and told Samantha about Blake. She'd seen him several times since he rescued her Alpha letter earlier that month—chance encounters in the hallway, mostly, where they would stop to chat. Just that morning, he'd wished her luck with the varsity soccer tryouts. She'd bitten back a smile, flattered that he'd even known about the tryouts, and responded by wishing him well in that evening's game. Blake chuckled. "Well, if we get far enough ahead, maybe Coach will stick me in for the final minutes. You know, just enough time to get me the reps but not enough to mess anything up."

"You'll do fine," she said, placing her hand on his upper arm. The gesture startled Janice, but it had seemed so natural, as if her hand was drawn to the purple mesh jersey, to the swell of his triceps.

She gave his arm a tentative squeeze, then drew her hand away.

"Thanks." His voice had sounded as soft as his dimples. "I'll remember you said that."

From the bleachers, Janis watched Blake run the second-team offense in the game's waning minutes. Coach "Two F's" Coffer mostly had him hand the ball off to the backs, but on the final play, Blake faked a handoff and sprinted around the end. With the goal line in reach, he took a knee. Screams collapsed to groans, but Janis understood. The game was won and Blake was showing class.

The cheers picked up again as the final seconds ticked away. Players clapped one another's helmets. Cheerleaders rustled their pom-poms. But from Janis's numb distance, the action seemed to be taking place among stage actors and collapsible set pieces.

This can all end, she thought. *This can all be blown away.*

She zipped her jacket slowly and pushed her hands into her pockets. "Hey, um, I think I'm going to catch a ride home with Margaret."

"What about the sleepover?"

"Yeah, I'm sorry." Janis tried to smile. "Tryouts whipped me pretty good."

"Oh. That's cool."

Samantha's voice sounded distant, as though a chasm separated them. Janis wondered if they hadn't started drifting apart that summer when she began having the strange dreams—dreams she'd been too weirded out to share, even with her best friend. Janis wondered, too, if her decision to stick with Alpha hadn't further separated them. After all, Alpha had deprived them of lunches together. And with Janis possibly earning a spot on varsity soon, they would no longer be practicing soccer together, either.

"We'll do it another time," Janis said. "I promise."

"It's cool," Samantha repeated but without looking up. "Well, my mom's probably waiting out front. I should get going." She turned and began picking her way down the emptying stands.

Janis stood watching her, wondering whether there would be another time after all.

18

"What are you seeing?" the man asked.

"Nothing out of the ordinary," the woman replied.

"I don't like it."

"Is something the matter, sir?"

"There have been no energetic disturbances around the girl's house since the end of last month. They've just stopped."

"I see."

"Similarly, the boy hasn't been on his computer in the same amount of time."

"Do you believe there's a connection?"

"I'm not sure yet. Have they been communicating with one another?"

"Negative, sir."

"I still don't like it."

"If it's any assurance, they both seem engrossed in high school. I don't believe we'd be seeing that if..."

"Keep a close eye on them, regardless," the man said. "We're entering a critical period."

"Yes, sir."

19

Friday, October 5
7:09 p.m.

"Not very many cars." Scott's father scrunched up his thick glasses and dipped his shaggy head to peer past Scott. "The front porch light isn't even on. Sure you've got the right house, Ace?"

Scott quickly read the numbers on the mailbox, then looked down at the invitation for the Alpha-Gamma gala, covering the address with his thumb. "It's supposed to be 2624. Let's see..." He pretended to search around. "Yup, says it right there on the box. I'm just a little early."

"Do you want me to wait to make sure?"

"Naw, I'm fine." He opened the car door and stepped out into the dusky street.

"All right. Well, call me when it's over. I've got *Christine* loaded in the Betamax. It's supposed to be a horror flick, but Jagu over at

Video World says it's a riot. Har, har, har! Then I've got the latest Dirty Harry flick, *Sudden Impact.*"

His dad cocked his head and started to squint, but before he could get off his horrendous Clint Eastwood impression, Scott closed the door. When he stood up, all he could see was his father's belly over the steering wheel. Scott half-waved, half-shooed at him, then took a couple of slow steps toward the affluent-looking house as his father's Volkswagen droned away. When the taillights had grown small enough, Scott headed toward the actual house, which was two blocks over.

Sorry, Dad, but tonight's too important.

And it would not be out of character for his father to shout something mortifying from the car as the front door was opening: "Don't feed him after midnight! Har, har, har, har!"

Scott walked briskly, touching his hair. He'd spent an hour in the bathroom with a blow-dryer and a comb, trying for a feathered style like Blake's. In the end, he'd rewet his hair and combed it over. At least the Bud Body fitness booklet had arrived that week. In the first exercises, Bud had him skipping in circles, pulling imaginary ropes, and slathering his body with vegetable oil in order to "succor the muscle tissue." Scott had been skeptical, but tensing now, he thought he felt the beginnings of a line separating his pectorals.

He winced when he cupped his bicep. He'd forgotten about the fading brown band on the inside of his arm. Another one marred his upper ribcage on the same side. They were from the day at the tennis courts a month earlier, when the fence he had clung to became ... electric? With his cervical nerves being crushed inside Jesse's pinch, Scott hadn't been able to feel more than a faint burning. But by the next morning, two raw bands had appeared, their surfaces mottled with blisters like toadstools risen after a humid rain.

Scott was still trying to make sense of it all: Jesse's strength ... Creed's speed ... And what about Tyler? Before Mr. Shine appeared, Tyler had been retracting his arm from beneath the windbreak. Had he shot an electrical current through the fence? Scott straightened his glasses. He couldn't exactly stroll up to Tyler and ask. Ever since the incident on the courts, he'd been taking extra care to avoid those guys, his ears attuned to the faintest rumbling of the Chevelle.

Penny loafers slapping the sidewalk, Scott squinted ahead. He spied Margaret Graystone's Prelude parked among the many cars cramming one particular driveway, making his heart bump in anticipation.

Ooh boy.

He fanned his face with the invitation. All the curtains on the ground level of the castle-like home had been pushed open, and light shone out into the yard. Inside, young men and women in formal attire sipped drinks and palmed cocktail napkins, some of them tipping their heads back in laughter.

You're out of your class.

Scott slowed at the foot of the walkway. It was the voice again, the one that had been haunting him since the first Gamma meeting. But he'd done fine so far, he reminded himself. The lunches, where he was beginning to feel comfortable with the other pledges, truly comfortable; the two Saturday morning service projects he had attended; even the push-ups and sprints the older members sprung on him from time to time—he'd done fine with all of them.

But the pledge period isn't even half over, Scott. There's still plenty of time for them to see you don't belong.

Scott shouldered the doubting voice aside and continued up the walkway. A couple was stepping outside when he reached the front porch, and he used the opportunity to slip through the front door. He found himself on a Persian carpet, marble columns standing like sentries beside two doorways. Conversation and music poured in from his left, Chaka Khan, from what little he knew of music.

He ran his hands down the lapels of his Miami-blue blazer, adjusted his pink knit tie, muttered a prayer, and stepped around the corner. The Alpha and Gamma members were spread over the living room. Several clustered around a sleek black piano, singing a rousing song Scott didn't recognize. Something about a piano man. Cologne and perfume commingled in an intoxicating bouquet. Scott's gaze flitted around for the other pledges, his damp hands alternately clasping in front of him and hiding in his pockets. He recognized several of the older brothers and raised his chin when they looked his way, but their eyes showed only the dimmest recognition.

That's what you get for hiding in the back all the time.

It was true. For the last month, Scott had been trying to have it both ways: participating without being seen—or at least without drawing attention to himself. And that's where he was still conceding to the doubting voice, to his beleaguered past. To be seen was to risk being singled out.

Yeah, but not to be seen is to miss out altogether.

At last he spotted the back of an Ovaltine-colored bowl cut across the room. Scott smiled in relief and made his way over. Sweet Pea was standing in front of a glass-topped table arrayed with drinks and platters of hors d'oeuvres. He glanced up. In his bowtie and too-small blue suit, he looked like Spanky from *The Little Rascals*.

"Whaddya say there, Stretch?"

"Hey, not much."

Sweet Pea was fixing a plate of food, though *loading* it was more like it.

Scott stepped up beside him and poured himself a Pepsi. "Been here long?"

"Long enough to pick out the four chicks I'm taking home."

Scott's laughter came out louder than it felt. When Sweet Pea turned, his plate was heaped so high with shrimp and cocktail sauce, he might as well have just taken the whole platter.

"Gawd!" Sweet Pea exclaimed around his first wet mouthful, wide eyes sweeping the room. "There's nothing but nines and tens in here. All right, maybe a couple of eights." He elbowed Scott in the side and lowered his voice. "What do you figure her for? Size D?"

Scott followed Sweet Pea's gaze, not knowing what he was talking about. They were apparently looking at a young woman whose breasts jogged inside her dress every time she laughed.

"Yeah, D sounds about right." Scott brought his cup to his lips.

"Well, she's not in training anymore, that's for sure." That got another elbow into Scott's side, and Sweet Pea snorted on cue. He suckled his fingers, then wiped them against his round thigh. He popped two more shrimp into his mouth. "Got your eye on anyone, Stretch?"

Scott's ears prickled. "Hmm?" He took a sip of Pepsi.

"You know—chicks, babes, broads, honeys—whatever you like to call them. Anyone in particular getting you hard?" He lowered his voice. "Better yet, any of them getting you off?"

The way Sweet Pea leered up at him, gobs of cocktail sauce ringing his lips, made Scott want to pack up his feelings for Janis and carry them someplace safe and distant.

"I guess I'm still looking," he said quietly.

"Playing the field, huh? I like that." Another shot to the ribs. He brought his hand to his mouth like a megaphone. "DID YOU HEAR THAT, LADIES? MY FRIEND HERE IS A FREE AGENT—

AND LOOKING! AND THEY DON'T CALL HIM STRETCH FOR NOTHING!"

Scott's face exploded with heat. He spun toward the table, head down, and pretended to fix himself a plate. "What did you do that for?" he hissed from the side of his mouth.

"Hey, I was doing you a favor. I thought there might be some takers."

Scott started to shake his head, but from his new vantage he could see into what looked like a den, where several other Gamma pledges mingled. And then his heart changed in tenor from the hard, humiliated thuds of only seconds ago to a fresh, fast thumping.

Janis was down there.

He pushed up his glasses and zeroed in. Yes, she was sitting on the couch, talking with another Alpha pledge. He watched the small movements of her head, her close-lipped smile, the way she palmed her drink in the lap of her black dress. Scott wasn't sure how he had missed her at first. Her red hair illuminated the room. To her left sat an empty couch seat.

There it is, Scott, your opening. Your opportunity.

"Hey, uh ... wait here," he told Sweet Pea. "I'll be right back."

"Don't you worry," Sweet Pea answered, fixating on a trio of young women chatting in front of him. "This puppy's not going anywhere."

Good.

He needed to concentrate, needed to focus. What he didn't need was Sweet Pea making his entrance behind him and trumpeting that same horrifying declaration to all of the pledges. Scott edged his way along the refreshment table. At the bottom of three white-carpeted steps he drained the last of his Pepsi and crushed the ice between his teeth.

This was the whole reason he'd pledged Gamma.

This was His Moment.

The couch sat on the far side of the room, beside a mirrored fireplace. And for a second, it seemed an impossible distance to Scott, as impossible as the distance separating their houses. He dropped his empty cup in a planter and began fording the room. Pledges in formal wear eddied around him. Scott never shifted his gaze. His focus, his everything, remained on Janis, on her smooth cascade of hair, on the perfect lines of her shoulders, on the unclaimed seat beside her. And the nearer Scott drew to that seat, the more certain he became that someone was going to appear from nowhere and plop blithely down. He tried to swim his limbs faster.

A Gamma pledge passed in front of the couch and paused. Sharp-dressing, smooth-talking Jeffrey Bateman. Disappointment guttered in Scott's stomach like cold fire. Jeffrey pulled up the knees of his slacks and began to squat, but then raised his hand to someone and strode from the couch.

And then Scott was beside her.

He sat. Air hissed from the leather couch cushion, and he felt himself sinking. Soon, his eyes were level with his knees.

It just can't be easy, can it?

He peeked over at Janis, who still faced the pledge to her right. For a moment, he was struck by the closeness of her hair, its smooth, almost glossy, sheen. Scott managed to scoot himself out of the hole and to the couch's edge. He perched forward, an elbow propped on his knee, and angled himself so as to appear interested in whatever they were discussing.

"...so we're going up there over winter break to tour the campuses," the girl with the frizzy hair was saying to Janis. "My dad was a Blue Devil, so that's his first choice for me, you know? But I sorta like Wake Forest."

Janis *hmm*ed.

Scott *hmm*ed behind her, but it was too soft, a low note buried in the chatter around them. The girl's rapidly blinking eyes never left Janis's.

"They're totally hard to get into, though. Dad says I should have some backups. You know, for just in case." She went on to list the lesser schools she was considering, none of them familiar to Scott.

He *hmm*ed anyway.

That got no reaction either. And he was sliding backward, sinking into the cushion again. Scott leaned against the back of the couch to slide himself out. And his seat flipped open. The couch featured a recliner on the end, but Scott didn't realize that, not at first. He believed he was overturning the whole thing. Someone screamed. He flailed an arm over to catch Janis, but his wrist jammed against the adjoining section of couch, which hadn't moved. When he rattled to a rest, he was nearly flat, the tops of his penny loafers staring back at him.

Laughter rose around him. Scott pressed his calves against the leg rest with such force that he was bolted upright and nearly launched from the seat. For a moment, the room jittered in his vision. This second maneuver earned him more laughter, and Scott could feel the old shame exploding over his face like a devilish case of acne.

"All ri-i-ight!" Sweet Pea cried from the top of the steps. "Now *that's* what I call a ten!"

The room cheered, and Scott realized then that the laughter hadn't been cruel or demeaning, just fraternal. His throat convulsed around a chuckle. Sweet Pea gave him a thumbs-up. And just like that, the room fell into jumbled voices again, the baking spotlight turned off.

Then Scott remembered the scream. He spun to find Janis's friend standing with one arm held out in front of her, looking from her black and white polka-dot dress to the cup, where whatever had sloshed out was still dripping from her fingers onto the glass coffee table.

"Oh, my god," Scott stammered. "I-I'm so sorry."

The girl glared at Scott, set the cup down, and stomped off in search of a bathroom.

Scott turned to Janis. "I really didn't mean to. Should I...?" He gestured to where the pledge had disappeared, not knowing how to complete the thought. He was waiting for Janis to curl her lip at him and go storming after her friend.

"Oh, she'll get over it." Janis waved her hand. "It's just water."

He exhaled. "Thank goodness."

Janis smiled and laughed, which made Scott laugh, too. He stooped to straighten his pant legs and, when he sat up, found her head tilted toward his. He breathed the clean scent of her hair.

"Actually, I should be the one thanking you," she whispered. "Debbie's been obsessing about colleges for the last month, but tonight it was reaching a whole new level. I didn't think she was ever going to shut up."

"Always happy to be of service." Scott winced at what he was about to say but said it anyway. "Need a conversation crashed? Call Scott Spruel. Should be getting those business cards printed up any day now."

Janis giggled and leaned against him. It lasted only a moment, but for that whole moment, Scott's senses swam.

She leaned away and looked at him thoughtfully. "You know, I was just thinking about you the other day."

"Really?" He tried to appear calm even as his mind blew apart.

"Do you remember how we used to play in the woods? When we were kids?"

"Yeah, of course."

You were the superior shark's tooth hunter, I'll admit, but I built the better forts. He was pretty sure that would have gotten another laugh, maybe even another lean, but he didn't say it. He didn't want to sidetrack her from whatever she was about to reveal to him.

"That's what I was thinking about," she finished.

"Um ... oh."

"Do you ever go in there anymore?" she asked.

Only the time I went to spy on you while you were practicing against your garage door.

He shook his head. "Not lately."

"No, me neither."

She was looking off to his right, and Scott wondered if the house and the party had become as distant for her as it had for him. He watched her eyes, green eyes, he remembered now. You couldn't see the green from a distance because it melded so cleanly with the chestnut spires of her irises. You could only see the green up close, face to face.

"It was our world in there, wasn't it?" she asked, squinting slightly. "Back then?"

He nodded, not quite sure what she meant.

She asked, "Do you remember how, when you went in far enough, especially in the summer, you couldn't even see the houses anymore? It was just the trees and creek and us, I guess. Whatever we were doing. Whatever we were imagining. The only time our parents ever came in after us was to call us home."

"I remember."

And Scott remembered because he was seeing it, experiencing it—an episode, anyway. He and Janis were walking along a towering oak that had recently fallen, giving them access to a part of the woods that sank into a low bog. They had always avoided the bog in the past. It smelled like toilet water, for one, and was next to impassable, for another. Plus, they imagined all kinds of creatures and dangers lurking inside, quicksand not the least of them.

How old were they? Eight? Scott wasn't sure. It was mid summer and they were pretending to be explorers—that much he did remember. As Janis stepped over a limb, she reached back for his hand to balance herself. She was maybe an inch taller than he, her cheeks splashed with bright freckles. And even though he was still aware of himself on the couch, he could hear the whine of mosquitoes and smell the stinging repellant his mother would spray over him in coats. And not only could he see Janis, the girl, he could *feel* her small hand around his own.

"Whatever you do, don't fall in." She stopped on the other side of the limb to help him over, then pointed with a stick she was holding. "That's where the water moccasins live."

Scott squinted into the reedy water but couldn't see anything.

"C'mon," she said.

He followed her down the trunk and along a treacherous path of limbs and bifurcations. Squinting, they pushed through showers of branches whose narrow leaves were already browning and flittering into the water. She clambered ahead while he took more care, kneeling down whenever he began to totter. The tree seemed enormous, as if they could keep walking along it forever. He really did feel like an explorer, and the water world they traversed, though only a few hundred yards from their street, looked foreign to him and strange.

Soon, the limbs narrowed and shifted under their feet. Janis took him down a limb that dipped into the bog before emerging again. They got on both sides of the dip and squatted. The tips of Janis's battered green Keds touched the brown water, but she didn't seem to notice.

They were peering into an alien world, where little black beetles sped on the water's surface in circles, like mercury squeezed out in drops. Long-legged insects skated past. And then they did see a snake, maybe even a water moccasin. It lay in a black coil at the bottom of the bog. Janis prodded it with her stick, and they watched it wriggle from sight, mud kicking up around it.

An alien world, yes. But best of all, it was *their* world, his and Janis's. She had been right about that, and he felt himself nodding even as he remained immersed in the memory.

Janis swatted a mosquito on her arm, then stood up and looked around. Scott straightened his plastic glasses and followed her example. From their vantage, they could see the cement wall of the levee through the trees. It ran from Sixteenth Avenue around the Meadows on the far side of the creek. Janis had told him her father said it was for when the creek flooded, which happened most summers. It wasn't to protect their neighborhood but the lower-lying ones around it.

"Hey, look," Janis said. "If we jump down there, we'll be past the swamp. We can follow the creek to the end of the Meadows."

That seemed like a grand idea to Scott. The Meadows consisted of a single street with three shorter streets coming off of it, Janis's street being the first one. The end of the Meadows, though modest in street distance, seemed really far away in woods distance. And they had never been that far in the woods before.

"All right," he said.

They made their way toward the end of the oak tree's branch and scampered down. The ground squished under the soles of their sneakers but soon became solid as they cleared the tall grass bordering the bog. They now looked out into more familiar woods of scrub oak and pine. The creek chuckled off to their left. Janis marched ahead, whacking saw palmettos with her stick as they passed. Scott did the same, imagining the palmettos were brigands come to steal their rations. Both of them had scratches on their legs, the ones suffered in earlier excursions already scabbed over. That always surprised Scott—they could bleed and heal without realizing their skin had been torn in the first place. It was part of the magic of the woods.

"Hey, is that Mrs. Thornton's house?" Scott whispered.

He aimed his stick off to the right where color showed through the trees. The Thorntons lived four houses from the end of the Meadows. Mrs. Thornton had one of those old-fashioned bikes with a metal basket in front, and she rode it through the neighborhood like the mean Miss Gulch from the *Wizard of Oz*. Her eyes stayed hidden behind brown sunglasses, lips pulled in as though she had just tasted something sour. She yelled at Scott once for "loitering" in front of her house on his clamp-on skates (he had fallen). Scott and Janis were sufficiently afraid of her that they skipped the end of the Meadows on Halloween, which was saying something.

"Yeah," Janis whispered. "We better stay back until we're past it."

They watched the house through the trees as they crept along, following the bank of the creek. The houses always looked different to Scott from behind than from the street—sinister, almost—as though maybe that was the side you weren't supposed to see. And Scott had never seen *these* houses from behind before. They made it past the Thorntons' and then the one beyond that. Through the slats of a fence, Scott could make out the aqua tiling of a swimming pool. Though they hadn't meant to, they were drawing nearer to the backyards, where tangled growth met fencing and barbered lawns. The course of the creek seemed to be pushing them there.

The next house stood large and dark, and Scott couldn't even remember it now from the street.

"Maybe we should go back," he whispered.

"Just one more, and we'll be at the end of the Meadows." Hoarse excitement scored Janis's voice. She was always the more adventurous. "We don't even have to go all the way, just to the edge of the last property line. But we'll still be able to say we went to the end."

He wanted to ask her about Samson. One of the houses down there was supposed to have an attack dog, though Scott wasn't sure which house. His mother was always telling him never to play at the end of the street, in case Samson got out. *Samson.* The name held a grave fascination for him, as if it belonged to a mythical beast. But standing there, Scott felt the fascination turning to dread, like a belt cinching his aorta. He was certain that the tall house with the iron fence was the one—Samson's house. He looked back the way they had come and then into Janis's determined eyes.

"Please," she whispered, squeezing his hand.

He agreed even as his fear centers begged him not to. The thing was, he liked Janis, liked her a lot. And being the only girl he liked— the only girl he really *knew*—Scott just assumed they'd be married someday. Janis smiled and led him forward again. The woods fell under a shadow as palmettos gave way to woody vines and a dim carpet of poison ivy. Janis seemed to know where to step to avoid the ivy without even looking down. Scott followed her until she pulled up.

"Did you hear that?" Her ponytail swished like a flame as she peered from side to side.

Scott listened. "You're just trying to scare—"

"Shh!"

And then Scott heard it too: a low growl that ended in what sounded like a dry cough. Gooseflesh broke over him until it felt as if someone was trying to lift him by his hairs. Scott saw him before Janis did. And what terrified him the most was not his nearness, but that he had waited until that moment to announce himself. How long had he been watching them?

"Get behind me," Scott whispered.

"What? What do you see?"

"We need to back away. Slowly."

He crouched and held his stick out in front of them. Thin and not very long, the stick looked like a wand with which he was trying to cast a warding spell. And in his mind, that's exactly what he was doing: muttering incantations, hoping beyond hope that Samson could hear him somehow and would heed him.

Stay right there ... We're leaving ... Please ... Please don't come any closer.

He placed one foot behind himself and then, very gently, his other. Janis clung to his shoulders. He could tell by the movement of her breath, first over his left ear then his right, that she still hadn't spotted him.

"Where?" she whispered.

He didn't answer. He couldn't afford to become distracted. He would learn later that you were never supposed to lock eyes with an aggressive dog, that the primitive part of its brain would interpret the signal as a challenge. But Scott was certain that the moment he dropped his gaze, Samson would charge. He could see the intent in the dog's obsidian eyes.

Scott took another step back. The Rottweiler sprinted from the shadows, barking savagely. In the time it took for Janis to scream, the beast halved the distance and pulled up, his scarred muzzle wrinkling from a pair of dagger-like canines. The muscles beneath his chest vibrated, as though the least stimulus would set them off. Pound for pound, he was bigger than either of them.

"Shhh," Scott whispered, not to Janis, but toward the dog. Fear had numbed his body into an insensate shell, like the papier-mâché globes they had made at school the year before with strips of newspaper and flour-based paste. And it felt to Scott as if he was peering out from the inside of his own globe, from that cool hollow where he had popped the balloon and pulled out its flaccid skin.

Strangely, his fear was the only thing keeping him calm. He hoped to project that calm onto Samson somehow.

"Shhh," Scott whispered again, the stick still held up in front of them. With his other hand, he felt behind for Janis.

Samson growled from the pit of his stomach.

Can I have your attention, please?

Scott started and found himself on a couch, Janis beside him. But she was a more mature version of the Janis he had just been with in the woods, a stunning version.

And then, with the same rapidity with which the party sounds and a Madonna song climbed around them, Scott remembered where he was, *who* he was. He straightened himself. Janis was looking down between them, and when Scott followed her gaze, he found his hand holding hers.

"Oh!" He fumbled to release her. "I'm so sorry—I didn't—"

Someone whistled sharply. "Hey! Can I have your attention?"

They looked up to where Britt, Gamma's sergeant at arms, stood. He was also Scott's older Gamma brother, who, as older brothers went, had turned out to be indifferent more than anything.

Behind Britt, someone turned down the music. Voices fell.

Britt smiled. "That's more like it." He waved the pledges toward the dining room. "The presidents of Alpha and Gamma would like to make a toast."

"I'm all right," Janis whispered to Scott, holding her own hand now.

When their eyes met, perplexity wrinkled the space between her brows. She stood and, with a backward glance, joined the other pledges filing up the three steps. Beyond their heads, Scott could see slices of Grant Sidwell and Margaret Graystone standing in the center of the dining room, drinks in hand. Scott followed the pledges but at the last moment veered down the hallway.

Squinting against the bright lights of the bathroom, Scott locked the door and leaned his arms against the marble countertop.

What in the world just happened?

That day in the woods—he hadn't been just remembering the experience, he had been *inside* of it, reliving it. Had he completely zoned out? Had he slumped there like a zombie while Janis sat watching him? He must have. And why was his hand holding hers? How had *that* happened?

He filled the sink with cold water and scooped it against his face, trying to drown the memory of that final bewildered look Janis had given him. *Way to go, Sport. Way to freak her out.*

Through the door, he heard shouts of "Hear! Hear!"

"All right," he told himself as he toweled his face off. "This thing goes until eleven. There's still time. There's still time to fix this." He cleared his throat and spoke into the huge mirror. "Oh, hey, Janis.

Sorry about blanking out on you a minute ago. I've got this weird epilepsy thing I contracted while, um, watching an episode of *The Space Giants*. No, no, I'm fine. And don't worry, it's not contagious or anything." He forced a weak laugh.

When Scott emerged, he found Janis across the living room. For a second he thought she was raising her hand toward him, but she was only pushing a strand of hair behind her ear, her gaze fixed on whomever she was talking to. It was not until he skirted a group in the center of the room that he saw the person in Janis's company: Blake Farrier. It was a bye week, Scott remembered—no football game.

Scott took another step nearer, but something about their closeness told Scott their conversation would not be welcoming of a third party. He'd get no points for barging in and spilling a drink this time. And Blake looked so solid standing there, so self-possessed. When Janis's lips turned up at something he said, Scott's heart crumpled into a wad.

He retreated to the refreshment table, where Sweet Pea was encamped again, a plate piled high to either side. Sweet Pea spoke through a mouthful of jalapeno poppers. "Still stag?"

Scott watched Blake's and Janis's faces from across the room. "Yeah," he mumbled.

The two were still talking when, an hour later, Scott went to the kitchen to call his father. As he returned through the pillars of the front hallway, he raised his hand to the living room, to no one, then went slouching out into the night, toward the house where his father had dropped him off.

20

"**B**lake asked me out," Janis said.

Margaret turned toward her. "*Out* out? Like on a date?" She smirked and returned her gaze to the road. "I was wondering why you were being so quiet." The Prelude's headlights swept an arc past the Oakwood sign at the entrance of their neighborhood. "How did he ask you."

"He said he was getting his driver's license this week and invited me to a movie next Saturday."

"And you said...?" Margaret was watching her from the edge of her vision, ready to critique any missteps in her answer.

"I said that it sounded nice but that, *yes*, I would have to check with Dad."

Margaret nodded her approval. "You always want them to know you have a father looking out for you. It separates the ones who are serious about you from the sleazeballs." She patted Janis's knee. "But I happen to know that Blake is one of the good ones. I'll be happy to put in a word to Dad for you."

"Thanks."

"He'll still want to meet him, of course."

"Yeah, I know."

"Well, how does it feel," Margaret asked, steering them into the Meadows, "your first time being asked out in high school? You seem sort of, I don't know, blasé about the whole thing."

Janis watched the road. How *did* she feel? In the moment it happened, it had seemed surreal. Blake had found her after the toast and congratulated her for making the varsity team that day. (She was the first freshman in eight years to be selected—and he knew that as well, somehow). From there, they had fallen into the kind of conversation typical of two people beginning to hope their interest in the other coincided: conversation that's intimate and excited but a little guarded at the same time, a little frightened. Then Blake was telling her about his driver's license. He was asking her about a movie together. And as Janis wrote down her number on his invitation, she realized that if they had still been in middle school, if it had been only a year or two earlier, she would have written it down on the palm of his hand.

Yes, *surreal* was definitely the word for it.

But with a little distance, Janis wondered whether the sphere of their conversation, his asking her out, had felt that way for the very reason that it was so far removed from the fear and strangeness that was becoming her life, her *reality*.

That week, Janis had become more attuned to the news during dinnertime, the international coverage seeming to conform to what her father had told her the week before. U.S.-Soviet relations were as tense as they'd been since the Cuban Missile Crisis. Reagan was talking about building a missile defense system in space—"Star Wars," he was dubbing it. Even Reagan's call for an arms reduction treaty seemed to fit. After all, why try to change the rules of the game unless the other team was winning under the old rules?

And during P.E. that Monday, Janis had overheard a fellow student—a nerd, she supposed—telling another student that "the Doomsday Clock" had been moved to three minutes until midnight that year.

"What does that mean?" she'd asked, her shoe propped on the gym bleachers where she'd gone to tie it.

At first the student had only responded by stroking his frayed mustache, grinning up in a way that made his smallish eyes press together. When he spoke, his voice was thin and arrogant. "Well, well, a neophyte doth seeketh a sip from the fountain of knowledge." He turned to an Asian student beside him. "What say you, Chun? Is this one worthy?"

"Oh, forget it," Janis muttered.

He spoke rapidly to her back. "The Doomsday Clock is a feature of the *Bulletin of the Atomic Scientists* put out by the University of Chicago. The minute hand represents the statistical probability of global nuclear war." He gasped for breath. "The scientists adjust it depending on how far or close we are. I was just telling Chun that they adjusted it up another minute this year."

"Is three until midnight really close?" she asked. "Is it bad?"

"Put it this way." Now that he had her attention again, arrogance crept back into his reedy voice. "It's the closest we've been since 1962, when things were really looking hairy. Two till midnight means we've probably crossed the point of no return. One till midnight, and we've actually punched the launch codes and are on alert for the final executive order before..." He traced out a trajectory with his finger while he whistled, then he threw his hand open. "Good night, sweet princess."

Beside him, Chun had nodded. "Affirmative, it's bad."

So maybe that's what it was, Janis thought, sitting beside Margaret. At the beginning of the school year, she had tried to leave her nighttime experiences for the normal, the everyday, only to learn in the last week that "the everyday" was three minutes from being blown to shit. But with Blake, she had a place she could feel normal and safe again, even if she knew it was illusory.

"I'm not sure how I feel." She turned to Margaret. "I probably just need more time."

"Well, there's no hurry. No need to rush anything." Margaret snapped off the headlights and killed the engine. "Just look at me and Kevin. We started dating as freshmen, too."

In the darkness, Janis rolled her eyes.

"If you ever have any questions, you can talk to one or both of us." Margaret unbuckled her seat belt and looked at Janis with a maternal tuck of her chin. "I mean it."

Janis thanked her dryly as she got out of the car. At the top of the hill and across the street sat the Spruels' house, a single-story white brick home like theirs, but with navy-blue instead of coffee-brown trim. The light was on in Scott's bedroom, Janis noticed. She caught her gaze lingering on the solitary glow as she followed Margaret up to the front porch.

While Margaret dug inside her purse for her keys, Tiger trotted up and began sideswiping Janis's legs with her body. The cat looked at her with dilated pupils, her meow ending in a question mark.

Janis stooped to scratch her behind the ears. "I'm going to stay out and pet Tiger a few minutes."

Margaret found the key. "Just remember to lock the door when you come in."

Janis waited for the front door to click closed before making her way back down the semi-circular driveway, Tiger padding behind her. When Janis reached the street, she looked toward Scott's house again. Tiger mewled and pushed her head against Janis's calf, no doubt wondering where her ear-scratcher had gone. Janis sat on the curb and let Tiger hop onto her lap.

Her and Scott's conversation at the party had begun normally enough. But when she looked at his face, she remembered her childhood in the woods. Or more precisely, she remembered she'd been thinking about it that week—a lot. The woods had been her refuge from the adult world. There was no one there to scold or shame her, telling her it's "this not that" or "that not this." No hydrogen bombs, no arms race, no Mutually Assured Destruction. No one hinting about her responsibilities in a future whose very existence looked doubtful to begin with.

The world beyond the cul-de-sac had belonged to them, and they to that world. It seemed funny to her that she'd tried to explain those feelings to Scott, that she'd opened up to him—and funnier still that he'd seemed to understand.

Janis looked down at Tiger, who was gouging her knees contentedly. Janis stroked her purring body and shifted her attention back to Scott's house. All year, she had barely recognized him as the same person. He was taller, neater, more appearance conscious, it seemed. Yet his eyes hadn't changed. She had realized that only tonight, seeing him up close. Yes, beyond the lenses were the same questioning eyes she remembered from when they used to play in the woods together.

And that's where things had really gone cuckoo for Cocoa Puffs. Without warning, she'd been in the woods again. Not just remembering being there, but *actually* there. She was a kid—eight, probably—on the summer day she and Scott had crossed the big tree and tried to venture to the end of the Meadows.

She had screamed when the dog came out of nowhere and charged them. She never used to scream—thought it was for a sissier class of girl—but the sudden appearance of the Rottweiler, huge and ferocious, had wrenched the piercing cry from her chest. Janis remembered looking at the twin rust-colored spots at its clenched brow because to look into its eyes or its mouth of bared teeth was too much. She would have screamed again. She squeezed Scott's shoulders, who eased them back, eased them away, his stick held out in front of them.

And then Britt whistled from the steps, and the woods and the dog vanished, the room oscillating back into being. She found herself on the couch, Scott beside her, holding her hand. Had she passed out? Had he been trying to revive her? But as her head cleared, as the room stilled and sharpened around her, he seemed as startled as she was.

Gazing on his window now, she wondered if something similar had happened to him.

A god of doorways, Mrs. Fern had said. *One face looking to the past. The other peering ahead, to the future.*

Janis thought about that. All week at tryouts, she had been seeing ghostlike images of soccer balls in motion. They were faint and fleeting, but they gave her just enough time to react, to position herself. Wasn't that peering into the future? She hadn't thought about it in that way, but wasn't it? And then this experience of the past—not just peering there but going there, *being* there.

And had she taken Scott with her, somehow?

Tiger protested when Janis went to set her aside, clinging gamely to her pantyhose. Janis stood, brushed the lap of her dress, and began walking up the street. Her flats beat a quick rhythm against the asphalt. She glanced back toward her front door. She had five minutes, maybe, but she needed to talk to Scott, needed to ask him. As crazy as it would sound, she had to know if he'd gone back to the summer of 1978, too—back to the woods of their childhood.

She was nearly to the top of her hill when Scott's window went dark. For a moment, Janis stared at the reflection of the street light against the glass, surprised at the weight of her disappointment.

You can always ask him on Monday.

But would she?

She turned to walk home. The shadow of the Leonards' second story rose through the trees in her leftward periphery. She sped her clacking pace as a breeze rustled the leaves. Janis rubbed her bare arms, feeling the cool of the fall night for the first time. A deeper chill brushed her spine as she caught a whiff of something faint but unmistakable.

Cigarette smoke.

Could be anyone's, she told herself, but without conviction. She fixed her gaze on the yellow light of her front porch. Tiger met her at the driveway and accompanied her the rest of the way.

Janis reached the front door a little out of breath, shaking her head at her own paranoia. She opened the door a crack and automatically positioned her legs to block Tiger from trying to squeeze past, but the cat wasn't beside her. Janis turned to find her at the foot of the steps, a low groan caught in her throat. She was peering toward the side yard, ears flattened.

Probably hears another cat—

The smell of cigarette smoke breezed past again, much stronger this time.

Janis patted her thigh for Tiger, let her inside the house, and then hurried to lock the door behind them. Leaning against the jamb, Janis began to shiver. She didn't need any special abilities to know that for the duration she'd been outside, Mr. Leonard had been watching her.

21

Scott stood in his bedroom, his rumpled shirt untucked, one finger hooked over the knot of his tie, staring at artifacts of an earlier hope. The rag and polish he had used to burnish his loafers lay beside his bed; the ironing board where he had pressed his shirt, its legs now folded in, leaned against his closet door; the dark-green bottle of cologne sat on his dresser, its cap still off. Only a few hours old, the ambitions they represented already felt forever out of his reach.

He yanked the pink knit tie from his neck and cast it away.

I told you. The voice again.

"Shut it."

It's not your place, Scott-o. Not your people. What did you expect? Your place isn't with them. It's above them. You know that. You know the powers you possess.

Scott didn't fight the voice this time. Instead, he found himself considering his computer desk. He had dusted and wiped it down with Pledge during the Big Clean, as he thought of it. Now it held his school books and some folders. But looking at it, he could think only of what it no longer held, what was missing.

He flicked off the light switch, and the room fell dark. The street light shone against his blinds. Margaret's car had turned down the street ten minutes before. He'd heard its signature from the family room, where his father had wanted him to watch the end of *Sudden Impact* (and Scott, feeling too miserable and defeated to say no, had sagged onto the couch). But now, like a desperate flicker, he felt his old hope pleading for a peek outside.

Just a single peek to see if maybe she—

Forget it, Romeo.

He left his room and walked down the hallway, through the blue glow of a television now silent, and past the bass snores of his father. He stopped in the kitchen for the cordless phone, slipping it into his back pocket.

In the garage, he moved the folding card table and the stack of empty boxes hiding his tunnel entrance. He ducked and edged his way through his father's hoard to the storage room, the crowded space smelling of sawdust. An aluminum-tipped string dangled from a single bulb. Scott jerked it. A long workbench blinked into view beneath a line of power outlets and a crumbling pegboard that had once held tools. Scott squatted in front of the cabinets. He pulled away concealing boxes and crumpled balls of newspaper and, one by one, stood with his pieces of equipment, setting them across the workbench: TRS-80, DC1 modem, printer, a box of floppies. He emerged with his cables and power strip last.

The next minute was like a familiar dance, something Scott would never blunder, never screw up. He inserted this cord here, that cord there, linking, making connections, enabling communication. With his small network complete, Scott plugged in the power strip and snapped its red switch. He waited a moment, then turned on each device in the proper sequence, finishing with the monitor.

```
TRS-80 Model III Disk BASIC
© 1980 by Tandy Corp. All Rights Reserved
READY
>
```

The sight of the flashing cursor sent a small detonation of excitement through him. *This is where you belong, buddy,* the voice whispered, *in here so you can navigate the greater networks.*

Scott reached behind the DC1 modem and drew up the one cable that remained inert. It was the telephone cord, but it hadn't a receptacle for its plastic head. *Which means you don't have jack, Jack.* Scott's face stung at his own joke. Without a phone jack, there was no way to plug in, no means by which to access the globe-spanning networks, to exercise his power. Scott sighed as he looked around the closet-sized workshop. Without a jack, his world was reduced to—

And that's when he spotted it. Down beside the bench, just above the short length of wood trim that ran along the floor: a basic wall jack. Over the receptacle sat a glob of dried paint that he had to pick away, but when he pressed in the modular connector, it clicked sweetly home.

Seconds later, the modem blinked to indicate a connection.

"Yes!" he hissed.

But was it a *clean* connection? Stooping over the computer, Scott loaded his COMM floppy and typed out a command to display the number he was dialing from. Within seconds, he had his answer: same exchange as their home phone, but a different line. Scott's fingers raced over the keys, commanding the modem to dial the number for automated time and weather.

> ATDP3721411
Dialing 3721411

Rapid pulses followed, and in each one, Scott could hear the number: ...(3) ....(7) ..(2) .(1) ....(4) .(1) .(1). He held his breath and waited. Then came the ring. But before Mrs. Time could answer his call, Scott punched the three-key command to hang up the modem.

"Dammit!"

He turned and paced the small workshop. Another delay, which meant this line was tapped as well. Any hacking adventures he undertook, whether here or in his room, would be recorded, stored as evidence, and read off to a grand jury one day as part of his indictment proceedings.

The muscles between his shoulders tensed, and for a second he pictured himself shoving all his equipment from the workbench to the cement floor. But the anger wasn't his, not entirely. It came from the part of himself he'd felt at the library computer in September, when he'd gone to print off The Pact. The part of himself that hungered for access and power—that craved it.

And now it was being denied.

But by what? By whom?

Scott rubbed the back of his neck. He had never shared any of his hacking exploits on the message boards. He and Wayne had always been ultra careful in that department. And compared to the big names in the hacking-verse, their own exploits had seemed small town anyway. Until U.S. Army Information, of course, but that had been Scott's final hack, his last time on the network.

Scott became distracted. At the far wall, something appeared off. He dragged away obstructing boxes, bags of instant cement, and a stack of paint cans. He'd perceived correctly—the wall was a propped up piece of painted plywood. Tipping it out, he managed to maneuver it against the door. The workshop widened by another seven feet. He walked inside the new space and stood in the dim light.

There was a smell of soldered metal, and Scott saw why. The space had been a metal workshop. A welding bench stood at one end, crowded around with hammers, a mounted vice, a drill press, cluttered shelving ... and was that a lathe? Sheets of metal leaned against it. He supposed his father could have acquired the equipment on one of his discount shopping sprees, but Scott doubted it. The workshop, with its aluminum siding and singed cement floor, appeared to have been used. The prior owners had just never cleared it out for some reason.

Scott pulled open the drawers beneath the welding bench. In one sat an acetylene torch and a row of soldering irons. Another drawer revealed a folded apron, gloves, and a welder's mask. Scott donned them, the mask cold against his face, and lifted out the torch. It still worked. The flame whooshed to life and then hissed as Scott honed it to a point. His old passion for model building sang inside him. But this wasn't plastic and model glue. This was the real deal.

Scott put everything away and returned the piece of plywood to the columnar indentations that marked the two sides of the workshop as separate. He scooted the boxes, buckets, and cans of paint in front of the false wall and stood back. The computer, the metal shop—he could have his old life back here, and no one would ever know. Scott cracked his knuckles as he considered it. No, not his old life—better. It was the *evolution* of his old life.

But what about the tap? the voice reminded him.

Scott frowned and brought a knuckle to his lips. He needed an ally. He needed ... Wayne. But for the last month, Wayne had been abiding by Scott's decree to the letter: *We're through. I mean it.*

No surprise there.

But what continued to puzzle Scott was why Wayne had been so dismissive of his warning about the phone tap. It seemed the sort of thing Wayne would have jumped all over—getting to play Whiz Kid, using his technical skills to demystify the puzzle, solve the rid—

Scott froze where he stood.

Unless Wayne's the one who tipped off the feds.

He began to shake his head, then stopped. He *had* heard stories about hackers ratting out other hackers. They popped up on the message boards from time to time. Some of the hackers had gotten busted themselves and made deals with the feds, while others had ratted out of sheer competitiveness and spite.

Scott thought of the fights he and Wayne had gotten into throughout the past year, all of them fueled by ... competitiveness and spite.

He took the phone from his rear pocket and dialed Wayne. His heart pounded in his temples as he waited for the numbers to pulse out. But just before the first ring, he hung up.

Better to confront him in person.

Scott turned off his computer equipment and began disassembling cords and cables. He disconnected the modem from the wall jack last and stood a moment contemplating the cord's plastic head. All that separated this lowly space in the back of his parents' garage from the rest of the world was one cursed tap.

And if Wayne was behind it, so help him.

22

Graystone house
Wednesday, October 10
Dinnertime

Mr. Graystone slowly wiped his napkin against his mouth and returned his gaze to the muted television—another commercial for Viper Industries. He had said nothing for the last minute. He grew silent like this whenever he weighed a momentous decision. All Janis could do was watch.

"How well do you know this fellow?" he asked Janis at last.

"Pretty well."

He remained looking at her, his face bearing the solemnity she'd seen in the parking lot almost two weeks before. For a man who dealt in sound thinking, *pretty well* was not the best answer, Janis realized too late.

Margaret, who had been the one to announce her upcoming date with Blake, spoke up again.

"Well, how well do you know anyone before a first date?" she asked. "That's what first dates are for. But what we both know of Blake"—she moved her eyes to Janis—"is that he's responsible, respectful, an A student. His father's a doctor and works in cancer research at the hospital."

"How long has he been driving?" their father asked.

"He got his license this week," Janis answered, again too honestly.

"*Which means* he's been driving with a temporary permit for the last year," Margaret finished, narrowing her eyes at Janis.

"Has he been driving at night?"

Margaret sighed. "What difference does it make?"

"It makes a considerable difference," her father answered. "Things are harder to see at night—lane markers, signage—especially if you don't have experience driving in the dark."

"Well, I'm sure he does," Margaret said.

Janis had been watching her sister's eyes, and now their color began to shift with the tone of her voice. *She's doing it again, eroding his convictions until her way seems the only, or at least the easiest, way.* The grooves of concern across her father's brow pouched and sagged like a sand sculpture facing a shallow but relentless tide. It was hard for Janis to watch. Even though Margaret was intervening on her behalf, this didn't seem right, as if she were upsetting some hallowed order. And it made their father look old and confused.

"I'd like to meet him," he said, looking back to Janis, blinking. "Have him come early to pick you up."

"Or how about inviting him for dinner?" her mother offered.

"That's a fantastic idea," Margaret said.

"Here?" Janis's ears prickled at the thought of Blake wedged between her parents and Margaret. "Nuh-uh. No way. Not on a first—"

Margaret's foot caught Janis in the shin. *Don't screw this up,* the kick said. *I just got a* major *concession from Dad for you.*

"All right, I'll *ask* if he can come."

And it was settled.

"And how about when that marshmallow guy came to life and started rampaging?" Blake asked, wiping a finger beneath his eyes. "Oh, man, I haven't laughed that hard in ages. I needed that."

"Yeah." Janis laughed at how hard Blake was still laughing. "Me too."

They were parked out in front of her house in Blake's Toyota MR2, a birthday gift from his dad. The car idled quietly, its interior dim except for the blue lights of the console. Just as Blake had promised Mr. Graystone at dinner—a dinner that, for all of Janis's worrying, had gone amazingly well—they had come straight home from the movie. Janis glanced at the clock display again, wondering how to stretch the next five minutes.

"And here I thought it was going to be a horror flick," Blake said.

Janis leaned away. "Starring Bill Murray and Dan Akroyd?"

The folds of Blake's purple letter jacket glinted softly as he laughed again. "I was going by the name. I thought, hey, it's Janis's pick. If *Ghostbusters* gives me nightmares, I'll have an excuse to call her in the morning."

You don't need an excuse.

But she didn't say it. All week, Margaret had counseled her about not being too forward, not showing too much interest too soon. "It's a mistake a lot of girls make," she said. "And it's a major turn off. Make *him* do the work." But Janis felt so comfortable in Blake's presence, so exclusive, that she wanted to shove off Margaret's advice for a change and say what she felt.

Instead, she gave his arm a playful punch. "If it gives you nightmares, blame the joke writers, not me."

"I'll do that." He turned toward her as his laughter wound down. "I had a great time."

Janis looked up at him. "So did I."

Is this where we're supposed to kiss? Her last time had been with Keith Rafferty, her last boyfriend. They had sneaked into his parents' basement during his birthday party and made out for a few minutes in the cool darkness. May, was it? Now Janis wondered whether five months was too long. Could she have gotten rusty in that time? Her stomach fluttered madly.

"Hey," he said, his eyes brightening with something remembered. "How did you know that old man was going to trip?"

Heat filled Janis's cheeks. "What do you mean?"

"Outside the theater. You lunged for him before he even started to fall."

"Oh, I..." She'd seen a ghost image. "I could just tell he wasn't paying attention to the curb."

"So on top of everything else, you're a superhero?" Blake smiled, then watched his hand jiggle the stick shift. "You know, when I saw the article about you in the paper this summer and read that you'd be attending Thirteenth Street High this year, I..." He gave an embarrassed laugh. "I was hoping that I'd have a chance to meet you. I remember thinking that. And now I'm really glad I did."

"Really?" Janis wrinkled her brow. "I mean, about the article."

It had never occurred to her that someone she'd never met—never even seen—could develop feelings for her from a couple of grainy pictures and a few columns of print.

"It's funny, I expected us to connect as athletes. I saw a lot of myself in that article. Your drive, your competitiveness. But now, having met you, talking to you, being out with you ... I don't know, it's like those pressures are a million miles away." The soft dimples returned, and he tipped his forehead toward her. "That's something I didn't expect."

"No, me neither," she whispered.

Whether she moved nearer to him or he nearer to her, she wasn't sure. But in the next moment, their lips were touching. His kiss felt strong and gentle. He brought his hand to her cheek and held it, her hair falling over his fingers. On the radio, Bryan Adams was singing "Straight from the Heart." How long they stayed like that, Janis couldn't say. She figured she must be doing something right because she felt warm and a little dizzy. She felt safe.

When they parted, Blake's blue eyes shone into hers.

"Well," he said, glancing at the time display, "I have exactly one minute before your father puts out an APB on a missing daughter."

They walked up the driveway in silence, Janis still feeling his close presence, his lips against hers. She wondered if he was thinking about the same thing. She hoped so. The sleeves of their jackets brushed as they walked. Even though Janis knew it was way too early, she caught herself wondering if this was something that might last through high school and into college.

On the front porch, Blake smiled and kissed her cheek. "In case your father's watching," he whispered, before standing back. "Call you tomorrow?"

She nodded and slipped her hands into the front pockets of her pinstripe jeans.

"All right. Thank your parents again for me."

"I will. Thanks for the movie."

"Sweet dreams."

His gaze lingered on hers as he wheeled to leave. And now Janis became aware of the darkness along the side of the house where Tiger had stopped to stare last week. She remembered the strong scent of cigarette smoke and the chilling sensation of being watched. She had spent the last week trying to explain the experience away, but as with everything else—the dreams, the soccer tryouts, the old man she'd saved from falling tonight—she was running low on rationalizations.

"Wait."

She hadn't said it loudly, and for a moment she hoped Blake hadn't heard. He turned toward her, eyebrows raised, then sauntered back and stood on the bottommost step to the porch.

"I was just wondering," she started. "That movie tonight. This is going to sound weird, but ... what do you think about ghosts and spirit worlds and all of that stuff? The supernatural, I guess you'd call it."

"So it *did* scare one of us." He laughed.

Janis smiled even though her heart was pounding madly. It suddenly felt important to her that she know. Was his mind open to such things, or was it as closed and resolute as Margaret's? Now, as he took another step higher, she didn't want him to answer. She didn't want to know. She looked around, wishing she had the power to take the question back.

He reached forward and rubbed her arms up and down. "Listen, they're great for movies, but that's all. They're not real." He kissed her forehead and lowered his face to hers. "Will that help you sleep?"

"Yeah. I think so."

They said goodnight again. Then Janis watched him climb into his car and drive away.

23

The next morning
Sunday, October 14
9:22 a.m.

Scott woke up early for a weekend morning—early for him, anyway—and, skipping breakfast, climbed onto his ten-speed Schwinn. He listened to the neighborhood as he pedaled out of the Meadows, relieved to hear only birds. As he gained speed. and wind began whipping his hair, his eyes flitted from house to house, marking places to hide should he hear the ominous belch of a certain Chevelle. It was more a precaution than anything. Jesse and company didn't strike Scott as early risers.

When he cleared the Oakwood sign, he turned left and began standing into his pedals to climb Sixteenth Avenue. He had planned to confront Wayne that week at school, but on Monday he realized that Wayne had Craig and Chun to hide behind, not to mention an entire student body. And Scott wanted Wayne to himself. He knew from sleepovers past that Wayne's parents were dutiful churchgoers themselves but allowed their son to sleep in. So not only would he catch Wayne alone, he would catch him by surprise, still groggy with sleep.

Wayne lived in a neighborhood not far from the high school. It was lower-middle class, Scott supposed: flat, one-story homes whose roofs were moss covered and most yards too sandy and limb littered to support grass, much less decent landscaping. Scott's bike rattled as he steered down its gravelly streets. Pebbles of asphalt, spun up by his tires, flicked into his hair and clinked off his glasses. *Maybe this is where some of Wayne's resentment comes from,* he thought, looking around at dumpy cars in plastic carports.

But ratting me out to the feds?

Scott cruised by Wayne's house once to make sure his father's burgundy Mitsubishi wasn't in the driveway. It wasn't. He circled back and pushed his bike inside a cluster of yellowing azalea bushes that stood in the no-man's land between Wayne's yard and the one next door.

At Wayne's door, Scott knocked with what he hoped sounded like authority, sharp and rapid. *Give him a scare.* When thirty seconds passed, he rapped again. He was about to try a third time when he heard tired shuffling in the hallway and, seconds later, the lock being worked from the inside. There was no window or peephole to peek out, which Scott considered another advantage. He fixed his face and stood tall, arms bowed out to the sides before deciding to fold them across his chest, his fists pushing out his narrow biceps.

When the door opened, a caramel-colored face appeared.

Scott sagged from his stance. "What the...? What are you doing here?"

Chun squinted in the morning light. And now Craig's face appeared beside him, flat and bleary, his T-shirt inside-out. Craig and Chun stood for several moments without saying anything. Finally, Chun spoke.

"We're under orders from Wayne not to talk to you."

"Is he here?"

"He's sleeping," Craig said.

"Well, he and I have something to discuss."

The two faces stared blankly from the half-opened door. Chun began to finger the mole above his nostril. It crossed Scott's mind to knock their heads together like a pair of coconuts. They had been *his* friends, not Wayne's. Hell, it was because of him that they even knew Wayne. And now they had Wayne, and Wayne had them, and Scott had ... no one. The memory of Blake's car idling in front of Janis's house last night only deepened that notion.

"All right," Scott said softly. "I see how it is. Just tell him that—"

He lunged at the doorway and was halfway inside before the other two knew what was happening. Chun recovered and tried to brace both arms against the door. Craig joined him, but the floor of the front hallway was covered in brown linoleum, and their tube-socked feet slipped and slid. Scott forced them back. A steady diet of D&D and video games had made dough of his friends' limbs while Scott's had toughened, thanks to the Bud Body program.

To want it is to become it, Bud said throughout his booklet. Repeating the mantra, Scott dug in with the toes of his Nikes.

With one final effort, Craig and Chun managed to slam the door shut, but Scott was already inside, marching toward Wayne's room. He was dimly aware of the familiar smells of his former friend's home as he waded deeper into its vapors: a mixture of cigarette smoke and stacks of secondhand science fiction books his father had amassed, their pages spotted with mold.

Scott wasn't sure if Craig or Chun grabbed his neck, but once there, the aggressor didn't seem to know what to do. When another hand fumbled for his shoulder, Scott slapped it away and spun.

"Look, you little minions," he panted. "This is between me and Wayne. I suggest you back the hell up."

Scott spoke more menacingly than he ever imagined himself capable—especially toward friends. He must have sounded convincing, because first Craig and then Chun backed away. When Scott turned and resumed his march down the hallway, the two followed passively.

Wayne's bedroom door was closed. A sign tacked on the outside read VULCANS AT WORK, with a curvaceous Saavik giving the Vulcan salute. The doorknob wouldn't turn. Scott raised his fist to pound, thought better of it, and reached into his back pocket. He had sworn off his alter ego Stiletto back in August, but he'd never removed the folding tension wrench and pick from the bottom of his wallet. A single hole pierced the center of the aluminum doorknob. The best tool for opening these, frankly, was a Q-tip with the cotton end cut off.

A metal pick worked too.

The lock clicked, and Scott threw the door open. He faced a cluttered room walled in mahogany-colored particleboard and smelling of Fritos. A thick blanket covered the window on the far wall. He flicked the light switch, but nothing happened. His gaze moved to the right side of the room. The outline of the bed came into focus, its sheets tangled, its mattress half stripped.

But no Wayne.

Scott stepped further into the room, venturing a glance toward the closet. He could feel Craig and Chun breathing behind him. He took another step. *Wayne must have heard me*, he thought, *must've hidden.* He craned his neck around the far side of the bed, then bowed to look under the computer desk. When he straightened, a point of metal met his low back.

"So you made it past my sentry, I see." Scott felt Wayne adjust his grip on his broadsword. "But you were foolish to underestimate my powers of perception. Now look at you! Fallen into my trap, like the stupid thief you are. Your disgrace and dishonor are complete."

"Ow!" Scott instinctively raised his arms out to the sides. "Be careful with that thing!"

"That's right," Wayne said. "Nice and easy."

Scott watched Craig's and Chun's shadows on the far wall. His own shadow blocked Wayne's, all except for the disheveled side of his head. Wayne had bought the used sword at a medieval fair the year before. Scott had been there; it was the real article. Wayne had even allowed him to handle it—not for long, but long enough that he could appreciate its keen edge. Even someone of Wayne's small stature could do damage with it. And if Wayne had stayed up D&D-ing the night before, as Scott suspected, lord only knew how much caffeine and raw adrenaline were swimming through his system.

"I just came to talk."

Wayne laughed, high and chopped. "Oh, is that what you call forcing your way in?" His shadow jerked its head.

Craig and Chun seized Scott by either arm, their morning breath slaying the air he inhaled. He probably could have shaken them off, but he let them wheel him around.

Wayne stood in front of the doorway, his back arched to counterbalance the cumbersome sword, his splayed toes grasping the shag carpet. A yellowing pair of Fruit of the Looms sagged from the brim of his pelvis. He tottered back against the closet and swung the sword toward the door.

"Deliver this louse from my sight," he ordered.

"C'mon," Craig whispered near Scott's ear. "I think he's serious."

Scott waited until they'd stepped into the hallway before calling over his shoulder. "I know about the tap, Wayne. I know you were the one who tipped off the feds. I know everything." He felt Craig's and Chun's grips falter. "So who's the louse now?"

"Halt!"

Craig and Chun released his arms, and Scott turned unimpeded. Wayne clasped the sword's pommel at his sunken navel and glared at him with his smudged-in eyes. Scott glared back.

"Say that again."

"Oh, choke on it," Scott said. "I know what you did."

Wayne's laugh was a single sharp note. "Oh, do you now?" He looked at Craig and Chun. "You remember the fabled tap, don't you, men? Scott's little ruse to worm his way back into our good company?"

"Sure," Scott said. "That's what you want them to believe." He turned from Wayne, who was struggling now to keep the heavy sword aloft, and faced the others. "Who's he going to rat out next, I wonder? Maybe you can make a little game out of it." He moved his finger between them. "Eenie, meenie, miney, mo."

Scott had pulled his bike halfway out of the azaleas when Wayne came after him. He'd stashed the broadsword and pulled on a pair of crumpled blue shorts with red and white racing stripes along the sides. He half ran, half pranced across the yard to avoid fallen limbs and bursts of stinging nettle.

"Wait!" he cried.

Scott wrested the rest of his bike free and huffed. "What is it?"

"You weren't crapping about the tap?" Wayne was hopping on one leg now, trying to brush something from the underside of his foot. "That was real?"

Scott had half a mind to punch Wayne in his clogged-up nose. Instead, he threw his leg over the fork of the bike. Wayne stopped hopping and blinked at the morning sunlight across his face.

"There was no tap, Scott. I checked."

Scott stopped. "What?"

"Not on my line, not on yours. No pens, no shoes. Nothing ordered through the phone company. I even went out and physically checked the corresponding B boxes. If our lines were any cleaner, we could eat off them." Wayne smirked at his own cleverness and smoothed his mustache.

"Why didn't you tell me?"

"I just thought you were being a putz. I thought you'd made it up."

Scott shook his head. "I didn't."

"Why did you think you were being tapped?"

"After the hack that night—you remember, the one I told you about—I thought I heard a delay on the line. It wasn't long, but it was long enough that I was sure someone was listening. And I know you don't believe me when I say stuff like this, but it *felt* like someone was listening."

"It's called hacker's intuition." Wayne recovered his conceit. "I've heard of it."

"But now that you tell me we're clean..." Scott laughed once. "Who knows? My brain was so burnt that night I could easily have heard something that wasn't even there. I mean, we're talking about milliseconds. And now every time I use the phone, I'm already convinced those additional milliseconds are there. I guess that's why I keep hearing them."

"*That's* called paranoia," Wayne said. "Next stop, Chattahoochee."

Scott smiled as his eyes met Wayne's. Both their gazes quickly fell back to where Scott was pushing his bike back and forth across a patch of sand. A self-conscious silence followed. Then an idea occurred to Scott.

"Hey, um, can I check something on your phone?"

Wayne shrugged his sloped shoulders and jerked his head. "Why not," he said. "Yeah, come on in."

Back home, Scott paced his secret workshop, his brain balling into a fist. He pulled the phone from his pocket and for the twelfth time that afternoon, dialed Mrs. Time. Seven series of pulses, a delay, and a ring—and *still* the delay was too long. He hadn't imagined it. And yet it wasn't tapped. Wayne had been exhaustive.

Doesn't make any flipping sense.

He suckled his vanilla Pudding Pop, going through Bell's schematics in his mind. He and Wayne belonged to the same exchange—376—which meant a call made from either one of their houses went to the same central office. As it turned out, their homes were roughly equidistant from that office (he and Wayne used to sift through their dumpster looking for cast-off equipment and technical manuals until a security guard ran them off), which meant the time discrepancy between pulse and ring couldn't be explained by distance.

And from that central office, the path was exactly the same. It went from the 376 exchange to the 372 exchange and finally to wherever Mrs. Time's computer lived. The time it took to connect should have been equal.

But it wasn't.

"Wait a minute," Scott muttered to himself. "You're not thinking."

Setting his Pudding Pop on its wrapper, he hopped onto the tall stool he had scavenged from the garage and leaned toward his TRS-80. He punched in the command to dial Mrs. Time and closed his eyes. The modem executed the dial, and he listened to the first faint ring.

Scott winced, gritting his teeth. It was the first time he'd exercised his ability in more than a month, and the sensation of his consciousness twining on itself tight-roped between lofty anticipation and crushing pain. Then he was inside, shooting along the lines, tandems, and switches, expanding over the network that connected him to Mrs. Time. Her automated voice crackled around him, blue and electric: "The. Time. Is ... One. Forty-two."

Scott extended himself as far as the connection would allow until he *became* the connection. The feeling was like that of someone who, having been crammed inside a three-foot-by-three-foot cell for a month, is allowed to stand and stretch at last. *Yes, this is where you belong,* a voice whispered. *Out in the greater networks.*

Reluctantly, he gathered himself at the terminal end, where the automated voice continued to report the time. From there he navigated the connection in reverse. Inside the 372 exchange, boxes hummed inside of boxes. Scott continued down the routing path to another exchange, the 376 exchange: his and Wayne's central office. The exchange was box shaped as well, but characterized by a different arrangement of giant batteries, frames, and switches. Just like the cars in his neighborhood, each exchange had its own signature.

And now Scott encountered ... something else.

The box was much smaller than a central office, its energy subtler, its signature nearly nonexistent. In fact, he had almost missed it, had almost sailed right past. But as he drew himself around the diminutive box, Scott became certain it was behind the delay he heard on the phone every time he went to make a call.

Was this what a tap felt like? he wondered. Could Wayne have erred?

Don't let it stop you, the voice whispered. *Short it.*

Short it? Could he?

Scott concentrated, gathering the parts of his consciousness still spread across the connection. He focused on the box-shaped obstruction. Behind his closed eyes, a red point appeared. It felt warm. He redoubled his concentration. The point grew to the size of a small orb, changing from red to orange, becoming hotter.

That's right, short it.

Sweat sprang from Scott's brow and trickled behind his glasses, but he couldn't stop to wipe it away. He was building something, gathering it into a single spot, like when you focused the sun's rays through a magnifying glass.

He strained harder. The orb swelled, verging on white. And then...

Scott climbed from the floor, his consciousness swimming up from some black void, his body tingling. The stool was down on its side. He knelt beside it a moment and straightened his glasses. Blinking, he could see the white orb—or what remained of it—as a bursting afterimage.

Is that how I ended up on the floor?

He shook his head and stood all the way up, using the workbench for support. The room wavered. The modem's red light blinked insistently. Beside it, his Popsicle sat in a spreading, custard-colored puddle. He faced the monitor and scanned the command lines. The final line indicated the call had been disconnected—he checked his watch—more than ten minutes ago.

Did I do that?

Scott turned on the cordless phone and lifted it to his ear. Just like with the modem, there was no dial tone. He mashed the phone off then on again, but still he heard nothing.

Both of the lines stayed dead the rest of the day, which agitated Scott's mother to no end. "I have *clients*," she kept repeating. At last, she turned her accusatory eye on Scott. "Do you know anything about this, buster?" He shook his head and remained silent. From his bedroom, he could hear her testing the phone and then huffing out another curse. Finally, she announced that she was driving to the real estate office for a few hours' work. "And you can bet your Benjamins I'll be calling Bell South while I'm there. I have *clients*, for pity's sake!"

That night, Scott dreamed about utility trucks rumbling past the house. In the morning, the dial tone was back on their phone.

But so, too, was the delay.

24

Citizen's Field
Thursday, November 15
8:06 p.m.

Janis stood in warm-ups with the other subs, watching the corner-kick go airborne off the Lyon player's foot. The ball hooked inward as it sailed toward the goal. Theresa Combs, Thirteenth Street's starting goalie, stepped out, her face tilted skyward. The opposing team's green jerseys multiplied inside the goal box, overwhelming Thirteenth Street's purple. Janis strained onto her tiptoes to see. In the next moment, the Lyon players ran shouting from the goal, arms raised.

The ball sat in the back of the net.

Janis thudded to her heels and looked at the game clock. With eight minutes to go, Lyon, the state's top ranked team, had just pulled ahead, two to one. That day, Principal Munshin had called an impromptu pep rally—a first for a girl's soccer game—and pledged in front of the two-thousand-member student body that if the undefeated girl's team won or fought Lyon to a tie, he would moonwalk the entire length of the field at game's end. Never mind that Michael Jackson was considered "out" by then and Prince "in," the students applauded wildly anyway.

Now, except for scattered shouts of support, the packed stands at Janis's back had gone mute. From their silence, a murmuring tide arose. At the same time the referee was waving his arms across his body to negate the goal, he was rushing toward Theresa. Janis brought her hand to her mouth.

Theresa, who had been one of the few players not to grumble when Janis, a freshman, made the varsity squad, who had remained after practice those first two weeks to help teach her the position, who had been playing her best game of the season, lay on her stomach, not moving.

And was that blood across her mouth?

Janis huddled with the other players on the sideline as the ambulance arrived and paramedics placed a collar around Theresa's neck. A stretcher waited beside her. Janis wanted to be out there, holding her hand, speaking words of encouragement—*something*— but the referees had cleared the field save for coaches and medical personnel.

"I saw the whole thing," Carol Hollis said. Janis and the other players edged closer to their co-captain. "I was right beside her. The Lyon player, the big one over there, smashed her in the mouth with her forearm. Had her eyes on Theresa the whole time. Never looked up for the ball."

"Why wasn't she ejected?" Janis asked, eyeing the refrigerator-sized player across the field.

"The ref said he couldn't toss her without having seen the infraction himself. He's going to give her a yellow card and award us a penalty kick." Carol shook her head. "Big whoop."

They watched Theresa being lifted into the back of the ambulance. The doors closed and the ambulance eased from the field, red lights swimming across the stands.

Coach Hall stormed to the opposing sideline as the siren began wailing from the street. "Is that what you teach your girls?" she shouted up into the Lyon coach's face. "Huh? Is that what you teach them? To break jaws and give concussions?"

The plodding coach shrugged his shoulders and turned away.

Coach Hall stalked back to the Thirteenth Street sideline and called her team together. "All right, we've got eight minutes left. I want you to play with the same intensity that got you here, but I also want you to play with the same integrity. No retaliation, understood? No cheap fouls. And protect yourselves." She turned to Janis. "That goes especially for you."

The words hit Janis like a lightning bolt. She was going into the game. She hurried to strip off her windbreaker and sweats, then scrambled out after the starters, shouts of support punctuating the applause from behind: "C'mon, Janis!" "Show 'em what the Titans are made of!"

Eight minutes. Air steamed from Janis's trembling lips. *Give them eight solid minutes.*

She tightened her ponytail and clapped her gloved hands together. *Thwat, thwat, thwat.* Carol Hollis turned and gave her a thumbs up, then took the penalty kick. Thirteenth Street High worked the ball to midfield before Lyon stole it back and came stampeding the other way. And that's what it looked like to Janis: a thundering stampede. Janis shuffled backward, her joints turning to ball bearings.

The shot came from the right side of the field, hard and low. Janis stumbled and stretched—*Watch the ball into your possession*—and caught the ball in both gloves as she landed on her side. The impact jarred the wind out of her. A Lyon player appeared above her. Janis grunted and curled around the ball. The player pulled up at the last instant, her thick leg cocked. She had meant to blast the ball from Janis's hands, broken fingers be damned.

Janis stood with the soccer ball to a mountain of applause, her breath returning in bruised gasps. The game clock showed six minutes. She bounced the ball twice and got off a solid punt.

For the next three minutes, the action remained on Lyon's side of the field. Janis used the opportunity to jog in place, windmilling her arms. Her muscles began to loosen. When Carol juked a defender and darted toward the goal, Janis's scream joined those from the stands. But the trailing defender recovered in time to knife Carol's legs, sending her tumbling. The fans' tenor changed from rapturous to outraged. "You're worse than Cobra Kai!" one student bellowed. Coach Hall threw up her arms. Another yellow card for Lyon, another penalty shot for Thirteenth Street High.

Janis watched the ball sail high, over the far net.

With two minutes to play, the Lyon coach signaled for his players to push up. Even the huskiest defenders trotted out to midfield, eyeing the large net Janis defended. Their hard-bitten faces said it all. They weren't leaving Gainesville without a win, even if it meant more ambulances.

For the second time since Janis entered the game, Lyon stampeded. The ghost-image was fleeting—almost too fleeting—but Janis reacted. She dove and tipped the ensuing shot out of bounds, a solid blast that would have grazed the near post en route to a score. She stood, heart pounding, breaths flaring her nostrils.

The side judge pointed her flag to the corner of the field to indicate a corner kick.

"Hey, *Cherry*."

The menacing whisper came from behind. Janis glanced around and found the Lyon player who had broken Theresa's jaw staring at her, eyes red-rimmed and fierce. Up close, her mud-smeared thighs looked as thick as truck tires. Janis turned and squinted toward the corner flag.

"What's your pain tolerance, Cherry?"

Janis kept her eyes on the girl poised to kick the ball even as her skin crawled.

"Hope it's better than your starter's."

The shot went skyward, starting out a distance from the goal but quickly hooking inward. It traced the same path as the last corner kick, the one that had doomed Theresa. Grunts and sharp cries rang out. Dark green jerseys collapsed toward the ball, and Janis made the same assessment Theresa must have. She needed to get there first, needed to jump high enough to punch the ball away.

Janis moved forward, gloved hands tensing into fists. The ball hooked nearer. She crouched to leave her feet, even as she sensed Theresa's assailant watching her from inside Lyon's thudding mass.

The image came an instant later: broken teeth and a goal.

Janis planted hard and staggered back to the far post, nearly losing her footing. The ball shot off the head of a Lyon player. Janis knelt low, elbows almost to the ground. A row of dirt-caked cleats raked her cheek. The ball bobbled between her hands and chest—*Watch the ball, Janis!*—then stuck.

Cheers crashed down from the stands. "Way to go!" Coach Hall yelled.

When Janis looked over, her coach was signaling for her to hold the ball, to burn clock. Janis nodded and bounced it, scanning the field of retreating players. She bounced the ball again. Less than thirty seconds to go. Tie score, one to one.

"I'm counting to five then I'm calling a delay of game."

The referee's voice startled Janis.

She stepped into the punt quickly, too quickly. It careened off the side of her foot and straight toward the player who'd just threatened her. The player saw her gift before the Thirteenth Street defenders did. By the time she met the ball with her chest, she had a five-yard lead on everyone else.

And she was fast.

Janis dashed out to meet her. It was what a goalie was supposed to do in a one-on-one situation. The nearer the other player, the larger the goal became, and the more angles she would have to score from. Still yards away, Janis was already bracing herself for the slide, the brutal collision. But the Lyon player had anticipated Janis's coming out. She cocked her leg.

The image for Janis this time was crystal clear.

She tried to beat a retreat, but the ball was in flight—lofty, with a tight backward spin. It was going to meet the net high but squarely in its center. Janis was that far out of position. The chip shot had come off the forward's foot that perfectly. Shouts climbed from the Lyon sideline.

Janis grunted and launched into her fading leap with everything she could summon. She stretched her arm—no, *pushed* her arm—until it felt like her shoulder was wrenching from its socket. She just needed to get her fingers on it, even one finger.

The ball spun above her.

Push! she screamed inside. *PUSH!*

And then the ground thudded into her. Up behind, she could see the movement of the net. Her fingers hadn't touched anything. And now the referee was blowing his whistle.

Janis closed her eyes and lay still. Seconds to go and she'd just blown the game. Thirteenth Street High had lost.

But the sounds around her didn't make sense.

She sat up. The Lyon players were sulking toward their sideline. And Janis's teammates were sprinting toward her. In the stands, the hundreds who had come out to support them were leaping up and down, throwing their arms around one another, breaking into primitive dance. The sound felt like a toppling wall. They heckled Principal Munshin, who was smiling and pulling a red Michael Jackson jacket over his purple Titans sweatshirt.

Before her teammates could descend on her, Janis craned her neck. The soccer ball sat off behind the net. The three shrill screams of the ref's whistle hadn't signaled a goal. They had signaled the end of the game.

Thirteenth Street High had just fought the state's top team to a draw.

The shot had missed.

"You're being awfully quiet," Blake said.

After the on-field celebration and Principal Munshin's frightful moonwalk (he looked like he was trying to wipe doggy doo from his shoes and nearly fell backward at the end), after being congratulated by her teammates and coaches, and after her parents had found and hugged her, Janis sat across from Blake at the McDonald's on Thirteenth Street. He had wanted to buy her a celebratory sundae or shake, but Janis opted for a Mr. Pibb instead. She bit down on the straw and drew thin sips.

"I would've thought..." Blake's smile looked confused. "You were fantastic out there. You know that, right?"

"Tell me about the last play."

She'd heard snatches of it from her teammates, the students, but she wanted to hear it from him.

"What's there to tell, Janis? The ball was about to go in and you vaulted up like Mary Lou Retton and tipped it away."

"You saw it go off my fingers?"

"Yeah, it popped into the air and went rolling down the backside of the net."

Janis glanced around. Except for a McDonald's employee who had unfolded a yellow CAUTION sign and begun pushing a mop under the tables, they had the dining area to themselves. She looked at Blake's questioning eyes. They had gone out on five more dates since *Ghostbusters*, and already the student body had them pegged as "an item." She shied from that title. How could they be an item if she couldn't be honest with him—about who she was, about what she could do, about what had happened at the game?

She pushed the straw in and out of the plastic top, listening to it squeak. "What if I told you that I never touched the ball?"

He laughed as though it were an odd joke. "What's that supposed to mean?"

"Blake..." She moved her drink aside and leaned nearer. "I never touched it."

"Of course you did. We all saw it."

Janis closed her eyes and shook her head.

"Well if you didn't, who did?"

It was a good question, a fair question. She replayed that moment in her mind when, the ball spinning above her, she had commanded her arm to *push* even though she knew she was never going to reach it. But she had felt something, hadn't she? A pulse shooting the length of her outstretched arm, beginning inside her chest and ending at the tips of her fingers? At the time, it had felt like the shock of a strained nerve. But now she wondered.

Spinning ball. Spinning plastic egg.

Janis shrugged. "I just didn't feel the ball."

Blake took her hands in his and bounced them playfully. "You were wearing thick goalie gloves, for one. Two, it was cold enough out there to numb your fingers. And three, your thoughts must have been going a hundred miles a second. I know mine would've been."

Janis dropped her gaze.

"Hey," he said, leaning nearer. "You were fantastic."

"Then why don't I feel fantastic?" *Why do I feel like a fraud?*

"You just need time for it to sink in."

Janis hadn't brought up the supernatural since the night of their first date. She knew Blake well enough now to know that such things were outside of his experience. She couldn't tell him about her strange dreams and couldn't talk to him about what had happened tonight—what she was beginning to *think* had happened. He wouldn't understand. It wasn't his fault, but he just wouldn't. They clicked in so many ways, just not there.

"I guess the whole thing kind of overwhelmed me," she said at last. "Sorry."

Even though Blake was still holding her hands, still smiling his concerned smile, he suddenly felt far away from her. "Don't be." A squeeze. A kiss. "C'mon. Let me take you home."

The McDonald's mopper tipped his paper hat to them on their way out of the restaurant. As Blake opened the car door for her, Janis thought of someone who might understand what was happening and, more importantly, who might be able to help *her* understand what was happening.

Blake checked to see that she was all the way inside before closing the door gently, then walked around the back of the car. Janis watched him in the rearview mirror, hating herself for lying to him. The next day, she would talk to this person, she told herself. Yes, the next day, after school.

25

Thirteenth Street High
Friday, November 16
2:31 p.m.

Janis waited for the final students to funnel out of the classroom while she pretended to organize her books. Two girls lingered at her back, whisper-chattering about so-and-so who had overheard so-and-so saying such-and-such about a third so-and-so and oh, the scandal. Janis gripped the back of her neck and dug at the tension. *Would you two scram, already?*

She tried to think of other things, like how Scott had been one of the first ones out of the classroom when the bell rang. He couldn't move quickly enough these days, it seemed, his head bobbing above the receding masses by the time Janis would get to the doorway. Since their conversation that night on the couch, he hadn't spoken a word to her, much less glanced over. And she'd long since lost the nerve to ask whether he'd experienced something unusual that night.

At the front of the classroom, Mrs. Fern sat at her desk in a mauve turtleneck and white woven vest, peering over the student papers just handed in. She laughed once to herself, her hair shaking like silver curtains. Finally, the two girl at Janis's back left the classroom, their chatter receding away. She took a deep breath as she stood, leaving her books stacked on her desk.

"Um, Mrs. Fern." She stepped toward the teacher's desk.

Mrs. Fern had been shaking her head as she continued to leaf through the typed assignments, several of them nearly opaque with correction fluid. Their teacher was an eccentric, for sure, but also a stickler for spelling and punctuation. "Even the most hallowed cathedrals of antiquity are nothing but for the soundness of plain brick and mortar," she often said.

"Hmm?" Mrs. Fern answered without looking up.

Janis glanced toward the door, then took a seat at a desk directly across from her. Soccer practice had been cancelled that day—Coach Hall's gift to them for last night's effort.

"I was hoping I could talk to you." She swallowed. "If you're not busy."

Mrs. Fern patted the papers back into a neat stack and blinked up. Her hazel eyes swam inside the thick lenses. Janis's gaze fell to the white crystal her teacher wore around her neck. She debated whether or not to use her Get Out of Awkward Situation Free card, which would be to ask for a few reading recommendations, thank her, and leave. But something in her teacher's expression told Janis that she was already aware of why she'd come. Mrs. Fern tilted her head, eyes glimmering with amusement and knowledge.

"The first day of class," Janis said, "you, um, you talked about a Roman god ... Janus?"

"Ah, yes, the god of doorways."

"Can you tell me more about him?" She decided to rephrase it. "What *you* know about him?"

Mrs. Fern grinned as though reading her thought process and sat back.

"Well, it's like I told you. The god Janus has two faces. One looks to the past, the other to the future. One face sees the world as most do, as it *appears* to exist. And the other ... well, the other sees another world, quite beyond the perceptions of most. It is what makes Janus so special."

"What is that other world?"

"Ah, it was much debated by the great thinkers." Mrs. Fern gathered her hair in back and let it fall. "Some believed it to be a realm that supports our physical world, that *manifests* it. Not a realm of people and objects, but of the passions and energies that constitute them."

When Mrs. Fern spoke this last part, Janis felt the familiar vibrations rise and oscillate throughout her awareness before settling down again.

"Do people go there?" Janis concentrated anew. "To this other world?"

"Why, artists go there all the time, writers of poetry and prose— some we've read in this course. And how fortunate we are that they share it with the rest of us. Think what our world would be like if it were just plain matter." Mrs. Fern brushed her fingers through the leaves of the potted fern that sat on the corner of her desk.

"I think what you're saying is that's where they get their inspiration." Janis hesitated. "But can people *actually* go there? Can they, I don't know, wake up and just find themselves there?"

"I suppose it can happen." Again, the amusement in her gaze.

A warm breeze smelling of fall leaves streamed through the open windows and rustled the fern's fronds. Janis frowned, considering how this had quickly become the weirdest conversation with a teacher she'd ever had. But she was getting somewhere. If she could just find the right question...

Mrs. Fern tee-peed her fingers beneath her chin.

"What would you say to someone who it happened to?"

Mrs. Fern smiled. *Well phrased,* the smile seemed to say. "I would tell her she had been given a unique opportunity. I would advise her to explore that world, to learn its laws, its rules—because they are said to be different from the rules governing our own world."

Janis watched the vertical lines above Mrs. Fern's lip.

"Similar in certain ways, the rules," Mrs. Fern continued, "but quite different in others. Time and space are not so ... absolute in that world. Past events can seem very present, as can future *probable* events—and that word, *probable,* is an important one, I would tell her."

"Important, how?"

"I would leave that to her to find out." Mrs. Fern's eyes became huge—and did one of them just wink? "If I told her everything there was to know, why, goodness, there would be nothing left for her to discover. And wouldn't that be a shame?"

Janis drew her brows together in thought. "If that world supports this one, can it also influence this one? You know, thoughts, objects—that sort of thing?"

"Here again, something I would leave for her to discover—oh!" Mrs. Fern clapped her hands. "I almost forgot to congratulate you on last night's *match nul.* I understand you made a spectacular save in the last seconds. I'm sorry I wasn't there to see it. Not something one witnesses every day, I wouldn't think."

"Thanks..." Janis eyed her teacher carefully.

Is it just coincidence she brought that up after my question about being able to influence objects?

"Well, I do have your papers to get started on before the weekend," Mrs. Fern said with a little waggle of her head. "But let me end by saying this. The worst thing anyone newly awakened into that realm can do would be to deny her experience of it. It can be frightening, I understand. But it is a tremendous source of *intuition*. It is how people come into intuition—some of us more consciously than others. Better to keep your eyes open, I think."

She just switched from third-person to second—from "her" to "your."

"Does that answer your question?"

"I think so," Janis said, not at all sure, and feeling the first stabs of a headache.

"Hmm, fascinating god, that Janus. So much from the ancients we still have to learn. If you're ever of the mind to delve deeper, my door is always open." Mrs. Fern picked up the battered leather satchel leaning against her desk and pushed the stack of papers into it. "Good day, then!"

Janis's headache worsened that afternoon, and by dinnertime, it had become almost unbearable—piercing red throbs. She left a message for Blake that she wouldn't be going to the football game that night. Her mother administered aspirin and came often to her bedside to change the warm towel across her forehead. Janis remained on her back. The effort to move, or even string together the smallest thoughts, had become a dozen strands of barbed wire winching her skull.

Little by little, the dissolving aspirin dulled Janis's senses until she became dimly aware of her mother removing the towel, kissing her forehead, and clicking off the bedside lamp.

Janis dreamed that she was back in Mrs. Fern's classroom. She was sitting at the front of the room again, but the fern plant on the teacher's desk was enormous, its hairy fronds writhing in whispers. Mrs. Fern appeared from behind the plant, and Janis realized she had been tending to it, burying crystals in its soil. When her teacher spoke, her voice sounded like a record player whose volume had been turned up and its speed slowed way down.

"PAST EVENTS CAN SEEM VERY PRESENT AS CAN FUTURE *PROBABLE* EVENTS."

As Janis looked at her teacher, she felt herself standing on an empty beach where black clouds gathered into an hourglass. She heard the ticking of a giant clock, its minute hand edging toward midnight.

"Nuclear war?" Janis asked Mrs. Fern. "Is that...?"

"PROBABLE."

Janis's eyes began to water. "Wh-what can I do?"

"KEEP YOUR EYES OPEN."

Mrs. Fern turned in her chair so her back was to Janis, her silver hair flowing down to where it disappeared behind the desk. She took her hair up in layers with her long, slender hands, turning it over the top of her head. When the final layer had fallen away, Janis saw a second face. It wavered in and out of focus but appeared to be a younger version of her teacher. The eyes shone with preternatural light.

"No longer can you deny the experiences, Janis." The face spoke clearly. "There are things to see. Things you have already seen."

"What? Tell me!"

"Things you have already seen," she repeated.

When Janis awoke, her head no longer felt like a spool of barbed wire. Her thoughts were clear. And she was standing in her backyard, beside the island of oak trees and azalea bushes, just out of reach of the English ivy that trickled away from the house. Janis peered around. A faint light similar to what she had observed in Mrs. Fern's eyes imbued the night. A familiar whooshing sound filled her ears—a sensation she'd denied herself for the last three months.

Now she remembered all the times in those three months she'd awakened in this state only to will herself back to her room, back to dreaming, to normalcy. The occasions must have numbered in the dozens.

Janis rose into the air and turned toward the back line of bushes.

Things you have already seen.

He wasn't outside tonight, wasn't pacing or propping his arms against the deck rail, the burning end of a cigarette illuminating his glasses. The deck was dark, as was the Leonards' house.

Janis flew to the place in the bushes that had pulled her through the last time. She remembered it was near the tree where her mother emptied compost from the plastic container she kept under the kitchen sink. As Janis extended her arms, she felt herself being repulsed. Then, like air inhaled through a straw, she was siphoned from the backyard.

WHOOSH.

The cement culvert wavered beneath her. She lifted her face to where the Leonards' chain-link fence stretched to either side, the house looming large beyond. Janis spotted the leaning shed, but it no longer stood in tall grass. A couple of days after seeing Mr. Leonard with the drill, she'd heard the roar of a mower and looked out to see flashes of his shirt beyond the bushes, moving in a line. He had since maintained the yard in a trim state, using a weed whacker to blast away the tall grass and weeds that had once grown along the fence.

The entire yard stood open and naked.

Janis passed through the fence at the edge of the yard and flew up to the shed. It had been a long time since she'd last flown, and a part of her sang with the rediscovery. But she glanced around as she went, making sure the shadows along the edges of the house were just that—shadows. She hadn't forgotten the last time. The horrific memory of the shed door opening on Mr. Leonard's pale face took form in her mind before Janis could stuff it down again.

Keep your eyes open.

Janis peeked up toward the deck before drifting around to the shed's front. She hovered before the lock, whose bolt seemed larger and more solid than the one she'd seen the last time.

He changes the lock. He mows the yard to eliminate places to hide...

Which could only mean that whatever secrets lay beneath his shed were worth protecting. Janis concentrated, her hands propped against the door. She fell through. The inside of the shed crackled to life around her. She rotated. It appeared the same as it had the last time, although perhaps a little tidier. The pile of kindling still stood in a heap beneath the shelving, but the roach-infested sacking was gone—replaced by a solid piece of plywood.

She probed the plywood with her thought-hands. Yes, the metal hatch remained beneath the pile, as did the electrical field surrounding it. Janis felt along the lines of energy, not pushing too hard. She feared the field had alerted Mr. Leonard to her presence the last time.

Janis withdrew her hands and listened outside before returning her gaze to the kindling. She nodded to herself. That was where the answers lay. Beneath the pile. Down below.

But how to get there?

The vibrations that sustained Janis's out-of-body state began to fade. Another dream was intruding on her experience, a dream about getting ready for a soccer game but not having the right jersey or shoes, finding holes in her goalie gloves. The vibrations diminished further. The scent of the sea drifted away, but before she could be whisked back to her sleeping body, where the anxiety dream awaited her, Janis pushed her hands beneath the plywood again. She had been so occupied by the hatch that she'd forgotten about the small, square-shaped panel embedded in the cement beside it. Her thought-fingers explored its three-by-three arrangement of blocks. It felt to Janis like a miniature typewriter.

No, a keypad. She would have to remember that...

26

Thursday, November 29
6:50 p.m.

"Who are you supposed to be, again?"

Scott's mother frowned past the steering wheel, then over at his outfit. Scott shifted in his seat and glanced down. He had borrowed the shoes from his father—seventies-era derby shoes, two sizes too big. They shifted over tube socks that showed half their length, thanks to a pair of rainbow suspenders that drew his pants nearly to his sternum. One of the front pockets of his shirt bulged with his scientific calculator, the other with pens and mechanical pencils. A plaid bowtie bloomed from the shirt collar. He tapped his old pair of glasses against his thigh, the thick plastic bridge and both bows bound with masking tape.

"It's Dress-up Night," Scott said. "We're supposed to look ridiculous."

"Well, you've certainly succeeded."

"Thanks," he mumbled.

Older brothers chose the costumes for their pledges, and Britt had come up with his—The Nerd Look. Scott kept telling himself it was just for fun and didn't mean anything, but apprehension stewed in the pit of his stomach. His mother wasn't helping the situation.

"I see what this is," she said. "I see *exactly* what this is."

"What what is?"

"*This.*" She jutted her chin toward him. "They're going to humiliate you."

Scott groaned inwardly. He had asked his mom to drive him because the risk was too high with his father. The sight of everyone in costume would have proven too much, shorting out whatever inhibitions his father possessed—and there weren't many there to begin with.

But now his mother was getting going with her own thing.

"All of the pledges are dressing up, Mom. It's fine. It's just for fun."

Scott reflected on how that week was the first time Britt had acted anything more than indifferently toward him during the thirteen-week pledge period. He'd smiled, but hadn't his eyes gleamed like ice when he handed over the suspenders and bow tie and ordered Scott to wear them?

"They're going to humiliate you, but don't let them, Scott. Stand up for yourself." She slapped the steering wheel with both hands, startling Scott. "For God's sake, *stand up for yourself!*"

Her shrill voice made his heart race.

"Mom, what are you—"

"That's what *grates* me about your father." Her eyes glared over the steering wheel, bearing the reflection of the taillights of the car she was tailgating. "He lets Larry walk all over him. 'You're supposed to be fifty-fifty partners,' I tell him. 'Oh, well Larry wants it like this,' your father says, or 'Larry wants it like that.'" She made her voice deep and stupid when she imitated his dad, and Scott didn't like it. "Now look at him. Look what he's become."

Scott watched the street lights passing and felt his heart shrinking inside him like a flaccid balloon.

"And here it is a week after Thanksgiving, and he still hasn't moved a goddamned thing out of that garage. What is it about the *men* in this family?" When she looked over at Scott, he saw ... disgust? And for the last three months, she had been gushing compliments over his room and his neat appearance.

"Just stand up for yourself," she said with an eerie flatness.

"It's ... it's just for fun, Mom."

"Don't be stupid. Their idea of fun is going to be a lot different than yours." She braked hard enough in front of Grant's house for Scott's seatbelt to lock against him. "Mark my word."

Scott barely had time to get out and push the door closed before she drove off. He stood a moment at the curb, listening to the cheery laughter from where the driveway wound down into trees, and lights twinkled from a two-story house. He wiped his eyes with his shoulders. Moisture stippled through his shirt. Sniffling, he donned his glasses and touched his hair, cold and slicked over with gel.

Just for fun, he reassured himself, and made his way down the driveway.

The first hour involved food and drinks in the backyard. The older members, wearing comfortable street clothes, smiled over their red plastic cups at the costumed pledges who mingled self-consciously in the flood of outdoor lighting. Scott was more than relieved to find the other pledges dressed as absurdly as he was. Jeffrey, who was supposed to be Peter Pan, kept tugging at his too-short frock, mumbling that his tights didn't leave much to the imagination. Someone—Brad, was it?—waddled around in a full Gumby getup. And Sweat Pea was dressed as, well, Swee'Pea from Popeye: powder-blue pajamas with footies, a big bonnet, and a pacifier on a string around his neck. Scott giggled. It was too perfect.

"Hey, laugh all you want, Stretch," Sweet Pea said. "But just watch the number of Alpha chicks who come over and pinch these baby cheeks. And believe me, I plan to pinch me some baby cheeks right back. Ain't that right, Peter Pan?"

He goosed Jeffrey's right butt cheek, sending him hollering and high-stepping away. The reaction looked especially hilarious in his green tights and little feathered hat. Scott roared with laughter along with the pledges, Gumby holding his belly.

"Goddamn." Jeffrey returned with both hands pressed to his backside.

But even Jeffrey was smiling. And that was the reason Scott had stuck with Gamma. Despite the disastrous first social, despite the fact that Janis felt as inaccessible to him as ever, that was why: his fellow pledges. As clichéd as it sounded, all of the days in Standards, the forced exercises and cafeteria lunches, the signing of The Pact—it *had* bonded the thirteen of them. Scott even began to suspect they were going to miss their lunches together. He knew he would. But while he had gotten along with all of the pledges, he hadn't become particularly close with any of them. The person he *was* the closest to, strangely, was...

"Blake!" the pledges called in unison.

Scott turned to find him striding down the driveway in full football attire—helmet, pads, and a red-and-blue jersey. Janis walked alongside him, her face creased with displeasure. Scott could see why. Her hair had been braided into pigtails and tied off with blue ribbons while her cheeks featured a constellation of large, hand-drawn freckles. And Scott knew from their childhood that she hated dresses. Passionately. The one she wore was high necked and frilly with blue stripes. Was she supposed to be Pippi Longstocking? The only things missing were the long, mismatched socks, but then Scott had it.

"Wendy!" Sweet Pea shouted.

The others laughed as it dawned on them, too. Yes, Wendy of hamburger-chain fame.

"Oh, c'mon, man." Jeffrey looked Blake over. "How is that supposed to be embarrassing? This is like a day at the office for you."

Blake arrived beside them and smiled sheepishly. "Grant knows about me and the Miami Dolphins. What better way to humiliate a Dolphins fan than to dress him up as a Buffalo Bill?"

"Yeah, well, I'll trade you."

"I already offered." Janis flipped up one of her pigtails. "He wouldn't go for it."

The others laughed, but Janis's face held its grimace. When Blake took her hand, Scott suffered a stab of longing so intense he had to turn away.

The thing was, Scott enjoyed sitting opposite Blake at lunch. The sentiment seemed mutual. They had spent much of the last month talking personal computers when Blake's family had been in the market for one. Scott appreciated that, appreciated him. Even when it became clear that Blake and Janis were an item, Scott found he couldn't distort his opinion of him for the worse. (And hadn't the X-Men's Jean Grey dated Angel before pledging her love to Scott?) If anything, he looked at Blake ever more as someone to model himself after—someone who didn't have to hide or reinvent himself. He was who he was, which was solid, someone Janis deserved. And on that point, Blake was a gentleman. No matter how much the other pledges prodded, he never went into detail about their dates, other than to say that Janis was a "great girl." And maybe that's what pained Scott the most—that Blake was getting to discover what he himself had known about Janis since childhood.

Scott slipped his hands into his jacked-up pants pockets and pretended to become interested in Grant, the Gamma president and host, who was plugging a microphone into a stereo system up on his deck. Van Halen's "Jump" ended abruptly. Grant descended the steps, unspooling the microphone's cord as he went. In the yard, members were setting up lawn chairs around what looked like a makeshift stage.

"You look about as miserable as I feel."

Scott turned to find Janis standing at his shoulder, also peering toward the stage. She was close enough that he could see the shine of outdoor lighting along each strand of her braided hair. The space around Scott began to revolve, just like it had that first day of school.

"On the bright side, this is the end of it," Janis said. "That's what I keep telling myself, anyway."

"Yeah," was all Scott could think to mutter.

Janis blinked and turned toward him. "You know, I've been meaning to ask you. Why this?" She reached for the front of his suspenders. "Why Gamma? I mean, what made you decide to pledge?"

"I, ah..." He watched the fingers of her hand trace the length of his suspender. "I just thought I needed to, um ... branch out ... you know, meet new people. Not too many from our middle school came to Thirteenth Street High."

Janis snorted as her hand fell away. "That depends on how you look at it."

Scott followed her narrowed gaze to where the three girls from their English class were chatting excitedly with some older Gamma members. The one dressed as a Playboy bunny, Amy, turned around for the guys to feel her puffy tail. "It's real rabbit's fur, I swear!" she exclaimed. The guys grinned at one another. Janis made a noise of disgust and turned back to Scott. He watched the soft green rings around her pupils grow as she inched nearer.

"Um, there's something else I've been meaning to ask you."

Scott's collar constricted around his throat. Her voice had a quiet, husky quality, almost intimate. He felt the sudden need to swallow but feared it would sound like an off-putting gulp.

"This might sound weird...," Janis started to say.

A trio of shrill voices burst inside their space, older Alpha members.

"Oh my *gawd*!" the one with feathered hair exclaimed, lifting Janis's pigtails. "Like, you look just *like* her!"

"How *adorable*!"

"For sure!" This one emitted a lengthy giggle.

"Yeah, well, you can thank Margaret," Janis muttered.

The one with huge, dark hair looked around. "Where *is* she?"

"Covering the evening shift at Penney's," Janis said. "She's coming by later."

"What a total, like, *bummer*."

Bummed or not, Scott hoped they would blow off just as quickly as they had blown in. He needed to know what Janis was about to ask him—especially while Blake was still occupied with the pledges behind them. Because for a moment, it had felt like just the two of them again, back in the woods.

"TESTING. TESTING."

Scott turned with Janis to where Grant was holding the microphone to his chin. The older members were settling into the rows of lawn chairs that now semi-circled the stage. Margaret's three friends squealed and fled from Janis's side, but Blake was there to fill the void, stepping up and taking her hand. Scott hardly noticed this time. The uneasy feeling was stealing back into the pit of his stomach.

A final hum of feedback sounded, followed by Grant Sidwell's resonant voice. "Yes, everyone take a seat, please. Not the pledges. I need you around here beside me. Right there is good. And in a line, please."

Scott followed the pack and took his place at the rear of a line that stretched along the back of the house, nearly to the trees. Outside the lights, he could more clearly see the faces in the audience, flushed and excited. His mother's words jabbed through his jittery thoughts.

They're going to humiliate you.

Grant lifted the microphone and turned back to the audience. "All right, all of you know how this works. When your little brother or sister takes the stage, you'll give them a scenario to act out. As always, you can team up and do a couples or group scenario. Our panel over here"—Grant indicated the four members in the front row—"will be awarding the points. Remember, humor and humiliation score highest."

Amid the laughter, Grant turned to the first pledge. There had been some jostling and rearranging in the line while Grant had been speaking, and Sweet Pea, by virtue of his pudginess and indifference, had been shoved to the front. He took the stage to a smattering of applause. Soon, his older Gamma brother was beside him, microphone in hand.

"Change his diaper!" someone yelled.

"Yeah, then make him eat it!"

Scott felt too nauseated to laugh. He had held his place at the back of the line by slipping farther into the darkness and then slipping back when the line had returned to order. For an instant, he had considered slipping away entirely, stealing off into the night and walking home. Oakwood wasn't too far away. But no, he needed to stay, needed to finish what he'd started. He stood on tiptoes, looking for Blake and Janice. He found them in the middle of the line.

"Swee'Pea, Swee'Pea, Swee'Pea," his older brother said, massaging his neck. "You are going to prove your loyalty to our esteemed club by singing the Gamma fight song three times. Do you remember the words?"

"Yeah, of course."

By Sweet Pea's surprised smile, Scott could practically read his thoughts. *That's it? That's all I have to do?*

His older brother raised a finger. "But you have to sing it in *goo-goo*s and *ga-ga*s. With your thumb in your mouth. Crawling around on your hands and knees." His grin looked positively devilish. "Got it?"

Sweet Pea's own smile vanished beneath a wave of laughter. He looked at his older Gamma brother another moment to make sure he was serious. He was. Shoulders slumped, Sweet Pea fixed his thumb in the corner of his mouth, sank to his knees, and started into a limping crawl.

"Goo-goo, ga-ga-goo, ga-ga, goo-goo..."

"Faster, baby!"

Scott cringed when Sweet Pea's older brother kicked him in the rear. That brought down fresh laughter.

"Ga-ga, goo-goo, ga-ga-goo..."

"I said, faster!" Another kick, this one harder. The laughter became riotous. "And aim your bonnet toward the audience when you sing!"

Scott's stomach roiled, and he placed his hands on his knees. He could see Janis saying something to Blake. Scott looked back to where Sweet Pea was receiving another kick, his older brother screaming above his ear now.

After two minutes that felt like two years, it was over.

Sweet Pea stood to a round of applause. His older brother hoisted one of his arms like a prize fighter just gone the distance. Sweet Pea looked appropriately dazed. They stood, waiting for the judge's decision. Two 7s and two 8s.

"Bitchin'!" Sweet Pea's older brother said. "A 7.5!" He clapped Sweet Pea's back, then hustled him into the audience where they would enjoy the rest of the show as spectators.

See, it's all in fun, Scott told himself through his shallow breaths.

The other scenarios went similarly, though not all of them were as physically abusive, Scott was glad to see. Amy, the Playboy bunny, was forced to give an impromptu speech on the importance of sex education, using a list of words she had been given—all of them crude, naturally. And every time she paused, said "um," or laughed, she had to hop in a circle like a bunny, which was often.

Before long, Blake and Janis's turn came. Scott lowered his head, not wanting to see her embarrassed. Since Margaret still wasn't there, Grant came up with a scenario for both of them. Blake was to get on one knee and propose to Janis, who was then to run around squealing. It was among the lamer scenarios, but Scott still found he couldn't watch. He stared at the tips of his father's derby shoes, the outdoor lighting branding the back of his neck.

"Janis," Blake said. "These last two months have been amazing. I mean that. And you would make me the happiest man in the world if you would only accept this ring and say, 'I do.' "

Pretend or not, the sincerity of his words crushed Scott.

"Yeah, yeah, I do," Janis said flatly. She gave a half-hearted squeal, then said, "All right, we're done here."

The audience protested, but when Scott raised his face, Janis was already leading Blake around to the back row to sit. The judging was unanimous: all 1s. Grant shrugged and turned to the next pledge, Peter Pan.

Jeffrey's dancing and prancing scored an 8.5, the highest so far.

Scott shuffled forward with a line that was becoming frighteningly shorter while the audience, with its retired acts, was growing larger and larger, spilling beyond the lawn chairs. Though the night was cool, the deck lighting that shone ever brighter over Scott made his body pour sweat.

It's all in fun, he repeated. *All in good fun.*

Don't be stupid, his mother's voice shot back.

By the time Scott's turn came, he felt as if he'd been cored out and strung through with frayed wires. His shirt stuck to his back, and he could feel a muscle at the corner of his mouth beginning to twitch.

"Last but not least," Grant announced, opening his arm toward Scott. "Britt, I believe this one's yours?"

Laughter burst from the audience, and when Scott turned, he saw Britt emerging from a sliding glass door beneath the deck. He was wearing a priest's robe and a white clerical collar. In one hand, he carried an ottoman, in the other, what looked like a large scroll. As Britt entered the light, the solemnity of his face evoked more laughter. He glanced over, the shine in his eyes speaking not to holy compassion but punishment, the fire and brimstone variety.

"Silence!" Britt commanded.

He set down the ottoman at the front of the stage. "Sit down," he told Scott.

Scott stepped forward, and all of Bud's training left him. His knees began to fold like a lawn chair before muscles jerked into action, throwing him upright. Pinwheeling his arms, he managed to steady himself. Laughter spouted from the audience. *Make them think it's part of an act.* Scott led with his hips now, chest sunk back, arms stiff at his sides. But the laughter that accompanied him was not the companionable kind; it wielded a cruel edge.

The muscle at the corner of his mouth began to jump again. Scott bit the inside of his lip to contain it.

"My faithful parishioners," Britt boomed into the microphone, "my flock, my herd..."

"I ain't your sheep!" someone shouted.

Britt didn't break stride. "It pains me deeply to inform you that there is a deceitful presence in our midst. Yes, a deceitful presence who came unto us like a thief in the night this past August, pretending to be someone he is not."

Scott's body stiffened.

"But he has been outed. Yes, he has been outed, my flock. Behold!"

When Scott turned, he found Britt holding open the scroll that was not a scroll at all, but a poster. Scott's first instinct was to leap up, grab it from his hands, and rip it to pieces. Instead, he remained rigid, his face becoming so hot he could feel the color leaching from it. He was staring at himself, or rather a ghost of himself past, one who had thick glasses, a disheveled head of hair, a smile as awkward and crooked as the collar of his shirt, and volcanic eruptions of acne across his brow. It was his yearbook photo from Creekside Middle School, from the year before. Copied, blown up, and pasted to the unfurled poster in Britt's hands.

"Ner-errrd!" a voice jeered.

Scott's breaths wheezed through a pinhole.

Some others took up the call—a few of them girls—but Britt raised his hand for their silence. "That's right, the nerd has been outed. But he is not lost. No, no, no, no! He is *not* lost. Not on my watch. Can you give me a hallelujah?"

"HALLELUJAH!"

"Can you give me an amen?"

"AMEN!"

Each shout felt like the report from a firing squad. Britt set the poster aside and stood beside Scott, pressing a hand over Scott's soaked brow.

Scott stopped groping over his pockets for the inhaler he no longer carried.

"Because, my flock, I sense that this nerd *can* be saved. I feel the Gamma spirit stirring deep inside him. But only if he is willing. *Only if he is willing!* Are you willing, son?" He moved the microphone to Scott's mouth.

Scott ran a furry tongue across his lips. "Y-yes," he gasped, his lungs allowing him that much.

"I said, *are you willing?*"

"Yes."

Britt threw his arms skyward. "Praise the lord!"

"PRAISE THE LORD!"

The crowd broke into applause, and when Scott glanced around, he found them all leaned forward, a keen hunger across their faces, sensing that whatever scenario Britt had cooked up for this last act—for him—was going to blow away all the others. Though he couldn't see her, Scott knew Janis was out there watching as well.

"All right, son," Britt said. Sweat shone through his crew cut as he stooped toward Scott's ear. He hadn't broken character once, and

Scott interpreted that as bad. Really bad. "We are gonna exorcise that nerd out of you. Do you hear me? Right out of your blessed soul! But you have to do what we say. Do you understand me?"

Scott nodded.

"I said, *do you understand me?*"

"Y-yes, I understand."

Scott watched someone hand Britt a large wooden paddle. Two lines of holes cored the varnished blade. Britt gripped the end of the paddle, propping the blade over his shoulder.

"Did you see *Revenge of the Nerds*?" Britt asked him. "Did you see that movie? Do you remember how those nerds laughed?"

Scott nodded, not moving his eyes from the paddle. Wayne's father had taken them that summer on the condition they not tell Wayne's mother. Scott remembered the laugh well. The three of them—Scott, Wayne, and Wayne's father—had brayed it most of the way home.

"Well, let's hear it," Britt said.

Scott learned nearer the microphone and emitted two soft honks.

"Now," Britt said, taking the microphone away, "you are going to bend over this here footstool, and every time I strike, you are going to give me one of those laughs. But it has to be loud, son. It has to be passionate. You have to convince me that my healing strikes are indeed driving the nerd out of you. Do you understand me?"

"Yes." Scott tried to keep his nose from sniveling. He turned over and assumed the position, conscious of the laughter still pelting down around him.

Just a few paddles, and you're done, he told himself. *He's probably not even going to do it very har—*

THWACK!

Scott's buttocks exploded with heat, and he bit into his lip to keep from screaming. The taste of warm copper trickled beneath his tongue.

"I didn't hear a laugh, nerd," Britt said from behind.

THWACK!

This time, Scott half honked, half grunted.

"Louder!"

THWACK!

Another half-honk, half-grunt.

"I wanna help you, son. I really do. But you have to want it!"

THWACK!

Scott's next honk emerged as a high grunt, almost a squeal.

"I just don't think we're getting through," Britt said sadly to more laughter, his breathing labored. "But it's all right. I've got a couple of parishioners who have volunteered to help out. Boys?"

Scott heard heavy footsteps land on the tarp and then felt his suspenders being pulled away. Another set of hands fumbled with the front of his pants. Too late, Scott realized what was happening. His pants were yanked to his calves. Cool air needled the skin of his raw buttocks. His underwear was down as well, he realized—also too late. Scott struggled to sit up, to reach back and reclaim them, but his neck and arms were being pinned.

"It's for your own good, son," Britt said above him.

THWACK!

A fresh clap of pain.

"I didn't hear you!" Britt bellowed.

They're going to humiliate you, but don't let them.

Scott turned his head toward the house as his chest began to wrack with strangled sobs.

THWACK!

Stand up for yourself.

Thicker, heavier sobs. And Scott realized in fresh horror that he was still trying to do the honks. Like with his sobbing, he couldn't stop. A swill of tears and snot began dripping from his face.

THWACK!

"H-a-a-wnk!"

Stand up for yourself!

It was no longer Britt striking him, but his mother, her shrieking face looming before his. *Stand up for yourself, Scott!* THWACK! *For God's sake, stand up for yourself!* THWACK! *For God's sake! For God's sake! For God's sake!* THWACK! THWACK! THWACK!

His honking became a series of retching screams, rising in pitch and urgency, occluding all else, even the sharp explosions of pain across his naked buttocks.

27

"Oh, god, do something Blake," Janis whispered. "Make him stop."

She had dropped her eyes the minute Scott was made to bend over the ottoman, sick to her stomach. But she could still hear the THWACKs of the paddle, each one landing in her gut.

"*Blake—!*" she whispered.

"He's stopping," he said quickly. She could hear his relief. "Look, he's stopping."

But when Britt spoke again, he was still using that creepy Southern preacher's voice.

"I just don't think we're getting through," he was saying. "But it's all right. I've got a couple of parishioners who have volunteered to help out. Boys?"

Janis raised her eyes as Bo and Shelton, two beefy jock-preps, descended on Scott and began wrestling with his clothes. And then his pants were down, his rail-thin buttocks, which had already begun to redden, bared to the world.

"It's for your own good, son."

Janis brought a fist to her mouth and clenched her eyelids.

THWACK!

The sound was starker this time, almost wet. And another sound was emerging. Janis couldn't tell if she was hearing it over the raucous shouts and laughter or if it was inside her own head, but it was unmistakable. It was the sound of Scott sobbing—just as he had that time in the woods with the Rottweiler.

Even when Samson growled, she remembered, even when he lunged, Scott had remained calm. For twenty minutes or more, holding the stick out before him, keeping her behind him, stopping occasionally to whisper a *shh*, he had remained calm. His stiff shoulders had felt cool beneath her hands. Only when they'd reached the safety of the fallen tree and climbed up, when Samson had returned to whatever hell-cave had spawned him, did Scott collapse and begin sobbing. The rhythm was exactly the same.

Janis jumped to her feet and began running toward the stage.

"Stop!" she cried.

THWACK!

"Stop, I said!"

THWACK!

And then she was close enough to see his head shivering, the skin on the back of his neck blanching where Shelton's fingers dug in. Janis grabbed the collar of Shelton's shirt and felt it rip when she yanked him backyard. Her assault on Bo, who was holding Scott's arms, was less a kick and more a pair of stomps—right in the side of his ribs. When he recoiled, his face was surprised with pain. Janis's only regret was that she wasn't in cleats.

"What in the hell's wrong with you?" she cried.

Her fury had swelled into a force beyond her. She turned to confront Britt, who had backed away a step, his thrashing robe gone limp. A strenuous sweat glistened along the sides of his face. The paddle was still suspended, poised to strike again, and in the huge silence, Janis could hear Scott's gasping sobs. They all could. Britt looked from Janis down to Scott, seeming to return to himself. He lowered the paddle. She grabbed it away and swung it against the nearest tree. The head of the paddle snapped at its neck and shot off into the bushes.

She turned her fury on the crowd. "Is this your idea of entertainment?" she screamed. "Huh? Beating someone who's defenseless?"

Blake was standing on the verge of the stage, his palms raised to her as though to say, *It's all right, babe. It's over. Let's all just cool down.* But she could see the pale shock on his face. Whether it was from what they had done to Scott or what she was doing to them, Janis couldn't tell.

Her gaze returned to Scott, who had gotten his pants back up and was pawing around for his glasses. His body was still hitching, but the sobs were thinner now, smaller. She glared once more at the crowd, at their shocked and stupid expressions, and knelt to help him. His taped glasses had ended up behind him somehow. She picked them up and offered them to him.

"Here," she whispered.

Scott stood and wiped a sleeve across his nose before accepting his glasses. With his face downcast, he pushed them on. He then began shoving his shirttail into his pants, as though trying to put himself back together. The pens and pencils that had been in his pocket were scattered around his feet. In her periphery, Janis noticed Grant approaching them.

"All right. I think we can all agree that one got a little out of hand." He spoke with the sober concern of a politician. He reached forward, as though deciding whether or not to place a hand on her shoulder.

"And you let it happen." Janis rounded on him, her voice shuddering with anger. "At your house."

She could see in his eyes and faltering hand the implication sinking in. The school took a hard line on hazing. Official notices were posted along the hallways. This was the sort of thing that could get Gamma hit with probation—or worse—not to mention the disciplinary actions against those involved, namely the president and host. Grant ran his fingers through his hair.

"At your house," she repeated.

"Oh, get over yourself," someone called.

Janis recognized the voice—just as she had recognized her handwriting years earlier.

When Janis turned, her former friend was sneering out at her, arms folded, head cocked to the side. She couldn't see the other hydra heads bookending her, couldn't see Alicia or Autumn, just Amy.

Amy, in her Playboy bunny outfit ("It's real rabbit's fur, I swear!"), legs crossed primly to show off her fishnet-clad thighs. Amy, who had slipped that note into her locker three years before, who had treated her and her friends like shit ever since. Amy, who had manipulated her emotions these last months for no other reason than to get into Alpha.

Like a fiery arrow, Janis shot toward her.

Gasps sounded like bottles of cola being popped open. Pledges and members alike cringed from her path. They had already witnessed her attack on Bo and Shelton. So had Amy. The sneer fled her red lips. Her large eyes flew around for someplace to hide. But in the cruelest of ironies, she was trapped between the two friends whom she'd sought safety in these last three years, their chairs pressed together and angled inward.

When Amy tried to stand, Janis shot her arm out. Janis had only made it to the second row of chairs, still a good fifteen feet away, but Amy was thrown backward anyway. One of her black heels snagged in the chair leg. The entire aluminum chair followed her somersault, bunny ears flying from her head. Amy and the chair landed in a clanking heap.

Maybe it was the terror of Amy's scream or the horror at what she herself had done, but Janis pulled up. Relaxed her fists. Forced herself to breathe. To everyone else, it would have looked like Amy had toppled backward in her attempt to scramble away. But Janis knew better. She had felt the pulse leave her hand, just like the night of the Lyon game...

Only stronger.

Alicia and Autumn, who had been cowering back, arms covering their faces, knelt to Amy's sides. With worried backward glances, they helped untangle their friend from her chair. When Amy peered over the upended seat, her hair flopped over half her face. One eye searched around and found Janis. In its naked fright, Janis saw that Amy had felt the pulse, too.

An arm slipped around Janis's waist.

"What's this?" Blake whispered. "What's gotten into you?"

She shrugged from her boyfriend's embrace and waded from the crowd, half of whom were craning their necks around at Amy, the other half still looking warily at her. Scott was no longer on the stage. She spotted the pale glow of his shirt at the dark end of the driveway, nearly to the street.

"Let's go," Blake said with a sigh. "I'll offer him a ride home."

"No, let me go to him. Alone."

"I have a car, Janis. Wouldn't it—?"

"You were supposed to do everything in your power to help him." Vehemence scored Janis's voice. "Wasn't that The Pact?"

Blake stood back in his bulky football costume, his gaze soft and uncertain. She had never become angry at him before, not like this. He started to say something, but she had already left his side. She clacked up the driveway, deaf to his calls, and then broke into a run.

By the time she reached him, Scott was making his way along the parked cars lining the curb, bracing his arm against them for support. His gait was stiff, almost a limp, and broadcast deep bruising.

"Hey." She arrived beside him. "Are you all right?"

Scott jerked and wiped his face. When he glanced over, narrow, puffed-up eyes looked out from a ruddy face. The street light caught a streak of moisture on his left cheek that he'd missed. He replaced his glasses and lurched back into motion.

"Guess I sort of l-l-lost it back there," he said.

He snuffled when he tried to laugh, and Janis thought it was one of the saddest sounds she'd ever heard.

"Yeah, well, that makes two of us."

"I-I'm sorry."

"For what?"

He was trying to keep his face turned from her while he spoke. "I didn't mean to get you in tr-trouble ... I had no business being there. Why don't you go on b-back. I'll b-b-be all right."

She watched his ribs starting to hitch again and could feel how desperately he wanted to be alone.

"Go back? *Pffft*. I'm done with Alpha."

Scott continued to limp forward.

"The only reason I pledged in the first place was because of Margaret. It's not me. It was never me."

Janis began yanking the bows out of her hair and stuffing them into her pockets. She groaned, remembering the freckles Margaret had drawn on her cheeks with a brown makeup pencil. They'd probably smear if she tried to wipe them away. She must have looked ridiculous attacking Bo and Shelton in her frilly dress and pigtails. *Wendy goes ape shit.* She was about to make a joke about it when she realized Scott had slowed down. He was peering over at her with the same searching eyes she remembered from their childhood.

"It was n-n-never me, either."

"Well, at least it only took us three months to figure it out instead of three years."

Scott managed another snuffled laugh. "Yeah."

She touched his arm. "Listen, I know a better way home. If we turn around and go to the back of the neighborhood, we'll end up at that greenway that connects Eighth and Sixteenth Avenues. We can avoid the streets. And when we come out, we'll be across from Oakwood."

Scott stopped walking, his gaze dropping to her hand resting on his forearm. He sniffled, appearing to contemplate her proposal, her touch.

"All right," he said.

Their route took them back past Grant's house. They kept to the opposite side of the street like a pair of exiles. Janis could hear voices down the driveway, thin and excited, the aftermath of a violent storm. She imagined Blake speaking with a concerned frown, hands held out. He could be very diplomatic—too diplomatic, sometimes. It was why he hadn't intervened on Scott's behalf. He would have eventually, Janis knew. But she also knew he was hoping the paddling would stop first.

Safely past the driveway, they resumed walking in the street. With the final parked cars at their back, Janis realized she'd chosen this route, not only for Scott's sake, but also for her own. She didn't want Blake pulling up, trying to exercise the same diplomacy on them, on her. Not tonight.

She felt guilty about this until she heard Scott snuffle again.

The street ended at a wooded cul-de-sac. A final street light stood against the night and the gathering trees. Beyond the curb, Janis could make out the beginning of a path that showed pale where the topsoil had worn down to a layer of limestone. She peeked behind them, glad to see no cars coming. Three or four street lights away, someone was walking a small dog. She turned back to the trees.

"There's just a short stretch of woods before the greenway."

"All right." Scott seemed more in control of himself. His breathing had softened, and his walking was not quite as stilted, as if the pain had lessened or he had learned how to move with it. Janis resisted the urge to take his hand as she might have when they were kids.

They stepped over the curb. Gravel crunched beneath their shoes. The path narrowed as it entered the trees, the tea-like scent of sweet gum leaves rising around them. Janis felt her pupils dilating as she waited for Scott to catch up. Inside the darkness, she found the courage to say what she'd wanted to say two months before, the night she had walked toward his window.

"I went back there, you know. That night."

"Back where?" His white shirt swam up in front of her.

"To the woods, to when we were kids. It was the time we—"

"—crossed the swampy area on the fallen tree," Scott finished for her. "The time we saw the dog."

She stood looking up at him as if someone had just landed on her back, knocking the wind out of her.

"I went there, too," he said.

"Wait, not just remembering being there, but *there* there?"

His glasses nodded. "I know what it sounds like, but..."

"It sounds like exactly what happened to me!" Her laughter was loud with surprise and relief. But then she felt her father's pragmatism creeping over her. "What was I wearing?"

It came out in a jumble: "Red shorts, one of those Florida halter tops with a smiling sun, and green Keds."

She laughed again, unreality spiraling through her. She wanted to tell Scott everything then: about her experiences at night, about her saving tip at the soccer game, about her confrontation with Amy just now, about her belief that she had done more than just remember their childhood that night, but that she had carried them both inside of it somehow.

Instead, she asked him a question. "Why did we stop going into the woods? I don't remember."

Scott shrugged. "Middle school, I guess."

They resumed walking, the moonlit streaks of limestone guiding them along. Janis thought about that. *Middle school.* And she saw that Scott was right. A longer school day followed by blocks of organized activities stacked one right after the other, abutting dusk and dinnertime. No room for the feral tangle of their woods. Even their middle school had been neatly cordoned—not just into seven periods, but into A and B teams, new blocks of friends.

"You were on B team, weren't you?" she asked him. "That's probably why I don't remember seeing you. What did you do after school? What sorts of things were you into?"

He seemed to hesitate. "Oh ... telephone systems, computers, rockets, D&D ... you know, cool stuff." The noise he made when he laughed sounded healthier. "You?"

"Let's see ... softball, soccer, foreign language study. You know, girl stuff."

His laughter followed hers, and before Janis was ready, they were coming to the verge of the greenway. Off to the right, she could hear the car traffic along Sixteenth Avenue, could see the phosphorescence of street lights through the trees. Scott shuffled up beside her.

"I know these aren't the same woods as the ones in Oakwood," Janis said. "But it's like ... I don't know ... like you're beyond the reach of the world when you're in here. Like none of that can touch you."

"Yeah," Scott said quietly.

She felt the strange urge to take his hand again, but now Scott was peering behind them, his breathing gone still. Janis listened, and soon she heard it, too, the tinkling of metal.

"Oh, it's just someone walking their dog. I saw them back on the street." She quickly added, "A small dog—not a Rottweiler."

They left the woods for the greenway and were soon climbing over the guardrail that ran along the south side of Sixteenth Avenue. After a dash across the four lanes (or in Scott's case, a hobble), they were at their neighborhood and beginning the steady ascent up Oakwood's main street. Beneath the glare of street lights, Janis and Scott walked quietly, self-consciously, maybe.

When Janis looked over, Scott appeared better. He had removed his bowtie and suspenders, undone his top button, and rolled up his sleeves. He'd straightened his hair as well. Except for his stiff-legged gait, there was little to indicate the torment he had suffered. And was that a shadow of a smile?

"What is it?" she asked.

"Do you remember the time we were playing down here and saw Mrs. Thornton coming down the hill on her bike?"

"You mean her broomstick? I thought we always ran away when ... wait!" She grabbed Scott's arm. "That wasn't the time we made a dare to see who could stay in the street the longest?"

Scott chuckled. "The ultimate game of chicken."

"I thought I was going to wet my pants."

"No, that was me. You were the one giggling."

As they passed over the spot where their eight-year-old selves had once stood facing the terrible Mrs. Thornton, Janis felt fresh giggles bubbling inside her. "What was that thing she used to say?"

Scott screwed up his face and shook his finger at the air. "The streets are no place to be mucking around!"

"That was it, *mucking around*. Oh, god."

"Then she'd tell us to go home or else she'd—"

"—*phone* our parents," Janis finished through more giggles. When she realized she was leaning against him, she released Scott's arm and looked up at him. "So what happened? Who won the dare?"

"Neither of us." Scott grinned and combed his fingers through his hair. "Mrs. Thornton braked so hard—to stop and lecture us, I think— that her bike wobbled, and she tipped over. We fled into the woods."

"Poor Mrs. Thornton."

When Scott laughed, Janis realized she had been bearing a yoke around her neck all school year because now she felt it splitting and falling away. She was going to have to answer to some people tomorrow—Margaret and Blake not the least among them—but for now, she was glad she'd walked Scott home, glad that it was just the two of them again. She hopped onto the curb and walked along it balance-beam style, like she used to when she was younger. Scott strolled along beside her, hands in his pockets, not limping at all.

Soon, the curb flowed into a driveway, and when Janis turned, she beheld a garage door the color of old teeth. A dark house rose around it. She felt the smile across her face wither. She steered Scott from the house, almost to the other side of the street, where the specter of cockroaches and sheds and hatches and yellow-tinted glasses couldn't reach them.

At the intersection that split Oakwood into its three subdivisions, Janis slowed. "I guess this is us." She cocked her head to the left. "The Meadows." The reluctance in her voice surprised her.

"Hey, um, that house back there," Scott said. "The brown one..."

Janis turned to where the second story of the Leonards' house loomed above the house on the corner, and she suppressed a shiver. *Why did you draw away from it?* she could already hear him asking. *Did something happen?* She looked back at Scott's eyes and studied their concern.

"If I tell you something," she asked, "will you promise not to say anything until I finish? Even if you think it's completely crazy?"

He nodded.

"I need to hear you say it."

"I promise," he said.

But she already sensed that he wouldn't think it was crazy. That he wouldn't think *she* was crazy. Her certainty went back to their childhood and the woods and the way their imaginations had once grown around and inside one another's. That connection was still living.

"Let's keep walking," she said, her heart already doing double-time. "Let's go up to the Grove."

When they had walked a block, she took a deep breath.

"I guess everything started this summer..."

28

Scott watched Janis's hands—hands that, when not holding the thick chains of the swing, shaped the night air in front of her, anxious to convey the truth of what she was sharing. It was a need Scott understood. There was more than one moment when he wanted to take her hands and tell them to be still, that of course he believed her. But he didn't move or speak. For the hour or more that she talked, an hour which had carried them into the Grove and onto the swing set where they eddied back and forth, he watched her hands, mesmerized.

There was her closeness, sure. There was their cocoon of darkness, where the street lights and distant houselights didn't quite reach. There was the cascade of events that had started with the gut-rending humiliation of being singled out and beaten raw in front of the others—in front of her—but that had led somehow to their walking home together. A magical, cleansing walk that seemed to have spanned years.

But what most mesmerized Scott now, watching her hands, were the very things their motion conveyed: out-of-body experiences, telekinetic powers, ghost-like images that sounded to Scott like precognition, and the whole business with Mr. Leonard and his shed. *Whoa.*

Maybe because he had spent so much time these last years taking the world of Jean Grey and Scott Summers and projecting them over Janis and himself—what he wanted them to be—little of what she told him jarred with his sense of the possible, the real.

If anything, her account deepened it.

Janis's hands stopped moving. Scott looked over to find her eyes, large and dark, peering at him through the night. Her hair was still braided into pigtails, her cheeks still dotted with fake freckles, but a tension drew on the contours of her face, making her appear much older than her fourteen years.

"So are we talking straightjackets and padded cells here or what?" she asked.

Only then did Scott realize she'd been waiting for him to respond. "No, no!" He twisted his swing to face her, his too-big shoes digging into the mulch. "That's not crazy at all."

"At all?" She smirked and lowered her eyes. "Now I know you're just humoring me."

Scott sensed then that she had tried to tell others—probably even Blake—and been looked at askance. Disbelief was what she had come to expect. "What I mean is *I* don't think it's crazy. Really. I believe you."

She raised her eyes but kept her head down, like she was waiting for the punch line.

He got up from the swing and gestured for her to follow. "C'mon."
"Huh?"

He walked several paces toward the teeter-totters, then turned around to face the four swings. Janis followed him. "That one, on the far right." Scott pointed. "Do you think, if you tried, you could make it move?"

Janis looked from the swing up to Scott and back.

"I don't know," she said. "The only times I've done it, I haven't really tried. Not consciously. Like tonight. I wasn't planning to knock Amy out of her chair. It just sort of ... happened."

"Try now," he encouraged her.

Janis remained staring at the swing. Then she pushed her frilly sleeve to her elbow and raised her arm. Scott watched the way her brow tensed down over her eyes, making them deeper and darker, more beautiful. He stood back to give her space. And then something in the air made his skin prickle, as if the molecules around them were being roused from their sleepy Brownian motion. The chain creaked. The black rubber seat began to rock and twist, back and forth.

Scott laughed. "It's working!"

Janis dropped her arm. "No, that's just the wind."

When Scott looked again, he saw that the other three swings were replicating the creaking motion of the first. The huge oak tree in the corner of the field rustled its dark leaves.

"But I felt something," Scott said.

"Yeah, me too. The wind." She shrugged in a way that said, *Sorry I couldn't prove it to you.*

Scott came over and placed one hand on the curve of her shoulder and the other on the soft underside of her wrist and raised her arm toward the swing again. It was the kind of contact that, as recently as that summer, would have sent him into conniptions even to *think* about. Now a deep calm moved through him, like the tide. It came from the night, from the spell of unreality that secluded them. He stooped until his sight line ran along her arm.

"I find it helps to picture the object as clearly as I can," he said. "Not just how it looks, but how it feel—"

Janis drew her arm away. "Wait, helps you do what?"

"I, um..." Scott rubbed the back of his neck.

For so long, he had wanted to tell someone, someone who would believe him or, at the very least, not call him an ass-wad. And here she was: Janis Graystone, the love of his young life. And therein lay the problem. How could he start popping off about modems, telecommunication lines, and ARPANet without coming off as a total stooge? The kind of person he had been working so hard to grow beyond? In his mind's eye, he saw his middle school photo, poster sized and unfurled. He remembered the raucous jeers. *Ner-errrd!*

Janis crossed her arms and arched an eyebrow. "Scott?"

His own arms sagged to his sides. He never could hold out long against that look. "Yeah, I guess I have something to tell you, too."

Janis took his elbow and led him back to the swing set. "Sit," she ordered, pointing. "Speak."

Scott did the first, removing his glasses. Then he told her everything. From his discovery that he could navigate the telecommunication system to his awareness of the tap—or whatever it was—and his attempt to short it. He picked away the masking tape from the bridge of his glasses as he spoke. It gave his hands something to do and made him all but blind to how Janis was receiving his words. The words came easily, though. In his own telling, he tapped into a resonance that existed between their experiences: projecting their consciousnesses, influencing remote objects, or in his case, remote data streams, being monitored, feeling alone in the experience ... until now.

When he was done, Scott wiped his lap of stray bits of tape and pushed his glasses back on. He had enough time to flinch before her fist met his shoulder. The punch was solid but not hard.

"That's for holding out on me, mister."

She looked at him another moment, head tilting to one side as if seeing him in a new light. Then she walked her swing backward and kicked out her legs. She swept past Scott and jackknifed her knees. The chains clicked and creaked as her pendulum reversed. Not knowing what else to do, Scott joined her. He modulated the kicks and pulls of his own legs until he and Janis were side by side, taking off and swooping back, the sweet scent of the playground's mulch streaming between them. Scott hardly noticed the biting soreness across his bottom.

When Janis spoke, her voice sounded close. "So where do you think they come from?"

"Our powers? Well, we haven't been subjected to high doses of any of the standard radiations—gamma, cosmic, that sort of thing—so we can eliminate the radiation cause. And neither of us are gods or demigods, so far as we know. Or from other planets. Or bearers of magical jewelry."

Scott cringed. *Like she's going to get any of those comic book references, you monumental dumbass.*

"Could be something in our DNA," he said carefully. "A genetic anomaly, maybe?"

Their legs flexed and extended in time.

"You know...," Janis said. "There *is* this thing my sister does. I used to think it was part of her my-way-or-the-highway resolve. But it's more than that. She goes inside your head somehow."

"Like mind control?"

"Sort of. But it's more like she weakens your thoughts, makes it so you can't impose your will. Not against hers, anyway. I don't even think she knows she does it. So maybe there's something to your DNA theory. Do your parents have any ... I don't know, special abilities?"

Scott snorted at the idea. "Other than my dad eating an entire pizza in his sleep once?" He shook his head. "How about yours?"

"No. Not that I know of. Too bad you don't have a brother or sister to test the idea."

Scott watched the tops of his shoes appear and disappear, the woods down the hill rising into view, a sweep of black, and then falling away. Inside those same woods was the clearing Scott had fled to the summer before, Jesse, Creed, and Tyler in pursuit. The clearing where he'd heard the radius and ulna bones of his right arm snap above Creed's giddy laughter.

Scott slammed down his heels, plowing two furrows into the mulch and nearly toppling forward.

"What is it?" Janis stopped kicking and let the ground catch her feet, rocking to a more elegant stop beside him.

"Creed and Tyler. You know, the Bast brothers?"

Janis's lips drew into a scowl. "Creed was the only boy to make me cry. Sucker punched me in the stomach when I was nine."

"Yeah well, there's something they do, too." Scott's words were already tumbling over one another. "Creed possesses some sort of super speed. One second, he's twenty yards away, and the next he's at your side." *Holding a blade to your throat.* "And Tyler, his power has something to do with electricity. I'm not sure how it works, exactly, but he shocked the bejeezus out of me at the tennis courts back in September. I think he ran a current through the fence when I was trying to climb over. Jesse got a dose, too. Burned like heck the next morning."

"What were you doing in the tennis courts with those creeps?"

Heat bloomed over Scott's ears. "I, ah..." *THAT'S OUR TEAM! GO, TEAM, GO!* "It's sort of a long story."

"So there's Creed and Tyler. Do you know of anyone else?"

Scott thought for a moment, then shook his head. "Jesse Hoag, but he's always been a freak of nature. Used to rip textbooks in half in elementary school, do you remember that? He got hold of one of mine once, one of those thick readers."

"Strange," Janis said quietly. She toed the ground with one of her blue flats. "You, me, my sister, the Bast brothers, Jesse. And even if we have to put an asterisk by Jesse's name, it doesn't change the fact that we all live in the same neighborhood." Her eyes narrowed. "Think about it, Scott. Of all the people we've known in our lives, our entire lives, the only ones with unique abil—all right, *powers*—live right here, in Oakwood."

He kept staring at her. How hadn't he seen that? His mind picked up the slack.

"So now it becomes a chicken-or-the-egg question," he said. "Which came first: our powers or moving to Oakwood?"

But Janis was peering past him now. When Scott turned, he saw it too: a pale halo against the giant oak tree, starting at the top half and swelling down and around it, becoming brighter. The drone of an approaching engine followed.

Janis stepped from the swing, and Scott stood beside her, his heart pounding the backside of his sternum. The car was coming up the hill quickly. High beams shot through chinks in the tree's leaf cover, penetrating their space. Scott instinctively moved in front of her, just as he had done that day in the woods when the large dog threatened them.

As the car entered the Grove, Scott sized up the headlights. He exhaled. "It's all right." He recognized the car's sound too. "It's your sister."

He followed Janis through the tall grass and threads of night mist to the curb, the car's golden light growing over them.

"Offer you a ride?" she asked.

Scott shook his head. "No, thanks. I'll just walk home."

"Hey, um, everything you told me ... I believe you."

Scott looked at her face, in full illumination now, and remembered the morning at the end of the summer when a square of sunlight had caught her perfection. He remembered how much it had hurt to look at from his sequestered distance. Now he stepped closer to her.

"I believe you, too."

The Prelude swerved up to the curb. The passenger side door flew open. Margaret leaned across the seat, glaring out at them. "Janis Graystone! You get into this car right this instant! Do you know it's almost midnight?"

Janis gave Scott a tired smile. "See you tomorrow?"

"Right. See you tomorrow."

"Sure you're okay?"

"Yeah." He found it hard to meet her eyes now. "And thanks for ... for what you did earlier."

Janis climbed into the car and pulled the door closed. The last thing Scott heard before the car wheeled around, its tires cutting sharply against the asphalt, was Margaret's harping voice: "You *assaulted* two of their members and tried to attack one of your own sisters?"

Scott pushed his hands into his pockets and set out for home. He could feel the late hour in his spent body and see it in the dark windows he ambled past. The entire street was sleeping save for a lone figure farther down the hill, walking his dog. Above the soft clopping of his own shoes, Scott could make out the distant tinkling of the dog's tags. But Scott wasn't thinking about that right now. He was thinking about the fading hum of Margaret's car, only minutes old, and how for the first time it hadn't sounded like a missed opportunity.

Not tonight.

29

Scott wasn't surprised when Grant Sidwell appeared in his first period biology class the next morning and asked the teacher permission to speak with him. He'd steeled himself for the eventuality. But when he found Britt waiting in the hallway as well, his gut quivered like gelatin. Only Britt looked nothing like the zealous priest from the night before. His stocky shoulders were rounded, his eyes downcast. In his lemon-yellow Polo, he looked like just another high school student.

"Listen, Scott," Grant said. "We, ah, we've come to apologize for last night. Things definitely got out of control."

"Yeah, man. Sorry." Britt barely raised his head.

"And we want to make it up to you." Grant placed his hand where Scott's shoulder met his neck and squeezed him companionably. Scott held himself rigid. "Forget last night happened, all right? You're in, man. As of right now, you're a Gamma brother. We're even going to waive your dues this year."

"Yeah," Britt put in.

Keep your mouth shut, and we'll take care of you. That's what Grant was really telling him. Sometime following the party, probably while he and Janis were talking up in the Grove, it was the solution Grant and the other officers had come up with.

"Thanks," Scott said, "but I'm not really interested in Gamma anymore."

"Did you hear me? You're in. You're a brother." He squeezed his shoulder again until it almost hurt.

"I heard you."

He could see the growing uncertainty in Grant's expression. And for the first time, Grant seemed to notice that, though Scott was wearing slacks and a nice shirt, he wasn't in Standards. No Gamma letter hung from his neck either. Grant's hand dropped away. "Last night was an aberration, Scott. It's not what Gamma's about and will never happen again. I promise."

Grant's eyes seemed to be pressing his now, but Scott's gaze didn't waver. He remembered that first meeting, in August, when the officers had all looked like magazine models. And that's just what they were, Scott understood, two-dimensional models. No substance. It was Grant who finally averted his eyes. His gaze seemed to search around a moment before seizing on Britt.

"Britt here's been put on probation," he said.

Britt's head whiplashed up, his eyes huge. A new development, Scott saw. Not something they'd discussed the night before.

"Now wait just a goddamned minute," Britt muttered.

Grant shook his head as if to say *not now*, then turned back to Scott. "We're willing to make this right, Scott. But we need you to tell us that you're willing to forget last night ever happened."

Hadn't Britt said something similar in the midst of swinging his paddle?

I wanna help you, son. I really do. But you have to want it!

THWACK!

"I'm trying to spare us both a lot of embarrassment here." Grant pushed out a chuckle.

Britt had paced a small circle and now spoke through gritted teeth. "Can we talk for a second?"

Grant shook his head again. He was in full self-preservation mode.

"The deal is this," Scott began.

Both of them stood watching him. Though his pulse raced, it was all Scott could do to keep from smiling. He counted slowly to five in his head.

"An Alpha pledge roughed up a couple of your members last night. You know who I'm talking about, right?" He waited for them to nod. "All right, then the deal is this. I'm willing to forget last night, but you have to forget last night, too. If I hear about Janis getting into any kind of trouble over what happened, I'm going straight to Principal Munshin. He'll hear everything. He'll understand there was a reason for what she did. You follow?"

Both of them nodded again.

"I didn't hear you."

"Yes," they said.

"How about we seal the deal with…" Scott studied the ceiling in pretend thought, then snapped his fingers. "I know, did you happen to see *Revenge of the Nerds?* Do you remember how those nerds laughed?"

Grant and Britt looked at one another.

"Of course you did. Let's hear it. Four of them."

Grant grimaced. "I really don't think that's necessary."

Scott started to turn away.

Britt's first honk-laugh ripped down the hallway. He elbowed Grant in the side and shot him a look that said, *C'mon, man, this is getting off easy—no probation for me, you're clear.* Grant sighed and joined Britt in the final three honk-laughs, though with far less enthusiasm.

"Not bad, gentlemen." Scott clapped Grant's shoulder. "For half a second there, you were almost half interesting." He watched their eyes trying to compute that. "Well, I've got to get back to class."

"Listen, if you ever want...," Grant started to say, but Scott didn't hear the rest. The door had already swung closed behind him.

The Steak 'n Shake past the university was about as far as you could go for lunch and still make it back in time for fifth period, depending on the wait. Janis peeked over at Blake, who was skipping his final lunch with the other Gamma pledges. Until that day, his pledge card had been perfect. She wondered if he'd brought her out here to break up. She wondered, too, why the idea only made her feel vaguely numb.

"So, is everything all right?" Blake asked her after they had been seated at a small corner table and ordered.

"Yeah. Sorry about last night." It came out sounding hollower than she meant it to.

"I've never seen you like that. You were really ... upset."

Upset? Her brain felt like it had been drenched in gasoline and set ablaze. But that part of the night seemed distant now, as if she had only stood behind that person, observing.

Janis watched their waitress twist back toward them, past tables of college students, brown-suited businessmen, and a group of telephone technicians with hard hats in their laps. One of the technicians seemed out of place, though Janis couldn't say quite how. When he caught her eyeing him, a polite smile appeared, more forced than reflexive, it seemed. The waitress delivered their fountain drinks, two vanilla Cokes. Janis looked up to find Blake's hand over his chin and his brows drawn together as though he was trying to decide who she was.

"Look," Janis said, forgetting about the technician, "Scott and I were good friends growing up. I was taller than him back then, so I used to pretend I was his older sister. I looked out for him." She shrugged as she traced a line through the condensation on her glass. "I guess the instinct's still there."

Blake took a swallow of his drink and set his glass down. When he looked out the window, the light paled his face. He crunched a piece of ice between his teeth, then let out a long breath.

Here it comes, Janis thought. *The "maybe we should be friends" speech.*

"You were right, you know," he said.

"About what?"

"The Pact. I should have done something before it went that far."

Janis's gaze fell back to her glass. "My dad says hindsight's always twenty-twenty."

"Is Scott okay?"

"I think so."

"I tried calling both of you last night. Him to see if there was anything I could do. And you to make sure you'd gotten home all right."

"Yeah, my dad gave me the message. Thanks."

She could see in his eyes that he was waiting for her to explain *why* she hadn't been home when he called. But what could she say? *Oh, a funny thing happened, babe. It turns out Scott and I took a trip to the past together a couple of months ago. That's right! Only neither of us knew that the other had had the same experience until last night. Ha, ha! So one thing leads to another, and next thing you know, I'm telling him all about my dreams of mushroom clouds and out-of-body experiences, not to mention this newfound power to tip away shots on goal and blast ex-friends who turn bitch. And Scott, he tells me about his power to fly inside telephone lines and blow up federal taps. So yeah, we decided to stay up late talking instead of going home.*

Janis couldn't even tell him an approximation of the truth, and a part of her mind clenched with anger—anger toward him for being so damned normal and anger at herself for holding his normalcy against him. She started to reach past the condiment basket for his hand, but the waitress returned, setting two steaming plates of steak burgers and fries between them.

"Well, it's too bad about the grounding." Blake uncapped the ketchup bottle and coaxed a fat dollop onto his burger. "My parents were really looking forward to meeting you."

She signaled for him to add some ketchup to her plate, beside the fries. "I was looking forward to meeting them, too."

The truth was, dinner in polite company with Blake's parents felt like the very last thing she wanted. Maybe the two-week grounding her father had handed down for her curfew violation last night wasn't such a bad thing after all. It would give her a reprieve, time to think.

Blake tucked a napkin over the knot of his tie, then paused, his burger poised in front of his mouth. "No Standards today?"

Janis looked down at her purple sweatshirt. She shook her head. "Not for me."

The realization crept over Blake's face. He set his burger down and wiped his hands. "But you're just one day from completing your pledge period."

"Margaret and I already had that conversation this morning, thanks."

"But have you thought it through?"

She stared at him.

"What I mean is..." He held up his hands in a gesture of diplomacy. "There are going to be service days, socials, weekend trips—I was looking forward to us doing those things together."

She kept staring at him, the french fry she held between her finger and thumb growing cold. "Do you honestly think I can just go traipsing back into that club all *fa-la-la* after what happened last night? You were there, Blake. You saw what they did to Scott. Jesus."

"Look, I talked to Grant afterwards. He and Britt are going to apologize to Scott and grant him full membership. They're even going to waive his fees."

Janis gave a sharp laugh. "Yeah, to save their own asses."

The muscles around Blake's jaw tensed. "At least they're willing to own up to their mistake."

"Big of them."

"What about you, Janis? Have you given any thought to the girl who injured herself trying to get away from you?"

The fry caught halfway down Janis's throat. She reached for her Coke. "Injured?" she managed after a moment. "Amy was injured?" The fight fell out of her like the checkers from a game of Connect Four.

"Sprained her ankle when she took that spill."

Janis closed her eyes and saw herself storming into the audience, her fury soaring inside her. She watched Amy's eyes fly wide as the pulse collided into her; heard her scream, a sound shrill with terror, with pain. And Janis could *feel* the pain. Because in the moment the pulse had hit her, they were connected, she and Amy. It hadn't lasted long, less than a second, but in that instant, Janis could feel her own ankle wrenching, the tissue tearing like a nylon stocking.

Janis pushed her plate aside and held the sides of her head.

"Hey, there's still time to make it right," Blake said gently.

"How?"

He took her hand. "I'm not supposed to know this, but early tomorrow morning the older Gamma brothers and Alpha sisters are going to surprise us at home and take us to breakfast to celebrate our first day as full members. Maybe you can use the opportunity to apologize to her." The thumb that stroked the back of her hand felt sensible and reassuring. "You should think about it, anyway."

Janis's gaze wandered over to the table of technicians, empty now. "I don't know," she said, but her head had already begun to nod.

Scott bit into his pizza slice, a paper plate poised under his chin to catch the dripping cheese. A cracked-open can of grape soda fizzed softly on the knob to his right. Nestled in the roots of a giant oak tree, he was in the same spot he'd eaten the first day of school. Indeed, he was eating the same lunch. But Scott didn't feel the same.

He peered around at the pair of food trucks parked at the curb, at the students spread over the leaf-covered lawn, most of them in jackets now, a cool wind tossing their hair. Scott's own jacket was padding the ground beneath his bruised bottom, but he didn't feel alone like he had on that first day of school. And better still, he didn't feel like he had to hide anymore. His worst fears had come to pass, and strangely, he felt freed from them.

Now tails, now heads.

Scott took a swig of the grape soda. That's what Grant didn't understand. It had never been about Gamma. The club had only ever been an access way to something else. To some*one* else.

For the untoldth time, Scott relived his and Janis's journey last night, through the band of woods, up Oakwood's main street, the past three years dissolving into a void, then and now sliding together. And where then and now met stood the same swing set on which he and Janis used to whisk past one another as kids, over the same sweet-smelling mulch. But their time on the swings last night had reached beyond the blithe doings of kids.

Far beyond.

"There's a wood shed in Mr. Leonard's backyard," Janis had told him. "I went inside twice, in my out-of-body state. Passed right through the wall. The first time I found a hatch hidden beneath the pile of kindling. It was surrounded by some kind of energy field that I couldn't push through. And then Mr. Leonard opened the shed door, and I flew, screaming, back to my body. Do you remember when I ran out of the classroom that first day of school? Well, that was me remembering. The next time I went into the shed, the lock had been changed, the floor covered with plywood. But I was able to feel a keypad beside the hatch. And that's when I knew for certain he had something hidden down there."

The details of her account remained with Scott. He wiped his hands and removed a letter from the small pocket of his backpack. It was a note, really, a few handwritten lines that had taken him all of third period to compose. After rereading the note, he folded it back up, more or less satisfied.

I'll give it to her seventh period.

The casualness of the thought was another way Scott felt different. It wasn't like those hand-wringing moments past when he used to tell himself he was going to approach her—*today is the day*, the chant went—and then shied away. Last night had changed that, too.

Which reminded him...

In his backpack, he swapped the note for a thick envelope, pushing it into his shirt pocket.

There was something else he needed to do that day.

He stood and shook the sand from his jacket and slung his pack over one shoulder. After depositing his trash, he veered toward Titan Terrace, toward the bend near the repaired tennis courts, where Jesse's black Chevelle leaned against the curb, Creed and Tyler standing beside it.

30

Janis reached her locker at the same time the bell rang overhead to start fifth period. With pale fingers, she began twisting out the combination on her Master Lock. After their perfunctory kiss in the parking lot, Blake had sprinted to make his next class, but Janis had drifted through the thinning students toward her locker. Being late didn't matter. Nothing seemed to matter—only what she had done.

I injured Amy.

The thought repeated itself like a self-flagellation. She could tell herself that Amy had asked for it, had deserved it. And maybe she had. But in the pulse, Janis hadn't experienced only their old connection; she had glimpsed something else, pressed deep down into the shadows of her former friend. A secret whose contours Janis couldn't quite make out. And underneath it ... a plea for help?

Janis yanked the lock free and hooked it over her finger. When she opened the metal door on her neat line of books and folders, something fluttered to the ground, a folded slip of paper. She knelt, her books pressed to her chest, and retrieved it. She looked up and down the empty hallway, then shook the note open. A cold sense of déjà vu seized her.

I was wrong. You're not a lesbian.
You're a freak.

This note had no signature, either. Janis let it fall from her fingers.

Creed, in his John Lennon shades, spotted Scott first and jerked from the driver's side window. His younger brother turned as well. A cigarette dangled from the corner of Tyler's mouth, and he squinted out at Scott through the smoke. Creed nudged him toward the sidewalk so the way was blocked.

But Scott's limping stride didn't falter, even as he glimpsed the narrow blades extending from the thumb and first finger of Creed's glove. Scott got as close as he dared, about two parked cars away, and stopped. Traffic hummed along Titan Terrace. Students streamed around him. He'd be safe as long as he didn't go any closer. He shifted his gaze to the enormous elbow sitting on the car's windowsill.

"Did you come to piss yourself again?" Creed asked.

"I came to talk to Jesse," Scott called back.

"Come and talk, then."

Scott shook his head. "Just Jesse."

Creed glared at Scott another moment and then palmed his bowler hat as he leaned toward the window. He said something, waited, said something else, then stood from the window.

"Jesse says the time for talking is over, shit face."

"I have something for him."

"What?" Suspicion narrowed Creed's voice.

"Something he's going to want."

Creed kept staring at Scott, then leaned toward the window again. Tyler watched from the sidewalk, not saying anything. He took a drag on his cigarette and blew an indifferent stream of smoke.

"Bring it over," Creed said when he stood.

"Not until you and your brother leave."

"Who do you think you're talking to?" Creed spiked his smoking butt into the gutter and began stalking toward Scott.

The elbow over the windowsill lurched, and a hand appeared. With two sausage-sized fingers, it waved Creed off. Creed looked from the hand to Scott and snarled. Then he backed away, jerking his head for his brother to follow.

Scott waited until they were up in the faculty parking lot before approaching. He watched the Chevelle's open window, his feet tracing a narrow path along the far edge of the sidewalk. Very soon, the elbow in Scott's view joined a giant shoulder and the shoulder a squat head that bulged from the collar of a black leather jacket. Scott stooped and looked into a pair of impassive gray eyes.

"I wanted to give you this." Scott pulled the envelope from his pocket.

"What is it?"

"There's more than three hundred dollars inside. I figured it would cover those charges on your phone bill from last year. Yours and Creed's. I didn't mean for your father to ... to do what he did."

Jesse's eyes didn't move from Scott's.

"What about last month?" Jesse asked.

"Last month?"

"We lost our phone service. Stayed out all night. Creed's, too. Happened on a Sunday."

"Look, I haven't done anything to your phones this year. I'm just trying to make this right. I want to get past this." He held out the envelope with the bills. It was the lunch money he'd been able to save over the last three months, plus some. His father had exchanged it all for tens and twenties.

Scott gave the envelope a shake. "Here."

Jesse's eyes remained on his, and Scott could see them assessing whether or not he was telling the truth. The gray eyes shifted to the envelope. And just as Scott was remembering how fast Jesse could move, Jesse's fist swallowed his wrist. He pinched the envelope away with his other hand.

"This doesn't square us," Jesse said.

Scott felt his bones mashing together. He twisted around and stifled a cry.

"You're still gonna get your arm broke," Jesse said flatly. "That was the deal. But here's what I'm gonna do." He held up the envelope of money. "Because of this, we're back to one arm. And 'cause I'm feeling especially generous, I'm gonna let you pick the time and place."

"Look, can't we just—"

Jesse's grip tightened.

"All right! All right!" Scott yelled. He tried to think, but the pain felt like the stab and twist of a dull knife. "Where it happened the first time—do you remember? We were in the Grove, I tried to run, and Creed caught me down in the woods, in that clearing. Remember?"

"All right. When?"

"After the holidays."

Jesse cinched his grip. "More specific."

"Ow! New Year's Eve! Midnight!" It was the first thing that flew into his mind. He knew his parents would be out that night. They went to Larry Habscomb's party every year. It was one of the few things they still did together.

Jesse's hand popped open, and Scott stumbled backward, clutching his wrist to his chest.

"You don't show up," Jesse warned, "and it's gonna be both arms when we catch you. And a leg. Now get the hell outta here."

Scott started to raise a finger. Something Jesse had said was just registering—

"Get outta here, I said."

When Scott glimpsed Creed and Tyler sauntering back, he nodded, deciding it wiser to heed Jesse's words. Still cradling his wrist, he retreated the way he had come, opening and closing his fingers. The pain faded to a throb. He glanced around at the Chevelle. Creed and Tyler were back beside Jesse's elbow, a thin shelf of smoke growing around them again. It wasn't the deal Scott had wanted, no, but he had just bought himself an arm and another month.

For now, that was going to have to be good enough.

Janis passed the typing teacher's desk, feeling no relief at its emptiness, and took her seat. Star was stooped over a crinkled sheet of newspaper. "More of the goddamned same," she grumbled, looking over. "Cut taxes for the rich, slash funding for the poor—that's food stamps, low-income housing, Medicaid..."

It was a familiar rant: the evils of "Reaganomics." Janis wasn't in the mood.

"That's not 'trickle-down,'" Star went on. "That's *pissing down* or, more accurately, pissing *on*. And don't get me started on the military budget. Do you know what he and his cronies are pushing for? Another trillion dollars over the next four years. A *trillion* dollars. That's a one with twelve zeros. Do you know how many people that would feed and educate?"

"Maybe there's a reason for that," Janis muttered, remembering what her father had said.

"Oh, and what would that be?"

Janis shook her head.

Star laughed. "Let me guess. The United States is vulnerable suddenly?" The derision in her voice rankled like hot needles.

"How would *you* know one way or the other?" Janis asked.

"Because anyone willing to exercise an ounce of their brain understands how these things work. There's only so much money in the budget, right? And everyone's fighting for their slice of the pie. So you have Defense running to the president and congress like a gaggle of Chicken Littles, screaming, 'The Russians are getting ahead! The Russians are getting ahead!'"

Janis pulled out her typing primer and set it on the metal stand beside the typewriter, away from Star.

"Meanwhile, the newspapers are printing 'leaked' intelligence saying the same thing, whipping the public's paranoia into full-fledged panic. And who's doing the leaking, you ask? Well, ask yourself another question: Who has the most to gain? It just so happens that when your business is defense, your greatest asset is..." She made her voice deep. "...*fear*."

Janis remembered the look on her father's face in the parking lot.

She stopped flipping through the primer and turned toward Star. "So you're saying the Russians *haven't* pulled ahead?"

Am I looking to Star for hope? Janis thought in disbelief. She studied her neighbor's spiked hair, ghoulish makeup job, and crumpled flannel shirt she'd worn more days than Janis could count. *Star?*

"I wouldn't bet on it."

Maybe it was the defiance in her posture or how Star's black lips scowled around the words, but Janis felt a sudden urge to hug her, especially after the ominous news that week of Soviet troop movements in eastern Europe and renewed threats to blockade West Berlin. If what Star said was true, then the United States and the Soviet Union were still on par militarily, their "peace" in place. Neither one could risk an attack on the other. MAD still ruled. Which meant the nuclear explosions in her dreams were just that—nuclear explosions in her dreams.

But instead of throwing her arms around Star, Janis leaned nearer and lowered her voice. "Hey, um, you mentioned something the first day of school about having a sister. Whatever happened to her?"

Star's scowl faded into an expression as flat as stone.

"Do you really want to know?" Her tone mirrored her face.

"Yes."

Wordlessly, Star began unbuttoning her green-checked flannel shirt. Janis looked around, alarmed, but Star stopped three quarters of the way down. She drew the two flaps of flannel apart, like theater curtains, to reveal a black T-shirt. Faded silk screening called for NUCLEAR FREEZE NOW! in yellow letters with a crossed-out missile underneath. The shirt had been stitched back together, Janis noticed, a long, wending scar. Star inserted a black fingernail into a small hole in the fabric, between her pointed breasts.

"That happened to her," Star said, "a bullet during an anti–nuclear weapons rally. There's a bigger hole in the back of the shirt, where the bullet exited." Star removed her finger and began buttoning her flannel shirt back up. "Blew her chest cavity to soup. She died in the emergency room that night."

"Oh my god." Janis's hand went to her mouth. "Who did it?"

"Someone who didn't like what she was shouting into her bullhorn, apparently."

"Were they caught?"

Star shook her head.

Janis didn't look over when the door banged shut and the roar of voices quieted to murmurs. Her gaze remained locked on Star, who looked down, a fresh scowl struggling to keep the film of moisture in her eyes from spilling.

"I apologize for being late," droned a voice from far away. "Your teacher, Mrs. Diaz, had to check out at lunch ... stomach virus ... I'll be filling in for the rest of the day ... open your primers to page 210 and..."

"I'm so sorry," Janis whispered. "If you ever want to talk about it, you can ... you know, talk to me."

As typewriters banged to life around them, Star moved her head in what might have been a nod. Then, having won her battle with her tears, she set her face in stone once more and opened her primer to a random page.

When Janis glanced toward the front of the classroom, the muscles around her eyes stiffened to ice. At the teacher's desk sat Mr. Leonard. His own eyes, which had been watching her, jerked away. He cleared his throat into his fist. Then he opened a newspaper and raised it in front of his yellow-tinted glasses until only the top of his pale brow showed, shiny with sweat.

He stayed like that the rest of the period as typewriters went off like gunfire around them.

31

Instead of going to her next class—sixth period Spanish—Janis slipped into the downstairs bathroom on C-wing, sealed herself in one of the damp stalls, drew the latch, and perched atop the tank, feet on the toilet lid. If she'd had a cigarette, she might have lit it and taken a drag, like Pony Boy from *The Outsiders*. That would have been another first for her, after skipping class.

The final bell rang outside.

Janis propped her head in her hands, her hair falling around her face like a tomato-colored curtain. "What's happening to me?" she whispered. The curtain shook back and forth. Just the night before, it felt as though her life was beginning to make sense again, to find grounding in a new normal. Thanks to Scott. But in the space of, what, twelve, fourteen hours, the stakes were all popping out. Her mind sped back through her argument with Blake, the revelation that she'd injured Amy, the note in her locker, the ghastly appearance of Mr. Leonard.

The shock of the last continued to tremor through her like the aftereffects of a Pacific quake. For a moment, she had been back in the roach-infested shed, his face staring down at her...

Janis stopped and inhaled the sharp odor of bleach.

And what about Star's story? *There's a bigger hole in the back of the shirt, where the bullet exited.* Janis's heart ached ... for Star, for Star's sister. She wished she had the power to go back, to warn them. But her powers seemed to come and go at their own choosing. And besides, she didn't possess the ability to influence past events, only to observe them.

What about future events?

Her thoughts zoomed in on her own sister. And then Mr. Leonard.

He'd followed Margaret to the beach that day. He watched their house at night. He safeguarded a hidden room beneath his shed, a room that would throw the dark curtain back on who he was. Janis knew these things, even if mostly in her gut. But hadn't Mrs. Fern called the out-of-body realm a source of intuition—a *tremendous* source of intuition? Yet what had she done with that intuition? Given Margaret a single meek warning three months ago?

Blew her chest cavity to soup.

Janis's hair shook above the toilet. It wasn't enough.

She hopped down, opened the stall door, and heaped cold tap water against her face. Then she paced the ten feet of bathroom for the next forty minutes—forty interminable minutes—until the next bell sprang her.

The three-headed hydra stood at the back of the English classroom, Amy balancing on a pair of chrome crutches, her right ankle cocooned in Ace bandaging. When her eyes met Janis's in the doorway, they swelled with fear and fresh hatred. She clanked backward, nearly losing her balance. Alicia and Autumn moved in front of her like a pair of bodyguards, their faces twisting and wringing until Janis thought their pores would start leaking makeup.

So much for trying to apologize.

She put her books beneath her seat and raised her eyes to Scott's desk. Her heart suffered a twinge of disappointment to find it empty. *Probably stayed home. And who can blame him after last night?* She pushed out a sigh. She'd wanted to talk to him so badly.

But just as the final bell sounded and Mrs. Fern stood to lecture, Scott scrambled through the door. He sat, legs splayed so his knees wouldn't knock the underside of his desk, and ran a hand through his hair. When he glanced over, his face startled before quirking into a crooked smile. For the first time that day, a smile touched Janis's lips as well.

I don't think it's crazy, she heard him saying. *Really. I believe you.*

After class, Scott walked up, hesitantly it seemed, and placed something on her desk.

Janis looked from the folded piece of paper to his face. "What's this?" she asked.

"Only ... only if you want to."

He stood a moment, appearing to mull the note over, then he tapped his fingers against her desk and walked from the classroom. Janis almost called after him but looked down and picked up the note instead. Nervous excitement fluttered through her as she opened it.

She read it a second time, nodded to herself, and tucked the note inside one of her folders.

32

That evening
7:32 p.m.

Scott stood in front of his closet mirror, freshly showered, in a towel-skirt. Pushing out his chest, he angled himself to one side, then the other. Not Scott Summers proportions yet, no. But lines and taut muscles appeared where there hadn't been any only a few months before. He wasn't imagining it anymore.

Satisfied, Scott pulled open the folding door on his closet. What to wear?

Jeans for sure. He slipped a pair off their hanger and tossed them toward his bed. A belt sailed after them. Blue-striped Oxford or green Polo? *Eenie, meenie, miney, mo* ... Polo it was. Knit vest? He shook his head. Too much. A jacket would suffice. He drew forth his latest acquisition, a black Members Only jacket, and draped it over the back of his desk chair.

Scott glanced at his bedside clock, his heart beating way too hard. It wasn't a date, no, not technically. But it would be the closest thing he'd ever had to one. His fingers shook as they worked buttons through holes.

A date that wasn't a date with Janis Graystone.

If *she agrees, buddy—and that's a big if.*

In the mirror, his shoulders sagged at the prospect of spending the evening clean, fragrant, well dressed, and alone. He stepped into his loafers and, after performing a few final tucks and teases in the mirror, pulled out an *X-Men* comic and retired onto his bed. It was issue #127, where the X-Men pursue the evil mutant Proteus. Scott flipped to the panels where Cyclops goads Wolverine—and soon the rest of the team—into a fight, to make sure they haven't lost their edge. A true leader's move. Even Wolverine says so afterwards.

Scott closed his eyes. *A true leader...*

He dreamed he was standing in the front yard, watching Mr. Shine rake leaves into small piles. The sun shone down from a brisk blue sky, and Scott realized it was the first time he'd seen their yardman since the day in the tennis courts, when Mr. Shine saved him from Jesse, Creed, and Tyler.

Scott stepped closer. "Hey, um, do you think you could show me that trick with the quarter one more time?"

A chuckle crackled from Mr. Shine's chest as he turned from the half-formed pile he was working on. He pushed his flat-topped straw hat farther back on his head and squinted toward Scott, propping the rake against his shoulder. But the metal rake had become a garbage pick, and the cuffed trousers and suspenders he had been wearing, blue coveralls like he wore at school.

Scott smiled. "How did you do that?"

"Jus' like you done that." Mr. Shine stuck out his chin.

When Scott looked down, he was dressed as Cyclops. He started to laugh, but then he noticed the array of thieving tools hanging from his red belt. And when he reached for his visor, the one Cyclops used to deliver his optic blast, Scott felt his own glasses and the edge of a hood—a thief's hood.

"You not there yet, but you closer," Mr. Shine said. "A little more diligence, a little more patience..."

He snapped a quarter into existence and flipped it toward Scott. When Scott tried to catch it, it bounced off his yellow gloves and into the street, where it started to roll along the gutter. Scott ran after it. He needed the quarter to perfect the trick, to complete his transformation.

"Best you hurry, young blood," Mr. Shine shouted behind him. "She's fixin' to jump for good!"

Scott saw what he meant. The quarter was headed straight for a storm drain. He pumped his arms and legs as hard as he could, but in the minute he'd stood talking to Mr. Shine, the sky had turned black with clouds, and now a hard wind pushed against him. The quarter became smaller as it rolled farther and farther away, hopping along the gutter as it went.

Clink. Clink-clink. Clink.

Just before it disappeared into the mouth of the drain, Scott jerked awake. His eyes took in the popcorn ceiling of his bedroom, his pulse swishing inside the channels of his ears.

Clink. Clink-clink. Clink.

The sound wasn't coming from a rolling quarter but the window. Scott checked his watch—8:02 p.m. *Shoot!* He leapt from his bed as the tapping sounded a third time. Snaking his hand behind the blinds, he gave the signal. He listened beyond his door a moment, then opened the blinds and slid open the window. The screen popped out in a shower of rust, and he lowered it outside.

Two sprays of mint breath freshener later, Scott climbed over the sill himself, closing the blinds and the window behind him. Around the corner of the house, in their old spot behind the juniper bushes, he found Janis. She was sitting with her back to the white brick, legs drawn in. Her combed hair flowed over the shoulder of a shiny purple and green athletic jacket and ran down her side. When she looked up, Scott struggled to breathe.

"Did I remember it right?" Janis asked. "The bug knock?"

The bug knock was a code they'd come up with one summer when they were nine—one tap, two fast taps, and then a fourth tap—meant to sound like a light-seeking insect to anyone who wasn't listening for it.

"Yeah, um, perfect." He tried to lower himself without crowding her. Their secret spot felt a lot smaller now.

"I wasn't sure my dad was going to let me out. I'm grounded, but I told him I was just going to pet Tiger and maybe take a jog down the street for exercise. I've got half an hour."

"All right," Scott said, even though he hadn't processed most of what she'd just told him. He watched her brush an auburn strand of hair from her eyes, and for a moment, he saw her not as Janis Graystone but as Jean Grey.

She raised her eyebrows in question.

"Oh, right, right," he stammered. "What I wrote..."

What he had written was:

Janis,
I think I can get us inside the shed. If you're available, come over at 8:00 tonight and we'll talk. Do you remember the knock?
Your friend,
Scott

He'd struggled over how to close it. That's what had taken him so many drafts to get right. Just *Scott* had seemed too blunt. *Fondly* or *Yours truly* too personal. *Your friend* won out by process of elimination.

The important thing was that the note had worked. She had come.

"You said the shed was secured by a bolt lock?" He was trying to make himself sound older, more practiced, like how he imagined Scott Summers would talk. But what came out was closer to Judge Wapner of *The People's Court*.

"He changed it between the first and second time I ... well, went in there. But, yeah, it was a bolt lock both times. Bigger the second time. It opens and closes with a key."

Scott dug into the back pocket of his jeans and pulled out a cloth wallet. "One of the benefits of being a nerd is that the things we obsess over sometimes end up having a use. I wanted so badly to be a thief—you know, the D&D kind—that I sent away for these." He unfolded the wallet to reveal a row of slender tension wrenches and metal picks. "I actually got pretty good with them. There's not a lock I haven't been able to open, anyway."

He looked away when he realized the last part sounded like a boast.

Janis didn't seem to notice. She reached over and drew a pick from its sleeve. "What about the hatch?"

"That's something else I've been pondering. The energy you felt—the electrical field—I'm wondering if it isn't a magnetic seal. A lot of the higher tech locking systems are magnetic."

"Is that something that can be picked?"

"No, but if I can get inside, I might be able to ... influence it."

He was preparing to explain what he meant, but she nodded. It was only their second day talking, and already they were discovering their own language again. He watched Janis turn the metal pick, examining each end. She slid it back into the wallet.

"What do you think he's keeping down there?" he asked.

A dark shadow passed over Janis's face, and she shook her head. "He subbed one of my classes today."

"Mr. Leonard?"

"Yeah, fifth period typing."

"Did—did he say anything?"

"No, he wouldn't look out from behind his newspaper."

Scott followed Janis's gaze beyond the junipers where the Watsons were out on one of their evening walks. Being able to observe the traffic on the street without being seen was one of the reasons Scott and Janis had chosen the meeting spot as kids. They would invent stories about their passing neighbors: their secrets, their past crimes, their current nefarious activities.

When Janis looked up at him, an odd light shone in her eyes. "Scott, are you sure you want to do this?"

"Huh? Yeah. Are you?"

He became certain she was going to say no. And with a *no* their renewed association, their rediscovered friendship would end, just like that. He could already feel his heart folding in on itself. Everything would go back to the way it had been at the start of the school year.

"I ... yes, I need to do this," she said. "I need to know. I just don't want to get you in trouble."

To this point, Scott had not considered the illegality of what they were planning. In its conceptual stage, it seemed as harmless as his old hacks: gaining access, looking around a little, not taking or damaging, leaving everything the way it had been. But to carry this out would be physical breaking and entering—and a lot easier to prove in court than hacking.

"Hey, it will be like one of our old adventures." He forced a laugh.

She studied his face closely. "All right, but if you ever have second thoughts..."

"I won't. I want to find out what's down there, too."

"We'll have to plan a time when he won't be there."

"How about at night, when they're sleeping?"

"That's the thing," she said. "I'm not sure he does sleep at night. During those early experiences, he was always out on his deck. Always watching. He wasn't out there the last time, but the weather's colder now. He could have been watching from inside. It felt like he was, anyway."

"Then we'll have to do it when he's not home. Maybe when he's subbing?"

"But how do we know when that'll be?"

"We don't ... unless we do."

The space between Janis's eyes pinched in.

"I can have Wayne call and say he's from one of the schools across town, Eastside Elementary, maybe. He could even capture one of their lines to make it look like the call is actually coming from Eastside—in case it's ever investigated, which I doubt it would be." Scott felt like a hacker again, his mind planning everything out three to four steps in advance. His mouth was having a hard time keeping up. "Wayne will say he has a teacher out sick, can Mr. Leonard come cover, et cetera, et cetera, the assignment will be waiting for him at the front office."

"But there won't be any assignment," Janis said.

"It doesn't matter. The time it takes for him to drive there, find out there's been some mistake, and drive back will take him, what, forty-five minutes? That should give us plenty of time to do what we need to do. We might even still be able to catch the bus to school."

"What about his wife?" Janis asked.

"Won't she be sleeping?"

"We don't know that."

"Then we'll need to figure out a way to distract her. Call the house, maybe? Keep her on the phone?"

"What's to stop her from looking out a back window?"

Scott grinned.

"What?" Janis said.

"You used to do the same thing when we were kids, poke holes in my ideas until I felt like one of those plastic heads you pump Play-Doh through. But that's good," he added quickly. "It's kept me humble these years."

She smirked with one side of her mouth. "Comes with being a Graystone."

When Scott realized he was staring, he cleared his throat. "All right," he said, affecting his practiced voice again. "Mr. Leonard's on his way to Eastside, his wife's in the house, maybe sleeping, maybe not ... I'll only need a couple of minutes to get inside the shed."

"I'll knock on the front door."

He began to shake his head.

"No, no, not like our old knock-and-runs," she said. "I'll have a story. I'll tell her our cat's missing and ask if she's seen her around. Mrs. Leonard will say no, of course, but then I'll describe Tiger. Her size, hair color, eye color. I'll keep her there as long as I can."

"Tiger's still alive?"

"Of course she is!" Janis slapped his arm. "She's only seven."

"But doesn't that make her like..." Scott pretended to count on his fingers. "...forty-something in human years?"

"Yeah, and how many forty-something-year-olds do you know who are keeling over from old age?"

Scott's laughter came out louder and dorkier than he would've liked, but it was the most honestly he had laughed all year. It wasn't just her wit, which he realized how much he'd missed. It was her friendship, which he'd missed so much more. He let his laughter taper off and adjusted his glasses.

"Hey, do you still have your walkie-talkie?" he asked.

"I think so..." She looked at him sidelong, as though he was going to crack another joke. "Probably in the garage."

Scott had gotten a set for Christmas when he was eight—one of those cheap plastic numbers—and given one to her. The idea of talking to each other from their bedrooms had excited them both. But the transmission beyond ten feet was dismal—mostly crackles against a background of thick static. The Morse component worked all right, but Janis hadn't been as enthused about learning the code as Scott, he remembered. After a month, his had ended up in the garage as well.

"See if you can find it," he said. "I'm serious. You won't even have to learn the code. The minute you hear Mrs. Leonard at the front door, you'll send me a beep, then turn off the talkie."

And just like that, the gravity of what they were planning fell back over them.

The Watsons returned from the end of the Meadows, both in blue jogging suits. They paused before Scott's house, looking as though they were debating whether or not to return up their street, before power walking toward the main road.

"What about getting back out?" she asked. "Won't you need another distraction?"

"Not with the lock already picked, no. I'll just need to clear out quickly."

Janis nodded solemnly. "When do you want to do this?".

"It's your call."

"How about Monday morning?"

"This Monday?"

"I'm afraid to wait too much longer," she said. "But Monday won't be rushing it, either. It will give us a couple days to work out the details and decide whether it's something we still want to do."

Scott knew she meant that last part for him. "I've already decided," he said.

She reached for the same place she had just given him a playful slap, his head swimming with her nearness, the promise of her touch. She patted his forearm twice, then held it close to the spot where his bones had once broken and healed, where his arm bent out a little.

"I'm glad we're talking again," she said.

The image of Jean Grey swam up in front of him, the dreams he still had for them.

"Yeah," Scott whispered. "Me too."

33

"The two have been talking," the woman said.

"Since when?"

"A long session took place on Thursday night, beginning at the entrance to the neighborhood and ending in the Grove. A shorter meeting took place outside the boy's house the following evening."

"The context?" the man asked.

"It appeared to be school related."

"No transcript?"

"No, sir. Too much interference."

"Coming from one of them?"

"Possibly."

"Hm," the man replied. "We still only have the two events of note from this fall: The phone outage in October, where a high concentration of energy originated from the boy's line. And the manifestation of energy in the girl's yard in mid November. But they're by far the most remarkable events to date."

"What's your read, sir?"

"Given their isolation, either the events in question are anomalies, or the boy and girl have a higher degree of insight and self-possession than we're giving them credit for. Which would make them a concern."

"Your orders, sir?"

"Be ready for anything."

34

Monday, December 3
6:30 a.m.

Janis stood in the street, hugging her arms, peering up at the glowing square of Scott's window. It was still dark out and cold. But the shivers that snaked through Janis's body and rattled her teeth seemed to come from some deep-down apprehension rather than the chill around her. Blowing warm air into the sides of her fists, she tried to remember if she'd had an experience the night before, a bad dream—something to warn her. But she couldn't.

"C'mon, c'mon, c'mon," she whispered, watching his light.

The thought of postponing the operation entered her mind again. She had only to explain her nagging feeling. Scott would understand. But like every other time that weekend that she'd felt her resolve starting to waver, she pictured the shirt that had once belonged to Star's sister, perforated and stitched together.

Turned her chest cavity to soup.

Then came the association between Star's sister and her own. What would happen if Mr. Leonard caught Margaret alone? Janis turned and looked at her sister's car parked in the street in front of the house. No, there could be no going back. Wheels were already in motion, and for better or worse, their fates were bound to this: hers, Margaret's, and Mr. Leonard's.

Scott's too, she realized.

When she turned back to his house, his bedroom window was dark. Seconds later, he appeared at the front door in slacks and a gray T-shirt, his blue backpack slung over one shoulder. He scampered down the lawn, the dark sweep of his hair bouncing, glasses jiggling. The tremulous apprehension returned to Janis.

"Wayne just called." His brown eyes shone keenly. "Nut took the bait."

Nut was their codename for Mr. Leonard after recalling how his thin upper lip remained stiff when he lectured, leaving his lower jaw to hinge up and down—like a nutcracker's.

Janis stood looking at Scott. Was it right to involve him in this?

"Okay," she whispered.

They moved toward the bus stop, their footfalls quick and quiet, neither one talking. Janis resisted the compulsion to smell her shower-damp hair. In her periphery, she noticed Scott pushing up his glasses. When they reached the intersection, Scott led them to the back of a bush that grew beside the Pattersons' garage door, hiding them from the street. They drew out their walkie-talkies, Scott's from his backpack and Janis's from the front pocket of her hooded Thirteenth Street Titans sweatshirt. Janis snapped hers on and twisted the volume to three.

"I know we've been over this a hundred times," Scott said, his eyebrows arching over the tops of his metal frames, "but..."

"I beep you when Nut leaves." She pressed the orange button on the side of her talkie and held it for one second. An insect-like whine sounded from Scott's talkie. "You beep me when you're in position. And I beep you again when Nut's wife is about to open the front door."

"And three quick beeps for any trouble," he reminded her. Three blips sounded from her talkie. Scott's lips shook around a smile. "Not that there will be any."

Janis almost called it off. There was a quality in his voice, an uneasy inflection that resonated with the ominous stirrings in the pit of her stomach. It was only then she realized she didn't fear for herself—not at all—but for him.

Janis peeked around the bush at the Leonards' house. It was emerging in the predawn, the sickly yellow shutters just beginning to stand out from the brown siding. In the dim light, the shutters reminded her of the rust-colored spots above the Rottweiler's eyes.

"All right," Scott said. "Wish me luck."

"Hey, maybe we should..."

But he was already jogging to the street. She watched him peer around and then slide feet-first into a storm drain that opened like a mouth beneath the corner curbing. As kids, they used to sneak down into the system of cement tunnels and explore their neighborhood's underworld on hands and knees, listening to the echoing *vroom* of cars passing overhead. They would crawl as far as they dared, which was never too far—at least not for Janis. Roaches lived down there.

The rest of Scott's body disappeared, and seconds later, Janis heard the faint sound of small wheels grinding over cement. The evening before, Scott had rolled an old skateboard into the drain. His plan was to lie belly-down and shove off beneath the Meadows, go fifty yards, and take a sharp left. There, he would wait inside the cylindrical opening that became the cement culvert running between Janis's and Mr. Leonard's backyards. "That way, the last place anyone will have seen me is walking to the bus stop," Scott had explained. "And with the skateboard, I'll be able to stay at the very bottom of the culvert until I reach their fence."

It made sense, Janis guessed. She looked down at his backpack, which sagged against her own stack of books. She peeked back at the Leonards' house. It remained dim and still. Janis's watch read 6:42. When would it be too late? At what point could they call it off?

The Leonards' garage door gave a shudder and began ratcheting open, the panels creaking and folding into the space above. Pale rear lights spilled out onto the driveway. Janis made herself as thin as she could behind the bush. When the green Datsun emerged, it appeared to not so much roll as feel its way backward, like a creature half-blind from being underground too long. The car lurched into the street at an angle, paused, and then started forward. The garage door ratcheted closed. Janis watched the dwindling taillights.

She hesitated, then pressed the orange button on her talkie, counted to one, and released it.

A second later, her talkie beeped back. Scott had received the signal.

Scott crooked his arm behind himself and pushed the talkie into the back pocket of his khakis. The skateboard on which he lay shifted beneath his stomach. He reached for the opening of the tunnel and braced himself. Rolling his narrow hips on the board, first one side and then the other, he was satisfied he could feel the flashlight in his right front pocket and the wallet containing his picking tools in the pocket opposite.

All systems go.

His heartbeats punched the flat of his skateboard. From his dim vantage, Scott squinted toward his target. He gauged the end of the chain link fence to be perhaps a hundred yards distant.

He took a deep breath, moved his hands to the lower lip of the opening, and pulled. The front wheels dropped down first, then the back wheels. Out in the open culvert, gravity took over. Scott tried to use his hands and the toes of his shoes to control his descent, but he was moving too quickly, the wheels grinding too loudly. Each time he met the edge of a slab, Scott winced at the teeth-rattling *click-clack*.

One of the advantages of using the skateboard, Scott had thought, was that were someone to spot him, he would look like a kid playing around in the culvert—not someone on a stealth mission. But so much for that stealth now.

grind, grind, grind, grind...

click-clack!

grind, grind, grind, grind...

click-clack!

He glanced up, glad to find the end of the corner lot approaching. The fencing to his left changed from steep wooden posts to chain linking. Steering to the near side of the culvert, Scott slowed himself. When he looked up again, he nearly choked at seeing the top of the Leonards' house. It was taller than he'd estimated, most of the second story in plain view.

Which meant he was in plain view, too.

His palms screamed fire when he braked. He shoved himself back up the culvert until he was behind the wooden posts again. He set his board sideways and examined his hands. The heels of his palms looked like a pair of red plums someone had tried to grate. They stung when he blew sand from them. With his fingertips, he reached for his talkie and held it gingerly.

Scott considered his distant position from the shed. Staying where he was would mean more valuable seconds to reach his target, but what choice did he have? It was either that or wait out in the open.

He pushed the orange button.

Janis jumped at the sound, even though she was expecting it—or maybe *because* she was expecting it. She answered with a quick beep and hid the talkie deep in her pocket. She knelt for her books and folders. When she stood and emerged from behind the bush, the world whorled and dove around her. *Head rush.* She staggered down to the street and held onto the stop sign. Two cars cruised by. Janis waited for them to fade down the main hill and for her head to clear.

As she crossed the street, books pressed to her stomach to keep the talkie from bouncing, she imagined Scott lying at the culvert's bottom just outside the fence. She wondered if his body felt as tense as hers, if his breaths were as feral. Her gaze led her sneakers along the rain gutter.

Too soon, she was standing at the Leonards' front walkway. When she raised her head, a yellow door stared back, like in her *To Kill a Mockingbird* nightmare. She checked her watch and drew a resolute breath. The door stood beneath a wooden balcony, where dead plants hung down from metal baskets. With each step, the odor of rotting soil grew stronger.

You haven't done anything you can't take back, she told herself. *Scott's in a public culvert on a skateboard. You haven't knocked on the door. Whatever normalcy your life still holds can be preserved.*

But Janis knew that wasn't true—not anymore. Whatever normalcy her life still held could only be prolonged. That was all. And that's why her legs continued to carry her forward. But when she was nearly to the front porch, another, more powerful thought entered her mind:

Don't do it! Call it off!

The apprehension was more than a vague stirring now; it clanged and banged like a fire alarm. It came from the part of herself that slipped out of her body at night, the part that experienced a world beyond the physical, that perceived both past and probable future events. And though Janis couldn't see anything—no ghost images— the danger she and Scott were about to fall into could not have felt more dire.

She nearly dropped her books as she dug inside her sweatshirt for the plastic talkie. The speaker crackled and hissed in her grasp. Her thumb searched for the orange button and found it.

Three quick beeps for any trouble.

She managed to press it once before the front door swung open.

Scott had been thinking about Wayne when the signal came. They had met up at Blue Chip Arcade on Saturday, where they went halfsies on the forty-tokens-for-five-dollars deal.

"Yeah, I remember Mr. Leonard," Wayne said, leaping back and forth across his joystick and hammering the fire button like a telegraph operator on speed. "I never saw anything wrong with him."

Yeah, well, you probably didn't see anything wrong with Rick Moranis's character in Ghostbusters, either—even after he became possessed.

"And you need him out of the house?"

"For an hour or so," Scott said. He gunned down a Burwor who strayed into his corner of the screen. "We just can't figure out how. The fact that he's a sub might be a starting point..."

Scott had long since learned that it was best to steer Wayne toward the solution you already had in mind and let him believe he'd arrived at it on his own, rather than telling him.

"Call him with a fake assignment." Wayne said it as though it were the most obvious thing in the world. "*Eat laser, turds!*"

"Yeah, but what if he calls the school?"

"Easy, you set it up so that whatever number you're supposedly calling from remotely call forwards to your number. That way, if he does call back, the phone will ring at your house. That is, until you take off the call forw—*you're mine, you cross-dressing son of a whore!*"

Scott moved his blue character out of harm's way while Wayne pursued the teleporting Wizard of Wor. The screen flashed with bolts and blasts. Wayne laughed maniacally, then screamed when the Wizard's lightning zapped him.

"Is it easy to do?"

Wayne scowled and jammed another token into the slot. "For some people. Just takes a little social engineering."

"Sounds dangerous."

"Ha! You always were a worm when it came to talking to the Bell techies."

"And you think you could pull it off?" Scott tried to affect just the right amount of skepticism. With too much, Wayne would go spazoid on him. He was like one of those chemistry kits in the hobby stores: overdose on a substrate and you'd end up with a foaming mess.

"I guarantee it."

When Wayne looked over, his pupils were huge—the result of two straight hours of video gaming, no doubt. But his eyes also shone with the anticipation of being able to solve something Scott couldn't. It was a look Scott knew well.

"Let's make it interesting, then," Scott said. "Your broadsword if you can't?"

Wayne's grin became so sharp it seemed to send a crease down the middle of his face. More than masterminding the solutions, Wayne loved being told he couldn't pull them off.

"You're on, numb nuts."

In the culvert, Scott's talkie beeped.

He very nearly signaled back before remembering where Janis was and that her talkie would be off now. As he clicked off his own unit and returned it to his back pocket, he pondered the shortness of the beep. It had lasted a half-second, tops, little more than the length of a confirmation signal.

Then he understood: Janis had had to signal to him *and* turn off her unit in the short space between Mrs. Leonard's unlocking the door and opening it. No wonder she'd rushed it. The important thing was that Mrs. Leonard was at the front of the house, which meant it was time for Scott to act.

He brought his wristwatch to his chin and pressed a small button. The timer function *blipped* to life, the hundredths of a second display scrambling madly. Three minutes. That's how much time he was giving himself.

He sat on his skateboard, aimed the pointed nose down the culvert, and let it roll. At the end of the fence, Scott skidded to a stop.

He turned the skateboard upside down and began scaling the steep slant of the culvert. His palms burned where the skin had rubbed away.

At the top, he found himself on a small ledge of grass between the culvert and fence line. He looked into a lawn shaded by early morning and then up at the house.

Scott remembered how the backs of the houses in Oakwood—the sides you weren't supposed to see—had looked sinister to him once. This one still did. He couldn't point to anything in particular; in fact, the backyard overlooked by the high deck showcased a certain middle-class normalcy. The grass, which had begun to brown with the colder weather, was trim and mostly naked of leaves. A plastic rake leaned beside a tidy coil of green garden hose at the side of the house. No, it was the *mood* of the house that bothered him: tall and brooding.

A house with secrets.

The leaning shed stood where Janis had drawn it on the map they'd made that weekend. Scott inserted the toe of a shoe into a chain-link diamond and pulled himself up. The fence shook softly. He dropped onto the lawn and crouched. A criminal now, he hurried up behind the shed until he was hidden from the house.

Thirty-one seconds gone.

Scott had selected only those picks and wrenches that worked with the widest range of locks. He moved them from the wallet to his mouth in a line and slid the wallet back into his pocket. He stepped around to the front of the shed. Doing his best to ignore the house at his back, he went to work.

Heart walloping, Janis managed to snap off the talkie. She wanted to believe she'd pressed the button more than once, that Scott had received the warning signal, but she knew he hadn't. The instant the door began to move, her finger had abandoned the orange button in search of the knob that controlled the volume and the talkie's power. Fortunately she'd twisted it the right way.

"Oh—ah—hi," Janis stuttered.

The woman's eyes peered at her like a spooked animal's from a nest of graying hair. Or maybe they only looked large and round to Janis because her mouth was so small, her lips nearly colorless. Janis's gaze fell to the woman's nightgown, as thin and sallow as her skin.

The reclusive Mrs. Leonard.

Janis recovered herself. "I'm Janis Graystone. I was up at the bus stop and decided to, um, ask a couple of neighbors if they've seen our cat. Tiger's her name. She left the house over the weekend, the one behind yours, and hasn't come back. We thought she might have ended up in one of your—"

With the same spooked look, Mrs. Leonard jabbed her finger past Janis. Her nightgown shuddered around her.

"I-I'm sorry?" Janis said, squinting. "Do you want me to leave?"

Only twenty seconds had elapsed, maybe fewer. Not nearly enough time for Scott. She tried again. "Because I just wanted to—"

The woman jabbed her finger with more force, shaking her head now.

No, she doesn't want me to talk, or she doesn't want me to leave?

Janis turned to where she was pointing. The newspaper! Protected by a plastic bag, it lay beside the walkway like a deflated balloon. Mrs. Leonard had been coming out to get it, Janis guessed, but now she was asking her to retrieve it for her. She probably didn't want to be seen in her nightgown. Or maybe she didn't want to be seen, period. Throughout her ten years of living here, Janis could count on one hand the number of times she had glimpsed her. And that's really all they had been, glimpses. The woman was Oakwood's version of Boo Radley.

"Would you like me to get the paper?"

Still pointing, Mrs. Leonard began to nod.

Thank God.

Janis set her books on the porch and returned down the walkway. The long bag dripped with condensation when she lifted it from the grass. Janis bounced it a few times from the neck of the bag, pretending to be concerned about its dampness. As she returned with it, she checked off another twenty-five seconds in her head.

Mrs. Leonard's lips torqued into an expression of gratitude as she accepted the newspaper. She was younger than she appeared from a distance, her brown eyes sharp and clear. Tucking the newspaper to her side, Mrs. Leonard began to retreat inside the house again.

"Oh, but wait, I haven't told you what my cat looks like."

The woman made a quick waving motion with her hand. There was an urgency to it, a pleading.

Come inside, the gesture said.

Janis looked from Mrs. Leonard up to the intersection. The sun had still yet to rise, and the street was blue-gray. "Oh, thanks, but my bus will be here any minute. I don't want to miss it."

The woman made a different gesture. She brought two fingers to her closed mouth and shook her head, and then with the same hand, mimed like she was writing something on the palm of her other hand.

"Ahh," Janis said. Mrs. Leonard was mute. That's what she was telling her. That's why she hadn't spoken. And now she wanted to write something down for her.

"I have a pen and some paper right here," Janis said, stooping for her books.

Mrs. Leonard grunted. When Janis looked up, the mute woman used her hands to explain her bad back and that she needed to sit down. Another reason she stayed indoors, Janis thought. Sympathy began clouding over the alarm that pulsed in the back of her mind: *Don't do it! Call it off!* Anyway, it was too late to call it off. Scott would be in front of the shed by now, and she'd promised to buy him at least three minutes, more if possible.

Come inside, Mrs. Leonard gestured again.

Janis wiped her hand against the side of her Levi's, her heart starting into a fresh cycle of pounding.

"All right," she said. "But just for a minute."

Swearing under his breath, Scott adjusted his pressure on the tension wrench in the bottom of the keyhole and reset his grip on the pick. At first feel, the lock had seemed like a standard five-pin chamber, which he could have opened in seconds. But these pins had to be pressed in a particular order, he learned; otherwise, they wouldn't stay trapped along the shear line and the bolt wouldn't budge.

Serious security, he thought, *and not something I've had a lot of practice on.*

He took a quick breath and blinked at the perspiration in the corner of one eye, trying to forget the fact that he was in plain view. The timer on his watch showed more than two minutes. He had figured out the sequence of the first two pins, but the third was proving a bitch. Every time he guessed wrong, he lost them all, and the pins were hard to set in the first place.

It took him twenty seconds to retrap the first two pins. The only good thing to be said for having already guessed and lost twice on the third pin was that it could only be the last one. He concentrated, probed the tip of the pin with his pick, pushed it up, and felt it click into position.

The penultimate pin would be a fifty-fifty shot. He chose the nearer one and pushed.

All of the pins fell out.

"Dammit!" he hissed, the spare wrench and picks nearly spilling from his mouth.

He reset the tension wrench, which had become slippery with the serous blood beading from his palms.

The timer raced past two and a half minutes.

The last time he'd done anything like this was when he hacked Army Information in late August. But he'd been under no time constraints then, the hack taking him nearly fifteen hours. The security lock was easier by comparison—far easier. It had components he could feel, fewer moving parts, and manageable probabilities. The disadvantage, of course, was that he had less time to sequence those moving parts—minutes, not hours. That, and he was standing in someone's backyard, not concealed in his own dark bedroom.

But Scott knew the sequence now.

He worked pin one into place again, then pin number two. Runnels of sweat circled the rims of his glasses, gathering at the bottoms of the lenses. As his hands worked, he thought about how the Army Information hack had led him here, in a strange way. Discovering the tap that night, hiding his computer equipment, promising himself that he would use his moratorium on hacking as a chance to embark on his maturation, to embrace it. To get out there.

Oh, you're out there all right.

He set pin three as he reflected on his exercise regimen, his updated wardrobe, old self out, new self in, Gamma—none of which would have happened without the tap. Neither would he and Janis have rediscovered one another.

Pin four clicked into place.

But to her, he knew he was just an interesting friend from her past. His transformation wasn't complete, not yet. Friday's confrontation with Grant and Britt had been a step, as was his attempt to negotiate with Jesse. But here he was, not the person he had envisioned, not Scott Summers. No, he was still Stiletto, pulse racing in terror and exhilaration over this, his latest stealth campaign.

He set the final pin and twisted the tension wrench. The bolt didn't move. He'd turned the wrench the wrong way. When he tried to recover and go back, his grip slipped. All of the pins fell out.

No, dammit! No! No! No!

The timer raced toward four minutes.

He snuck a glance at the fence above the culvert, knowing he'd blown it, that his time was more than up. He imagined the front door closing in front of Janis.

With the weight of the house bearing down on him, Scott cut his gaze back to the keyhole. He blinked the sting of sweat from his eyes. He reinserted the tension wrench, hesitated, and then followed with the pick.

35

Janis closed the door behind her and followed the ghost-like image of Mrs. Leonard through the dim front hall. The air inside the house smelled almost pleasant, like cakes of makeup. But within paces, it became apparent that the powdery fragrance concealed a cruder understench of cigarettes and dampness.

A living room opened to their right. A faded, floral-patterned couch and two chairs sat over a dull white carpet. Thick beige curtains covered the windows. Something told Janis that the room had never seen company, not while the Leonards lived here. To her left, a staircase climbed steeply into darkness. Mrs. Leonard led them back to a kitchen, Janis wincing as the soles of her sneakers, still damp from the grass, began squeaking over the black and white tiles. Only then did it occur to her that if Mrs. Leonard was mute, she was probably deaf as well.

"Excuse me," Janis called, testing the idea.

Mrs. Leonard didn't turn.

When Janis lifted her gaze, she stiffened. Beyond the round kitchen table stood a sliding glass door, and beyond that lay the deck, the same place Mr. Leonard had spent summer nights watching her house. From her vantage, the backyard where she and Margaret had grown up playing hide-and-seek and "colonial times," and where Margaret still sunbathed sometimes, looked dangerously exposed. But it wasn't the view of her own yard that worried Janis. In a few more paces, they would be able to see down into the Leonards' backyard as well.

Janis recovered and edged ahead of Mrs. Leonard to the far side of the table. She dropped her books and pulled a chair for her host, all the time shifting her body to block the view through the glass door.

"Rest your back." Janis said where Mrs. Leonard could read her lips. "I'll get you something to write on."

She pulled up a chair beside Mrs. Leonard. Her fingers shook as she opened one of her notebooks and drew out a sheet of college-ruled paper and a blue pen. When Mrs. Leonard had taken them, Janis peeked behind her. In front of the shed, head bowed to the lock, stood Scott.

Janis turned back to where Mrs. Leonard's hand traced thin scrawls on the paper. *Good, she writes slowly.* Janis kept her torso rigid, fighting the urge to twist around again, to watch Scott to safety.

She leaned toward Mrs. Leonard instead and noticed a fragrance about the woman. It was the smell of the house—fine and powdery on the surface but musty underneath—a smell redolent of illness and sorrow and being shut in. It was the smell of someone who didn't go outside, not even for her own newspaper. Opposite where Mrs. Leonard had set the newspaper, Janis observed a black coffee mug.

Or maybe someone prevents her from going outside.

And now Janis became certain that this woman was as in the dark as anyone. Whatever Mr. Leonard kept hidden under his shed, whatever his past crimes, whatever designs he had on Margaret, his wife knew nothing about them.

Mrs. Leonard pushed the piece of paper in front of her: *Your cat comes into our yard sometimes, but she hasn't lately. I'm sorry.*

"So I guess you already know what she looks like?" Janis said.

Mrs. Leonard took the paper back, nodding, and wrote something else, something a little shorter.

I've seen her through the window. She's pretty.

"Oh, do you like cats?"

Mrs. Leonard bent over the paper again.

By her mental clock, Janis guessed it had been about four minutes. Scott had said he would bail if he didn't have the lock picked within three. She peeked behind her. The top of his head was still stooped toward the door. Her toes began curling inside her white Keds, right foot, left foot, as if that could speed his progress. She turned back to the table just as Mrs. Leonard finished.

Yes, but I can't have one.

"Why not? Cats are really easy to care for, if that's, um, your concern. They're very independent."

Janis labored to speak slowly, to stretch out the seconds. She'd never been one for small talk, had never seen the point, but now that it was vital she string sentences together, her mind was coming up painfully short.

Mrs. Leonard shook her head and wrote out a fourth line.

My husband.

The word shot through Janis like a bolt, but she composed her face as she raised it back to Mrs. Leonard's. "Oh, is he allergic?" Janis pointed to her own nose. "Do cats make him sneeze?"

But Janis knew the answer. She could read it in Mrs. Leonard's conflicted eyes. Her husband had already decided she wasn't to have a cat, no matter how badly she wanted one, no matter how isolated she felt. And maybe that was the point—to keep her isolated, to keep her dependent on him.

As if to confirm this, Mrs. Leonard shook her head again and began writing something else. And in that moment, Janis found that she was glad to be imparting a little company to this lonely woman.

Mrs. Leonard pushed the paper back in front of her.

He's here.

Janis thrust herself up. The coffee mug tottered on the tabletop. She hadn't heard the rumble of the garage door, but it wasn't the door to the garage that was opening. It was the front door.

Footsteps landed in the hallway.

Janis spun to where Scott's glasses were just fading into the darkness of the shed, the door closing behind him. And then she looked down at Mrs. Leonard. The deaf woman stared back at her, her face taut.

Wait a minute. How could she *have heard? Unless—*

"In here!" Mrs. Leonard called clearly.

It took another second for the full horror to dawn on Janis: Mrs. Leonard had been killing time, too.

Scott snapped on his flashlight and swung it around the shed, the stress of the lock-picking exercise still gripping his neck. Janis had expressed doubts about the things she perceived in her astral state, but the inside of the shed was exactly how she'd described it: shelves, old woodcutting implements, gloves. The space felt as claustrophobic as she'd described it, too. He ran his beam along the solid frame, then down to the pile of kindling.

Clamping the end of the camping flashlight between his teeth, Scott stooped and began moving the kindling to the shelves.

The wounds on his palms stung as he worked, but Scott couldn't stop to brush away the flecks of bark. Outside, his race had been against Mrs. Leonard returning inside the house and seeing him. Now, safely inside the shed, his race was against Mr. Leonard returning home in the next thirty minutes, give or take.

At last, Scott pried the plywood board up with his fingers and shook away the final layer of kindling. A few roaches scrambled away. He set the board against the door, took his flashlight from his mouth, and shone it down.

"I'll be damned," he muttered, kneeling.

The metal hatch was almost the size of a manhole cover. It was solid with a thick hinge on one side and a crescent-shaped depression on the other for grasping. But even using both hands, Scott found he couldn't budge it. *A twelve-hundred-pound holding force*, he guessed. *At least.* Embedded in the cement beside the hatch sat a basic keypad. Scott smiled around his labored breaths. That more than proved it: Janis's abilities were the real deal.

Now it was time to establish his own credentials.

He closed his eyes and focused on the hatch. He guessed there was a magnet mounted in the frame and an armature plate around the hatch itself, the two bound by an electromagnetic force. He just needed to locate the source.

He reached with the part of himself that hungered for distance and control, for power. His consciousness twined in on itself, and in the next moment, DC current stormed around him. *I'm in!* Scott pushed against the stinging current, feeling his way toward whatever spoke to the relay. Two lines plunged underground, one leading to a battery backup, he guessed, the other to some sort of central command. But there had to be something local, something associated with the keypad.

And there it was: a small circuit board.

From far away, Scott felt his fingers resting over the blocks on the keypad. His hacking instinct urged him to probe for the code. But how long would that take? No, better to concentrate on the relay between keypad and hatch, to short it.

Scott pulled his energy in. As always, it was a struggle, as if the energy didn't *want* to be harnessed, straining against him like a herd of cats. But at last, Scott contained it. He focused on the tiny relay that directed current to the solenoid—the generator of the magnetic field. A red point appeared in his mind's eye and then grew, changing color, becoming hotter.

It's not the concentration of energy so much as its release.

The thought came spontaneously, and with it, Scott understood what had happened the last time, with the tap. The strain to hold the energy in one place had overwhelmed his mind, rendering him unconscious. Free from his control, the energy had exploded outward in a mini-Big Bang.

The trick, then, was to build the energy up and release it consciously.

The orb in his mind's eye swelled to orange. His head went swimmy. *Just a little bit longer* ... The orb verged on white. Before his awareness could waver away, Scott let go.

He staggered from the flash and the sensation of being blown from the system. He had been kneeling at the hatch's edge, but coming to, he found himself slumped to one side, the flashlight fallen from his grasp. Its beam shone across his shoes. Standing, he seized the hatch with both hands and pulled. It swung open. Scott fell onto his backside, rattling the shelves around him.

Where the hatch door had been, rebar rungs descended into darkness. Scott got to his feet and shone his light down. The cement cylinder ended in a room, maybe fifteen feet below.

He lowered his legs inside the cylinder, hooking his fingers around the rim, then the top rung. As he climbed down, his breaths echoed off the smooth wall in front of him. With his next step, it felt as though his foot had broken into open space. He moved his leg back in a circle to be sure. Cool air stirred past him.

Scott was too far down now to see the keypad above, too far down to notice that the bottom-right key had begun to pulse red.

He stepped from the ladder and cast his beam around.

"I said, what are you doing here?"

Janis's voice had become trapped inside her constricting chest. She looked at Mrs. Leonard, whose face remained tense, then back to Mr. Leonard, who stood at the entrance to the front hall. He had come in just seconds before, a black bag hanging from the shoulder of his crumpled gray shirt, his long brow still collapsing into a bed of creases over those awful yellow glasses.

"My cat." It came out in the wrong key, like when you accidentally hit a minor note in a major chord. "My cat's missing."

Mr. Leonard looked at his wife. "When did she come?"

"Right after you left. She was just about to knock on the door."

His gaze fell back on Janis. "Who called this morning?"

"What do you mean?" She tried to appear confused, but she was no actress. Her eyes felt too large, and she couldn't stop blinking.

"Who called me this morning?"

Janis's gut shrank beneath his raised voice. She edged back from the table.

"I-I don't understand..."

"Don't con me!" He charged into the kitchen, aiming his finger across the table at her like a weapon. "Don't you *dare* con me! Someone wanted me out of the house. The schools don't call me— we have that worked out. I parked one street over, waited, and came back. And now you're here. Who put you up to this?"

Janis's thoughts had been colliding into one another, but now they found common direction.

"I was up at the bus stop. I saw your car leave. And that's what made me think to come over and ... and ask your wife if she'd seen our cat. I swear I didn't call you."

It was as close to the truth as she could possibly come. Maybe that's why her face felt more natural around the sounds her mouth made. She watched Mr. Leonard watching her. He wasn't looking down and to one side, like he used to do when he subbed, wasn't hiding behind his newspaper. Beyond his lenses, the whites of his eyes appeared fierce and jaundiced.

"Did anyone see you come?"

"See me?" Fresh alarms clanged in Janis's head. *Yes! Yes! Say yes!*

She opened her mouth, but Mrs. Leonard spoke first: "I didn't see anyone."

Mr. Leonard looked back at Janis.

"I told my sister I'd be asking some of the neighbors about Tiger, so she probably knows..."

Did his eye just tic at the mention of Margaret?

"And you say you came from the bus stop?" he asked.

Janis nodded, not knowing whether it was a good thing or a bad thing to be admitting. He turned and paced off into the front room. *He's looking out the window. He's checking to see if anyone else is at the stop.* When Mr. Leonard returned, he appeared less harried. He set his bag on the floor.

"Sit down," he told her.

"I don't want to miss my bus."

"If you miss it, we can take you," Mrs. Leonard said, resting a hand on her arm.

This coming from a woman who just faked being a mute. Janis felt like a trapped mouse. Her gaze skittered between Mrs. Leonard, who blocked escape to her left, and Mr. Leonard, who stood ahead of her to the right.

"I-I really have to go."

She jerked around to the sliding glass door and saw with relief that it was like the door at their house, the one between the kitchen and back patio. It had a slider lock. *Tall means locked, short means unlocked,* she used to recite as a little girl. Janis jammed down the lock and yanked the handle.

The door opened an inch, then banged to a stop. At the same instant Janis saw the broom handle in the door track, Mrs. Leonard was around her.

"Get off!" Janis screamed.

Mrs. Leonard pinned Janis's arms to her sides with one arm and clapped a hand over her mouth with the other. She was not infirm. Her back was fine. The muscles that restrained Janis felt like steel cords. Janis wriggled and shoved against her, but the woman hardly budged.

Beyond the glass door, she could see the light on in her own kitchen, where her parents would be eating breakfast, her father reading the newspaper. When she kicked the door, it only shuddered. She tried to scream through her sealed mouth. "*Mmmfff!*"

Mr. Leonard moved in front of her, holding his hands out.

"We're not going to hurt you," he said.

His voice was calm, but his eyes jittered behind his lenses. Janis leaped up and got a heel into Mr. Leonard's lean gut. With a low grunt, he stumbled backward. When Janis went to stomp her captor's foot, Mrs. Leonard anticipated her. She stepped back and tightened her grip.

"Janis," she said into her ear. "We just want to talk to you."

Mr. Leonard recovered and drew something from his pocket. It was about the size and shape of an electric razor. When he cocked his wrist, the object hummed to life. Lights on either side of it blinked red.

"I don't want to have to use this," he said, recovering his breath.

Oh God, what is that thing?

Janis squinted away as the blinking device drew nearer. It smelled like a hairdryer beginning to overheat. Then something sizzled, not a sound but a *sensation*—inside her head. When Janis tried to scream again, saliva spilled against Mrs. Leonard's fingers and turned cold against her own lips. Gray lights began to flash around the periphery of her vision.

Don't pass out, she pleaded with herself. *Whatever you do, please don't pass out.*

She stopped struggling.

Mr. Leonard stared at her another moment, then withdrew the device and flicked his wrist. The smell and sensation faded with the red lights, and Janis blinked until her vision cleared.

"That's better." Mr. Leonard was just returning the device to his pocket and opening his mouth to say something more when the phone in the hallway rang. Janis's gaze followed his, faint hope flickering inside her. *Maybe someone saw me walk into the house. Maybe they told my parents.* But Janis had never heard a ring like this before: half ring, full ring, half ring.

"Someone's inside," Mrs. Leonard said.

Janis watched Mr. Leonard's eyes dart from the phone. The pale light through the glass door shrank his pupils to points. "Who is it?"

But he wasn't asking his wife. He was looking at her.

Janis shook her head.

He dug his hand into the front pocket of her sweatshirt and pulled out the walkie-talkie. He held it up in front of her face.

"Who is it?"

She hadn't stopped shaking her head.

"Goddammit!" Mr. Leonard wheeled and spiked the talkie against the floor. It burst apart. One of the batteries rolled toward the den. "You have no idea what you've done," he whispered through bared teeth. "Put her in the bathroom."

Janis writhed and tried to scream again, but Mrs. Leonard's grip held firm. She felt herself being half carried, half dragged around the table. Mr. Leonard strode ahead of them and punched a code into the wall beneath the staircase. A door appeared, and Mr. Leonard pushed it open.

Scott!

Mrs. Leonard released her at the same time she shoved her through another doorway. Janis fell against a sink. By the time she turned, the door was slamming closed. A bolt clunked home, its sound solid and final.

Scott's flashlight hung down by his side, still on but forgotten. Upon dropping from the ladder, he had found himself in a room with a row of locked cases. Scott considered picking them open, but the cold, flickering glow from a room down the corridor had drawn him forward instead.

"Ho-ly smokes," he whispered.

The wall monitors looked like something from the security room of a major department store. There were twelve of them, four across and three down, black and white screens. Some were still and some oscillated, but all showed the same thing: the Graystones' house.

"And I thought *I* was the voyeur."

In the top left monitor, Scott found himself looking at the Graystones' front porch. By the angle, Scott guessed the camera was mounted somewhere on the street light—perhaps in the light fixture itself, where it would be hard to see. The top-middle and right monitors showed the garage side of the house. In one shot, the edge of a leaf fluttered in and out of view. The image was being fed by a camera in the woods.

All of those hours Janis practiced against the garage door...

Scott left the thought at that, coldness worming through his gut.

It wasn't that he had distrusted Janis's intuition about Mr. Leonard's intentions. But to this point, that's all it had been, her intuition. Now the truth was taking ghastly shape. Indeed, looking at those monitors was like peering into the mind of someone meticulous and pathological. And if Mr. Leonard had gone this far, there was no question he had plans to go further still.

Beneath the lowest monitors, showing the patio and windows at the back of the Graystones' house, sat a control panel. Scott eased onto the chair, its caster wheels squeaking over a square of balding carpet. Dials lined the panel, numbered one through twelve on clumsy red label-maker strips. Each dial probably corresponded to a camera.

A switch beneath each knob seemed to toggle between functions. *Focus? Zoom? Brightness?* Scott didn't dare test them to find out.

His gaze moved from the controls to where the panel formed a desk. It was empty save for an olive-green military phone and a flat book.

Scott cannoned the book open. It appeared to be a ledger of some kind. He adjusted his glasses and flipped back a couple of pages until he saw writing. Frowning, he ran his middle finger down the columns.

No, not a ledger. A logbook.

The leftmost column held what appeared to be codes, several of them repeating. The middle and rightmost columns listed dates and times—military times, some with asterisks beside them. Scott started to flip to the beginning of the book when he heard the *chuff* of a distant door opening. He snapped his head toward the sound, a primal yell lodged in his brainstem.

Descending footsteps followed, wicked in their soft cadence.

Scott rose to his feet. He looked down the corridor where the sound of the footfalls continued to grow, masculine footfalls. Scott wasn't sure how he knew this, but he did. *Mr. Leonard? No, too soon.* Unless he'd returned to the house for something he'd forgotten.

Scott eased the chair back in place. One of the casters squeaked thinly. The footfalls paused, then resumed, coming faster. Scott looked around. The military phone, the notes in the ledger, the bunker, the disturbing obsession with security. Was Mr. Leonard a Vietnam veteran? Someone who had killed in the field? Who had no compunction about killing again?

He turned and fled the way he had come. When he reached the room with the ladder, Scott cut his flashlight and listened back. The *whoosh-whumps* of his heart filled his ears. He pulled himself up the ladder. The column he entered was black, but he couldn't risk a light.

His raw palms screamed around the rebar rungs. He swam an arm overhead, feeling for the opening, for the rim. At last his hand collided with the underside of the hatch, jamming his wrist.

He shoved the hatch, but it wouldn't move. Locked again.

The footfalls entered the room beneath him.

36

" Janis, we're not trying to hurt you."

The thick door muffled Mrs. Leonard's voice. Janis had already tried the handle. That had rotated fine, but the door wouldn't budge, and she could see no means by which to operate the bolt from the inside. A bathroom that only locked on the outside. Janis's chest began to shudder.

"When Tom comes back, he'll explain."

When Tom comes back...

Janis felt the life leaving her legs. Every part of her wanted to collapse in the corner, to shrink between the sink and toilet and close her eyes, to not have to think about what would happen when Tom came back. A minute before, she could see the soft light through her kitchen window. Now she might never see her house again—Dad, Mom, Margaret, Tiger...

Stop it. Pull yourself together.

She wiped her eyes with the back of her hand and studied the door again. The part where she'd heard the bolt close was at shoulder level, too high to kick out.

She backed herself to the sink, then turned to the wall. No mirror above the sink. She tried the cabinet doors underneath, but they were fake, adhered to the wooden frame. She trained her gaze on the toilet.

The ceramic lid came off the holding tank with a dull scrape, and Janis held it to her chest like her most fervent hope. The lid was oblong and heavy, maybe fifteen pounds. She turned back to the door and moved the lid to shoulder level, testing the weight again. Would fifteen pounds be enough? She gripped the edges until she felt her fingers blanching.

She'd know in a second.

In two lunging steps she heaved the end of the lid against the door's lock like a battering ram. Something cracked, and the lid fell into two pieces at her feet, shattering against the tile.

She seized the handle. The door rattled in its frame but wouldn't open. The lock had yielded to the blow but only a very little.

"Janis, please," Mrs. Leonard called from the other side of the door. "You just need to—"

Janis backed up and kicked the door. She did it again and again, her heel aching to the bone. She switched legs. Every time she struck, the door vibrated, but it wouldn't swing out, wouldn't fall open. She imagined Mrs. Leonard on the other side, bracing it with her deceptively sturdy body.

"Janis, listen to me."

"Shut up!" Janis yelled.

With her back to the sink, she reassessed the brown door. She needed to think. A crusty indentation showed where the lid had met wood. The floor was littered with the aftermath. Janis pulled off her sweatshirt and tossed it away. She picked out the sharpest length of ceramic and slid it into the back of her jeans beneath her shirt, the smooth side against her skin. For when Tom came back.

"Janis, you and your—"

"Stop it!" she yelled, covering her ears.

Her breaths exploded from her lungs. She hoped Scott had escaped, that he wasn't hurt. She would never forgive herself if anything happened to him. And in the midst of that thought came a familiar electric sensation. Soon, her body was thrumming with the energy of her nighttime experiences. When she uncovered her ears, the air crackled around her.

If Mrs. Leonard was still talking, Janis couldn't hear her. And if she was still bracing the door, God help her.

Janis stood from the sink and raised her arm. This wasn't going to be like the night at the swing sets. She set her legs as the space around her pulsed with violent energy—energy she controlled. Though three feet separated her hand from the door, it felt like those three feet didn't matter. Not anymore.

With everything she could summon, Janis *pushed.*

Footfalls echoed up into the cylinder where Scott clung to the rungs, the sounds narrowing, zeroing in. Scott imagined his pursuer moving past the cases. *Gun cases?* He suppressed the horrifying thought and concentrated. His mind twined and entered the locking system, finding the relay. It was open again, somehow, current flowing to the solenoid.

Once more, Scott drew his concentration around it.

Build it up, build it up...

And then he released.

Scott's chin dipped, and his grip slipped from the rung. A sensation of falling, back scraping. A dull blow to the base of his head. Scott gasped and flailed his arms. His hands found a rung. With his feet still planted on the rungs below, he had fallen backward and become lodged in the cylinder.

Now he pulled himself upright and reoriented himself, pawing for the hatch overhead. He found it and shoved. The lid swung out, the hinge reaching its terminus with a dull *clank*.

"Hey!" The voice below was a throbbing echo.

Scott scrambled up into the shed and slammed the hatch door closed. Seeing the pulsing red button on the keypad, he understood: a passive detection field. That made him even more terrified of his pursuer. The voice that had shouted up at him *had* been male, and Scott imagined Mr. Leonard racing up the metal rungs still slick with his sweat and blood.

Scott seized the plywood board that had covered the hatch and wedged it between the hatch and the metal brackets of the lowest shelf. A second later, another shout called out, this one from mere feet away. The hatch door jittered. The wedged board and shelves rattled, but held.

As he turned to flee, a paralyzing thought came to Scott: *The shed door is bolted again. It's bolted, and you won't be able to open it. You won't be able to pick it. There won't be time.* The thought carried such certainty that he could already feel himself bouncing off the solid frame and landing beside the board he'd just propped up. The board that, with the next jitter of the hatch, shifted another inch.

But the shed doors flew wide, and Scott blinked out into morning light. He reached with his first strides, covering precious ground, taking the straightest line to the fence. He leaped for the chain linking, threw himself over, and tumbled down the side of the culvert. *Cripes, ouch, ouch, ouch!*

His right hip bore the brunt of the landing. Seizing his skateboard by the trucks, Scott staggered to his feet. He hobble-ran toward the opening beneath the street. The fence rattled to stillness behind him.

You might make it yet.

Less than a yard from the adjoining lot, Scott heard the shelving inside the shed collapse. *Crap.* His brain crunched the numbers:

Three seconds for him to climb from the hatch, another second to emerge from the shed, three to four more to cross the lawn and see the entire culvert.

Scott had seven seconds to get out of sight. He leaned into the steep hill, the skateboard tucked to his side, his talkie, flashlight, and tools swinging in his pockets, their motion fighting his own. He considered ditching them, but there was no time. Besides, he didn't want to leave any evidence of himself behind. Mr. Leonard hadn't gotten a look at him, didn't know who he was.

Behind him, the shed door clapped open.

Three seconds left.

Scott pressed his glasses to his face and moved the skateboard to his stomach. He took four more hobbled steps and heaved himself, headfirst, toward the opening beneath the street. He squinted his eyes, half expecting to crack his skull against the top of the cement tunnel. But the only thing to strike him was the sudden coolness of the space. Both sets of wheels landed inside—a nearly simultaneous *CLACKCLACK*. The momentum drove him toward the junction with a long tunnel running parallel to the street.

Heaving for air, Scott turned.

It was like looking out from inside a straw, but what Scott could see of the cement culvert was empty. He imagined Mr. Leonard arriving against the fence, peering up and down the steep length of the culvert—and finding no one. Scott closed his eyes. Fireworks burst behind his lids.

I owe you, Bud Body.

Still gasping, he began pushing himself toward the bus stop. His hip was bashed, his palms raw, and he could feel the place where he'd scraped his back, hot and bleeding beneath his shirt. But his only thought was returning to Janis and telling her that her intuition had been true all along.

He paused to illuminate his watch face. If he hurried, they might still catch the bus. At school, they could call the police and tell them about the cameras and the monitoring room. Scott suspected the locked cases held unlawful things as well. Mr. Leonard wouldn't be able to dismantle and relocate everything in time. The secret he'd been keeping all these years, locked and concealed beneath his house, was as extensive as his evident sickness.

A sickness that can't harm Janis's sister now, Scott thought as he rolled nearer the falling wedge of light.

Or Janis.

Janis lodged her back foot beneath the base of the cabinet. Aiming her arm toward the door again, she resummoned the energy. Her first attempt hadn't moved the bolt, but she had heard, had *felt*, the wood fracture around it. She had also felt herself slipping backward, disrupting her focus.

"Whatever you're doing, Janis, please stop." Mrs. Leonard's voice was clearer, less impeded, and Janis saw that her last attempt had opened a fissure along the frame. "Tom wants to *help* you. We both do."

Sure you do.

A jaggedness scored Janis's thoughts, a meanness that delighted in the fear she heard in Mrs. Leonard's voice.

She *pushed* again.

The door groaned its protest and then crunched away. The top half collapsed down. The bottom half exploded out. Mrs. Leonard shrieked. Amid the flying wood, Janis caught a flash of her sallow gown and the flailing of her arms. Her body thudded into the opposite wall.

A scarlet joy flourished inside Janis. She kicked through the debris and out into the hallway.

Mrs. Leonard scooted backward on one hand and both bare feet toward the kitchen. A patch of blood grew inside the gray-brown hair above her temple. Janis stalked Mrs. Leonard, her lips drawing from her teeth.

"Please," Mrs. Leonard said, her voice small and dazed. "Please, don't..."

"I'm sorry, I can't hear you," Janis taunted. A small part of her recoiled. She'd never spoken to an adult like that. She drew the ceramic shard from the back of her jeans and pointed it toward Mrs. Leonard.

"Your powers..." Mrs. Leonard sagged against a kitchen chair. "Yours and ... and your sister's. Don't let them see..."

Janis's arm faltered. She knew about her and Margaret's abilities?

"Don't let *who* see?" she said.

"Don't let them know..."

"Who?" Janis cried.

"Please..."

Mrs. Leonard's face was ashen, her eyes round and spacey.

She's in shock. Janis had heard the phrase uttered in untold television dramas over the years—so-and-so's "in shock"—the actor's voice grave and knowing. Janis had always accepted the diagnosis, never quite understanding what it meant. But now she was seeing it for herself.

Her gaze fell to the woman's left arm lying limply across her body, the palm turned up at an unnatural angle, the balls of her fingers purple and still. And then Janis understood that Mrs. Leonard's shock came not only from the blow to her head; her shoulder was broken. Janis covered her mouth when she spotted a shard of bone poking the inside of her gown.

"Wait here." Janis's joy evaporated. The vibrations vanished. "I-I'll go get help."

"No, you can't..." Tension creased Mrs. Leonard's brow, but her eyes remained glassy. "You mustn't..."

"You're going to be all right."

Janis wheeled and made for the front door on flimsy legs. A single thought repeated in her head like a skipping record: *You did that to her. You did that to her. You did that to her.*

Through the dust of the demolished bathroom, she focused on the front door at the end of the hallway. She needed to get outside, needed to go to the neighbors'. *Call the police,* she would tell them. She couldn't even think of the neighbors' names. *Call an ambulance.*

The knob turned inside Janis's grasp, but not from her own power.

The surprise on Mr. Leonard's pale, sweat-streaked face must have mirrored her own, but he recovered first. He pinned her arms to her sides, just as his wife had done. But he was larger, his strength more bracing.

Janis's scream pierced the open doorway, echoing out into the neighborhood.

Swearing, Mr. Leonard kicked the door closed and spun with her. A hand clamped over her mouth, fingers and a thumb digging into the corners of her jaw. His leg wrapped around hers, and Janis pitched to one side. She tried to writhe free, but there was nothing to push against. He'd stolen her leverage.

"Colleen!" he called.

Janis twisted her gaze toward the ruined hallway. In the kitchen beyond, the slumped-over Mrs. Leonard looked like a garage-sale doll. The patch of blood had spread to her ear and now dripped from her lobe, staining her gown near the jut of bone. She raised her good arm and pushed it out.

"Go," she mumbled.

Above her, Janis heard Mr. Leonard swallow.

"Go," she repeated more urgently. "I'll take care of myself, but you must go."

Janis could feel Mr. Leonard's breath inside her ear now. She squirmed and tried to scream against his hand. He shook her once.

"I only have a minute, so you need to listen to me." He panted as he spoke. "You're part of a program, a deadly program. It's your abilities. I tried to reach your sister, to warn her, but there are too many eyes. Nothing is what it seems, and no one can be trusted. Do you understand me? No one. Not even the ones who will investigate what happened here. Especially not them. Do you understand me?"

She had no idea what he was talking about but tried to nod anyway.

"Your one chance is to hide your powers. Never use them. Never speak of them again."

He seemed to notice the sharp length of ceramic she still clung to. Moving his hand from her mouth, he twisted her wrist in a way that didn't hurt but made her fingers turn numb. He eased the shard from her grasp. Why she didn't scream again, Janis couldn't say. There had been a quality to his voice, his words, to the way he held her now that felt almost ... paternal.

Tom wants to help you.

"You'll understand this one day," Mr. Leonard whispered and drove the shard into her side.

The faint scream echoed past Scott, like a specter. He stopped to listen, the hair bristling along his nape. He heard nothing more, but the sound, hoarse and high, had been unmistakable. It belonged to Janis.

Scott grabbed for the smooth cement ahead of him. The skateboard veered up the tunnel wall and he nearly tipped over. Scott jerked the board back on course. His legs pistoned at the darkness behind him. The wedge of falling light, still twenty yards away, didn't seem to be getting any closer. A desperate heat broke over Scott's body. He was trapped, entombed. He gasped for air.

The second scream to reach him was more of a grunt—a sheared-off beginning with no middle or ending.

Also Janis's.

In a flurry of kicks and shoves, he pulled himself into the leaf-strewn cylinder beneath the storm drain. Cold air washed around him. He stood and peered from the opening out into the street. Mr.

Leonard's green Datsun sat parked in front of the house where Janis had gone. And then Mr. Leonard appeared, alone. He ran down the walkway. An army-green duffel bag bounced from his shoulder. Peering around, he jerked the driver's-side door open.

Scott writhed through the storm drain, fingers grasping at asphalt. He heard the door bang closed and the Datsun shake to life. By the time Scott emerged, the car was halfway down the hill. Its engine droned into the distance. Scott jerked his gaze around to the Pattersons' garage door.

In the thin morning light, the bush stood alone.

He couldn't feel his legs as he sprinted toward the Leonards' house, not even his bashed hip.

"Hey," a man's voice called from behind. "Is everything all right?"

Scott twisted his head to find the Watsons emerging from the Downs in their matching blue sweat suits. Mr. Watson's hand made a visor above his eyes.

"Call the police!" Scott gasped, still sprinting. "The Leonards' house!"

The Watsons looked at one another and back at Scott.

"Please!"

Maybe it was the way the *please* tore from his throat, but they began running toward the Meadows, Mr. Watson stripping his wrist weights, then hopping to do the same with his ankle weights.

Scott leaped the curb and hurdled a bush. Dew kicked up around him. Beneath the balcony, the yellow door stood ajar. Scott slowed. Was that the heel of a white shoe beyond? He pushed the door open.

No.

Janis was lying on her side, her back to him. Hair fell from her head and onto the dull carpet like a spilled drink. Her white T-shirt was eerily bloodless where a narrow shard stood from her ribs.

Nothing moved. Nothing breathed.

Please, no.

In two blinks, Scott's eyes took in the ruined hallway and the slumped and bleeding woman beyond.

Then he was on the floor in front of Janis. He found her eyes open but empty, the soft rims of green around her pupils thin and hard to see. One hand held a small gold pendant at her neck.

"Stay awake," he pled, stroking the side of her head. "Help's coming."

Her eyes shifted slightly at his voice. She was breathing, he saw, but each breath was so thin that her torso remained rigid. He took her hand in both of his, forgetting the injuries to his palms.

"Can you hear me?" His voice was starting to tremble, to come apart. "Stay awake."

He kissed her hand and pressed it to his cheek.

"Please," he said.

Her fingers curled around his and held tight. They remained like that, Scott and Janis, until the distant wail of sirens grew around them and a cadre of footsteps pounded up the walkway.

37

"We've suffered a containment breach," the woman reported.

"What? External?"

"It appears internal."

"Casualties?"

"One down, one missing. And the girl, sir. She's being taken to the hospital."

"How in the fucking hell did this happen?"

"We're looking into it, sir."

"Listen to me," the man said. "Damage control first, risk assessment second."

"Yes, sir."

"All resources, all means. Be goddamned thorough"

"Understood."

"It's what I hired you for."

"Yes, sir."

"Don't you dare let me down."

"No, sir."

38

Eleven days later
Friday, December 14, 1984
2:51 p.m.

Scott stood in the street in front of the Graystones' house, hands in his coat pockets, shoulders shrugged to his ears. The wind blew gray around him. Turning, he could see his own bedroom window up the hill. It appeared eye-like, set back behind the bushes, the half-raised blinds a hooded lid. And no wonder. It was the same place from which he'd looked out for three years, watching the very spot where he now stood, the spot that always seemed so far away.

Only someone else had been watching, too.

Scott raised his face to the street light at the end of the cul-de-sac. He'd come home from school one day the previous week to see a police technician standing inside a bucket lift, dismantling a camera. Scott assumed they'd done the same in the woods and around the Leonards' house. For the entire week, yellow police tape had crisscrossed the Leonards' front door and fluttered over the gate to their backyard, making the house look sinister from the street, too.

Scott exhaled through pursed lips, turned back to the Graystones' house, and limped up the semi-circular driveway. The hip he'd landed on in the culvert remained sore. In front of the door, he hesitated. A Gobstopper-sized lump filled his throat. He tried to swallow, but it wouldn't move.

Shoe on its side, violent spill of hair, jagged shard...

He removed his glasses and rubbed his eyes. This was proving harder than he'd anticipated. Replacing his glasses, he reached for the illuminated doorbell. But before he could press the button, the door opened.

Bundled in Thirteenth Street sweats, purple and white, her hair gathered in a loose ponytail, she looked stunning, a picture of divine resurrection. Scott recovered his legs in time to keep from staggering. As she stepped toward him, her pale lips leaned toward a smile.

"Hey, stranger," Janis said hoarsely.

Scott tried to smile back. "Hey yourself. How are you?"

She winced as she raised her right arm overhead. "They took the stitches out yesterday, before my discharge. It's still a little sore, and I still get short of breath, but every day's better." Her arm eased back to her side. "Thanks to you."

Scott's gaze fell to his shoes. "No, I just..." He tasted salt in the back of his throat and was afraid that if he tried to say more, the salt would climb into his tear ducts and spill out.

Janis closed the door behind her.

"I was wondering when I'd get a chance to talk to you," she said. "My dad won't let me go anywhere until I'm all healed. I would've called, but ... well, what you told me about your phone."

Scott shifted his weight. "When I went to the hospital, there were police outside your door."

Janis shook his shoulder. "They weren't there to keep you out, dummy."

"Yeah, I know. I wasn't sure."

Both times Scott had tried to visit—a handwritten get-well card clutched behind his back—Blake had been at Janis's bedside. Both times, Scott had continued past her room, slipped from the hospital, and biked home.

"I heard they found him," he said.

"Yeah." Janis sat on the top step and clasped her hands between her knees.

Scott sat beside her.

"They found his car at a rest stop in Georgia. A trucker remembered seeing someone fitting his description climbing into a semi bound for South Carolina. That's where they found him, in an interstate motel outside of Florence. His body, anyway. And the rope around his neck."

"So that's it, I guess?"

"I gave a detailed statement while it was still fresh in my memory. They've linked him to some unsolved cases in the state. Kidnapping, abduction..." She hesitated. "...other things."

"And his wife?"

"She confessed to acting as an accomplice. Prison after her arm heals."

Scott peeked behind them and then lowered his voice. "Did your powers do that?"

Janis watched her clasped hands. She nodded.

"So what did you tell everyone?"

"I stuck to the story about Tiger. Said that I was worried when I didn't see her outside in the morning. Thought maybe she'd wandered off, et cetera. I told the rest more or less how it happened, leaving certain parts out."

Scott listened as Janis gave him the play-by-play, from the moment he dropped into the storm drain until he found her in the front hallway. Scott lined up her experiences aboveground with his experiences below. When she finished, Scott had a complete picture.

"How did you get your powers to work this time?" he asked.

"It was my emotions, I think—fear, anger, desperation—all swirling inside me. It triggered something, turned something on. I suddenly felt in control of my space, of the objects around me. I reached for the door, and I ... I drove all of those emotions against it. Of course, I told everyone else that I'd battered it down with the lid to the toilet tank."

For a second, Scott felt like they were inside the panels of one of his comic books.

"They believed you?"

"I think so." She looked over. "What did you tell the police?"

"That I was at the bus stop when I heard you scream. Course, I was still making my way back up the tunnel."

They both looked out into the street where the sweet gum leaves were skittering and piling into drifts. Janis leaned her head against his shoulder. Her ponytail fell between them, alighting on his thigh.

"You were down there when he went into the basement?"

"I got out before he saw me. But the sophistication of his security system, Janis, the cameras, the whole setup ... I've never seen anything like it. I mean, it was beyond even what Bell does at their big central offices." Scott's next words tumbled out. "How in the hell could he have done all of that on a military pension and the little he gets substitute teaching?"

Janis unclasped her hands and looked at him.

Scott's face flushed with heat. "Oh, but don't listen to me. Curse of the nerd brain." He knocked his knuckles against the side of his head. "It never stops working, I'm afraid."

But Janis was nodding. "No, I've been wondering the same thing."

"Really?"

"There was this small device he threatened me with. When he turned it on, it made my head buzz, and I felt like I was going to pass out. I'd never seen, much less heard, of anything like that, have you? We have our official versions of what happened—I was looking for Tiger, you were waiting at the bus stop. But what if the information we've been given about the Leonards is an official version, too? You know—who they are, what they did, their pasts. Their names, even."

"What do you mean?"

"The special investigator, a woman named Agent Steel—cropped hair, chilly blue eyes, gave me the creeps." Janis shivered. "Anyway, she kept referring to Mrs. Leonard as Susan. But in the house, I heard Mr. Leonard call his wife Colleen. He yelled it when he saw her injured in the kitchen."

"Maybe that's her middle name."

"No, the forms I signed had her whole name: Susan Patricia Leonard. And the Leonards knew about our powers—mine and Margaret's, anyway. Then there were the things he said about a dangerous program and not letting them see our powers, not letting them know."

"Who's *them*?"

"He didn't say."

Scott started to open his mouth, then clamped it closed.

"'Nothing is what it seems, and no one can be trusted.' I kept thinking about that when Agent Steel was questioning me. And I kept thinking, too, about what he said after he helped me to the floor. Right before he left."

"Mr. Leonard?"

"'Lay low until I contact you.' That's what he said."

"Well, I guess that won't be happening anytime soon."

Janis placed her hand against her side, over the place Scott had seen that awful length of shard protruding. "The wound—the doctors keep saying that it couldn't have happened in a better place. A punctured liver still functions, still does what it's supposed to do. And mine's going to heal completely. I'll just have a small scar between these two ribs."

"You think he picked that spot on purpose?"

Janis fell silent. "I don't know."

"I wasn't going to say anything about this, but..." Scott still wasn't sure whether it was a good idea, but maybe there was a connection with what she was telling him. "Well, I've been probing the tap I told you about, exploring it."

"And?"

"I don't think it's a tap, Janis."

"You're not being monitored?"

Scott fidgeted with the hem of his jacket. "Yes and no. It's more like a switchboard, like the ones hotels have. Or very similar. You know, you call a hotel, a receptionist answers, you tell them the room number, and they connect you, right? With some hotels, you can dial the room number directly, but the call still passes through the hotel's switchboard. The receptionist can still listen in." Scott looked at her. "I don't know how to explain this, Janis, other than to say that it feels like Oakwood has its own switchboard."

The idea had begun with Jesse Hoag. The day Scott had given him the money, Jesse mentioned losing his phone service on a Sunday—

Creed had lost his, too. Janis later confirmed hers had gone out as well. And while Scott hadn't been able to follow up with Jesse for obvious reasons, Janis remembered that her outage had happened on the afternoon of October 14, the day after her first date with Blake—the same day Scott had shorted what he thought had been a personal wiretap.

Janis's eyes widened.

Scott nodded. "Which would mean *all* of our phones are being monitored."

"Then who's the receptionist?"

"I thought it might've been the Leonards—I saw some telephone equipment when I went beneath the shed—but all that stuff's been tagged and warehoused, I'm sure. No longer operational, anyway. And yet there's still a delay on my line. Yours, too, I checked. I'm still trying to figure it out."

Was the answer also a *them*?

Janis wrapped her arms around her knees and rested the side of her head there. When she spoke again, her voice sounded older, tired.

"There are things I'm still trying to figure out too, I guess. So much has happened and ... don't take this the wrong way, Scott, but I need a break. What you just told me, I ... I can't think about right now."

Scott swallowed and looked at his hands. *Way to drop a load on her, dimwit.*

"I'm not going to be at school next week," she said. "My parents decided we should leave for Denver early, spend a longer holiday with Grams. They thought it best that we get away for a while."

"I understand." But the thought of not seeing her in all that time made Scott's insides feel hollow and metallic. The last week and a half had been hard enough. He studied the gray street.

"Oh! I almost forgot something." Janis patted his hand. "Wait here."

Scott turned as she disappeared through the front door.

She returned a minute later, a slender paper bag crackling in her hands. Her eyes shone with excitement as she held it out to him. Scott nearly lost his balance when he stood.

"What's this?"

"An early Christmas present."

He took it. "Oh, you didn't have to—"

But then he had the gift partway out of the bag, and a startled sound sheared his words. The front of the comic book showed a battle-torn Scott Summers and Jean Grey fighting side by side, taking on the Shi'Ar Imperial Guard.

"How did you know?"

Janis laughed. "You told me about it, remember? Up at the Grove that night. You mentioned it was the only one missing from your collection. I guess the issue number stuck in my head."

He *had* told her everything that night, hadn't he?

"But where did you find it?" Now Scott was laughing.

"Well, Margaret felt bad about not believing me about Mr. Leonard. I'd tried to warn her back in August, but Margaret being Margaret..." Janis rolled her eyes. "Anyway, she said she owed me. Turned out the guy at the hobby store near school had the issue in his personal collection."

"You mean Tully? And he *sold* it to her?"

Scott had tried for years to get him to part with the issue but only ever received a condescending smirk in response, no matter what he offered.

"Margaret can be very persuasive."

Scott kept staring at the cover. *Uncanny X-Men #137.* "I-I don't know what to say. I didn't get you anything."

"Do you remember what you said when you found me?"

Stay awake. Help's coming.

"I think so."

"Seeing you there, Scott. Hearing your voice. Knowing that you were all right." Her eyes began to glimmer, even as she smiled. "That told me that I was going to be all right, too. That was your gift to me."

She rose onto her tiptoes and kissed his cheek.

"Merry Christmas, Scott."

"Merry Christmas, Janis," he whispered. For the first time, he noticed the fragrant evergreen trim around the Graystones' front door, the red and white stockings hanging beneath the door's small windows.

"So..." Her hand lingered around his another moment. "See you in 1985?"

He tried to think of something Scott Summers would say to Jean Grey, something special, something that would capture the dizzying enormity of what he felt for her in that moment.

But all he could come up with was, "You bet."

When Scott reached the street, he flipped up his jacket collar. He'd have Jesse to face soon, a switchboard to figure out, and Mr. Leonard's cryptic message to decipher—if it could even be believed. But for the moment, his thoughts were on one person.

Halfway up the hill, he turned, surprised to find Janis still on the front porch, still looking after him. Scott raised the comic book, smiled as she waved back, and then hunched his shoulders against the December wind, the touch of her lips still warm against his skin.

The Series Continues...

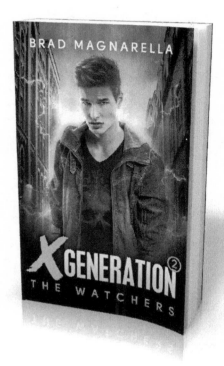

XGeneration 2

The Watchers

THE XGENERATION SERIES

by Brad Magnarella

YOU DON'T KNOW ME

THE WATCHERS

SILENT GENERATION

PRESSURE DROP

CRY LITTLE SISTER

GREATEST GOOD

DEAD HAND

About the Author

Brad Magnarella is an author of speculative fiction. His books include the *XGeneration Series* and the allegorical trilogy, *The Prisoner and the Sun*. Raised in Gainesville, Florida, he now calls various cities home. He currently lives and writes in Washington, D.C.

www.bradmagnarella.com